I0748431

DOWN STYPHON!

KALVAN SAGA: VOLUME VIII

JOHN F. CARR

Pequod Press

DOWN STYPHON!
A Pequod Press Adventure Novel

First Edition

Manufactured in the United States of America
First Printing 2016

V 10 9 8 7 6 5 4 3 2 1

ISBN: 978-0-937912-67-6

On the cover: Alan Gutierrez, *Down Styphon!*

Pequod Press
P.O. Box 80
Boalsburg, PA 16827
www.PequodPress.com

Kalvan Novels

by John F. Carr

Down Styphon!
Gunpowder God
The Fireseed Wars
Siege of Tarr-Hostigos
The Hos-Blethan Affair
Kalvan Kingmaker
Great Kings' War

Paratime Police Novels

by John F. Carr

Time Crime (H. Beam Piper & John F. Carr)

The Lord Kalvan novels are based on H. Beam Piper's Paratime series and his 1965 novel, **Lord Kalvan of Otherwhen**.

DEDICATION

To my Russian Princess, Victoria

ACKNOWLEDGEMENTS

Special thanks go to Pequod Press's Editor Victoria Alexander for her hard work and efforts to make this book as professional as possible.

I would be remiss, if I didn't mention and give thanks to James Landau who has been my primary continuity editor for the past 30 years.

I'd also like to give thanks to all the members of the Copyediting and Post-Proofing Team, Dwight Decker, Dennis Frank, Richard Oakley, Larry Hopkins, Wolfgang Diehr, and David Williams.

Special mention goes to Dennis Frank for all his work on the maps. Dennis is also in charge of the John F. Carr Archive at St. Bonaventure University where he serves as Archivist. Visit the John Carr Archives at:

http://web.sbu.edu/friedsam/archives/carr/index.html

Thanks go to Alan Gutierrez who came up with the cover design and executed it so well; he has been the cover artist for the entire Kalvan saga, starting with **Great Kings' War** in 1985. He also drew the fine interior maps.

Hostigos Town
Tigos Mountains
1. Ptosphes' Palace
2. Yirtta's Temple
3. High Temple Of Dralm
4. Hostigos Apothecary
5. Guild Hall
6. Galazar Shrine House
7. Royal Armory
8. Fynos Mill
9. Tranth's Hall
10. The Royal Hos-Hostgos Bank
11. Lytris Shrine
12. Saturday Market
13. Gull's Nest
14. Ptosphes' Almshouse
15. Royal Foundling House
16. Royal Army Barracks
17. Tranth's Temple
18. Red Halberd Inn
19. Silver Stag
N
Great Kings Highway
Ryphos Road
Old Tigos Road
Lyssa Street
Market Street
Bear Creek Bridge
High Street
Prince Zythanes Road
Darro Creek
Cannos
Axyon Street
Great Kings Highway

Tarr-Hostigos
Hostigos Gap
14
Xych Street
15
Styh Street
Ivros Road
Thal Road
Market Street
16
Malthos Road
Coopers
nners Way

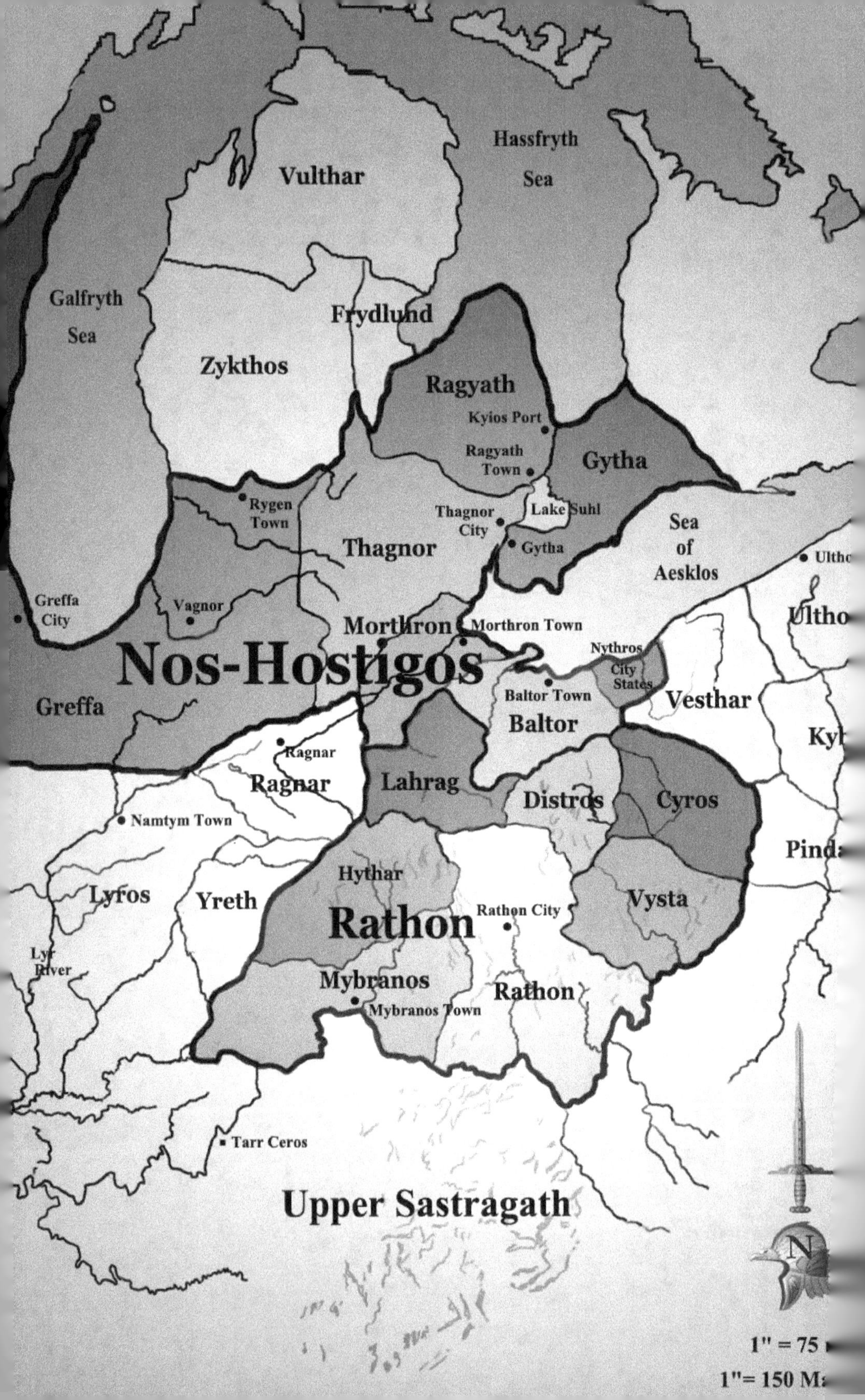

Hassfryth
Sea
Vulthar
Galfryth
Sea
Frydlund
Zykthos
Ragyath
Kyios Port
Ragyath
Town
Gytha
Rygen
Town
Thagnor
City
Lake Suhl
Sea
of
Aesklos
Thagnor
Gytha
Greffa
City
Vagnor
Morthron
Morthron Town
Nos-Hostigos
Nythros
City
States
Greffa
Baltor Town
Baltor
Vesthar
Ragnar
Ragnar
Lahrag
Distros
Cyros
Namtym Town
Hythar
Lyros
Yreth
Rathon
Rathon City
Vysta
Lyr
River
Mybranos
Mybranos Town
Rathon
Tarr Ceros
Upper Sastragath
N
1" = 75

Hos-Harphax
Upper Sastragath
Sephrax City
Sephrax
Thebra City
Thebra
Imbraz City
Listros
Listros City
Mykronos Town
Mykronos
Zacryth Town
Imbraz
Chaliphax Town
Chaliphax
Zacryth
Lantos Town
Lantos
Mythrax
Hos-Ktemnos
Mythrax Town
Ktemnos
Mentron
Mentron Town
Ktemnos City
Cythlos Town
Hos-Bletha
Cythlos
Balph
N
Scale: 1" = 67 mi.

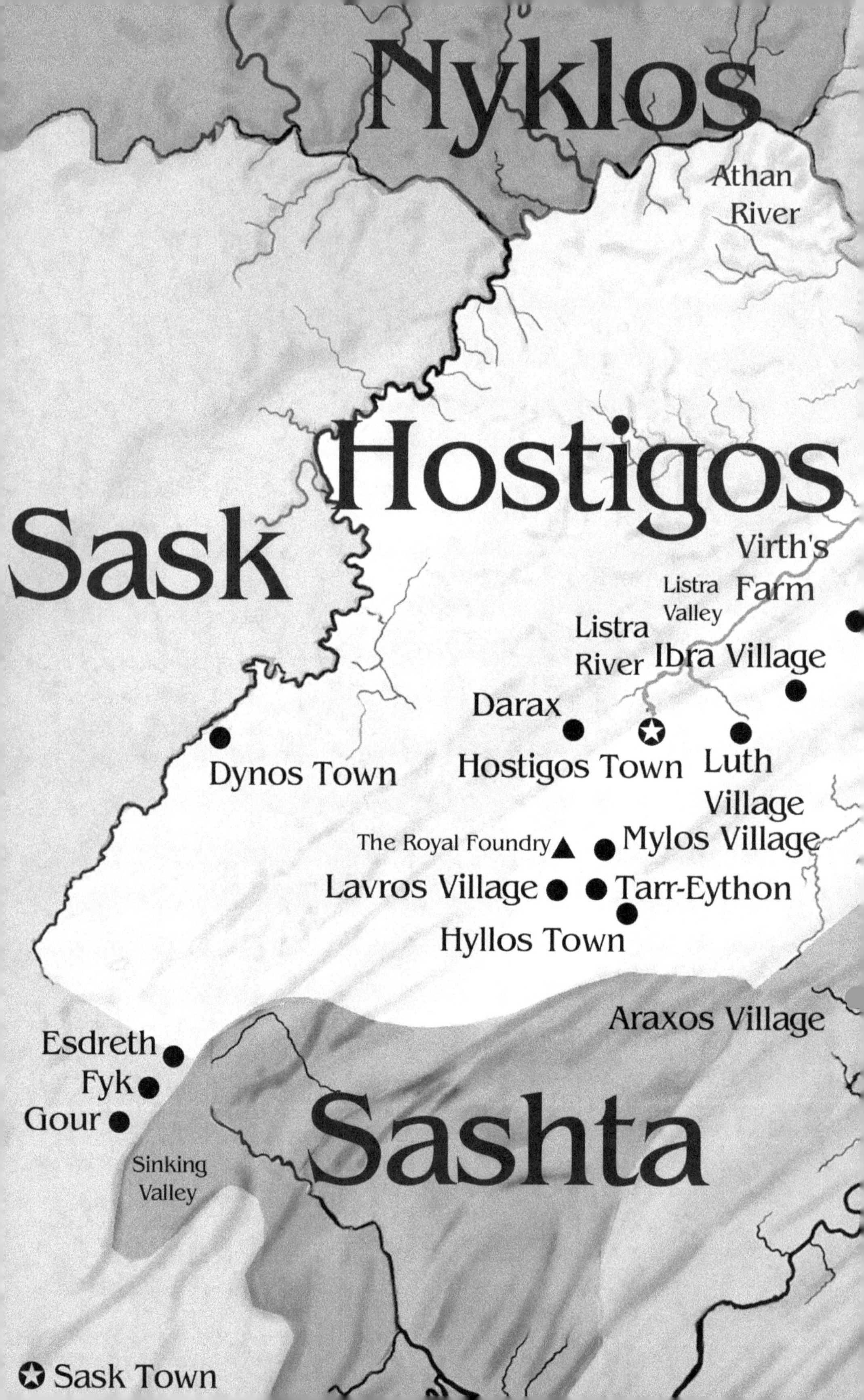

Nyklos
Athan River
Hostigos
Sask
Virth's Farm
Listra Valley
Listra River
Ibra Village
Darax
Dynos Town
Hostigos Town
Luth Village
The Royal Foundry
Mylos Village
Lavros Village
Tarr-Eython
Hyllos Town
Araxos Village
Esdreth
Fyk
Gour
Sinking Valley
Sashta
Sask Town

Nostor
Gorge River
Nirfd
Nostor Town
Narza Gap
Dyssa
Seven Hills Valley
Systos
Listra Mouth
Dombra Town
Fitra
Wolf Valley
Athan River
Ryx Village
Beshta
Harph River
N
Besh River
Hos-Harphax
Scale: 1" = 8 mi.
1" = 16 Marches

The Great Kingdoms
The Saltless Seas
Karphya
Vulthar City
Fryttander
Grefftscharr
Thagnor
Upper Middle Kingdoms
reffa
Morthron
Trygath
Tarr-Ceros
Upper Sastragath
Lower Sastragath
Hos-Zygros
Zygros City
Hos-Agrys
Giarth City
Agrys City
Ulthor Port
Hos-Hostigos
Dyssa
Lista River
Nostor Town
Hostigos Town
Hyllos Town
Beshta Town
Tarr-Beshta
Tenabra
Harphax City
Mrathos
Hos-Harphax
Thebra City
Hos-Ktemnos
Hos-Ktemnos
Balph
Bletha Town
Hos-Bletha
Dalthax City
Eryn Town
Cythros Town
N
Scale: 1" = 200 mi.
1" = 400 Marches

DRAMATIS PERSONAE

HOS-HOSTIGOS & ALLIES

Alkides—Artillery general in the Royal Army.

Aspasthar—Son of Harmakros and false heir to the Hos-Agrys Throne.

Chartiphon—Great King of Hos-Rathon.

Demia—Princess, Kalvan and Rylla's daughter.

Ermut—Rector of the University of Hostigos.

Errock—Captain-General of the Thagnori Army.

Hectides—Old wolf hunter and scout for the Royal Army.

Herad—Admiral Herad, Supreme Admiral of the Royal Nos-Hostigos Navy.

Hestophes—Captain-General of the Army of Hostigos.

Kalvan—Former Penn. State Trooper and Great King of Hos-Hostigos.

Klestreus—Head of Hostigos Security.

Leukestros—Grand Constable of Thagnor and Colonel in the Royal Army.

Mnestros—Prince of Eubros and Kalvan's ally.

Mytron—Chancellor of Nos-Hostigos and Highpriest of Dralm.

Nathros—General, Rector of Engineering College.

Pheblon—Former Prince of Nostor.

Phrames—Prince of Gytha and Captain-General of the Royal Army.

Rylla—Former Great Queen of Nos-Hostigos, Kalvan's wife and co-ruler.

Sarrask—Former of Prince of Sask.

Skranga—Chief of Hos-Hostigos Intelligence now in Hos-Bletha.

Tharses—Uncle Wolf Highpriest of Hos-Hostigos.

Vanar Halgoth—Captain of Kalvan's Tymannian Guard.

Vinaldos—Count, Acting Intelligence Chief.

Uncle Wolf Xanthos—A Hostigi Uncle Wolf under Highpriest Tharses.

Xykos—Grand-Captain of Great Queen Rylla's Own Horse Guard.

PARATIMERS

Aranth Saln—Kalvan Study Team Military Expert now undercover as Ranthos.
Danthor Dras—University Professor and expert on Styphon's House Subsector.
Danar Sirna—Former Member of Kalvan Study Team and Phidestros' mistress.
Hadron Dalla—Verkan's wife and Paratime Police Chief's Special Assistant.
Hadron Tharn—Dalla's power-mad brother.
Hadron Zinganna—Dalla's adopted Prole sister. Undercover in Greffa as Zinna.
Kostran Galth—Paratime Police Inspector, Head of the Greffan Study Team.
Ranthar Jard—Paratime Police Inspector.
Tortha Karf—Former Paratime Police Chief.
Verkan Vall—Paratime Police Chief.

STYPHON'S HOUSE

Anaxthenes—New Supreme Priest and Styphon's Own Voice.
Aristocles—Grand Commander and second in command of the Order.
Baphocles—Archpriest, one of Anaxthenes supporters.
Cimon—Inner Circle Archpriest called the "Peasant Priest."
Danthor—Paratime Professor's undercover identity as Styphon's House Archpriest.
Dimonestes—Archpriest, formerly one of Roxthar's followers.
Dracar—Archpriest of Inner Circle, formerly Roxthar's puppet.
Drayton—Styphon's House Treasurer.
Euriphocles—Archpriest, one of Anaxthenes' co-conspirators.
Grythos—Archpriest of the Inner Circle, Prince-Regent of Hos-Agrys and Military Advisor.
Haltor—Highpriest of the Agrysi Great Temple.
Heraclestros—Archpriest, former Highpriest of Agrys City.
Lesthros—Archpriest of Bletha Town.
Neamenestros—Archpriest and one of Anaxthenes allies.
Phyllos—Highpriest of Harphax City Great Temple.
Sarmoth—Knight Sergeant of the Order of Zarthani Knights. Soton's aide-de-camp.
Soton—Grand Master of the Order of Zarthani Knights.
Symnos—The High Marshal in charge of the Ktemnoi Sacred Squares.
Timothanes—Archpriest, one of Archpriest Dracar's supporters.
Yagos—Anaxthenes' Special Deputy and spy master.
Xenophes—High Marshal of the Styphon's House Temple Guard.

ALLIES OF STYPHON'S HOUSE

Geblon—Great King of Hos-Harphax.

Lavena—Baron Sthentros' daughter and Great Queen of Hos-Harphax.

Lyphannes—Chancellor of Hos-Harphax.

Lukthos—Great King of Hos-Ktemnos.

Niclophon—Great King of Hos-Bletha.

Sthentros—New Prince of Hostigos.

HOS-BLETHA

Archimanes—Chancellor of Hos-Bletha.

Althaphon—Baron and old enemy of Gasphros.

Basilron—Blethan Prince of Syragon.

Carthames—Blethan Prince of Drathor.

Kosklos—Blethan Prince of Artigos.

Lykron—Captain-General of Hos-Bletha until sent to Balph.

Mythros—Blethan Prince of Pytha.

Niclophon—Great King of Hos-Bletha.

Theodoros—Captain-General of the Hos-Blethan Royal Army.

Vythron—Blethan Prince of Taurnos.

NEUTRALS

Arminta—Phidestros' wife and Great Queen of Hos-Zygros.

Hyrum—King of Dorg.

Kyblannos—General in the Hos-Zygros Army and Phidestros' chief military advisor.

Olmnestes—Uncle Wolf Highpriest.

Phidestros—Former mercenary, now Great King of Hos-Zygros.

Ranjar Sargos—Var-Wannax, or Great Chief, of the Sastragath.

Ranthos—Former Paratimer Aranth Saln who is undercover as a mercenary Captain.

Roldolf—King of Xiphlon.

Theovacar—King of Grefftscharr.

PROLOGUE

Styphon's Voice Anaxthenes should have been filled with elation, since over the past two years all of his plans had come to fruition. With Archpriest Roxthar dead, he was now the most powerful priest in all the Five Kingdoms. Unfortunately, that no longer meant what it had before the mysterious arrival of the Usurper Kalvan, and the revolt of the bastard mercenary Phidestros, who was now perched firmly on one of the Great Thrones.

Once this hallowed hall had represented the apex of power in the Five Great Kingdoms, but that claim was now in doubt. Rats were nibbling at all sides of the Temple's hegemony. True, the Usurper Kalvan had been exiled to the Middle Kingdoms, but he had created a new kingdom there that was as strong, if not stronger, than Hos-Hostigos had been at its peak. In the north Great King Phidestros ruled over Hos-Zygros, while his henchman, Geblon, ruled as the Great King of Hos-Harphax. Of all the northern kingdoms, only Hos-Agrys was still firmly in the Temple's control. While to the south, Hos-Bletha was divided into two kingdoms, neither one great nor a true kingdom.

The thirty-three archpriests seated at the Triangle Table were not the strongest reeds, either. However, they were an improvement over the previous crop, most of whom had been in the thrall of Roxthar and his Holy Investigation. Since every archpriest within five hundred marches had arrived, except the archpriest of Hos-Zygros, who was dead, the Archpriest of Hos-Harphax, who had not wanted to brave the weather, and Archpriest Grythos who was acting Prince-Regent of Hos-Agrys: it was time to begin.

Anaxthenes rose to his feet, looking from side to side. "I have called this Council to discuss several important issues. First and most importantly, the Temple is faced with a grave threat. This morning a boat arrived from Zygros with a terrible cargo."

He could see that he had the full attention of all the seated archpriests. He had just received the news of the atrocity early this morning and put a lid on it. However, he knew by evening every priest in the holy city would know all about it.

"Aboard the boat were the pickled heads of over four hundred Zygrosi Styphon's House priests!" All the faces at the table paled at this grave news. "It appears that the bastard Phidestros has rejected our overtures and made himself our deadly enemy. To say nothing about the treasure he has looted from the Zygrosi temples."

Several of the archpriests began touching their throats, as if wondering when the headsman's ax would fall upon their own necks.

"I, as Supreme Priest, declare the False Great King Phidestros anathema, a pretender and archfoe of the Temple. Any merchants, noblemen or soldiers who deal with him will be declared adversaries of Styphon's House. Styphon's Will Be Done!"

There was a round of "aye, aye" from the assembled archpriests.

"It is long past time we talked frankly about the Temple's future." That got everyone's attention, since frank talk was a rarity under the Golden Dome. "We are surrounded by enemies. The Pretender Phidestros and Great King Geblon to the north, the Usurper Kalvan and his minion, King Chartiphon, to our west and another pretender, Valthros, who calls himself Great King of Hos-Bletha, to the south. Since the war with Daemon Kalvan and the conquest of Hos-Agrys, we no longer have the military might and soldiers to impose Our will upon all the great kingdoms. Grand Master Soton has seated himself at Tarr-Ceros and refuses to leave until he has restored the Order of Zarthani Knights to their former power, which could take him more winters than he has left to live. Styphon's Own Guard has lost close to half their number and are having a hard time finding new recruits. Our own Great King Lukthos is still trying to rebuild the Royal Army of Hos-Ktemnos, and is reluctant to commit his troops to another campaign—although he will do so if pressed."

Most of the archpriests looked shocked at the dire news he was presenting, although they should have figured it out on their own long ago.

"There are few unattached free companies left in the Five Kingdoms: those not under long-term contract to us have either joined with Kalvan or Phidestros—or died in the Fireseed Wars. Furthermore, it appears the best captain-generals are all fighting for the opposition. To put it bluntly, the future does not bode well for the Temple's continued dominance."

The room was as quiet as a tomb, none of the usual tittering or whispering.

Anaxthenes knew he held their complete attention. "So, we're going to expand our business."

"What do you mean by that, Your Divinity?" Archpriest Dimonestes asked.

"First, we are going to move substantial assets to our new staging ground in the west. We have made groundbreaking progress with the Ros-Zarthani west coast city-states. I call on Archpriest Prythos to brief you on our progress and future plans there."

The broad archpriest rose to his feet. He no longer had the big belly he'd had when Anaxthenes had first met with him. Three trips, back and forth along the long Iron Trail, had put him in fighting trim. "My fellow archpriests, Supreme Priest Anaxthenes had the wisdom to suggest moving some of our operations to the west coast when I informed him of the Ros-Zarthani prowess as warriors in the war against the Usurper Kalvan. We both believed the situation there was ripe for exploitation. Few of you recognize me because I've spent most of my time negotiating and palavering with a few other select upperpriests who have been working on this project for the past three winters.

"I recently accompanied the Ros-Zarthani force, after they left the Grand Host and returned to their city-state of Antiphon under Arch-Stratego Zarphu. The Ros-Zarthani soldiers impressed everyone in the Grand Host of Styphon's House with their steadfastness and courage. I was very taken with the Arch-Stratego and got to know him very well on the return journey. He asked all manner of questions about fireseed and the various weapons that use it. Zarphu is the kind of man that could be a valued friend, or a dangerous foe.

"On my previous visit to Antiphon, I had established a small temple with the priests who had accompanied me. Lord Tyrant Dyzar, a most ambitious and paranoid ruler, allowed us this in exchange for a wagonload of old calivers and arquebuses and our promise to build a fireseed mill. Before we left, I purchased enough slaves for a temple farm and sent scouts out to search for a local source of brimstone.

"Meanwhile, while under the command of Grand Host of Styphon's House, the Arch-Stratego Zarphu not only earned the respect of his fellow commanders, but had picked up as many discarded fireseed weapons as he could conceal. He returned to Antiphon to great acclaim from the populace. So much so that it threatened the Lord Tyrant and in response he sent some of his bodyguards, called the Eternals, to assassinate the Arch-Stratego. However, Zarphu was well protected by his men and the Eternals proved to be quite mortal. The people of Antiphon did not take the attempted assassination well. The next day a huge crowd stormed the palace and killed everyone who tried to stop them. They were led by the troopers who had accompanied the Arch-Stratego across the Sea of Grass and into the Five Kingdoms. The mob took the Tyrant out to their grand plazos where he was literally pulled apart."

The archpriests looked properly cowed and fearful. Anaxthenes knew that to a man they feared that someday a mob would sack their palaces and tear them to shreds. One of the reasons why Kalvan had become the most feared man in the great kingdoms.

"The following day Zarphu was unanimously granted, by the Council of Nobles and the Merchants Guild, the title of Tyrant of Antiphon," Archpriest Prythos continued. "I was granted an audience with Zarphu several days later and he agreed to allow Styphon's House to build temples and introduce Styphon to the city. The Ros-Zarthani are fond of war gods and Styphon has proved to be quite popular with the commoners and nobility. Many of them are anxious to obtain fireseed arms for themselves. Supreme Priest Anaxthenes suggested we accelerate our expansion into the west coast in lieu of recent developments here in the Five Kingdoms."

Anaxthenes nodded, and Archpriest Prythos sat back down. "Well said, Prythos. My plan is to send a large party of archpriests and highpriests with proper attendants under Archpriest Prythos' leadership to not only introduce Styphon's House to Antiphon, but eventually to all the other west coast city-states."

None of the assembled archpriests looked happy with this new idea. Not that he expected them to welcome it, not this band of prosperous and indolent priests. *They had better get used to the idea quickly*, he decided. "I'm going to send ten of you along with a hundred highpriests and two thousand lowerpriests to accompany Archpriest Prythos along the Iron Trail. I want this party to leave early in the season so as not to attract attention."

By that, he meant Kalvan's notice. There were mutterings and heated whispers among the assembled archpriests, but no one dared raise his voice in objection. *They're smarter than I thought*, he concluded.

"Archpriest Neamenestros, Prythos will head the delegation and you will be his Hand in all things as Highpriest of the new Antiphon Temple. I will let you pick those highpriests whom you would like to accompany you on this expedition."

"Yes, Your Divinity," Neamenestros replied. He had been forewarned and, although unhappy about his new post, he had understood its necessity. Nor was Neamenestros pleased to find himself subordinate to Archpriest Prythos, but Prythos knew the Archstratagi and the lay of the land.

Anaxthenes knew his final proposition was not going to go over well. "Next, we are going to start selling guns and fireseed to the Mexicotal."

Archpriest Dracar, his naked head sticking out of his cowl like a baby bird's, cried, "You can't, Your Divinity! They're flesh eaters! Cannibals!"

Anaxthenes nodded to one of his guardsmen at the door. The man moved quickly over to the table and swung his halberd at the Archpriest, taking Dracar's head off his shoulders, severing the carotid arteries. The head flew to one side, landing on an archpriest's lap, while the red arterial fountain splattered blood over the nearby archpriests.

"Any more complaints?" he asked. He fought to suppress the smile that threatened to break out upon his face. Dracar had long been a thorn in his posterior and he welcomed this opportunity to pull it out.

The chamber was as silent as a tomb. Many of the archpriests were looking down at their blood-splattered robes with distaste and fear.

When there were no replies, he nodded to the guardsman who cleaned his halberd head with Dracar's yellow robe, then went back to his station.

"It's taken several winters to set this up," he continued. "But my Special Deputy, Yagos, has done an excellent job of learning the language of the Mexicotal." He knocked twice on the table and Yagos, wearing armor, a helmet festooned with feathers and brandishing a turquoise club in the shape of a snake, entered the chamber. "Meet Huitzilopochtli, the Hummingbird God of the Mexicotal."

Yagos jabbered for a short while in the unfamiliar language, then nodded at Anaxthenes.

"It appears that the Mexicotal view Yagos as some sort of deity. This has provided a great advantage with our negotiations. We will need a core of five archpriests and a score of highpriests to begin our talks at Tenochtitlan, the Mexicotal capital."

Anaxthenes looked to his right where Archpriest Danthor sat. He would have been Anaxthenes' ideal choice, but with all the challenges he faced in Balph and throughout the Five Kingdoms, he needed Danthor here. His next best choice was Archpriest Baphocles, a long-time supporter and excellent negotiator. "Baphocles, you will lead the expedition. Yagos will help you select your team. Some of the Mexicotal priests believe he is their Hummingbird God come to life, which explains his costume. Others are not so sure, but it has kept him safe from their sacrificial rites which have claimed our earlier emissaries.

"We will keep these negotiations a Temple secret and anyone who speaks of them outside of this temple will forfeit his life." He pointed to Dracar's head which was still leaking blood upon the floor. "Is that understood?"

"Aye, ayes," came from all around the Triangle Table.

"Good. Neamenestros, Timothanes and Yagos, you remain behind. We have much to discuss. The rest of you are dismissed."

SPRING

ONE

I

Kalvan sat on a high-backed chair bouncing little Ptosphes on his knee. The child giggled in response; it was one of their favorite games.

"Giggly, giggly, giggly. Giggly, giggly, Joe," he said in a sing-song voice.

Ptosphes laughed even louder, as he bounced up and down. He was at the toddler stage, but soon he would grow out of it and tire of playtime activities like this.

Demia watched with disdain, as though she were too old for such amusements.

One of the worst things about being the indispensable man was you didn't have enough time for both what you wanted to do and what you needed to do, although this activity fell into the former category. So Kalvan tried to enjoy these few stolen moments with his children whenever he had the opportunity.

Their game was interrupted when Rylla, her face pinched, burst into the chamber.

Oh no! Kalvan thought. *What now?* His body temperature began to heat up in the sweltering Michigan air. *Sometimes it's thick enough that a fish could swim in it.*

"Astrath!" she cried out. "It's time for the baby's bath."

Astrath was the new royal nursemaid, a buxom young lady with a special rapport with the children. They both loved her. Ptosphes catapulted out of Kalvan's lap and ran over to the nursemaid as fast as his wobbly little legs would take him. His sister, a pretty little child with her mother's upturned nose and complexion, followed behind.

When the children had vacated the chamber, Rylla turned to him. “We need to talk.”

Not again, he winced.

She caught his expression and frowned. “Husband, I know you’re tired of hearing about it, but Our people want to return to their homeland.”

Not all of our subjects, he thought. *Or even most of them*. The commoners had it better here in Thagnor than they’d ever had it on old Hostigos. Many of them had their own servants and owned small businesses, or worked for one of the busy royal firms. All they had left in Hos-Hostigos were ruined lands and demolished buildings. For that reason and others, Kalvan didn’t share Rylla’s urgency.

“This land is nice for a visit,” she continued. “But we are exiled from our homeland. Most of us will never feel comfortable in this cold and foreign place. Even Prince Sarrask agrees that it’s time to retake our home lands from the Harphaxi.”

Kalvan sighed. “You know we can’t leave here with King Theovacar poised at our back like a dagger. We’d be playing right into his hands.”

“We could leave a strong garrison. Not even the Grand Host was able to breach the walls you built here.”

“True, but now that Verkan has left Greffa we no longer have him as a threat to King Theovacar.” He had been sorely distressed when a letter had arrived from Verkan, telling them that on her return from Xiphlon City Dalla had been kidnapped. Verkan was unsure whether it was the Mexicotal, the Ruthani tribesmen or just bandits. Regardless, he was off to rescue his wife. And Kalvan couldn’t blame him one little bit. He couldn’t imagine what he would do if Rylla were taken from him. He knew one thing for sure: he would never rest until either she was rescued, or he found her body and took his revenge.

“I know that it’s a terrible thing that happened to our friends,” Rylla said sadly. “But King Verkan placed his friend Prince Kostran on the Greffan throne. I’m sure the prince will support us.”

Kalvan shook his head. “Prince Kostran is an administrator, not a warrior. Verkan needed someone he trusted and he’s counting on the walls he built to keep Theovacar at bay. But, the prince will not come to our aid. Theovacar could cause Styphon's Own deviltry while our army is away. Destroy our farmlands, outbuildings and feast upon our allies. I've told you about the Romans in the Cold Lands and how they sowed the lands of their worst enemy with salt. Such behavior is not beyond a tyrant like Theovacar. He could even destroy our fleet. We don't dare leave until he's been vanquished."

Kalvan knew that might take years, maybe a decade if he dragged it out long enough, with new projects and armaments that had to be perfected, before he was ready to leave. He had no desire himself to return to the war-damaged and wasted lands of Hos-Hostigos. True, he was the ultimate exile, since there was no way he would ever return to his own world. *Could that be why I'm so stubborn?* he asked himself. Maybe, but only partially. Mostly, it was because he knew how difficult it would be to reclaim and hold those blasted lands again. Hos-Hostigos was better left in the minds of men as a myth, like Camelot.

Nor would the new Great King of Hos-Harphax welcome their return. They would have to battle Great King Geblon, as well as outlaws and any armies that Styphon's House brewed up. It might take them a decade to finish off their opponents, and how would they replenish those wasted lands while fighting battles against both human and natural opponents? No, their enemies now held claim to those lands that comprised Hos-Hostigos. It would be a long time before the Hostigi were strong enough to hold their new kingdom securely enough that they could strike out and reconquer their old homeland.

"I'm sorry, love, but we need to build up our forces here and defeat Theovacar and our other enemies in the Middle Kingdoms before we return to Hos-Hostigos."

Rylla shook her fist in anger. "That could take two hands of years! I hate it here! The winters are too cold and the summers too hot and muggy. Too many children will be born in this blasted land never knowing their true home. Our children, too! I'm beginning to believe that you don't want to return to Hostigos. Is this or is this not true?"

She was right, but he knew the truth was not going to play well in

Detroit. "What I want is whatever makes you happy, kitten. Of course, I want to go back to our home, but when it is safe to do so. What I don't want to do is risk our family and home here in Nos-Hostigos; not after all the sacrifices we've made to get here. You have my word, that once Theovacar and the Grefftscharrer armies and fleet have been vanquished, we will return to Hos-Hostigos as conquerors."

Rylla shook her head. "I see you are trying to evade my question. Kalvan, you are as slippery as a Saltless Sea eel."

Kalvan only shrugged in reply. *What can I say…?*

II

Great Queen Arminta made her way down the stone passageway, holding her candle before her to light the way. She enjoyed being able to move freely inside the summer palace without being accompanied by armed bodyguards. This had only become possible when her husband had outlawed Styphon's House throughout Hos-Zygros and looted their temples, banking houses, temple farms and other holdings. Then he had all the highpriests put to death and exiled the underpriests and their ardent followers, most of whom had gravitated to Agrys City which was held in thrall by former Archpriest Grythos as regent for the young Agrysi heir apparent.

All this was done in payment for her kidnapping by the Inner Circle of Styphon's House. Her husband was not a man to play fast and loose with as both his father, now in exile, and Styphon's House had learned to their everlasting displeasure.

However, his new subjects felt quite differently. And not just because he was widely known—having been the only commander to beat Kalvan in battle—as the greatest soldier of his age. Phidestros, as Great King of Hos-Zygros, had made a number of major reforms, many of them at her suggestion—similar to ones Great King Kalvan had made in Hostigos. First, he had outlawed slavery, put selected commoners forward as judges instead of nobles and lowered taxes—which the gold recently looted from

Styphon's temples had helped pay for. Next, he had reformed the guild system, giving more power to the apprentices, and had formed royal guilds with much more liberal entrance requirements. Then Phidestros had provided free land to those soldiers about to retire, as well as find positions within the royal government for those with battlefield injuries. He had even established sanatoriums for those soldiers with afflictions too severe to work.

She was proud of both these reforms and her husband, who had acted upon her advice. To be both loved and accepted were gifts she had never expected in this life. She prayed her thanks to Yirtta Allmother, the source of life and fertility, every night.

Finally, Arminta arrived at her husband's workroom where he spent most of his limited free time working with his tools. As a youth, Phidestros had been apprenticed to a cabinet maker and he still enjoyed working with wood, woodworking tools and building things like this new *desk* of his. The chamber was well-lit by oil lamps placed in sconces around the room. The Great King was busy sanding the top of a huge burl that she guessed was to be the top of the *desk* he was working on. Her husband had based his design on a similar piece of furniture that he had seen and studied in Kalvan's palace in Hostigos Town during the Siege of Tarr-Hostigos, which one of the Hostigi prisoners had called a "desk."

Not everyone in court thought his wood-working hobby was dignified or proper enough to serve as a great king's hobby, but Phidestros didn't give a flying fig, as he put it, about what "other people thought." One of the many things she admired about him.

"Hello, husband. How goes your new *desk*?"

His face looked lupine when he looked up. "I'm making good progress. As soon as I have this burl smooth, I'm going to wax it which will bring out the color. Anything to take my mind off those high-born idiots I have to deal with all day!"

"Rough day?"

"Yes, some of those hard-headed Zygrosi nobles haven't had it pounded deep enough into their skulls that things are different now, and that they can no longer treat commoners as their personal chattel or as slaves.

Fortunately, some of the younger ones are more amenable to new thoughts. Those who refuse to bend to the new ways will be replaced."

"Please, my husband, go slowly and carefully in replacing the scions of the older houses with your officers. I understand you need to reward your men, but it could also alienate some of those we need to support our reign. Not everyone was thrilled when you brought the Temple down."

Phidestros nodded wearily. "I know, I know. But it had to be done. I had to show Styphon's treacherous dogs that we were not to be trifled with. They'll think twice before they raise their hand against us again."

Not for the first time, Arminta wondered who had suffered most during her confinement to Balph. She had certainly hated it there, surrounded on all sides by the false priests of Styphon. On the other hand, her husband had been forced to bend himself to another's will; something he hated at the best of times. It had certainly created a complete breach with Styphon's House. Fortunately, thanks to Great King Kalvan, the Temple no longer had the power or manpower to enforce its will.

They had certainly made an implacable enemy in her husband. "I'm surprised Great King Geblon hasn't renounced them as well," she said. Geblon had been her husband's loyal sidekick ever since he started the Iron Company.

"Geblon is right next door to Hos-Ktemnos and the center of Styphon's Power on Earth. There's not much they can do to punish me without raising another grand host and I don't think they could find enough manpower to do it again. However, Geblon doesn't have a big army and if Styphon's Voice had Soton raise a large force against him, he would be in real trouble."

"You could always come to his aid," Arminta pointed out.

Phidestros stopped his sanding and looked up. "Not if Soton raised an army quickly and invaded Hos-Harphax. Hos-Zygros is a thousand marches away and we would have to fight our way through Hos-Agrys to get to Harphax. While there's not enough Styphoni troops in Agrys to do more than delay us, it might give Soton enough time to topple Geblon and have him assassinated or imprisoned. That is why Geblon has refrained from sacking Styphon's temples, although I'm certain he has been tempted. The way that wife of his spends money, he can use all he can steal, raid or borrow!"

Arminta nodded in accord. Great Queen Lavena was as spoiled as she was beautiful. Arminta had spent enough time at the palace in Harphax City to thoroughly detest Lavena, but not enough to wish her ill. However, if her spendthrift ways put Geblon's throne in jeopardy, that would change.

TWO

Great King Kalvan moved his backside uncomfortably on the Fireseed Throne as he looked down at the long line of petitioners, all of whom wanted favors or justice. Few, he knew from past experience, would leave satisfied. He had been at this all morning and it appeared that his chancellor had scheduled enough supplicants that he would be here all day. Mytron knew him well: how much Kalvan hated the pomp and circumstance of the ritual of the presence chamber, so he had stocked the chamber accordingly, removing all the time-wasters and blowhards. Unfortunately, it was still necessary for him to adjudicate disputes and dispense rulings, in order to establish both his authority and the rule of law.

Kalvan removed his pipe from his belt and took out his tobacco pouch. He needed something to occupy his mind as Chancellor Mytron, the Highpriest of Dralm and chief healer, introduced the next supplicant. This one, a duke, was from Dorg, and a long way from home. *I wonder what he wants?*

The Dorgian went down on his knees as he approached the Throne.

Kalvan, irritated by the man's slavish behavior, signaled him to rise. "Men do not come to me on their knees, no matter what you have heard to the contrary, Duke."

"Yes, yes, Your Majesty. I'm sorry, I did not mean to offend—"

Rylla, who sat in her own matching throne at his side, made a knowing smile. She knew all his quirks and idiocrasies. Or at least, that's how she saw them. Kalvan saw them as democratic principles that did not translate well into Zarthani society.

"I'm not offended, yet."

The Duke quickly rose to his feet, his face beet red. "I have come to petition Your Majesty's support against the vile creature, King Hyrum, who sits upon the throne of Dorg."

"Why should I take up arms against a fellow king?" Kalvan asked. He got similar requests about twice a month, most of them directed against the King of Dorg. He saw no advantage to overthrowing King Hyrum and earning the reputation of usurper of other kings' rule. Besides, if he conquered Dorg, he'd then be responsible for putting a competent ruler in Hyrum's place, as well as ensuring the kingdom's peace and tranquility. He had enough on his plate keeping the lid on Nos-Hostigos and its allies.

To say nothing of preparing for Theovacar's next move and the possibility of another Styphoni invasion force.

"Your Majesty, King Hyrum is a tyrant of the worst kind. He kidnaps our women, right off the street, regardless of rank!"

Now, I know what rankles, Kalvan thought.

"He then takes them into his palace from which they never return. It is rumored that the Tyrant Hyrum commits all types of abominations upon their persons, then has them stuffed as one would stuff a dead owl or trophy stag! He then dotes upon his assembly of death, doing all manner of unspeakable things—"

"If these words are true, why do the nobles and commoners of Dorg put up with his transgressions?" Kalvan asked.

"King Hyrum has a strong household guard and the loyalty of the Royal Army. We do not have the arms or experience to defeat him, which is why we need your aid, Your Majesty."

"And why should I embroil Nos-Hostigos in a war against the rightful ruler of Dorg that your fellow citizens will not undertake for themselves?"

"Because of Your Majesty's reputation as a fair and good ruler, and because you know in your heart that Hyrum is an abomination before both the gods and men."

"Nice words, but they won't refill my coffers nor reanimate the many Hostigi soldiers who will die in such a war."

"We will pay, Your Majesty," the Duke stammered. "I can promise you in advance two hundred thousand ounces of gold and five times that of silver. Plus, you can plunder the Royal Treasury of Dorg, which is known to be the wealthiest in the Middle Kingdoms, now that Theovacar has been unseated from Greffa."

"I'm sorry, Duke. My army cannot be bought with gold or sad stories of misrule. If you want to depose King Hyrum, do it yourself. I will not do it for you."

"But, but... Your Majesty!"

Chancellor Mytron took the Duke by the back of his ruff and led him away from the throne.

There was a sudden ruckus, and Kalvan reached below for one of his pocket pistols.

It was one of the palace guardsmen, pushing his way through the throng of petitioners. "Your Majesty," he called out. "There is a messenger from the sea wall who wishes to speak with you."

"Bring him to me," he said with obvious relief. *Maybe I can get off this throne and get back to work.* "I will be in my private audience chamber."

Kalvan and Rylla were there for only a few minutes before the messenger arrived. He was dripping wet, although whether from running in the moist air or from the lake breeze, he couldn't tell.

While the messenger regained his breath, Kalvan said, "Cleon, bring the poor man a glass of wine."

Cleon nodded, departed and returned with a goblet of wine.

The man downed the wine in three big gulps. "Thank you, Your Majesty. I have news. A boat bearing the flag of Grefftscharr has entered the harbor."

"How was the flag displayed?" he asked. This was an important question: according to Middle Kingdom custom, an upside down flag indicated a truce or parley was requested.

"Upside down, Your Majesty."

Ever since Kalvan had evicted Theovacar from Greffa City, the former capital, he had tightened his control over Grefftscharr tighter and tighter until it was not uncommon to receive Grefftscharrer merchant vessels requesting sanctuary. King Theovacar was not a popular ruler, but he was a dangerous one; not only to his people, but to his neighbors.

"Upon your return to your station, have the vessel's captain and whatever emissaries it contains brought to the Presence Chamber."

"Yes, Sir."

"Cleon, tell one of the pages to go find Captain-General Errock and tell him to meet me in the Presence Chamber as soon as possible."

His manservant turned and left.

"What do you want with Errock?" Rylla asked.

"Errock is from Greffa and he knows many people. I may need him to verify these people's story."

Kalvan sat impatiently waiting for the visitors, or whatever they were, from Grefftscharr to arrive. Captain-General Errock had just arrived and was still catching his breath from running up the castle stairs. Rylla sat next to him, while Chancellor Mytron paced back and forth in front of them. He was glad to see that Mytron had regained most of the weight he had lost during the exodus from Hostigos. Mytron still fretted too much, but he had been an excellent choice as chancellor since he knew how to separate church from state. Something his predecessor, Highpriest Xentos, had not been willing or able to do.

As the Grefftscharr delegation entered the audience chamber, it was obvious this was no rag-tag band of refugees or outcasts. The delegates were dressed in rich robes with ermine and mink collars. The thick gold chains around their necks told the world these were rich and prosperous men. Kalvan wondered who or what they represented within the Grefftscharrer government. Had Theovacar regained his sanity and decided to sue for peace?

No, that is unthinkable, he decided.

After Chancellor Mytron made the pro-forma introductions, one of the men in a wine-colored robe stepped forward. "Great King Kalvan, I am Duke Utharn of Ult-Greffa. We have come here to inform Your Majesty that the Despot who was formerly titled Theovacar, King of Grefftscharr, is now dead."

Kalvan could feel his jaw drop. He looked over at Rylla and saw her eyes bulging at this proclamation.

"What happened?" he asked, feeling as if someone had just pulled the rug out from underneath his feet.

The Duke bowed deeply, then began to speak: "The despot Theovacar raised taxes and fees to the point where the entire populace of our kingdom was suffering. His temper knew no bounds and he frequently murdered or imprisoned anyone suspected of harboring ill will against the Throne. Many of these people were innocent of all charges, but the tyrant refused to rescind their sentences. Finally, the Assembly of Lords and Council of Merchants agreed together that Theovacar's rule must end.

"When pressed, Theovacar's bodyguard arrested him. He was judged by the Assembly of Nobles and declared a despot. He was put to death by beheading. Now we, the leaders and spokesmen for the new government, have come here to sue for peace with Nos-Hostigos. There is no conflict between our kingdoms and we would like to openly trade and exchange ambassadors with Your Majesties, Nos-Hostigos and its allies. The war between our peoples is over. Long live Great King Kalvan!"

Everyone in the chamber joined in with a chorus of "Long Live Great King Kalvan!"

The Grefftscharri must have been inspired by Verkan's takeover of Greffa, Kalvan decided. Of course, the end of hostilities was good news for Nos-Hostigos, but not good news for Kalvan. "I am very pleased to learn that your tyrant is no longer in office. It will open a new period of peace and trade between our two kingdoms.

"Yes, Your Majesty. It will bring an end to an unnecessary and unjust war."

Kalvan was unable to find anything in that statement he disagreed with. It just was that peace so unexpected and poorly timed. After what he had said earlier to Rylla, he would never be able to block the Return to Old Hostigos movement.

"Who is the new king of Grefftscharr?" he asked.

"King Wydmar, Theovacar's oldest cousin from his mother's side. He is now the ruler of Grefftscharr and its colonies. He has sent us as his personal delegation to sue for peace."

"He is a wise ruler," Kalvan replied. Or smart enough to end a war he wasn't going to win. And couldn't afford to pay for.

Rylla leaned over, saying, "We need to talk."

He nodded. "Duke Utharn, I suggest you meet with Chancellor Mytron to work out the details of the peace terms between our two kingdoms. When you have come to a meeting of the minds, the Chancellor will present the terms to Us."

"Thank you, Your Majesty," the Duke replied, followed with a bow. He and his party quickly followed Mytron out of the presence chamber and into the Chancellor's office.

He turned to his wife. "I agree that we need to talk, but first I need to question Captain-General Errock."

"Captain-General, does this story ring true to your ears?"

Errock tugged at his goatee for a few moments. "Yes, Your Majesty, I believe they are telling the truth and that this peace treaty is sincere. Duke Utharn is well known throughout Grefftscharr as a fair-dealer and honest man—for a member of the gentry. If this were a ruse, his life would be forfeit. Furthermore, King Theovacar is too proud and self-loving to ever allow even a rumor that he was deposed to circulate. If Utharn says the despot is dead—he is no longer among the living. And good riddance!"

"That is good to know," Kalvan said. Errock had fled Theovacar's court under penalty of death, and while his brother had remained in Grefftscharr, Errock had relocated in Thagnor to escape the headsman's ax. His knowledge of the Middle Kingdoms, as well as his ability to lead men, had made him a real asset to Nos-Hostigos and Kalvan.

"Now, I want you to join with Chancellor Mytron and aid him in his questioning of the envoys. If anything rings hollow, leave and let me know at once."

"Yes, Your Majesty," Errock said, as he turned around and left the audience chamber.

Kalvan turned back to his wife. "It is time we talked."

"Yes, husband, it surely is," Rylla replied with a cat that ate the canary smile.

I've really done it this time, he thought. *I've boxed myself in good. I don't even think that Duke Skranga could talk his way out of this dilemma.*

He could see she was beaming. "I can't believe it. Allfather Dralm must have listened to my prayers! Now that Theovacar is dead, my husband, you can lead our people back to their homeland!"

Kalvan felt the beginning of a massive headache, one he knew wasn't going to go away anytime soon. He nodded, not trusting his voice.

"When do we leave?" she asked.

"There are a lot of preparations that need to be made before we start talk of leaving. First, we need to know where we are going. Since most of Old Hos-Hostigos is now a wasteland, as Great King Lysandros discovered to his dismay, we need to find another route into the Five Kingdoms."

"It is the fastest route," Rylla said. "Don't we have enough provisions for an army?"

Kalvan shook his head. "To take and hold Hos-Hostigos, we would need an army of at least upwards of forty thousand men, with fifty to sixty thousand horses and oxen to carry the supplies and provisions we would need. By the time we arrive, we might be facing the combined forces of Hos-Harphax, Hos-Ktemnos and the Zarthani Knights backed by Styphon's Own Guard. Maybe as many as fifty to sixty thousand men."

"That many?"

"Maybe. We can't be certain. Maybe Grand Master Soton will have trouble bringing troops from the Sastragath. However, we can be certain that the Inner Circle of Styphon's House will do all it can to ensure that we do not retake our homeland. In addition, Great King Geblon will not only have the Royal Army to face us, but a substantial levy from his princes."

"What about the south?" Rylla asked.

"The south is blocked by the Zarthani Knights and Styphon's House. The northern routes are dangerous since we cannot afford to fight Styphon's House, Archpriest Grythos of Hos-Agrys and Great King Phidestros at the same time."

Rylla nodded. "Maybe it is time to send an envoy to Hos-Zygros to meet with Great King Phidestros and enlist his aid."

Kalvan shook his head. "I'm not sure it's going to be that easy. After all, the new great king of Hos-Harphax is Great King Geblon, one of Phidestros' former generals. Geblon holds that all of our former kingdom is now part of Hos-Harphax." *As it was before my arrival*, he thought to himself. "I don't believe that he or his wife will relinquish their claims upon our lands just because we want to return to our old homeland."

Rylla's face took on a grim cast. "Lavena will never relinquish Hostigos, not as long as her father claims to be prince of Hostigos. What an abomination! We will have to kill them all."

Kalvan held up his hands, palms facing out. "Darling, it's not going to be that easy. Phidestros left behind a rebuilt Harphaxi army when he left for Hos-Zygros. And that's not including Phidestros' own holdings in Greater Beshta where he left behind another army to hold his lands. I don't know that we could beat a combined army of Zygrosi and Harphaxi troops. Nor can we count Styphon's House out, either. The minute we move into the Five Kingdoms, Styphon's House will be putting an army together to attack us. They will support any force that opposes us, along the lines of 'the enemy of my enemy is my friend.'"

"Yes, I've heard that before."

"Which makes it no less true," he replied.

"After their losses at the Siege of Thagnor, Styphon's House is depleted and as weak as it will ever be. The time to strike at Balph, the serpent's nest, is right now!"

"Darling, it's not going to be that easy. To get to Balph, we either have to go through Hos-Harphax, or go through Hos-Ktemnos, which means fighting Grand Master Soton. We need to call a meeting of the General Staff and discuss our options."

"Good idea. I'll start drawing up some plans for the invasion...."

Kalvan wondered if she didn't already have something worked out. Was it possible that she'd learned about Theovacar's death before the envoys arrived? *No, I'm just getting a little paranoid. And just when things were going so well....*

THREE

I

Archpriest Danthor decided to visit the Balph Study Team in person rather than attempt another call. For some reason, no one was answering. He knew their cover hadn't been compromised because, as a member of the Innermost Circle of Styphon's House, he would have been informed the moment it happened. No, there was something going on, and for some reason no one had bothered to inform him. *Maybe I need to spend some time on First Level, if for no other reason than to remind these jokers that I'm not someone to be trifled with.*

He'd even tried to call Chief Verkan, but he wasn't answering, either.

The Balph Study Team had its headquarters at a goldsmith's shop. It was usually a busy place, but today Danthor noticed that the door was barred and none of the interior lights were on. *What's going on? And why am I out of the loop?*

The main street was full of shoppers and travelers, including a number of priests.

Danthor feared he had been undercover in Balph for too long, and he was growing complacent. He entered the jewelry store that sat next to the goldsmith's shop.

"Your Sanctity, can I help you?" the owner asked.

"Do you know where the owners of the shop next door have gone?"

The jewelry shop owner shook his head. "I'm sorry, Your Sanctity, but the goldsmith, along with his masters and apprentices, closed up the shop and left over a moon-half ago."

"Did they say where they were going before they left?" Danthor asked.

"Yes, they said that the political situation in Grefftscharr had worsened and they had to return home. One mentioned that the Hostigi were making inroads upon their territory." He paused to add, "Praise Styphon, the Daemon Kalvan is causing mischief there and no longer in the Five Kingdoms!"

"As Styphon Wills it," Danthor added, as he nodded his head. He held up a large key, saying, "I will be entering their shop to see if they left my special order behind."

"Of course, Your Sanctity."

One advantage to being a Styphon's House archpriest was that no one dared question anything you did. Danthor used his keys to unlock both the outer lock and the magnetic lock that kept the shop secure from thieves and agents-inquisitory. Inside, all the golden wares were still on the counters and in the display cabinets. Danthor used the thumb-lock to get into the door leading downstairs where the Balph conveyer-head resided. The room was empty of the dome-shaped conveyers and anything else. *If I didn't know better, I'd think they had bugged out.*

Now he was worried. It would have taken a real emergency for the Balph Study Team to have vacated the premises so completely. *What in the Styphon is going on?*

Danthor used his communicator, designed to look like a small golden idol of Styphon, to call the other Kalvan's Time-Line study teams. No one was answering. Why had he been left behind? Was it merely an oversight or were things so bad that no one had the opportunity to contact him? He got small comfort from either answer.

II

The General Staff of Nos-Hostigos met in the Great Hall of Tarr-Thagnor, with flags and banners on one side and colorful tapestries depicting past Hostigi victories on the other. Running down the middle of the room was a wooden trestle table ringed by a score of high-backed leather chairs. Seated at the head of the table was Great King Kalvan as Commander-and-Chief with Great Queen Rylla, as Chief of Operations, to his right and Prince Phrames, his Chief of Staff, to his left. Sitting down on both sides of the table were the kingdom's top military and political leaders: Uncle Wolf Tharses, Highpriest of Galzar and Chief of Chaplains, as well as Highpriest Mytron, Highpriest of Dralm and Chancellor of Nos-Hostigos. Everyone of importance was there, including Captain-General Hestophes, Grand Constable Leukestros, Chief of Intelligence Klestreus, Admiral Herad, Pheblon, former Prince of Nostor, Baron Halmoth, Prince-in-Exile Mnestros of Eubros, elevated to prince after his father died when the Styphoni overran the Agrysi Princedom of Eubros, Prince Sarrask and Captain-General Errock. Only King Chartiphon of Rathon was absent, being too far away to be able to make the meeting. Expecting his absence, Kalvan had sent him a letter describing the latest developments in Grefftscharr.

Kalvan rose to his feet. "First, I want to announce an important political development, maybe the most important since we arrived in the Middle Kingdoms two years ago." He had everyone's undivided attention. "Yesterday morning a delegation from Ult-Greffa arrived to sue for peace."

The room was as still as if he'd announced a bomb was about to go off. Captain-General Hestophes froze, a burning splinter only inches from his pipe.

"There has been a popular uprising in Grefftscharr resulting in the execution of King Theovacar," Kalvan announced.

Everyone at the table looked up in surprise. A few "Praise, Dralm's" were said.

"The new King sent a delegation to Thagnor to request peace. The war with Grefftscharr is finally over."

"Praise Dralm and Great King Kalvan!" shouted a dozen voices.

"This means we'll be able to focus all of our attention on our real enemy, Styphon's House," Prince Pheblon said.

"Down Styphon!" Prince Sarrask of Sask added.

"Exactly," Kalvan said. "Now that we no longer have an enemy to our rear we now have the opportunity to decide our future." He paused to look over at his wife. "The question before us today is whether or not we will return to Old Hostigos now or in the future. I realized that there are many among us who long to return to their former homes."

"Not me," Prince Pheblon grumbled. "All I have waiting for me in Nostor are broken buildings and tombstones. My former princedom is nothing but a graveyard."

"Enough of your defeatist jibber-jabber, Pheblon," Prince Sarrask cried. "Stab me, but are we going to be condemned to live our lives as exiles in this godsforsaken land because of your fears! Not me. I want to return to Sask and rebuild my palace and my subjects' homes. It is my birthright!"

Sarrask's words were followed by cheers from a dozen voices, including Great Queen Rylla's.

Kalvan felt a sinking sensation. He needed to take control of the meeting. "There are a number of factors we have to take into account before we willy-nilly hare off on a military expedition to liberate Old Hostigos. First, while we no longer have to fear an attack from the rear by former King Theovacar, we cannot write-off Styphon's House and the Order of Zarthani Knights. Plus, since we left the Five Kingdoms, there have been a number of important changes among the ruling houses. Prince Phidestros, our sworn enemy, is now seated on the Ivory Throne of Hos-Zygros, while his paladin, Great King Geblon, holds the Iron Throne of Hos-Harphax which he believes holds suzerainty over our homeland of Hos-Hostigos.

"However, it does appear that certain fractures have occurred within Styphon's zone of control. I'll let Chief of Intelligence Klestreus give you the latest news."

Klestreus slowly rose up from the other end of the table. "We have just received a message from our spies in Hos-Ktemnos that a boat arrived from Hos-Zygros containing as cargo the heads of several hundred Styphon's House priests. If that isn't a declaration of war against the Temple, I don't know what is?"

Kalvan had ordered his spymaster to keep this news quiet until today's meeting. It was his hole card, and he was hoping it would introduce some sanity to the proceedings.

"Maybe we can forge a peace treaty with Great King Phidestros," Prince Phrames said.

Kalvan nodded. "I believe this is an avenue we should approach."

Rylla shook her head. "More delays! We're already past the second moon of spring. How much longer do we have until we can no longer mount an effective campaign this season?"

"Not long, Your Majesty," Sarrask said. "We need to move quickly and decisively."

"But where and how?" Kalvan asked rhetorically. "One path is to go north to Ulthor City and work our way through Hos-Agrys; certainly, the surviving League of Dralm Agrysi princes will welcome and join with us, more than offsetting those who joined forces with the Styphoni. According to our intelligence operatives, we know that Soton took most of his army back to Hos-Ktemnos last year and has returned to Tarr-Ceros.

"Moreover, what will Great King Phidestros do while we're attacking his neighbor? Will he welcome us, or view us as a threat? I fear the latter. We do not have enough men to fight both the Agrysi and Zygrosi armies at the same time, especially since Phidestros took at least thirty thousand or more well-trained and veteran troops with him into Hos-Zygros.

"Plus, when we advance upon Agrys City we will be close enough to Hos-Harphax that Great King Geblon, even without Phidestros' support, could march north and attack our siege party. Then we would have to face both the Styphoni and Harphaxi armies.

"I'm sure that if you have any questions about it, either Prince Mnestros or Captain-General Hestophes will fill you in on the situation in Hos-Agrys after the meeting. As far as returning to Hostigos directly, there's no way we can retrace our route through Hos-Hostigos. According to our intelligence reports, Great King Lysandros' men fell upon the land like a plague of locusts, eating everything that was alive including their own horses and oxen. Those farms and outbuildings that survived our passage were burned or leveled by the Harphaxi as they made their way home. It's far too late in the year to establish food depots and arsenals for our army in those destroyed territories."

"There must be another avenue," Rylla interrupted.

"I suggest we attempt a two-pronged attack," Prince Sarrask offered. "First, we send an envoy to Hos-Zygros to talk terms with Great King Phidestros. Meanwhile, our army can strike the Styphoni to the south, hitting the Zarthani Knights—starting with Tarr-Ceros, then once it's destroyed, roll up the rest of their forts along the Great River like a rug."

When did Sarrask get so damn smart? Kalvan wondered. Or was this plan Rylla's idea? It sounded like something Gonsalo Cordoba might have come up with during the Italian Wars when the Spanish took Sicily and worked their way up the Italian peninsula.

"Once the southern border has been secured," Sarrask continued, "our forces can join up with Skranga and Democriphon's—or Great King Valthros' or whatever he calls himself these days—Royal Army of Hos-Bletha. Both armies will outnumber Great King Niclophon's forces by three or four to one. Once Niclophon is dispatched we can run through Hos-Ktemnos like a dose of the salts, killing all the Styphoni and their minions throughout Niclophon's lands. He has long suckled at the Temple's breast; now he will pay for his infamy. Our intelligence tells us that the great king of Hos-Ktemnos has not had the men or time to rebuild the Sacred Squares. Once we have destroyed the rattlesnake's nest that is Balph and cut the head off Styphon's snake, I would bet my treasure train that Great King Lukthos of Hos-Ktemnos will surrender or sue for terms."

"Hear, hear!" cried out a number of voices.

Kalvan shook his head in wonder. Sarrask—most likely with Rylla's aid—had come up with a workable plan. One that would be impossible for him to shoot down, Dralm-damnit!

To salvage what he could from this debacle, Kalvan held up his cup of wine. "To Sarrask, for a whale of a good idea." Prince Sarrask had come a long way from the time he had arrived on that cross-time flying machine, when he was one of Hostigos' biggest enemies. Now, Sarrask was one of their most loyal paladins, right up there with Baron Hestophes and Prince Phrames.

Rylla was beaming, as was Sarrask—his face bright red with embarrassment.

"We will start drawing-up plans for the investment of Tarr-Ceros at first light," Kalvan announced. He knew one of the secrets of good leadership was knowing when to fold one's hand while being gracious about it. Obviously, not everyone shared his desire to stay in Nos-Hostigos. Sarrask's plan wasn't foolproof, but it was better than anything he had come up with—or had wanted to.

"This will be our second siege of Tarr-Ceros. The first was a partial success, but we left without pulling down the walls. This time we will stay until we've cracked the heart of this tough nut and killed or captured Grand Master Soton and his top aides."

Captain-General Errock nodded. "I agree, Your Majesty. We cannot afford to leave the Grand Master at our backs while we besiege the other Order forts and tarrs. However, Tarr-Ceros will be, as you said, 'a tough nut to crack,' and I doubt we can do it before the weather turns bad."

Kalvan nodded. "A good point, Captain-General. However, the invasion plan—as presented by Prince Sarrask—is not time-dependent. Although I agree, the sooner we can take Tarr-Ceros the less time Styphon's House will have to prepare for our march upon the unholy city of Balph. Meanwhile, we will inform Duke Skranga and Great King Valthros of our plans so they can prepare for our arrival."

"Good idea," Errock interjected. "Tarr-Ceros has adopted many of Your Majesty's defensive tactics since your investment of their fort. Their walls are now protected by earthworks, bulwarks and more guns. It will not be easy to break through their defenses."

Kalvan nodded. One of the problems with introducing novel tactics and weapons, both defensive and offensive, was that one's enemies often quickly adopted them as well. From what his spies had to say, Phidestros was developing his own rifle corps, while even Styphon's House was working on transitioning from muskets to rifles. However, no one else had developed their own explosive artillery shells and the last two years had seen some great improvements on the Hostigi versions.

"We have a lot more guns and shells than we had during our earlier siege," Kalvan stated. "I plan to rain shells down upon Tarr-Ceros like Thanor's Hammers falling out of the sky!"

"Huzzah and Down Styphon!" shouted voices from a dozen throats. "Huzzah and Down Styphon! Huzzah and Down Styphon!"

When the chant had quieted down, Kalvan continued, "We need to send one of our most trusted men and advisors to Hos-Zygros to parley with Great King Phidestros and win him over to our side. Or, barring that, keep him neutral. I plan to send Captain-General Hestophes, who's already been in Hos-Agrys, and knows the lay of the land, to Zygros Town to set up talks with Phidestros. As his advisor, I plan to send Highpriest Tharses."

Prince Sarrask noted, "We will miss his generalship, Your Majesty, but Baron Hestophes is the right man. And, by Galzar, so is Uncle Wolf Tharses!"

Even Rylla nodded in accord.

Kalvan bent over to speak to Prince Phrames in private. "How anxious are you to return to Beshta, Prince?"

Phrames shook his head. "Not at all, Your Majesty. I only ruled the Princedom of Beshta for a short time, but it had been so badly managed by Prince Balthar that I was only able to introduce the most rudimentary reforms. I—unlike most of these fools—am very happy here as Prince of Gytha and have no desire to leave Nos-Hostigos to return to Beshta."

Kalvan sighed. That solved one problem, since—no matter what accommodations they reached—Phidestros would not be willing to abandon Greater Beshta. Sashta didn't matter since its former prince, Prince Balthames, was dead and buried in an anonymous grave.

"Hestophes, you will meet me in my private audience chamber after the meeting and we will discuss the details of your mission."

"Yes, Your Majesty," the stout Captain-General replied.

Kalvan could tell from his tight-lipped response that he wasn't happy about the assignment, but as a good soldier would do as ordered. Hestophes had already spent most of a year in Hos-Agrys working as head of a Hostigi fifth column. Now, he'd be going to Hos-Zygros to meet with Phidestros. Meanwhile, his wife was on permanent assignment, as nursemaid and guardian, to Harmakros' son, Aspasthar in Agrys City. The way the war was going it was likely to be a long time before they would get together again. He wondered if he could tolerate such a long absence from Rylla. Probably not, he decided.

He turned to Admiral Herad, "I would like to meet with you, as well, Admiral."

The Admiral stood up and bowed. "At your pleasure, Your Majesty."

Mental note: *Write long letter to King Chartiphon and tell him what's going down.*

FOUR

I

Grand Master Soton smacked his knee with a fist in frustration. A delegation from the Inner Circle had arrived from Balph and he didn't care one whit about whatever it was they wanted. It was just more time-wasting nonsense. He had more important things to worry over. There were rumors that the nomads were gathering again on the other side of the Great River—weren't the Ormaz-spawned bastards satisfied with all the booty they had taken after attacking Dorg and overrunning Wulfula last summer?—and several of the border forts were still in need of major repairs. Plus, he was having little success in getting new recruits for the Order.

He picked up his mace and began to swing it back and forth. Slowly, he felt himself begin to relax. A knock at the door to his private chamber brought him back to the world and its many problems.

"Yes, Sarmoth?"

"I have Archpriest Danthor to see you, Grand Master."

"Send him in," he replied. Of all the archpriests of the Innermost Circle, Danthor was one of the canniest and most down to earth. He could be reasoned with, unlike so many others. It could easily have been worse; Styphon's Voice Anaxthenes himself could have come, or sent Archpriest Neamenestros or one of his other vile minions.

Archpriest Danthor, a tall man who walked with a commanding stride, entered the chamber. He was also one of the few archpriests with a full head of silver hair; probably more common in Hos-Bletha—where he was from—than in Hos-Ktemnos where most of the upperpriests shaved their heads. However, it did mean that he stood out in a crowd of highpriests like a flamingo among a flock of pigeons.

"Your Worthiness," the Archpriest said, "it is good to see you in good health."

Soton nodded. "Welcome, Danthor. Although, I suspect I will not welcome any requests you have brought with you from Balph."

Danthor smiled. "I believe not, Your Worthiness. However, I do have fresh news: Have you heard about Great King Phidestros' latest betrayal?"

"No, what has that jumped-up bastard done this time?"

"Phidestros sent a boat to Balph containing the severed heads of all the upperpriests and loyal lowerpriests in Hos-Zygros. Styphon's Voice and the Inner Circle have sent me to ask you to respond in kind."

"With what?" he asked, his voice rising. "I have barely enough troops to garrison the Order's forts. Would the Inner Circle rather have a nomad invasion next spring, or Phidestros' head on a silver platter?"

Archpriest Danthor shrugged. "Both, probably. There is no end to their desires, real or pretend."

"Exactly," Soton roared. "I've spent the last three years fighting Kalvan and conquering Hos-Agrys. The cost has been abysmal; I've lost over twelve thousand Order troops, most of them irreplaceable. Our recruiters have to compete with depleted mercenary bands, Great King Lukthos' muster parties and with Styphon's Own Guard's recruiting efforts—all here in the Sastragath or in Hos-Ktemnos since our enemies or neutrals control the other four kingdoms. So, from where am I supposed to gather this army that the Inner Circle wants me raise? It will have to be a big one in order to beard one of the greatest generals in the Five Kingdoms. Don't they know that Phidestros took over twenty-five thousand veterans of the Fireseed Wars with him when he left Hos-Harphax to claim the Ivory Throne?"

"I doubt that they took that into consideration, Your Worthiness. Before the Usurper Kalvan arrived, the members of the Inner Circle never had to deal with such contingencies. Now, they hide their heads in the sand and make orders that only the gods could carry out."

"Truer words have never been spoken," Soton said, nodding his accord. "Take a seat, Danthor. Are the archpriests such fools as to believe that Great King Geblon will allow me passage through Hos-Harphax to attack his former master? Even if we were to travel to Hos-Zygros by boat, we would be forced to land on inhospitable shores that our enemy owns and rules. To successfully attack Phidestros, I would need at least fifty thousand well-trained soldiers and hundreds of big guns. Now, unless the Inner Circle has a sorcerer who can magically procure these items, there is no way that I can raise an army to fight in Hos-Zygros, even with all the gold in Balph at my disposal!"

The Archpriest nodded his agreement. "I will return with your words, although they will not be welcome to the Innermost Circle."

Soton shook his head in wonderment. "What do these cow-faced morons think Kalvan will be doing if I hare off to fight Great King Phidestros? We just received word that King Theovacar has been murdered and his killers have made peace with Nos-Hostigos."

"King Theovacar dead! This news has not yet reached Balph."

"Of course not, we just learned about it ourselves. Apparently, there was a palace revolt and Theovacar's nobles rose up against him, overthrew him and had him beheaded. Now, the Usurper Kalvan has lost his only enemy in the Upper Middle Kingdoms, and is free to resume his war against the Temple."

"Will he strike soon, or bide his time?" Danthor asked.

Soton shrugged. "Only Styphon knows for sure. I suspect the Usurper will wait until next spring before he makes any military move against us. However, Kalvan has built his reputation on not doing what others have predicted that he might do. Our agents-inquisitory have told me that he has used this time of peace to rebuild his army and now more than two-thirds of his shot companies are armed with rifles."

"That is very bad news. I will have to leave sooner than anticipated. Styphon's Voice Anaxthenes will want to know of this latest development."

"Yes, and maybe it will make him reconsider his war against Phidestros. It would be the gods' own disaster if Kalvan and Phidestros forged their wills together and became one against the Temple."

"The very foundations of Balph tremble at the thought," Danthor replied.

II

Kalvan realized, as he waited for Hestophes, he'd been out-maneuvered and out-flanked by the Return to Hostigos Party, but that in large part it was his own fault. He was the one who'd told Rylla that the major obstacle was King Theovacar and the Grefftscharr fleet. Once that threat had been neutralized—and had it ever!—well, he would either have had to change his position, which Rylla would never forgive him for, or make good on his word. The problem with making good on his word was that it would embroil the Kingdom in a major war that could go on for years.

Just as he was becoming accustomed to the peace of the last year, he had to give it up to make preparations to attack Tarr-Ceros. They'd had enough problems with that fortress during their previous siege; fortunately, now they had much better tools. It was too bad they hadn't finished the job then, but Kalvan had faced other problems such as a nomad invasion and a Styphon's House inspired invasion of Hos-Hostigos.

Kalvan used his tinderbox to light up his pipe and drew in some smoke. The problem was they were going to have to level Tarr-Ceros, which was the biggest and strongest castle here-and-now; it reminded him of one of the old Crusader fortresses, only bigger. Unfortunately, everyone was waiting for him to come up with another miracle, like last year's Greek fire. Well, he didn't have any new weapons to pull out of his hat, but they did have lots more cannons, as well as shells that only misfired two out of every ten times they were used, versus the older ones that went off prematurely, or not at all, one of out of every three or four times.

Plus, two-thirds of the Royal Army's musketeers were now armed with rifles. That would help keep the Knights from skirmishing or attacking from sally ports.

He heard a knock at the door.

"Come in," he said.

"Your Majesty," Hestophes said as he entered the room, holding a large jar. "I figured if we were going to talk, we might need some of Ermut's

Best to lubricate the wheels of thought."

Kalvan nodded. "Good idea." While he had greatly decreased his input of spirits the last couple of years, a few drinks every once in a while didn't seem to hurt. Maybe it would help allay some of the anxiety he was feeling over the latest turn of events.

While the Captain-General was filling their goblets, he said, "Hestophes, I know you'd rather stay with the army and help orchestrate our attack on Tarr-Ceros, but I don't have anyone else with your credentials and background to negotiate a deal with Great King Phidestros."

"How about Prince Phrames?" he asked.

Kalvan shook his head. "I need Phrames here in Thagnor. He is going to rule Nos-Hostigos in my stead while I'm off fighting Styphon's House. I need someone in command here I can trust implicitly and who understands what I've been trying to achieve."

"Aha," Hestophes said, nodding. "Phrames is a good choice. But won't Phidestros be insulted if the head of negotiations is a mere baron?"

"Good point," he replied. "From now on, you are Duke Hestophes."

"Thank you, Your Majesty, but I wasn't fishing for a new title—"

"I know, but you deserve one. And once this war is over, I'll give you lands here or in Hostigos commensurate with your new title."

"Thank you, Your Majesty."

"I believe Highpriest Tharses will be of great help as Phidestros is a stalwart worshipper of Galzar. I'll let you pick the rest of your negotiating party. Just don't take too many soldiers. I have a feeling I'm going to need every damn one of them."

Hestophes smiled. "Understood. What kind of terms are we talking about?"

"Since Phidestros has just sacked all the Styphon's House temples in Hos-Zygros, I don't think he'll be looking for gold. Maybe revenge upon Styphon's House for kidnapping Princess Arminta?"

"Maybe that'll be enough. However, he may want a share of the spoils when you sack Balph."

"You can tell Phidestros, I'll give him half of all the gold, silver and jewels we find, if he joins us. If not, I'll give him a third. He can even send one of his generals to oversee the disbursement of the spoils."

Hestophes' eyebrows shot up. "That's *very* generous, Your Majesty."

"Yes, but it's still cheaper than a war we could lose."

Hestophes nodded, as though he couldn't find anything wrong with the proposition. "However, sire, Great King Phidestros is going to demand some guarantees regarding his holdings and his friend Geblon's claims upon Old Hos-Hostigos."

"You can tell him that we have no claim upon his lands in Great Beshta, and welcome him as a neighbor. However, we will want to have suzerainty over the rest of Hos-Hostigos, including the princedoms of Hostigos, Sask, Nostor, Ulthor and Nyklos. We are even willing to pay Great King Geblon for any *improvements* he has made in those lands."

Hestophes laughed. "That will cost the treasury only a few phenigs since as far as I know Geblon has made no efforts to reclaim those territories, other than sending a few nobles there he wanted to exile from his court."

"Great King Geblon may not see it that way. I doubt that his wife or father-in-law, Sthentros the Traitor, will agree. I'd rather pay a reasonable ransom in gold than risk war with Hos-Zygros and Hos-Harphax at this time."

"Good point, Your Majesty. Although, I doubt Queen Rylla shares your views. At the least, she'll want the self-proclaimed Prince of Hostigos' head on a platter!"

Kalvan gnashed his teeth together. "This war was her idea but I won't brook any interference in the way I run it. The Royal Treasury is fat with gold and I'd rather spend some of it than risk losing more men in a never-ending war."

"I agree," Hestophes said. "The war has been good for me, but it has cost Hostigos dearly."

Kalvan nodded. "This time I want to make sure that the butcher's bill is mostly paid by Styphon's House. I want to see the False Temple destroyed and pulled down around Styphon's Own Voice's ears in Balph."

The Captain-General paused to drink from his goblet. "I agree, Your Majesty, but Styphon's House has more heads than a nest full of serpents."

"True, but if we can build an alliance with Phidestros, who's proven his hatred for Styphon's House by the mass murder of hundreds of their priests, we may have an opportunity to put them out of business for good."

"I will do my best to see that it happens. What route should I take to Zygros Town?"

As Kalvan recalled, Zygros Town was located on the same site as Quebec City back home. "Bypass the land route through Hos-Agrys. We have some secret supporters in Hos-Agrys, but there are too many Styphoni in that kingdom. I suggest you travel by boat through the Sea of Aesklos to Narth Town, a small Zygrosi trading port west of Port Glarth. From there you can ride over the land bridge to the Skirlos Sea and from there hire a boat and sail to Port Itya. At Itya you should be able to contact the right royal officials who can help you reach Zygros Town."

"That's a sound plan, Your Majesty."

"For communication, we're going to be using homing pigeons."

"Pigeons?" Hestophes asked in surprise. "I thought they were only good for eating."

The Zarthani or Urgothi tribes, during one of their migrations, had brought the homing pigeons with them from Asia or Europe, since squabs were a popular delicacy here-and-now. No one, until Kalvan had arrived, had come up with the idea of using them for carrying messages.

"Yes, homing pigeons were used in my homeland for flying messages to distant places. They're an unknown tool here and in Hos-Zygros, so no one will be looking for them."

"How will they know where to go, Your Majesty?" Hestophes asked, frowning.

"I've had some students at the University training them for the past couple of years. When you arrive in Zygros Town make sure you rent a townhouse running at least three or four stories. You can set up a pigeon pen on the roof; if anyone asks, you're a bird fancier. After all, you're a nobleman; some might find it eccentric, but they'll accept it. I'll include several pigeon handlers with your party; they'll feed and care for the birds, as well as send and receive messages."

The expression on Hestophes' face warred between doubt and excitement. "Sire, if this works, it means we can send messages in days that would ordinarily take a moon-half or more!"

Kalvan smiled. "That's the idea. Communication is as important a part of warfare as are maneuverability and fast movement. Of course, accidents can happen; sometimes birds are intercepted and killed by hawks or other birds of prey. So, we'll send two pigeons for each message or release them at different times. The messages will be sent in a code that only the handlers will be able to decipher."

"It will be a great boon, Your Majesty. And much safer than the semaphores we used in Hos-Hostigos."

Kalvan didn't want to think about the semaphore line they had used to transmit messages from Hostigos to the border of Beshta. When the traitor Sthentros had sold the secret of their operation to Great King Lysandros, he had sealed the fate of Hos-Hostigos.

"The pigeons are only to be used for important messages. When you meet with Great King Phidestros, it will be your job to talk him into some kind of a working arrangement between our two kingdoms. What I'd really like would be his help in vanquishing Styphon's House, but the biggest obstacle in our way is Hos-Harphax. I need to know how loyal he is to Great King Geblon, and whether or not he will try to keep us out of Hos-Hostigos."

Hestophes took out his pipe and knocked out the heel against his boot. "This could be tricky. From everything I've heard about Phidestros and the Iron Band, the Great Captain is extremely loyal to his comrades. Geblon used to be his banner captain, and has been with him since the beginning when they formed the original Iron Company in Hos-Zygros."

He paused to fill this pipe barrel with fresh leaf from his tobacco pouch. "The only other old comrade that he listens to is Captain-General Kyblannos, head of his artillery. If I could meet with Kyblannos on the sly, I might be able to get a better reading of Phidestros' current state of mind. I understand that Great Queen Arminta plays an important part in his court; she may be in favor of our cause. After all, she was the one kidnapped by Styphon's House."

"Where does Captain-General Kyblannos hang his helmet these days?"

After lighting his pipe, Hestophes continued, "Probably in Zygros Town with his wife, children and guns. It'll take a while to arrange a parley with Phidestros; I'll do my best to arrange a meet with Kyblannos before I see the Great King."

"I'll see to it that you have enough gold for any needed bribes and expenses. The mission you're conducting is probably more important than the siege of Tarr-Ceros. If Phidestros doesn't back our claims, we may have to be satisfied with putting Styphon's House out of business and forget about returning to Hostigos."

"Great Queen Rylla won't like that."

"Don't I just know it," Kalvan muttered.

FIVE

I

After Duke Hestophes left, Cleon ushered in Admiral Herad. The Admiral walked in stiffly, his face frozen in a mask of indifference. Kalvan wondered if he thought he was going to get reamed for some slip-up. No, there was no reason for him to be unhappy with Herad. *Aha! He's worried that now we are at peace with Grefftscharr, I'm going to make cuts in the Royal Navy.*

"Your Majesty," the Admiral said, bowing stiffly.

"Admiral, I need your advice about the attack on Tarr-Ceros."

The Admiral's face brightened. "What can I do to help? Are you worried about the Orders' galleys?"

"Not directly," Kalvan replied. "They don't really threaten the siege since we'll be attacking above the river banks. However, they might try and having some of our ships outside Kythar Town should keep them from mounting any flanking attacks from the river."

Herad nodded. He knew full well that the Hostigi guns would keep the galleys on the Lydistros River at bay.

Like the Spanish after the Battle of Lepanto, the Styphoni relied primarily on galleys; the Mississippi galleys were lighter than those of Styphon's Atlantic fleet, but still the dominant vessel. Galleys were different than strong-sided sailing warships; they could be propelled in any direction, regardless of the wind, or the lack of it. They could be brought to a dead stop, or maneuvered like guardsmen on parade. They were inexpensive; if one were sunk, the loss was not great. Of course, the officers and their soldiers might be lost. And the rowers would go down with the boat, but galley oarsmen were all slaves and of little value. They were worked hard and long and not expected to last long anyway.

Galleys never went far, but they went fast. They had no rigging to be fouled, nor did they need to carry large casks of food, water and fireseed. While they sometimes had platforms for catapults, they were too thin-sided for real guns. True, they could be used for ramming, but their primary purpose was to swiftly—and in concert with its companions, for they always worked in formation—grapple and put a band of soldiers aboard the enemy. Ramming was more of a threat, something to sow panic among the enemy. Primarily, they relied on army tactics, only applied at sea—a smooth sea at that.

Galley warfare was a matter of moving forces here and there, not personal combat. As far as Kalvan was concerned, their time was in the past. He was going to bring modern naval tactics and warfare to the Great Northern Ocean.

He took Admiral Herad into his confidence: "Admiral, my plan—after we take Tarr-Ceros and the other Order fortresses—is to gather our forces in Xiphlon City before we sail to one of the Blethan ports."

The Admiral nodded.

"We'll need most of our transports and warships to go downriver, since we don't know what we might be facing at Xiphlon. Even if we don't need the warships, we will need them afterwards to make our way to Hos-Bletha."

Herad nodded again, as if he understood. "I take it, Sire, that you don't completely trust High King Roldolf."

"That is correct," Kalvan replied. "Whatever treasure and loot we take after the sack of Tarr-Ceros, I will have them shipped back to Thagnor Town, so that's not what I'm worried about. Many of these Middle Kingdom monarchs have a history of treachery and backstabbing. I don't want to give Roldolf any ideas. Instead, I want to rent some of his merchant ships to help take our army to Hos-Bletha."

"And you would like to have the Royal Navy along for protection," Herad surmised. "And the transports for future operations."

"Exactly. For what I have in mind, I will need at least thirty of our largest gaff-rigged two and three-masted schooners, all of them fully manned and gunned. Plus, all the transports you can pull together."

"That's almost all our heavy craft," Herad said, raising his eyebrows. "That will just leave the Navy with sloops and gunboats."

"True, but the larger boats won't be needed here in the Upper Middle Kingdoms now that the Grefftscharri threat has been neutralized. If the schooners need more guns, contact my Chief of Ordnance and he will guarantee that you get them."

"That will help us greatly, Your Majesty. However, six or seven warships should be enough to quell any traitorous thought Roldolf might harbor."

"I'm not worried about Roldolf. Once our troops have arrived, we could besiege Xiphlon City quite easily. What I'm worried about are the Styphoni ocean fleets. I plan to guard our fleet with our own warships."

"What about the hurricanes?" Herad asked.

"They don't arrive until late in the summer. I hope to have our fleet out of Xiphlon City by early summer."

"That makes sense, Your Majesty."

"What I need our warships for is to keep the Styphoni galley fleet at bay. With our cannon and Greek fire, we can destroy the galleys long before they are within boarding or ramming range."

Herad actually grinned. "Our warships will rip through them like a shark going through a school of tuna."

Kalvan returned his smile. "My question is, can we get them across the Greffan Canal in time?"

The Admiral stroked his chin whiskers.

Kalvan knew that the Chicago Portage, or the Greffan Canal as it was called here-and-now, had been used by the Indians. The Grefftscharrers had improved it by turning it into a canal, but he wasn't sure that it was deep enough for the draft of the schooners' hulls. It was a damn good thing he had an ally sitting on the throne of Greffa.

"A lot of merchant ships have used the Greffan Canal since King's Verkan's ascension, Your Majesty. I can send most of our sloops, which have less draft than our schooners, to the Lydistros River to keep the

Order Galleys at bay. Meanwhile, I'll have my engineers survey the canal."

"The canal can always be dredged and widened if necessary," Kalvan said.

"It would take a lot of manpower and most of the University's engineering staff to do so."

"I don't care. Have your top engineers do a quick survey of the canal and report back to me. I will write a letter to Prince Kostran of Greffa explaining our predicament; I'm sure he will give us his help and cooperation. If you need workers or money, I can provide both—as much as you need. This is a top priority job. The good news is that you'll have several moons to do it in. I don't expect that Tarr-Ceros will fold quickly."

Admiral Herad nodded. "I will put my best men on it, sire. With your full support, it will be done."

Kalvan smiled. *Now, that's what I like to hear!*

II

As Kalvan rode his horse down the paving stone street toward the University, he was surprised by the heavy congestion, lots of wagons, carts, caravans and pedestrians were crowding the road. For one thing, it showed how prosperous Thagnor Town had become since his arrival a few years before. Of course, some of the traffic was the movement of victuals, armaments, troops and supplies for the new campaign against the Zarthani Knights. He couldn't help but wonder how many of the men preparing to leave their homes would ever return. It was a good thing he didn't have to explain to their families why they didn't return.

Both Kalvan and his horse escort were attracting a lot of eyeballs. He wondered if they were directed at him or Vanar Halgoth and his Tymannian Guard, which looked like a band of Vikings out of Kalvan's own past. He didn't like traveling with an escort, but Halgoth—who was charged with his security—wouldn't allow him to leave without at least five members of his bodyguard, although Halgoth preferred a score. Security at the gates was pretty tight, but so far this year three Styphoni agents had made it inside the city and had made two attempts upon his life, indicating that no matter how far away he was from their center of power, Kalvan wasn't safe until Styphon's House was torn down and ground into the dirt.

Still, having Halgoth along allowed him the opportunity to talk with his chief bodyguard in private. "Halgoth, I've got a mission for you."

"What for, Your Majesty?" Halgoth asked in a growly, deep voice loud enough to raise the dead.

"As you know, we are going to besiege the Knight's biggest fortress, Tarr-Ceros."

The big man smiled openly, showing large teeth in the shape of tombstones. "It's about time we got into the field again."

"No, no," Kalvan replied. "I've got something else in mind for you."

"What?" he asked.

"I want you to find Warlord Ranjar Sargos and give him a message from me."

"Does that mean I'll miss all the fighting?" Halgoth asked, his voice ringing with disappointment.

"No, there'll be plenty of fighting this year. Tarr-Ceros is only our first target. I plan to destroy all the Order forts all the way from Tarr-Ceros down to Tarr-Syklos, the southernmost castle. I don't know how long it will take, but I expect at a minimum it will be most of this year's campaign season. Fortunately, the warmer southern weather means we can stay in the south, rather than having to return to Thagnor to winter."

Happier now that he knew he wouldn't miss all the fighting, Halgoth asked, "When do I leave, Your Majesty?"

"Today, if possible. Take along as many men as you'll need for safety. I'll give you my message verbally, so you can memorize it after we return to the palace."

"What about your personal bodyguard?" Halgoth asked.

"Who do you suggest?"

Halgoth paused for a moment. "Edrick the Bald would be my suggested replacement."

Kalvan said, "Good choice. Tell him before you depart for the Sea of Grass."

"Yes, Your Majesty."

The walls of the University of Hostigos reared up above them. The gates swung open even before they arrived and a bunch of men swarmed out of the building.

"Your Majesty!" cried Rector Ermut, who was leading the pack. He was accompanied by about a dozen faculty and students in maroon robes. "I'm glad you could make it. We have new things to show you."

Kalvan felt his heart race as he dismounted and tied his horse up to a hitching post. He enjoyed tinkering around at the university much more than fighting battles or settling disagreements in his presence chamber. "Good, since this will be my last visit this year."

"Why is that, Your Majesty?" Ermut asked, as if he'd made some unrecognized faux pas.

"War is heating up again."

"Are the Styphoni gathering another army?" he asked, his voice rising.

Kalvan shook his head. "No. We're going on the offensive. The Return to Hostigos crowd wants their homeland back...."

Ermut shook his head, and spun his index finger, as if the whole concept were crazy. "We have a better and more secure home here in the Upper Middle Kingdoms, than we ever had in Hostigos. Fewer enemies, too."

Kalvan shrugged. "That's what I believe. But not everyone shares our feelings. Anyway, enough of that; I'll have to deal with this nonsense for the next year or two—or more. What about that demonstration Nathros said was ready?"

Kalvan followed the Rector and his staff through the open courtyard and into the engineering building, which looked like the former keep at Tarr-Hostigos. The idea being that if the town was ever sacked by enemies, the University of Hostigos would act as a defensive fort within the town. The fact that the military school was next door gave some credence to its defenses. However, if it looked as if the university were about to be overrun, there were enough emplaced fireseed charges to ensure the entire facility went up like an erupting volcano. Kalvan did not want his crowning achievement to fall into enemy hands, regardless of the cost.

They walked up four flights of stone stairs, much wider than the typical Zarthani interior castle stairs, to the engineering laboratory where the new steam engines were being perfected. The room smelled of oil and burnt machine parts. The earlier cylinders, made of hammered steel, were okay for the primitive steamboats, but improvements were needed if they were ever to get the railroads off the design tables and into the field. Realistically, Kalvan knew that large railroads wouldn't be built during his lifetime; the Hostigi would have to build and develop a major iron industry first. But his grandchildren might live to see such a world.

As a child, Kalvan had become a big railroad enthusiast after getting his first Lionel train for Christmas when he was seven years old. He had grown up within hailing distance of the Juniata railroad yards in Altoona, a town steeped in railroad history and steam engine innovation.

One of the apprentices met them at the door. "I'm sorry, Your Majesty, but Master Nathros is late. He should be here with your model soon."

Ermut said, "While we wait, Your Majesty, how about some winter wine?"

Kalvan shook his head. Having a drink was not the answer to all problems, although it seemed that almost everyone here-and-now took that approach. He suspected his top artificers and engineers might have had a hard time assembling the model, which would explain the delay.

After a long wait, Nathros finally came into the chamber, his long maroon robe dragging on the floor. There were dark bags under his eyes and he appeared woe begotten: "I'm sorry, Your Majesty, but we've had some problems with the model I wanted to show you. My apprentices should be along shortly."

The minutes soon dragged into a candle-half. It was stuffy in the room and Kalvan found it difficult to keep an even temper. Finally he had had enough. "Nathros," he said, "I thought you told me that demonstration setup I wanted you to build would be ready by now."

Nathros went to the door and peeked out. "Looks like they're just coming with it now," he said nervously.

A couple of burly apprentices were horsing a brass tank through the door. It looked like a cross between a small wash boiler and a milk churn, with a base about two feet in diameter and a hollow cylinder about four inches in diameter and about eighteen inches in length protruding from the top. In the middle of the cylinder a rod about half an inch thick stuck out. The whole thing was festooned with petcocks and valves, as well as a large screwtop cap that was mounted on the side of the wash boiler.

Kalvan gestured. "Put it down on that grate over the fire there." He went over, unscrewed the cap, and poured in a measure of water.

"I don't know what this is, but I'm sure it is important," Nathros commented speculatively.

Kalvan handed him a plate with a fixture in it. "Put this on the rod, put those rocks on the plate, and sit and watch," he said quietly.

Nathros did as he was told.

Presently he heard a hissing noise. The plate, rocks and all, was slowly rising up

"What in the name of Dralm's Staff is this?" Nathros cried out.

Kalvan gave a satisfied laugh. "That'll be enough. Help me get this thing off the fire and onto the floor before it explodes."

Together they lifted it onto the floor. Nathros said "Is this the same thing as the steam engines we used in the steamboats?"

Kalvan shook his head. "Something better. We can use this to make machines that move by themselves on land, as well as water."

"My King, if you had not shown us many things I would not have believed it possible," Nathros commended, as he studied the contraption. Now that it was off the fire and cooling, the plate was slowly sinking down under the weight of the rocks.

Kalvan pointed to the rod holding the plate. "What would you say if I told you that this rod could be made to move back and forth with great force and rapidly?"

Nathros gave it a wall-eyed look and then caught himself. "But how? It takes a long time to heat up, and then it takes a long time to cool down."

Kalvan turned to the table where there were some diagrams. "You do it this way. First, you separate the boiler from the cylinder, and then you set it up using valves so that steam is admitted to the cylinder when the piston is near that end of the cylinder, and that steam is exhausted to the air when the piston is at the other end of the cylinder. You do this on both sides of the cylinder."

Nathros studied the drawings. "Yesss...but nobody can turn the valves that fast and get it right all of the time," he said pensively.

Kalvan pulled another piece of paper out of the stack. "This is going to take some experimentation, but this is how you can get the valves to open and close when they should. These rods control slide valves and they are worked by this connecting rod, which has stops to make the valves move when they should. You put a swivel here on the connecting rod and then another rod to this crankshaft here"—he pointed to the crankshaft—"and it will run itself."

Nathros was excited. "Sire, I'm beginning to see how it can be done. It will take considerable experimentation to get it right."

Kalvan clapped him on the back. "And you are just the man to do it."

SIX

I

The newly appointed Duchess Danar Sirna did her best to hide her dismay as Great Queen Lavena berated one of her royal dressmakers for making the waist of her new gown too loose.

"What do you think I am, some sort of fat cow?" Lavena shrieked, while striking the poor woman about the head and shoulders with her fists.

"Please, Your Majesty," Sirna interrupted. "The poor woman just made an error in measurement."

The dressmaker was now huddled on the stone floor, sobbing with her face buried in her arms.

The truth was Lavena had put on weight, or hadn't lost a lot of the weight she had gained since the birth of her daughter—another failure in Lavena's mind since she had wanted an heir to cement her control over the destiny of Hos-Harphax, not a mere daughter. Of course, it was easier to blame the tight fit on the dressmaker than to lose the weight she'd gained.

The Queen was one of those people for whom good enough was never sufficient. Her sudden rise from the gentry to the highest of nobility should have been enough to guarantee her happiness, or at least satisfaction. Instead, it appeared only to have fueled the ambitious monster that resided inside.

"I ought to send her to the headsman," Lavena muttered.

The scary part was she might have done it if Sirna had not been there. Sirna was the only friend Lavena had and the only person, including Great King Geblon, to whom she was willing to make concessions in order to keep in their good favor. What the Queen didn't realize was that she had already lost Sirna's respect and friendship; all that was left was her self-serving determination not to become another one of the Queen's victims. If the Queen ever realized how little she valued her, Sirna knew that she might quickly make her own acquaintance with the headsman's ax.

The dressmaker quickly hustled her way out of the Great Queen's private quarters, giving Sirna a shy smile of gratitude as she fled. Sirna wished she could join her.

"What's the matter, Your Majesty?" Sirna asked. "And don't tell me it's the size of the garment."

"You know me too well," the Great Queen said. "I just received another note from my father."

Sirna nodded. Prince Sthentros was the kind of person who could poison a well from long distance just by thinking about it. He was demanding, overweening, narcissistic and insecure. In Lavena's case, the poisoned apple hadn't fallen far from the tree. "What does he want this time?"

Lavena giggled, which made her appear a decade younger and nicer.

Sometimes it's hard to remember she's just a kid, Sirna thought. *A spoiled and arrogant child, just the same. Yet, Rylla's only a year older than her cousin, but she's decades more mature.*

The Queen quickly sobered. "Poppy wants more gold. He claims that we insulted him with the paltry twenty-thousand ounces we sent him a moon ago."

Sirna wasn't surprised. Sthentros' original demand had been for two hundred and fifty thousand ounces, commensurate with his position as one of the leading princes of the realm. This was completely untrue since his princedom of Hostigos was underpopulated and needed rebuilding. Sthentros didn't have a clue as to how lucky he was that Great King Geblon doted on his wife and gave in to her every whim. It had been Lavena herself who'd cut back her father's demands when the Great King told her that most of the gold would come out of her personal allowance.

Geblon was rightfully worried that his subjects wouldn't put up with another major tax increase, not after the last tithe to refurbish the palace that Lavena had demanded. There were rumblings in the streets of

Harphax City about the Queen's frivolous ways and the high taxes that were shuttering businesses and filling the debtors' prisons. Recently graffiti had appeared on public buildings reading: "We want King Kalvan!" and "Down with King Geblon and Styphon's House!" The last was ironic since Geblon only dealt with the Temple because he owed their Great Banking House so much gold.

Lavena had been trying to talk him into sacking all the Styphon's House temples to fill the Royal Treasury, as Great King Phidestros had done in Hos-Zygros. Geblon had refused: "We live next door to those godless money grubbers. If we sack their temples, next we'll have Grand Master Soton pounding at our city gates demanding *our* heads!" Instead, they had borrowed more gold from Styphon's Great Banking House.

His argument hadn't quite convinced Lavena, although it had shut her up on the subject. Sirna believed that Geblon was absolutely correct; there was no way Styphon's House was going to allow a neighboring kingdom to desecrate its temples. The Temple's response would be all-out war. One that Hos-Harphax would probably lose without Phidestros' support.

Great King Phidestros was far away from the Temple's center of power and had a large enough army to keep them away. It had been several months since they'd heard about the shipload of priests' heads that Phidestros had sent to the docks of Balph and, so far, there had been no response. Of course, that would change if Styphon's House ever regained the power they'd lost since Kalvan's arrival.

She had tried to contact Field Agent Maldar and tell him about Phidestros' bold strike against Styphon's House, but he had not replied. What was it now: eight or nine ten-days ago? Nor had she been unsuccessful in raising anyone at the House of Olthos, the mercantile firm that the Harphaxi Study Team used as a safe house. She was beginning to get worried. What if she'd been abandoned here on Aryan-Transpacific, Styphon's House Subsector, Kalvan's Time Line? Would she have to spend the rest of her life dependent upon Lavena's mercy and good humor? Now that was a nightmare scenario.

"My father's also unhappy," Lavena continued, "that he has so few subjects. He wants my husband to order several hundred merchants and guildmasters to relocate to Hostigos."

Sirna had to stifle a laugh, and ended up grunting and snorting instead.

Lavena broke out with laughter. "Can you imagine some of these high-born snobs living in the ruins of Hostigos Town! It would almost be worth the open rebellion it would cause to see the looks of horror on their faces!"

Sirna was gratified to hear that the Queen realized the consequences of sending prosperous merchants to Hostigos. Not even the poorest of the poor were willing to emigrate to Hostigos, despite free land grants and a dozen silver crowns. A few thieves had taken the silver, but lost their heads when they shortly reappeared in Harphax City. Hostigos was like a penal colony without the trappings.

"What are you going to do about his latest request?" Sirna asked.

"My husband suggests we empty the City gaols and the castle dungeon, then send all the thieves, robbers and murderers to Hostigos. He believes that's the only way we'll ever fill Hostigos with subjects. Of course, I rejected it; my father would be very angry and hurt. Unfortunately, the better sort—the very ones he wants—will never emigrate there. I find it so frustrating that Our subjects will not do as we command that I want to pull my hair out!"

"Well, there's another way to look at it, Your Majesty. Those well-off subjects that your father wants in his realm are the very ones that contribute the most to the Royal Treasury. I suspect you would be sorely pressed financially if they did emigrate to Hostigos."

Lavena broke out in a smile. "That's why I value you so, Sirna. You're so thoughtful and wise. Yes, that's a very good reason. Of course, I can't tell my father that. He'll just have to make do on what we send him."

II

Kalvan decided it was time to make a trip to the Royal Hostigos Artillery Works to see how much progress had been made with the rifling project. He heard the whoop-whoop of guns being fired outside in the proofing field. He knew from reading about the Civil War that cannon rifling would not only increase accuracy, but double the range of their fire.

Most rifled cannon back on otherwhen were breech-loading guns. Since they didn't have the time to rediscover how to construct breechloaders, Kalvan decided to try something the U.S. Ordnance Board had done just before the Civil War. They had converted the older smoothbore cannons by simply cutting grooves into their bores.

After some experimentation on some older guns, the Artillery Works had been able to cut the proper grooves into the gun bores. Now, the problem was designing the right kind of projectile to shoot out of the guns. Since time was short, Kalvan had ordered them to develop winglets for the cannonballs, which fit into the rifling grooves.

Captain-General Alkides met him in the main office where his desk was covered with papers and small to medium-sized round shot. Alkides, who had become head of the Royal Artillery after the death of Captain-General Thalmoth, was rail thin; Kalvan noticed that he'd recently lost the pot belly that used to balloon out underneath his breastplate.

"Your Majesty, I'm glad you were able to be with us as we test the latest prototypes. Since these guns will be used mostly on the field of battle, rather than for siege work, we've limited our work to the eight-pounders."

Alkides held up one of the new cylindrical-conical shells which had six little winglets, and passed it to Kalvan.

"Nice work, but how does it shoot?"

"Let's go out to the testing field and see, Your Majesty."

Outside in the proofing field, the gunners were using ropes to pull a brass eight-pounder in position. They were firing into sandbags set against a thick stone wall. The last thing anybody wanted was to damage one of the neighboring houses. After swabbing the barrel, the gunners put in the fireseed charge and followed that with one of the winged cannonballs.

"They're harder to load than the smoothbores," Alkides noted. "The balls have to be carefully guided into the gun or the winglets can get bent."

Kalvan watched as three artillerymen loaded the rifled artillery piece. Once the cannonball was put in place, it was followed by cotton wadding, then the fuse was lit and the gunners quickly pulled back.

He put his hands over his ears when the gun match was lit.

The gun fired with a loud boom.

There was a brief explosion and a cloud of gray and black smoke. The ball hit the side of the wall with a loud *whuumph!*

"Now that we've proofed the new gun," Alkides said, "next, we'll take it to the firing field so we can get a better idea of how far the ball will travel. Would you like to join us, Your Majesty?"

"No, Alkides. I've got too many things to oversee for the expedition to Tarr-Ceros. Let me know how far it travels by courier. I'd like to take one or two batteries of these new eight-pounders with us when we go into Hos-Ktemnos, if it's at all possible."

"So far we've proofed six guns, Your Majesty. Another twenty are in various stages of production. But, there's no way in Ormaz's Caverns we'll get even one complete battery ready before you depart."

Kalvan nodded, thinking to himself: *We'll be stuck outside Tarr-Ceros for three or four months, at least.* "The eight-pounders are too small to be of much value during the siege. See what you can do to provide me with at least one battery, possibly two, before the siege ends. You can send them to me when Tarr-Ceros falls."

Alkides let out a breath of air he'd apparently been holding for some time. "Thank you, Your Majesty. I can promise you one battery of the new guns, but more than that I cannot guarantee."

"I don't expect miracles, only the true gods can provide those. Just do your best, Alkides."

SEVEN

I

It took another moon-half for Kalvan to gather the supplies, map out the logistics, take part in a score of staff meetings and finally get his massive army, which included eight thousand cavalry, fourteen thousand foot and over two thousand artillerymen, on the move as well as several hours to say good-bye to Demia and little Ptosphes.

Rylla, despite all his hinting around that it would be better for the children if she stayed home, had decided to accompany the army. He could tell that Rylla was worried that he might not be as avid about returning to Hos-Hostigos as she was. Well, she was correct, but he knew when it was time to throw up the white flag.

Of course, not everything depended upon him; if Phidestros decided to back Great King Geblon with an army to block their return, it would be a fool's errand to try and win back Old Hostigos. His biggest worry was that he would be unable to convince Rylla of that and they would be forced into a war that might be impossible to win. Or one that might not only cost them their army, but their very lives.

Due to the huge supply train and the large number of artillery guns accompanying the Hostigos army, they were lucky to make ten miles, or twenty marches in local terms, a day. The new road between Thagnor and Rathon was only partially built and most of the army was obscured by clouds of dust. Even though they were in vanguard, Kalvan had to put a handkerchief over his nose to keep the dust and stench of animal excrement at bay. He would have hated to be in the baggage train at the rear of the army, eating their dust. They came to a halt when they reached the Kirfryn River, or the Maumee River as it was known back in otherwhen. The river was too deep to ford and about a quarter-mile wide.

After a twelve-mile detour upstream, they came to a new Roman-style arched bridge over the river. Fortunately, the road didn't peter out for another twenty-five miles or so beyond the bridge. This was all friendly territory so the outriders didn't have anything to report. It took the army almost a moon-half to reach the outskirts of Rathon Town where King Chartiphon had a royal escort waiting.

His former chancellor met them in his private audience chamber. Chartiphon looked good to Kalvan's eyes; his formerly gold imperial beard was now streaked with gunmetal gray, but his blue eyes were sparkling and his skin tone was good. He looked happy to see them.

"How are the girls?" Rylla asked. "And your new son?"

"Wonderful, the new boy is a big one," the proud papa replied. "I've named him Harmakros; I believe he'll do our former friend justice. As for the girls, two for one. Can you believe it? Twins, and at my age!"

"You're only as old as you feel," Kalvan said, who with all his responsibilities felt as old as Methuselah. He was pleased to see their old retainer in such good spirits. Chartiphon had been an emotional wreck after the retreat from Hos-Hostigos and the destruction of Tarr-Hostigos. Not only had the new responsibility of kingship been good for him, but it appeared his young wife had helped bring him back to life.

"I received Your Majesty's message about the attack on Tarr-Ceros. How many additional troops do you need and what type? Do you have enough cannons? And do you have a place for this old warrior?"

"Your support is greatly appreciated, old friend. However, I will need you here. With King Verkan gone—"

"What happened to Verkan?" Chartiphon asked worriedly.

"Dalla was kidnapped," Rylla interjected. "On her return from Xiphlon to see how her family fared during the Mexicotal siege."

"That's terrible," Chartiphon said with the anxiety of one who was familiar with fears about the safety of his loved ones.

"Yes, Verkan left with an armed escort to rescue her, or at least find out what happened." Kalvan suspected the news was not going to be good, and that his friend would not return for some while—or at least until he found his wife's remains. "Which is why I need you to keep the majority of your army here just in case Styphon's House puts together another force. And to keep our so-called allies honest."

King Chartiphon nodded. After several decades of soldiering, he well understood the fickleness of allies and how alliances could change as fast as the favor of Lystris, the Goddess of Weather and Fortune. After all, their biggest enemy in the Middle Kingdoms had just been deposed and decapitated.

"However, as far as your offer goes, I could use two or three thousand of your Sastragathi irregulars. I will need them for scouting and chasing the enemy's light cavalry and the Order's oath-brothers after we destroy Tarr-Ceros. My plan is to take down the Order forts, one at a time, until they're all destroyed. I mean to finish Styphon's House once and for all."

"It's the True Gods' work, praise Dralm!" Chartiphon cried. "It's about time. The Temple has been a black plague upon the Five Great Kingdoms for hundreds of years. I will do my best to keep the peace and Your Majesty's realm safe."

II

Grand Master Soton looked anxiously at the stone walls, covered with Order banners and tapestries depicting great battles, which surrounded him in his private chamber deep within Tarr-Ceros. For the first time in his career, they were not reassuring; in fact, he was beginning to feel like a rat in a cage. Ever since he'd heard about the large Hostigi army leaving Rathon and headed toward Tarr-Ceros, he'd felt skittish and irritable. He knew that Kalvan was coming for him, to destroy everything he'd built and shatter the peace as well. And, finally, kill him and bring an end to the Order of Zarthani Knights.

He took out his corncob pipe and filled it with fresh tobacco. His fingers fumbled as he tried to work the tinderbox striker. He set the tinderbox down and used a candle to light a splinter to fire his pipe.

This time, Soton was afraid Kalvan might succeed in destroying Tarr-Ceros and the Order. There was no Grand Host of Styphon to distract him, nor did Soton have the manpower to stop the Hostigi. They'd lost too many veteran and irreplaceable soldiers in the Fireseed Wars. The only thing that might save the Order of Zarthani Knights would be if the Sacred Squares of Hos-Ktemnos came to their rescue. And, he didn't see that happening. Not if it would mean leaving Balph unprotected. Anaxthenes and his minions cared more about their own hides than all the Order's great achievements. They would let the Order and its master die rather than jeopardize their dainty bottoms.

Regardless, he would send his oldest friend, Grand Commander Aristocles, to Balph and request reinforcements from the Inner Circle. Not that they'd send them, but at least his protégé would be saved from a useless death. Maybe at some point in the future, if Styphon's House survived the coming storm, Aristocles might be able to resurrect the Order. A very slim reed, indeed, but it was all he had to comfort himself in his final days.

There was a pounding at the door. "Who is it?" he demanded.

"Grand Commander Aristocles has arrived," his adjutant Sarmoth said.

"Bid him enter."

Aristocles came into the room, looking around to see what was up.

"Please take a seat, my friend."

Aristocles sat down, taking a moment to fill his pipe and light up.

When he was settled, Soton said, "You've heard about the Hostigi army headed our way."

Aristocles paused to exhale a cloud of smoke. "I take it that the Usurper plans to besiege Tarr-Ceros and level it to the ground."

"That is my assumption. I don't believe he—or the she-bitch he calls his wife—will settle for anything less than our complete destruction."

"That will not be easy," Aristocles replied. "It's been tried several times before, but no one—not even Kalvan himself—has been able to breach these walls."

"True," he replied. "However, in this case Kalvan has time on his side. Unless Styphon Himself comes to our aid, we are doomed."

"Don't talk like that!" Aristocles cried. "That's defeatist talk; you've always decried such."

"Not in this case, I'm just being realistic. Kalvan has us badly outnumbered and our scouts have reported a huge artillery train follows his army."

"Have the other tarrs send us reinforcements," Aristocles said. "They could harry the Hostigi from the rear."

"I will give no such orders," Soton said. "If we send them all together, they would be defeated. There are less than a score of Lances left, most of them badly understrength due to losses in Hostigos and Thagnor over the past three winters. At best, they could all together mount a force of fourteen to fifteen thousand men. Kalvan would dispatch them with his new rifle corps like hunters shooting pigeons out of trees. We do not have the firepower to match his rifles, nor enough men to make a difference. If they were to make harrying attacks, Kalvan would defeat them in detail and the remaining tarrs would be vulnerable." He didn't bother to mention that if Kalvan was of a mind to destroy the Order he could do it a castle at a time and there was nothing he—nor they—could do to stop him.

"I want you to journey to Balph and present my request for any army to Anaxthenes, Styphon's Own Voice."

Aristocles shook his head. "Neither Styphon's Voice, nor the Inner Circle will listen to your entreaty. It's a waste of time. Let me go directly to Great King Lukthos, maybe he will listen to reason. He has as much, if not more, than the Inner Circle to lose if Tarr-Ceros and our other border forts fall. All of Hos-Ktemnos will become the playground of the barbarians from the Sastragath to the Sea of Grass."

"True," Soton said. "However, Lukthos is Anaxthenes' creature and he will not make a move on his own without running it past Styphon's Voice."

"Then why bother to go at all?" Aristocles asked, his voice rising in anger.

"Because, my brother, we are doomed either way. And, if a miracle happens, and Anaxthenes gives the right order to Lukthos, Tarr-Ceros and the Order might be saved."

"Aargh. I will do as you order, Master. However, I still believe it to be a complete waste of time and effort."

Not if it saves the life of my best friend, Soton thought to himself.

EIGHT

I

The Hostigi Army followed the Ohio River, or Lydistros River, past the small town named Tild, which was located in the area of otherwhen Kalvan knew as Cincinnati. From there they followed the north bank of the Lydistros downstream to Tarr-Ceros. The area was relatively unsettled with few permanent villages and farms. Most of the land was heavily forested, first-growth trees for the most part. The few villages were deserted by the time the main Hostigi force approached. Not that Kalvan could blame them. The local war bands were voracious foragers and, if they didn't take the villagers captive to sell as slaves, they stripped them of foodstuffs, young women and valuables.

The army didn't run into any resistance until they were about fifty miles east of Tarr-Ceros. Small bands of Sastragathi and Ruthani raiders—some of them Order oath-brothers—began to attack the baggage train and scouting parties until Kalvan put Chartiphon's Sastragathi irregulars to work. He used them as outriders in large bands of a hundred to a hundred and fifty men. Each band was accompanied by five riflemen who acted as snipers. The raiders were spooked when they found out that the Hostigi rifles could fire accurately at ranges unheard of with smoothbores.

After a few lessons on the advantages of superior weapons, the light cavalry backed off and the rest of the way to Tarr-Ceros was left open. Kalvan wasn't surprised when Soton didn't send out a larger force of his Knights to harry them; the Grand Master knew he was outnumbered and outgunned. It was unfortunate that he wouldn't surrender, although

Kalvan would have preferred it. The Order, other than its connections to Styphon's House, was reminiscent of the Christian Knights who had fought in the Holy Land and in Prussia. Had the Zarthani Knights surrendered, though, the problem would have been what to do with Grand Master Soton. From all he'd heard, Kalvan knew he was a believer in Styphon and probably wouldn't recant, even upon the threat of death.

Well, that was one problem he wasn't going to have to face.

By the time they reached Tarr-Ceros, the town of Kythar across the Lydistros River (Louisville, Kentucky) was a ghost town. Normally a thriving outpost, bustling with commerce and industry with galleys, barges and riverboats tied up to the wharves, it was now deserted. From a local trapper, Kalvan learned that the townspeople had fled by boat, horse and foot when they learned that the Hostigi were coming. It appeared that Styphoni propaganda, which painted Kalvan and the Hostigi as demons and devils, had worked.

If nothing else, the Kythar Town would be a good source of firewood and construction lumber. Kalvan sent out several companies of the Mobile Force to hold the town in case the locals returned, or the Order was using it as a ruse. The return reports verified Kythar was as empty of people as last night's jug.

The outer works of Tarr-Ceros started about a quarter mile from the river bank. They had been mostly wooden palisades when Kalvan had besieged the Order's fort five years ago. Now, the wood timbers had been replaced with stone and earthworks. Along Wall-1 there were some small guns, four- to six-pounders mounted in towers at regular intervals of about fifteen feet. Kalvan's first response was to take them out. To do that, he had three batteries of thirty-two pound guns brought up to the front line Kalvan had established as their attack zone. The thirty-two pounders made quick work of the smaller guns, most of them old-style bombards, although it took most of the afternoon before the last of them were blown off their mountings and destroyed. Few of them would ever fire again.

While the batteries fired, the Mobile Force Second Sharpshooters Company took care of the enemy artillery crews, shooting them with their rifles whenever they rose above the palisades. As a result, there was very little return gunfire. Since Wall-1's walls were buried up to two-thirds its height behind earthworks, the Hostigi guns were useless for taking them down. Fortunately, the other six walls were farther up the hill and were not defended with earthworks.

Kalvan turned to Prince Sarrask who was sitting in the command pavilion beside him. "It's unfortunate that the townspeople evacuated Kythar Town. We could have used them to help haul away these Dralm-damned earthworks!"

Sarrask nodded, then another battery of guns fired and the sound clapped their ears like a rough pair of hands. The Prince paused for his hearing to return before saying, "By my count, Your Majesty, there are seven ring walls we'll have to break through before we get to the heart of Tarr-Ceros. It's going to take the better part of two seasons to blast through those walls."

Kalvan paused to wipe the gray dust from his face. "We don't have to knock all the walls down, just make strategic breaches in several spots."

"Yes, so the enemy can't concentrate its fire on any one position," Prince Sarrask noted.

Kalvan had to restrain himself from patting Sarrask on the head like a student with the correct answer. The Prince was beginning to develop strategic thinking. At one time, he would have never credited Sarrask for having that much horse sense. He'd grown a lot during the last five years; unfortunately, so had their enemies. "The walls behind those earthworks are thick, three to three rods. But before we can hit them, we have to remove these earthworks."

"How about using the Styphoni dogs in the Basog Prison?" Sarrask asked.

"We still have some five thousand prisoners of war," Kalvan noted. Most of them were former Styphoni guardsmen or Zarthani Knights captured from the Holy Host of Styphon who couldn't be trusted not to take up arms against Hostigos in the future. His choice had been to keep them as prisoners, rather than kill them. Kalvan had put them to work in chain gangs, helping to repair war-damaged buildings in Thagnor Town and doing road work.

"I'll send a note to Prince Phrames to have them escorted here. It'll take about a moon before they arrive, but we don't have time to wait for them. Besides, we're going to need a lot more shovelers and hewers of stones and dirt than we have prisoners."

"That's what foot soldiers are for," Sarrask said with a smile.

"Yes, but if we don't knock down those parapets first the Styphoni will slaughter them." In his mind's eye, Kalvan could see the Knights protecting themselves from the foot soldiers by tipping oil down from the parapets onto the soldiers, or throwing burning torches and grenades. Plus, their horse archers would be shooting arrows over the walls to rain down upon his men. This was beginning to remind him of trench warfare, the scourge of World War I. Without manpower, the only way to remove the earthworks was by explosive shells. But that would be a slow business and he would need a hell of a lot more shells than they had with them.

"We're going to have to knock down these upper walls with our artillery until they're level with the top of the earthworks," Kalvan continued. "Once they're down, we can send work parties to remove the earthworks.

"That's going to take time, Your Majesty," Sarrask said. "I remember our last siege and those walls, even at the top, are as wide as a man is tall. Fortunately, only Wall-1 has any earthworks, or we'd be battering these walls until Galzar's Final Muster!"

Sarrask was right; even so, it was a daunting job. The big problem was that there was a hellacious amount of dirt, stones and tree trunks. What he wouldn't give for even a small bulldozer or skip loader. At least he'd thought far enough ahead to bring plenty of picks, shovels and wheelbarrows.

He told his orderly to fetch Captain-General Alkides.

II

"What is it, Your Majesty?" Alkides asked. He looked hopeful, as if waiting for Kalvan to come up with another of his "miracles."

Kalvan's top hat was empty, no more rabbits to pull out. He leaned forward so that he could be heard over the thunder of artillery fire. "Your guns are going to have to take out the entire upper-section of Wall-1, from that pillar to the next two. Everything that rises above the earthworks has to be smashed or blown down." He used his hands to describe the area he was talking about. It was about the length of a football field.

Alkides eyebrows rose. "That will take some time, Your Majesty."

"It will take a lot less time than trying to remove those earthworks a shovel at a time under enemy fire," he replied.

Alkides nodded. "Of course, I should have thought of that. The Styphoni could rain down molten lead and oil on their heads from those parapets and we wouldn't dare fire our guns for fear of hitting our own men."

"Exactly," Kalvan replied. "That's why we're going to hit them with everything we've got."

It took until the next morning to prepare for the first real attack. He had all twelve batteries, each made up of ten guns from eight-pounders—including one new battery of the rifled eight-pounders—to the big thirty-two pounder siege breakers, fire upon the areas of the stone wall they wanted to breach.

When the guns fired in unison, the ground shuddered and the air was filled with gray and black smoke as well as the stench of brimstone. Kalvan made a mental note to fire off a missive to King Chartiphon and have him send all the fireseed he could spare.

It took several days before there were any visible results, other than stone shards and flying splinters of rock. Kalvan was pleased when an entire section of the upper wall, some twelve feet high and thirty feet wide, collapsed onto the earthworks and slid partway down the slope.

The artillery immediately went to work on the next section of the wall. Occasionally a cannonball would hit the earthen slope and bounce over the parapet top. With the infantry staying behind the Hostigi guns, the Order had no way to fight back. So far, it was a one-sided battle and the cannons were doing all the work.

Knowing it would be almost impossible, under enemy fire, to move the guns over the raised earthworks, Kalvan had his infantrymen shoveling out dirt and stones on the section of the wall where the upper wall had collapsed. The Knights attempted several counterattacks, but as soon as the enemy was sighted, the Hostigi horns were sounded and the pick and shovelers quickly ran down the slope to hide behind the forward line where wooden barriers had been erected. A few were killed or wounded by musket fire, but casualties were light since the Knights were unable to move over the parapets quickly enough to get their musketeers in position for volley fire.

Meanwhile, the artillery and riflemen would make quick work of any of the Order troops who lingered on the earthworks. The best the Knights could do was to halt the pick and shovel work for an hour or two.

As soon as a section of the lower wall was exposed by the diggers, the artillery focused in and fired at the exposed stone wall. The only good news, as far as Kalvan was concerned, was that there were no earthworks protecting the inner six walls. Once inside the first ring wall, it would be a simple, but time consuming, demolition job to take down the inside walls.

NINE

I

Grand Commander Aristocles walked impatiently back and forth in the large antechamber outside Styphon's Seat. He had no interest in the fine tapestries and wall hangings depicting Styphon's ascension to his Sky-Palace, nor the ornate golden statuary. A flickering oil lamp more correctly represented his state of mind. The Temple was in dire danger and all the priests in Balph cared about were their luxuries and privileges.

It had taken him several days, and a big bribe, to arrange his audience with Styphon's Voice. *These idiots have no idea how bad things are*, he decided. Aristocles was no believer, like Grand Master Soton, in Styphon or his divinity. He was a warrior and the Order had provided him with both battles and advancement commensurate with his abilities. For that he owed Styphon's House his loyalty, but not his life. He was only putting up with the temple-rats' arrogance and stupidity for the sake of his friend and mentor, Soton.

If Tarr-Ceros were to fall, all of Styphon's holdings as well as the Kingdom of Hos-Ktemnos would be in danger of conquest. Kalvan was an implacable opponent and he had a stack of grievances against Styphon's House as tall as the highest tree. The only general of Styphon's House who had ever beaten Kalvan was Grand Master Soton; if he went down, woe be unto the Temple.

Things were bad all over: the Temple had foolishly alienated Great King Phidestros by kidnapping his wife, and he had retaliated by killing all the Styphon's House priests in Hos-Zygros. Great King Geblon was an uncertain ally since he was Phidestros' creation. With few allies, the

Temple needed to act quickly and decisively if it were to save itself. If it weren't for Grand Master Soton, Aristocles would already be in the wind.

At long last, a black-robed underpriest came out of the Seat and announced, "Grand Commander, His Divinity will see you now."

"About time," Aristocles muttered under his beard.

Styphon's Voice, wearing the flame-colored robe of primacy, was seated in a bejeweled and gold encrusted throne worthy of a great king. "Welcome, Commander. What news do you have for Us?"

"As you no doubt have heard, Your Divinity, the Usurper Kalvan has besieged Tarr-Ceros with a mighty army."

"We have heard. I'm certain that the Grand Master will make the Daemon Kalvan pay fearsomely for his arrogance."

As Aristocles feared, the head temple-rat had no clue as to how dire their situation was. Nor would he be pleased by the man who informed him of the truth. *So be it*, he decided. "Your Divinity, the Usurper has put together an army of some thirty thousand men against the twelve thousand Knights who garrison Tarr-Ceros. He has also assembled more guns to batter Tarr-Ceros than have ever been brought together in a single siege. Without relief, the Order's greatest fort will fall within a season."

Styphon's Voice reared back. "Our spies have brought us news of Kalvan's host, but this news you bring cannot be true. Tarr-Ceros has resisted every attack upon its walls for over three centuries. Why would it succumb now?"

"Because Kalvan will be bringing with his army a great artillery train with over a hundred guns to blast our defensive walls. Not even the great walls of Tarr-Ceros can resist this many cannon. On top of that, the Order has been bled dry by the wars against the Usurper, and no longer has enough men to resist this latest attack. Even if the other Order tarrs were emptied of their garrisons—which means there would be no one left to stand against the Sea of Grass nomads and the Sastragathi barbarians—the Order would still not have enough men to engage with Kalvan and win."

Styphon's Voice appeared nonplussed by this answer and took some time before asking, "What about King Theovacar of Grefftscharr?" he sputtered. "He was our ally against the Daemon before. We can send him two hundred and fifty thousand ounces of gold and a hundred tons of fire-seed. That should buy his aid."

Aristocles shook his head. "King Theovacar is dead, Your Divinity. Murdered by his own subjects, an alliance of merchants and nobles. Theovacar was a tyrant, greatly hated and feared by his subjects; he was beheaded and buried in an anonymous grave."

"This is sorrowful news!" Styphon's Voice cried out. "First, it's this popinjay Phidestros killing our priests; now, it's subjects murdering their rightful ruler. This is the first we've heard of his ignoble death. How about Theovacar's successor? Will he take our bribes?"

"No, Your Divinity. The first thing the regicides did to legitimize their claim to the throne was to sue for peace with Nos-Hostigos. Of course, Kalvan welcomed them to his court. Otherwise, he would not have dared to attack the Order for fear of Theovacar's fleet."

"So, what is it you wish from Us?"

"Grand Master Soton requests that you ask Great King Lukthos to send as big an army as he can assemble and come to our aid immediately."

The head of the Temple massaged his chin while he thought out his reply. "If We were to order such, and Our army of deliverance were to be defeated, where would the Temple be then, I ask you?"

"In truth, Your Divinity, if the Army of Hos-Ktemnos were to be defeated, Balph would be open to invasion by the Daemon and his allies. However, if Tarr-Ceros falls, Kalvan will most likely go straight through Ktemnos to conquer both Ktemnos City and Balph. Where will you be then?"

Styphon's Voice's face turned as white as a novice's robe. Aristocles knew that Anaxthenes was not often given arguments he could not brush away with the sweep of his hand.

"I will have to consult with the Inner Circle before making a decision on something this important to the Temple's future."

Aristocles nodded. "Yes, Your Divinity. I will be awaiting your decision." Meanwhile, he needed to come up with a distant land to make a new life. A place far enough away that Styphon's House was but a rumor and where Kalvan was unknown. Once word of the siege got out, he knew that he wouldn't be the only Knight seeking sanctuary. Maybe he could band together with other men wise enough to know when it was time to run for safety.

II

The Hostigi were still digging away at the earthworks on Wall-1 when the prisoners arrived and were put to work digging and hauling away the resulting debris. Work went faster then, as Kalvan ordered the Styphoni prisoners to work in the front ranks, the most exposed position. By then, the Knights had stopped their sorties as they were taking too many casualties. Still, the occasional sniper would pick off one of the shovelers. Out of boredom, some of the Mobile Force riflemen would place themselves among the workers and retaliate.

Kalvan was growing tired of the constant noise of the guns and the dust that swirled everywhere, getting into his nasal passages, his food, even his clothes. He wondered how he was going to survive another six months of this. Even with the cotton ear plugs he had everyone using, he was having problems hearing when the guns were quiet.

When the final section of the wall fell down, his sergeants had to restrain the infantrymen from charging up over the remaining earthworks and into the breach with their picks and shovels!

It took another quarter-moon to level the ground in front of the breach. They'd only had to fight off one sortie party. Once the cannons started firing the Knights couldn't retreat fast enough. They'd killed about fifty men and taken a score of wounded as prisoners. After that the Knights had stayed behind their walls.

III

For this quickly called council meeting, only twenty-two of the seats around the Triangle Table in the Great Council Hall of Styphon's House were filled. Most of the assembled archpriests wore worried expressions. These council meetings were rare and the ones called hastily were usually reserved for bad news. Archpriest Danthor wondered what new disaster had befallen Styphon's House.

Styphon's Own Voice looked haggard as if he hadn't slept for the past couple of days which did not bode well. Unlike his predecessor, it took a lot to unnerve Anaxthenes. He was intelligent, decisive, self-serving, completely amoral and not intimidated by anyone or anything. Even former Archpriest Roxthar had given him lots of room.

"I called this council," Anaxthenes began, "at the request of Grand Master Soton's representative, Grand Commander Aristocles of the Order of Zarthani Knights."

Danthor was familiar with Aristocles' reputation. A valiant warrior who was not one to raise unnecessary fears. *Things must really be getting bad at Tarr-Ceros.*

"As we all know, the Daemon Kalvan has besieged Tarr-Ceros, the greatest Order fortress on the western frontier. Grand Commander Aristocles has informed me that Grand Master Soton is worried that the fortress will fall before the end of summer."

This brought about a collective gasp from around the table. No one, including Danthor, had realized that the great fortress of Tarr-Ceros was in such a precarious position. If the grand fortress fell, the rest of the Order's forts would follow like autumn leaves. From there, it was a hop, skip and jump to Balph. It was time to start working up a contingency plan in case he had to bug out of Balph quickly. Normally, he would rely on the Paratime Police or the University to spirit him away, but too many ten-days had gone by without a word from Chief Verkan or the Balph Study Team. It looked like he was on his own. *What in Styphon's Sky-Palace is going on?*

"Soton has requested," Anaxthenes continued, "that we urge Great King Lukthos to send the Sacred Squares of Hos-Ktemnos to Tarr-Ceros. If such is done, it is uncertain as to whether or not the expedition will succeed. The Hostigi have assembled a great army of some thirty thousand men."

Archpriest Timothanes cried out, "Your Divinity, if the Sacred Squares are defeated, who will remain to protect us from the Daemon?"

Danthor ran through the figures. There were ten bands of Styphon's Own Guard, or some five to six thousand men in and around Balph, not counting Anaxthenes' own Sephrax Guard, another thousand. There were another two or three thousand guardsmen at Mykos Town, the Guards' headquarters. At most, roughly ten thousand men could be assembled quickly to defend Balph against an invader. More than triple that if the Royal and princely Sacred Squares of Hos-Ktemnos were added to the mix. In truth, he doubted Styphon's House could count on half that many since most of the princes would be more concerned with protecting their holdings against Kalvan rather than saving Styphon's House's bacon. All in all, there was not much love for Styphon's House among the Ktemnoi nobility, many of whom were deeply in debt to the Temple.

By the long faces worn by the other archpriests, Danthor figured everyone else had reached the same conclusion.

"If the Sacred Squares and Ktemnoi forces were defeated, other than Styphon's Own Guard and our loyal bodyguards, we would be on our own," Styphon's Voice answered.

"Then, we must think of ourselves first and foremost," Archpriest Timothanes replied. "The Order can be replaced over time, Balph cannot. If the Holy City were to fall to this Usurper Kalvan, it would mean the end of Styphon's House On Earth."

Danthor suspected that they were all making plans for a quick departure should a Hostigi army appear on the horizon. He was going to have to step up his own plans; fortunately, his digs were modest comparted to most of the archpriests who owned palaces and great manors. He would only take with him what could be packed on a single horse. Too many of Balph's upperpriests would be assembling entire pack trains full of gold and other precious items. All guaranteed to slow them down as well as make them tempting targets for bandits.

"Then I take it," Styphon's Voice said, "you all agree that Grand Master Soton will have to depend upon his own resources and that we will not send any relief force to Tarr-Ceros."

"Aye, aye," all the assembled archpriests said together.

Danthor had met Soton and been impressed by the Grand Master.

Soton was a realist and he doubted that the Innermost Circle's decision would come as a surprise. He wasn't sure why Soton had even bothered to send a delegation at all unless he had an ulterior motive—like saving the life of an old friend. Soton and Aristocles had been bunkmates as novices and great friends ever since. Yes, that made sense, more than this dog and pony show did.

TEN

I

Kalvan called his high command to join him in his stone-walled headquarters. The walls were lined with deerskin maps of Tarr-Ceros and the Upper Sastragath; they had interrogated the few prisoners they'd captured and the maps were quite accurate. Prince Sarrask was the first to speak:

"Your Majesty, when do we bust out through the gap?"

Great Queen Rylla, Captain-General Halmoth, Admiral Herad, Prince Pheblon and Captain-General Alkides all looked at him intently waiting for his reply.

"In about three candles. The Knights will be waiting for us in force. They know that we will be unable to use our artillery until it is brought through the breach and then emplaced, which will take about two or three candles, depending upon their resistance. There will probably be four or five thousand of them. All of them on foot, even the cavalry, since there's not enough room between the walls to maneuver horses. A lot of the terrain is hilly with gullies and washes. Most of the Knights will be heavily armored and they know how to fight. The ground will make for close fighting which will minimize our firepower advantage.

"What we'll do is lead with our men-at-arms and heavy cavalry. If we can hit their front lines hard with our heavy horse, we will break them."

"I thought you said that the land between the walls wasn't roomy enough for the Knights to maneuver cavalry," Halmoth said. "So why are we using our horse?"

"Because, by attacking from the front, we have room to charge, and then evade if we need to. The Knights don't. Remember, they have to use the gates from Wall-2, both coming and going, and space is limited. They won't be expecting to be hit by heavy cavalry and it should disorder their line. From that point on, it'll be a general melee."

The horn players and sergeants were given their orders. The Hostigi infantry at the front of the gap began to move aside to let the cavalry get by. The small rise beyond the breach was lined with hundreds of fully armored Knights with halberds, poleaxes, glaves and swords. The Hostigi horns sounded and the heavy horse, by squadrons, began to move through the passageway cut into the earthworks towards the breach.

The deep-toned Zarthani war horns sounded and the heavy infantry moved in an orderly fashion towards the breach, forming an iron curtain five ranks deep where the stone wall had formerly stood.

II

Since Grand Commander Aristocles had left for Balph, Grand Master Soton had put Commander Sarmoth in charge of the attempt to stop the Usurper Kalvan and his army from breaking through the large breach in the first wall protecting Tarr-Ceros. It was a job that Sarmoth was pleased to take. Finally, the Order could take direct action against the godless Hostigi.

The last few moons had been a nightmare, nothing but constant artillery fire and shells going off day and night. Sarmoth's head throbbed from the pain in his ears, to say nothing of the headache that bedeviled him. Now the Hostigi would pay!

As commander of the fort's six lances, his first inclination was to order his men to mount up on their chargers and prepare to charge the enemy as they came through the breach in the first wall, taking the fight to the Hostigi. However there was too little space to maneuver their heavy chargers, since there was a steep rise, leading to the second wall, about six rods from the wall. If Kalvan sent his riflemen to the front lines, they could shoot the Order cavalry like ducks in a pond. Instead, Sarmoth ordered his Knights, over five thousand strong, to don their heavy armor and fight as dismounted men-at-arms. They would be backed by the Order Foot, mostly musketeers and those armed with halberds and poleaxes.

Sarmoth was surprised when he saw the Hostigi heavy cavalry at the forefront of Kalvan's attacking force. As the cavalry made their way up the rise, where the earth had been dug away, he ordered his musketeers forward to hit them with a volley. His ears were so clogged from the wadding he had in his ears, he barely heard their concentrated fire. About a score of the enemy were hit and several horses went down. But the cursed Hostigi continued their advance; most of the dead and wounded horses were pushed aside and the musketeers' gunfire didn't appear to do much more than temporarily slow the enemy advance. There was time for two more ragged volleys before the lead heavy cavalry, their lances down, hit the Orders' line.

His Knights used their polearms to take the fight to the Hostigi heavy horse, but many were hit by lances or knocked aside by the jammed together chargers. In a few moments the fighting was so intense, he couldn't see what was going on more than three bodies ahead. He saw a fountain of blood up ahead when one of the Order's halberdiers stuck an enemy horseman's helm. Then he watched as a bunch of his own men were pushed forward, caught between their own troops and the oncoming Hostigi horse.

Sarmoth realized that the Order's entire line was being pushed backwards into the rise behind them. If the Hostigi kept coming, his men would be trapped against the stone wall behind the rise and the Hostigi cavalry in front. He grabbed the nearest sergeant and told him to find the nearest Hornmaster and sound retreat.

His men fought with everything they had, but it wasn't enough. The Hostigi continued to advance, squeezing the Knights back against their own ranks. As he watched in frustration and growing impotence, his men fell back against the wall of Hostigi steel. Then, the horns rang out, rising above even the battle din.

"To the gates!" Sarmoth cried out. His sergeants picked up his command and the Knights slowly began to retreat. Victory was not to be. As he made his way to the nearest gate, he gathered a phalanx of men to guard the gate to ensure that only the Order troops made it inside.

III

"You have to give them credit," Kalvan said to his top command. "If the Knights had broken we could have made our way through the gate."

Captain-General Alkides said. "Yes, and saved my guns!"

Two big artillery pieces had blown-up in the last month, from the constant firing, and Kalvan knew that Alkides was worried that more would follow their fate. To the artillery commander, his guns were like children.

Kalvan looked at Wall-2, which was almost as thick and stout as Wall-1, and said, "It's going to take us half a moon to blast another breach."

"Well, the Knights were stout foes," Sarrask added. "They didn't break, and only Galzar knows how many of them we sent to his Hall."

Kalvan agreed. The Knights had retreated, dragging most of their wounded and dead with them. He figured that they had killed or seriously injured four to five hundred of them. He hated to waste his time killing good men, only because they were in thrall to a false god. But Grand Master Soton had a head as hard as his mace and would fight to the last man or his own death—whichever came first.

"Alkides, how long before we can get your guns in position?" he asked.

Alkides tugged his beard. "If our Sharpshooters can keep the walls clear of musketeers, we should have them seated by tomorrow afternoon. We have plenty of horses and my men are anxious to get back to work."

"Good," Kalvan replied. All morning he'd had the prisoners working on smoothing out the small rise leading up to the breach. They'd spent most of the evening celebrating their victory, as limited as it was. But Kalvan knew that letting his men blow off steam was important; this was only the first leg of a long journey.

By morning, they will have moved up the artillery and started work on the second outer wall, Wall-2.

ELEVEN

I

Duke Skranga was sitting in his office on the fifth floor of Tarr-Pytha when one of his agents cleared his throat outside the doorway. Skranga, as a matter of principle, always kept his door open. He set his pipe down, saying, "Come in."

"A letter from Great King Kalvan has just arrived. It has been decoded and readied for Your Grace's perusal."

Unlike many Hostigi raised by Kalvan to the nobility, Skranga had been born into a wealthy wine merchant family and taught by scribes how to read runes and do his sums. The family had later fallen on hard times after a long-time customer, who had received a very large order of wine, died before payment had been rendered. The wine had been for a Styphon's House temple and they had laughed at his father when he'd asked for payment; Skranga still believed that their customer had been poisoned so that the local highpriest could forego paying for the wine. The man's heirs had pleaded poverty; in the end Skranga's father had lost their house and business.

"Please, let me see it," Skranga said excitedly. Communications from Nos-Hostigos, due to distance and travel through enemy-held territories, were rare and treasured when they arrived. It had been over a winter since they had received one from Kalvan himself. He started to read it, but had to stop when his hands began to shake.

"It's finally happening!" he said out loud.

The agent asked, "What, Your Grace?"

Skranga waved him away with his hand. "You'll learn about it in due time."

He went back to his reading. King Theovacar was dead; murdered by his own subjects. He could hardly believe it. If anyone was too evil to die, that person was Theovacar.

He was very pleased to read that Kalvan was now going to return to Old Hostigos. *It's about time!* He was tired of living in this heat-baked land where the sun was constantly beating down upon his head and the humidity lay over the land like a wet blanket. He wanted a real winter, with snow—yes, and even ice!

Instead of tracking through the desolation left by the Grand Host of Styphon, Kalvan reported that he was going south and laying siege to Tarr-Ceros. Skranga wasn't sure that his Great King would have an easy time besieging Tarr-Ceros, but with enough guns even that mighty fortress was vulnerable. According to the note, Kalvan intended to destroy the Order's fortresses one at a time, then winter in Hos-Bletha. There he would join forces with Democriphon and the Army of Hos-Bletha.

We'll sweep through Niclophon's princedom like a broom through a cobweb! Skranga thought excitedly.

He needed to meet with Democriphon and share the good news. *Won't he be surprised*, he thought. *Just when we'd just about given up on ever leaving this blasted land....*

II

Captain-General Alkides, arms akimbo, stood next to one of his brass thirty-two pounders like a proud father. All and all, the artillery head appeared to be in his element. He picked up a red flag and waved it, then cupped his hands over his ears. Kalvan quickly followed suit.

A series of explosions went off like rolling thunder. *All that's missing is sheet lightening*, Kalvan thought. Even with the cotton plugs and his hands over his ears, the concussion from the nearby thirty-two pound guns, firing nearly simultaneously, was enough to make his body rock and his ears hurt. The stench of brimstone was so strong he almost gagged. He didn't know how Alkides stood it, standing by the guns hour after hour, day after day.

There was a sudden burst of activity around the guns from the artillerymen as cannons were swabbed and cleaned for the next charge and reloading. Watching over them, Alkides appeared as happy as a proud papa.

Kalvan pointed over to his new headquarters, a hastily built stone block building. "Let's go inside," he ordered.

Between the stones, taken from the fallen walls, and cotton padding, the HQ's rooms were relatively quiet. Another barrage went off and the building rocked, sending up small clouds of gray dust. Kalvan paused to fill his pipe with tobacco from his belt pouch and light it. Alkides also took this opportunity to fire up his own corncob pipe. Soon the odor of tobacco combined with the smell of burnt fireseed. He had to grab his nose and pinch to keep from sneezing.

When the urge left, Kalvan pointed to the pyrographed deerskin field-map of Tarr-Ceros which covered a sizeable portion of the back wall. The map was based on what the Royal Cartographers had learned from the First Siege of Tarr-Ceros along with their observations and measurements regarding the new walls and the original fort.

"It looks like Wall-2 is just about ready to collapse. What's your reading, Alkides?"

The Captain-General paused to run his fingers through his tangled brown hair. "We're almost there, Your Majesty. It'll be down before the sun falls. It's the next to last of the new curtain walls that replaced the old wooden palisades. Once we blast through Wall-3, our job is going to get a lot tougher. These inside walls are thick, some of them are three rods or more, the thickness of three tall men laid end-to-end."

"What's the best way to bring them down?" Kalvan asked. Siegecraft was not his best subject.

"We need to dig tunnels underneath the section of the wall we're blasting, then prop up the foundation stones with wooden timbers. Of course, we don't want the enemy to know what we're doing so we'll keep up the artillery fire. When enough stones have been replaced, we'll put in some small barrels of fireseed, and then set fire to the timbers so that whole section of the wall will collapse.

"On a lot of the older tarrs, the walls are square and easy to undermine.

We're fortunate that these walls were designed long ago and there are no buttresses to worry about. Unfortunately, Tarr-Ceros' inner walls are circular and there are no obvious places to undermine except the old sally ports."

"What about using shells on them?" Kalvan asked.

Alkides shook his head. "Too much of the explosion fires outward from the walls, that is, if you actually strike the walls where you want to and if the shell doesn't go off prematurely."

Kalvan knew that was a problem; it was hard to get the fuse timing right with the available technology so that the shell exploded when it struck the target instead of in the air or after it fell down. The shells would be much more useful once the walls were down and the citadel itself was under attack. Once they landed on the buildings it didn't matter when they exploded.

"I'll go talk to the engineers and let them work up some plans for undermining the next wall," Kalvan said.

"Good," Alkides said, as he knocked the ash heel out of his pipe barrel. "I doubt the Wall-2 will last another four or five candles. We'll be busy tonight!"

III

Aspasthar sat patiently in one their secret hiding places in a small chamber only accessible by one of the long-forgotten passageways that ran through the old Agrys palace like termite-riddled wood. The three-hundred-year-old building was a veritable warren of known and lost tunnels and passageways, some which led to bolt holes and escape hatches. Life at the palace as a pretender to the Agrysi throne and spy had proven much less exciting than Aspasthar had expected, but also far more dangerous. Prince-Regent Grythos was a ruthless and vicious man; not one to be underestimated or trifled with.

Only a few moons ago, a palace footman had accidentally held a candle too close to the Prince-Regent, spilling hot tallow on his hand. The punishment meted out had been quick and brutal; the man's eyes had been gouged out and he'd been sent to the dungeon never to return. Rebels and partisans, proven or unproven, were treated to summary execution by quartering or burning at the stake.

Aspasthar, undercover as Prince Dementros, was fortunate to be blessed with two valued companions whom he completely trusted and were as anxious for adventure as he was. One of their jobs was to spy on the Prince-Regent's private audience chamber. The audience chamber had a secret screen behind one of the trophy cases that lined the wall. He suspected it had been used by ambitious underlings to keep an ear on their master's doings. Or, as Lady Tymolara had put forth, by one of the old king's wives to keep an eye on her husband and his concubines.

The boys had discovered it during one of their many forays through the forgotten palace passages. All three of them, having studied cartography under Colonel Nathros at the Hostigos Military Academy, were able to draw detailed maps of the tunnels that crisscrossed the palace and its environs. They had devoted moons to following the various tunnels, which had paid off when they had run across a secret tunnel leading to the great king's private audience chamber.

Rythor had morning watch today, while Athos had the afternoon and early evening watch. Aspasthar usually took the late evening watch and slept in. He was gaining a reputation as something of a layabout which was good coloration for his real job of spying on the Prince-Regent and other Styphoni priests who visited the palace. Some of the servants had reported to Grythos' chief-intelligencer that he slept late and often missed his lessons. Grythos seemed to think this was a good thing, demonstrating a lack of ambition on Prince Dementros' part.

Aspasthar knew that it was important to hide his strong will and intelligence under a cloak of indolence since he was coming close to his majority, the time he would be enthroned as Great King of Hos-Agrys. Something that Archpriest Grythos would only allow if he believed the young prince to be malleable and under his thumb. Otherwise, Grythos—without compunction—would have him quietly assassinated or smothered in his sleep.

There was a quick triple knock at the hidden door of the chamber, indicating that Rythor was back. He opened the panel and let his friend inside.

"Prince, I have news!" Rythor cried out. Even in their private meetings the boys always referred to him by his title or as "Your Royal Highness." This had been pounded into their heads, over and over, by Lady Tymolara, their governess and protector.

"Out with it, Rythor!" the Prince whispered. Even in their private cubbyhole they knew that other ears were nearby. Many of the new royal servants had been brought from Balph and were Styphoni agents here to keep an eye out on the boys, as well as search out traitors.

"A courier just arrived from Balph with news about Great King Kalvan," he said.

Aspasthar felt his pulse quicken. Kalvan was his Royal Guardian and the man his father had sworn allegiance to. A father he had barely known before he had died during the Siege of Tarr-Hostigos. Still, his father's name, Harmakros, was known wherever Hostigi settled or roamed.

"The courier reported to the Prince-Regent that our Great King has launched an attack upon Tarr-Ceros, the lair of Grand Master Soton."

Aspasthar let out a deep breath. "Then it has begun…."

"What's begun, Your Royal Highness?"

"The final war against Styphon's House."

IV

Kalvan sharpened the nib on his goose quill pen, and then, when it was sharp enough, dipped it into the ink well. Mental memo one thousand and one: *introduce steel nibs ASAP.* As he recalled from one of his Princeton history professor's lectures, bronze and copper nibs were far inferior to quill nibs.

Prince Phrames,

My good friend and trusted advisor, the siege here is going on as expected.

The bombardment of Tarr-Ceros continues day and night. We just breached Wall-3, and there are only 4 more walls to go. However, these are the thickest and oldest walls; they will not be easy to blast through or undermine. But down they will come!

The noise of firing guns is so loud and continuous I've been forced to rotate the gun crews twice during the day and twice at night in order to save them from permanent deafness. The regular troops guarding the walls are rotated on a daily basis or otherwise, I fear, we'd have rebellion in the ranks. How those poor devils inside Tarr-Ceros are bearing this, only Galzar knows.

The Knights have stubbornly refused our offer of terms of surrender, as everyone predicted. I had hoped for better, but in my heart knew that this great fortress would, in the end, have to be reduced to rubble. It's unfortunate, since the Order's forts are the defensive backbone of the lower Great Kingdoms and their loss will be felt for decades, as the Sea of Grass and Sastragathi barbarians move into the hole their loss will create.

We have finally received word back from High King Roldolf of Xiphlon. You were correct in your assessment of his character: he is indeed a wily negotiator. In return for shipping our army to the eastern coast of Hos-Bletha, he wants much more than mere gold and silver. He is requesting a dozen guns and their crews, along with two bands of fireseed crafters and a team of cannon founders. I would quarrel with his terms, but it would be murder to march our army overland through the swamps and quagmires of southern Hos-Bletha. We might lose as many as a quarter of our men through disease, not to mention sneak attacks by swamp dwellers and the native Ruthani.

I want you to go through the battle-spoils we have accumulated during the last few years and find the guns we need. Make sure that all of them are the old-style bombards. I see no reason to be overly generous. As to the cannon makers, founders and fireseed crafters, accept volunteers only. They will be heavily rewarded; not only will High King Roldolf pay them a generous salary, but that salary will be matched with Royal funds upon their return to Thagnor

Town. When you have gathered the guns and assembled the necessary guildsmen, send them on barges down to Kythar Town, where they will stay until our departure for Xiphlon. Be sure to send sufficient warships along with the barges to ensure they are not captured by the Dorgi ships or any others along the way down the Great River.

It is my suspicion that Roldolf will try to "buy" off as many of our guildsmen as he can, and his terms will be most generous. See that Captain-General Klestreus includes several of his intelligencers among the crews; he can teach them how to respond to bribes and ferret out secrets. I see no reason to trust Roldolf, and it will be to our long-term advantage to have some of our agents working in Xiphlon under High King Roldolf's protection.

I expect this siege to continue on for at least another two moons, maybe longer—

There was a heavy knock at his oak door. *Halgoth must be back*, Kalvan decided. No one else he knew could make that much racket pounding on oak without busting his hand, or using a mace.

"Come in!" he shouted, so as to be heard over the crashing cannon.

Halgoth came in with a sheepish look on his face. He shrugged, then said, "I'm sorry, Your Majesty, but Warlord Sargos will not be attacking the Black Knights…."

"What happened?" Kalvan asked.

"The other chiefs and sachems refuse to go to war this summer. They are still counting the loot from last year's raids against Dorg and their attack on Wulfula City. Chief Sargos ordered me to beg your forgiveness, but his power is limited in time of peace. He wishes you great luck in your attack on the Great Fortress and will pray to the War Gods for your success."

Halgoth looked so distressed at having to give this bad news that Kalvan felt sorry for him. "It's all right, Halgoth. We are not dependent upon Warlord Sargos' help."

The Captain of his bodyguard made a wide smile that left him looking like a jack-o-lantern. At moments like this it was easy to forget that Halgoth was basically at heart a killing machine, much like a wolf pack leader, instead of the friendly shaggy dog he so often resembled.

"There is still plenty of fighting to come," Kalvan added.

Halgoth let out a deep breath. "Good, Your Majesty. I was afraid I might have missed the real battle."

Kalvan shook his head. "No, it'll be at least another two moons before this castle is destroyed and the surviving Knights are forced into a fight. You'll get your fill of fighting then, I guarantee it!"

FALL

TWELVE

I

Great Queen Rylla watched as a red flare bloomed overhead in the night air, illuminating the broken walls and the armored men waiting in case of a sortie by the inhabitants. The ground shuddered and she covered her ears as another ear-splitting salvo of gunfire went off. Chunks of rock and splinters of stone sprayed downwards from the walls. One of the high towers that flanked the gate finally toppled, the big old gun rolling out and striking the ground with an audible thud. It rolled a few times and came to a rest, its hulk reminiscent of a dead bison.

Her husband's orders were to bombard the walls day and night; he was hoping to shatter the morale of the Knights huddling inside the massive fort as well as the ramparts.

"Darling, why don't the Knights have better guns?"

Kalvan smiled, his teeth glowing in the flickering red and yellow light of a big bonfire some two rods away. "First, the Order never needed better guns; most of their fights were against lightly armed nomads from the Sastragath or the Sea of Grass. Secondly, before the Fireseed Wars, cast cannons were made from brass and prohibitively expensive; they were only available in Grefftscharr and Hos-Zygros; both areas well-known for casting brass bells. Lastly, Styphon's House went to a lot of effort to ensure that no one bought them, since the old bombards used a lot more fireseed to less effect. No one was molding guns in quantity until we built the Royal Foundry in Hostigos."

"Aha," she said in reply. That was another one of the many innovations her husband had brought with him from the Cold Lands. Another reason that his life must be protected at all costs. *If only he realized how much he meant, not only to me, but to the future of our children and our people.* "How much longer before we breach this section of Wall-4?"

"It's holding up pretty well. The tunneling is proceeding, another reason we're now attacking at night as well as during the day. Our tunnelers ran into some old tunnels underneath the walls, but they were filled with rocks. I can't imagine what it's like inside the citadel with all this noise and constant bombardment. The Knights have been putting up with this for over two moons."

"How much longer will the siege go on?" Rylla asked.

Kalvan shook his head back and forth. "Another moon, maybe more. It's hard to tell. If the rest of the walls are as thick as Wall-4, it's going to take some time. Then, we'll have to bombard the old fort itself; and it's very well made. Fortunately, we'll be able to use our shells and they will rain Regwarn itself down upon the Styphoni!"

Rylla shrugged. The ground shook again as another concentrated salvo sounded off. She put her hand on her husband's shoulder to keep from falling down. She wished there was another route to Hostigos; she was tired of being an exile. She wanted to return to her home, even if her father and so many other friends were no longer among the living. Hostigos might be in ruins now, but it would be repaired. Maybe not in her lifetime, but certainly in her children's. Was it so wrong to want them to grow up in their homeland…?

Another mortar shell went up and exploded prematurely, bathing the front of the wall in fiery red.

"I just wish they'd surrender," Kalvan postulated.

"Why? We'd only have to fight them again at a later date."

Kalvan shrugged. "I admire the Order; they're among the best troops in the Great Kingdoms. They've done a great job of protecting the march lands from the nomads for centuries. It's a shame to see them dying to protect the old order."

"Darling, you sent them reasonable terms. It wasn't your fault that Grand Master Soton rejected them out of hand."

"I know, I know. I just keep wondering if I couldn't have presented them in a manner that wouldn't have sparked outright rejection."

Rylla shook her head. "Soton is a true believer. You can't reason with such men. Do you remember Xentos and how he deserted us for his god shortly after he arrived in Agrys City?"

Kalvan nodded. "Yes, I never realized how stubborn and ambitious he was. Well, he paid with his life for his error."

Rylla felt her eyes burn. Even though he turned on them, she still had fond childhood memories of Xentos, the former Hostigos highpriest of Dralm. Like Hostigos itself, her father, Harmakros, and so many others, they had all been lost in the war against Styphon's House. She felt her grief turn into anger. "Then, let them all die! The Knights made their beds when they did Styphon's dirty work!"

II

Grand Master Soton thought he heard the sound of someone knocking on his door. It was hard to tell as the very walls and foundation creaked and groaned from the weight of iron the Hostigi were throwing against the castle walls.

"Come in!" he shouted.

His adjutant, Knight Commander Sarmoth, came bursting into his inner chamber. "Sir, we've finally located one of the spots where the Hostigi are tunneling underneath the wall."

Finally, they could take action rather than sit passively as the walls of Tarr-Ceros came tumbling down about their ears. "Good. Send a tunneling party to locate their tunnel and kill the lot of them!"

"I already have men waiting, sir," Sarmoth said with a smile.

"Good. I suppose you'll want to command the tunnel party." He tried not to grin; he remembered a time when he was as anxious for action as his adjutant. By Galzar's Mace, he'd love to lead them himself instead of sitting here in his chair impotently while the Hostigi battered down the walls of his fortress one wall at a time. Well, at least, someone would be doing something.

"Thank you, sir!"

Sarmoth all but ran down the corridor leading to the western stairwell. The time had come to turn the tables on the Hostigi and he was the man to do it. He quickly made his way down the stairs to the armory where he removed his black tunic and put on a back-and-breast and the rest of his armor. From the armory he went down a ramp to the upper dungeon where several hundred Order foot were gathered and a score of miners, their tunics smeared with dirt and soot.

The head miner, a graybeard wearing a dirty canvas hat, said, "Sir, we stopped digging just less than a joint-length from the enemy's tunnel. We could hear them talking and the sound of their shovels. One of them mentioned fireseed barrels…so we should be careful that we don't use any open lamps."

He handed Sarmoth a large candle inside a circular brass-wire gauze screen with a wide metal base. "The screens keep the candle flame from setting off any gas in the tunnels. They should do the same for the Hostigi fireseed."

"How many of these candles do you have?" Sarmoth asked.

"About four hands worth," the miner replied.

"Bring them here and hand them out to my men."

The miner turned and left with his companions to bring back the lamps. While they were gone, Sarmoth gave his men orders about their mission. He finished with, "Leave your muskets and pistols here. Most importantly, do not let your candles near any fireseed barrels. And kill as many of the Hostigi swine as you can!"

They all nodded in concert. He didn't have to remind them how deadly an explosion could be inside such a confined area.

It wasn't long before the miner and his men returned with the lamps. He let the head miner lead the way down to a tunnel leading to the western sally port. When they ran across another passage going north/south, the miner turned right, saying, "This is the right passage. The sally port is about twenty rods from here."

As they walked down this smaller and more confined tunnel, Sarmoth discovered that his wide shoulders barely fit through the passageway. His breastplate squealed when it rubbed against the limestone walls. He felt his heart starting to beat faster. He didn't like being confined down here deep in the earth; it reminded him of childhood tales of Ormaz's Caverns of the Dead.

The only benefit of being below in the tunnels was that the pounding of Kalvan's guns was now reduced to a distant murmur. He had grown so accustomed to the sound of their thunder it was as if his ears had been reborn.

The miners came to a sudden halt at the place where they had been digging earlier. The head man held up a finger to his lips to quiet some of the soldiers, several of whom were complaining about the dark and how small the tunnel was. "Sir, if you put your ear to the wall, you can hear the Hostigi talking."

Sarmoth pressed his ear against the limestone wall. He heard the muffled sound of picks striking stone and some spoken words, but was unable to discern what the enemy soldiers were saying. Turning to the miners, he said, "When I give the word, break through this section of the wall."

Those miners encumbered with lamps handed them off to the nearest soldiers.

When they all had their picks raised, Sarmoth said, "Strike now!"

Soon the small passageway was filled with the sound of metal striking stone. The noise was so loud that Sarmoth was certain it would alert the Hostigi that they were coming. When he voiced his concern to the head miner, he shook his head. "They're making too much noise digging themselves to hear us, unless one of 'em's right up against the wall. It was Lystris' own luck that one of my men picked up their voices before they heard us."

Sarmoth nodded, sword in hand. It seemed to take forever before the wall was breached and they could hear the Hostigi talking amongst themselves. It took several dozen heartbeats before the hole was widened enough to allow a man passage. Sarmoth pushed his way through the gap, leading the way and slashing the first man he ran into in the face with his blade.

The Hostigi reared back, howling and then crumpling when Sarmoth's sword entered his eye socket. In an eye-blink the small chamber was filled with the clanging of swords amid the cries of desperate and dying men.

After his easy victory, Sarmoth became engaged with a Hostigi captain, with gold inlay on his morion helmet, who knew how to use his blade in a manner Sarmoth had never encountered before. He found himself, despite his bigger size and longer arms, being pushed back against one of the stone walls. He was parrying the enemy's blade when the man pricked his cheek with a knife. He reared back and fought with renewed vigor. During the fight, they knocked over a fireseed barrel which broke open, splashing fireseed powder all over the floor.

"Watch out!" he cried.

One of the lamp holders took a sword blow to the head and fell, his lamp upending amidst the fireseed.

Both Sarmoth and his opponent lowered their swords, and looked at each other with wide eyes. Neither could see an escape route.

A breath later, there was a bright flash—as though the sun had broken through the walls in all its majesty—then utter darkness and the thunder of falling rocks….

III

Archpriest Danthor stepped warily up to Styphon's Voice's private audience room where the Captain of the Guard silently motioned him to wait. Which reminded him that all of the Sephrax Guard, that is those who personally attended Anaxthenes, had their tongues removed so they would be unable to gossip or reveal his private conversations. He understood that the pay was good, but the price seemed awfully high to him.

These were tumultuous times and all of Balph was in an uproar over Kalvan's attack upon the Order's greatest fortress. Many of the archpriests were fearful that his next stop, after Tarr-Ceros, would be the Holy City. He knew better; Kalvan had too good of a military mind to get bogged down in a fall or winter attack. He would wait until next spring, then all of Regwarn would break loose in Hos-Ktemnos. Besides, it would be months before the last of the Order's forts fell.

Danthor knew from the briefings by the Blethan Town Study Team that Kalvan had orchestrated the "Orphan Prince scam" that had put Democriphon forward as a claimant to the Ivory Throne. It was possible that Kalvan planned to link up with Duke Skranga and Democriphon in

Hos-Bletha, put Great King Niclophon out of his misery and then, with his combined force, invade Hos-Ktemnos.

He wondered what Anaxthenes had in mind to stop Kalvan. Or was he planning to bug out himself, as so many of the upperpriests were planning to do. The biggest problem the upperpriests faced was that all their possessions were owned by Styphon's House, which made it difficult to cash in their bonds at Styphon's Banking Houses or remove their treasures from their manors or, in the archpriests' cases, palaces. Anyone caught transporting gold, silver, jewels or other treasure was subject to beheading. Stealing from the Temple was Styphon's House's worst offense and demanded the death penalty—with no exceptions, regardless of rank. Many in Balph were wondering whether they had more to fear from Styphon's Own Guard or Great King Kalvan's cannons, since he was believed to have a penchant for shooting Styphon's priests out of big guns.

After about a quarter-candle wait before Anaxthenes' private chamber, a captain of the Sephrax Guard escorted him into Styphon's Voice's presence. He nodded to the big man as he passed by.

Styphon's Voice was seated before a long table filled to overflowing with parchments and scrolls. He had his head buried in a large scroll as Danthor entered his private chamber, but still managed to motion Danthor to sit down.

When Anaxthenes finished reading, he looked up—his eyes pinning Danthor to his seat. He reminded Danthor of a bird of prey about to strike with its talons or sharp beak. "You're one of the smart ones, so I don't have to remind you of the threat we face from the Daemon Kalvan."

Danthor nodded his head in agreement.

"While the Daemon methodically destroys the walls of Tarr-Ceros, most of our priesthood concerns itself with how much gold they can smuggle out of Balph before he tackles *our* walls, which as you know are old and not as strong as I'd like. The price for the Temple's three hundred years of peace and success. I, however, am not going to sit idly by and watch as Kalvan destroys our work."

"What is your plan, Your Divinity?" he asked.

Anaxthenes smiled. "Good, you came right to the point. My plan is to bring Great King Geblon of Hos-Harphax to our defense. What do you think of that?"

Danthor stroked his chin. He knew that Geblon was a former general under Great King Phidestros, who had recently cleaned his house of all of Styphon's priests, beheading most of them. The question was: Would Geblon go against his former boss's will? Rumor also had it that Geblon was firmly under the thumb of his wife, Queen Lavena, who spent money like water. So it all came down to a question of loyalties.

"Your Divinity, it all depends upon whether or not Great King Geblon is more beholden to Great King Phidestros or his wife."

Anaxthenes smiled predatorily. "Good answer. From the size of his recent loans from our Banking Houses, I would suspect the latter. It will be up to you to convince him where his true loyalties lie. You will be my personal envoy to the Court of Great King Geblon. I will give you five hundred thousand ounces of gold to convince him of our sincerity. All of it to be spent on bringing the Harphaxi army up to fighting trim. You can also inform him that if he brings his army in support of Balph, we will forgive all his debts."

Danthor asked, "And how much might that be, Your Divinity? It has not even been a winter since he was enthroned."

"Great King Geblon is already in debt to us for over a million ounces of gold."

Danthor whistled despite himself.

"Yes, he's deep into our pockets, which was our intention. Most of the money was to build a new palace, which had to be done in less than five moons. Geblon doesn't know it, but we helped raise his costs by hiring many of the Harphaxi builders to work for us. And, already, his wife is talking about more additions to the palace. This has not raised his popularity in Harphax City, which has seen its taxes raised twice since Geblon was seated upon the Iron Throne."

"It's unfortunate that we cannot purchase Great King Phidestros loyalty, as well."

Anaxthenes shook his head sadly. "It was my unfortunate idea to kidnap Princess Arminta, falsely thinking that it would give us more leverage over Phidestros. Obviously, it ricocheted back on me. However, at the time, I had no idea that the Prince was so ambitious and ruthless; his ascension to the Ivory Throne caught us all unaware."

Danthor nodded. Even the Zygrosi Study Team had been caught off guard by Phidestros' takeover of Hos-Zygros and the exile of his father.

"Is there anything else I can use to persuade Geblon to come to our aid?" he asked.

"Yes," Styphon's Voice replied. "Tell him we will give him half a million ounces of gold in advance for the defense of Balph and another million when the Usurper Kalvan is defeated."

"What about Princess Lavena?"

"Make certain that she is informed of our generosity. Her avarice is our greatest ally in this endeavor. Furthermore, she has a deeply personal stake; her father is Prince of Hostigos and her hatred and jealousy of Great Queen Rylla is legendary. Furthermore, Prince Sthentros is considered a traitor by all Hostigi and is high on Kalvan's death list. If the Daemon Kalvan sacks Balph and defeats Great King Lukthos, Hos-Harphax and Old Hostigos will be next on his agenda."

"When do you want me to leave, Your Divinity?"

"As soon as the weather improves. I will have a large galley prepared for your leave-taking."

THIRTEEN

I

Grand Master Soton found himself sitting on a wooden bench in the Styphon's House chapel deep inside the keep. He was the only one present; the highpriest and his underpriests, who had conducted the weekly services, had all fled for Balph when word had arrived that Kalvan and his army was coming to besiege Tarr-Ceros. None of the Order Knights or lesser soldiers had come into the chapel for worship since the beginning of the siege. *Be honest*, he reminded himself, *fewer and fewer have been coming here for a long time.*

The Knights believe that Styphon's House no longer values them for anything but cannon fodder and they may be right. Most of them now spend their time at Galzar's chapel. I should probably be there with them paying for a place in Galzar's Hall for my valued officer Sarmoth who died during the execution of my orders. He died gladly in my service, I must say. If anyone does, he truly deserves a spot at Galzar's Table with the other heroes.

Soton examined the rich tapestries and wall hangings that decorated the chapel, as well as the golden idol of Styphon and all the accoutrements. *This is no place for a soldier*, he decided.

A sudden stab of grief dropped him to his knees upon the stone floor. He was going to really miss Sarmoth; he was an up-and-coming commander and a good man—and friend. He could not be replaced.

He had lost too many friends already, but at least Aristocles had escaped this charnel house. Even here deep in the keep he could hear the booming of Kalvan's guns and smell the brimstone. *Am I wasting the Order on a fight it cannot win?* The thought brought him nothing but pain. *Have*

I wasted my life in support of a rotten house?

Where is the support from the Inner Circle and Styphon's Voice that I begged for? Not a single soldier has come to our aid since the beginning of the siege. I wonder if Anaxthenes even bothered to consult with Great King Lukthos about rescuing the fortress? Probably not.

No help would be forthcoming and he would get to watch as ten thousand men under his command were buried alive in the rubble of Tarr-Ceros. It didn't have to be this way, he decided. *But what can I do?*

One thing he could do was visit the place where his men congregated. Galzar's chapel and infirmary were outside the main keep and among the castle's outbuildings. The Brotherhood of Galzar maintained the Order chapels and infirmaries. He had once asked the chapel highpriest why. His answer had been succinct and to the point: "Because you do good work here by protecting all our borders."

Outside the keep, the thunder of Kalvan's guns beat upon his ears and he could feel the ground quiver. While it felt and sounded as if they were in the midst of a great storm, the sun was shining and the sky bright blue. Already some of the enemy shells had reached past the inner walls, and he came across big gouges in the earth and outbuildings that had been blasted into ruins. Many of them were stables, now fortunately empty; almost all the horses had been sent away before the Hostigi Army arrived. The big chargers, especially, were too valuable to spare and had been sent south. The few horses that remained were the smaller and faster ones; they were now stabled inside the keep where they would be safe—*but for how much longer?*

The small chapel of Galzar was filled to overflowing, although his men made room when they noted his arrival. Many were seated on rough wooden benches, while others kneeled before the wolf-headed statue of Galzar, with its ruby-red eyes. *They know that Styphon has abandoned us and are making peace with Galzar before the end.*

The Uncle Wolf in charge, upon noting his appearance, made his way to Soton's side. So accustomed was he to Styphon's priests that Soton quite expected an entreaty for more funds, goods and protection. Instead, the highpriest welcomed him to their chapel and told him it was good for morale. He had to fight the tears that threatened to well up his eyes.

I have been a fool for too long; even Aristocles has chided me for my thick-headedness.

"Grand Master, will you accompany me to the infirmary? It will do the men good to see your face and know that they are in your thoughts."

"Of course, Your Worship," he said, as he followed the Uncle Wolf past the altar and down a short corridor.

Soton was shocked by the scene that met his eyes. Men crying or lying on cots in tight balls. "Are these men wounded?" he asked.

"Some have wounds from falling tiles and collapsing walls," the Uncle Wolf reported. "But most of these men are suffering from battle shock. Even though they have not been in battle yet, the constant bombardment and fear of the future have brought about this terrible malady."

He was familiar with battle shock, but this was a first time he had run across it before the fighting had even begun. However, the tarr had been under bombardment for almost two moons and even his nerves were on edge from the constant din. It also came to his attention that the chamber was filled to the bursting with sobbing, weeping and traumatized men. "What has brought this about?" he asked.

The Uncle Wolf shook his head. "The constant barrages of artillery fire and exploding shells with no way to reply."

Soton nodded. Never had he seen so many victims in one place. There wasn't enough room in the infirmary for half this number. Suddenly, it hit him where there was room to spare. "Move these men to Styphon's chapel. All the priests have fled and there's lots of room. From now on, it will be Galzar's new temple."

The Uncle Wolf seemed dazed. "Thank you, your Eminence. Men, go get the litters and help move the wounded and battle-shocked to our new home."

Soton fell to his knees and he began to pray, this time to Galzar, the Wargod.

II

Great Queen Arminta greatly enjoyed the early hours of evening after supper; it was her only alone time with baby Soligon and her husband. Other than her time asleep in their bed chamber it was her only escape from her duties as great queen. Not that she minded her obligations, but it was nice to cuddle her newborn and sit next to Phidestros, who was resting in his armchair smoking a pipe, staring into the fireplace.

"What's on your mind, my dear?" she asked.

"I just received word that a delegation from Hostigos has entered our territory."

"How large a delegation?"

"It's a small party. Some fifty men, most of them soldiers—for protection, I'd assume. It's not a big enough force for anything else."

"Anything smaller could be perceived as an insult. Which, from what I know about Great King Kalvan, is not what he intends," Arminta said.

Phidestros exhaled a small cloud of smoke. "I agree. I'm just not sure what to make of it. What business could Kalvan possibly have with us?"

Arminta went over the latest news from the east. "Didn't we recently hear that King Theovacar was removed from his throne?"

"Yes, my love. And that is the most generous description of a beheading I've heard in some time," he said with a laugh. "Theovacar's head and body were separated, as I understand it. Maybe there's a lesson there for all of us...."

She laughed. "Yes, for tyrants. Not for kings, like you, who are beloved by their subjects."

Phidestros shook his head in bemusement. "I'm not used to all this *love*."

"Well, you exiled a particularly nasty tyrant—even if he was your putative father—from the Ivory Throne, rescinded the worst of his taxes, and then gave the people of Zygros City a weeklong enthronement celebration at our expense. Not to mention all your reforms. I think that's grounds enough for gratitude, if not outright love."

"It's not just me. You were the force behind those reforms: no more slavery, no more debtors' prison, an independent judiciary, and so forth. They're lucky I married you instead of some shrew like Lavena."

"You're right there, husband. Speaking of Great Queen Lavena, maybe she might have something to do with why Kalvan has sent a party to confer with you."

"What do you mean?" he asked.

"Well, for one thing, with King Theovacar no longer a threat, what's there to keep Great King Kalvan from returning to Hos-Hostigos?"

Phidestros choked, almost spitting out his pipe. "Several things, starting with Styphon's House! They went to great expense and effort to expel him from the Five Kingdoms. I don't suppose their hatred of him has decreased since he's cost them a fortune in gold and filled half of Galzar's Hall with their dead."

"True, but Styphon's House is no longer the monolith it was when Kalvan arrived. We've expelled them from Hos-Zygros, and they have a pretender in Hos-Bletha who has desecrated and sacked their temples. In addition, they must have spent several large fortunes buying mercenaries and armies to fight Kalvan. We know that they are stretched thin in Hos-Agrys. At this time, Styphon's House would be hard-pressed to gather a new host to fight Kalvan."

"Very good points. I can see I was a wise man to marry so well."

She laughed. "It certainly wasn't for money, since my father spent it faster than he could collect it."

"Let's hope our son, his namesake, does better with the funds we leave him." Seeing her pointed look, he added, "With you as his mother, I can see he will do much better."

She smiled. "You're a wise man. I suspect that King Kalvan would like to return to Hostigos, since I believe that is what his wife wants."

"They have a nice home in Thagnor: why would they want to leave it for the wreckage that is Hostigos Town? I know how ruined the town is, since I was one of those who helped sack it."

Arminta shook her head. "Husband, not everyone is a born wanderer such as yourself. You are happy wherever you can hang your helm. Most people want to live and die in the place they were born."

Phidestros said, "Look at yourself, you were happy enough to leave Argros and Hos-Harphax behind. Why should Queen Rylla be any different?"

"That's because I had good reasons for wanting to get away from the Princedom of Argros. I wanted a home of my own; I was tired of always having to fix my father's and my brothers' messes." She paused to look down lovingly at the bundle in her arms. "And you've given me what I've always truly wanted."

He smiled at her. "We are fortunate to have found each other."

"Yes, and to have a nice home to call our own. I believe that's what Great Queen Rylla wants—to go back home."

"Then they've got a problem," Phidestros said grimly. "After all, I own the largest holding in what was once Hos-Hostigos—Greater Beshta. And I'm not about to give it up."

"I agree, even though we are far more comfortable here in Hos-Zygros. It is your demesne, fought and paid for in blood."

"Besides," he added, "I have obligations to Great King Geblon—"

"Fa!" she replied. "If anyone owes anyone, it's Geblon. Without our support, he would count himself fortunate to be a rural baron."

Phidestros exhaled more smoke, looked thoughtful, then said, "There's truth in your words. I could have sat upon the Iron Throne myself, but I didn't want the headaches that came along with it. Especially that she-devil, Lavena."

"She certainly has Geblon wrapped around her thumb. He doesn't dare leave for the privy without her say-so."

Phidestros looked down, hiding a grin. "You're right. Lavena would never rest if Kalvan returned to Hostigos, nor give Geblon a moment's peace. The poor bugger would have to fight Kalvan whether it made sense or not. It's not as if his subjects are vying to settle in Hostigos."

"Exactly, and she would play right into Styphon's House's plans, my dear. You do see that."

"Yes, it profits the Temple to have great kings at each other's throats."

"The question we should be asking is: does it profit us?"

III

While he didn't like to admit it, Kalvan was getting used to the constant artillery barrages. He feared his hearing, even with the cotton ear plugs, might never recover from the siege. But, as bad as the noise and stench of fireseed was outside, it had to be ten times worse inside the fortress of Tarr-Ceros. *Why don't they give up and surrender? God only knows, Styphon's House cares nothing about their sacrifices. It's unfortunate that Grand Master Soton is one of the few Temple commanders who actually believed in Styphon. A more practical man would have asked for terms a month ago.*

Still, they were making good progress. Tarr-Ceros would fall within the next moon or two, then they would move on to the next Order castle and besiege that one. He doubted that many of the Order's tarrs, after Tarr-Ceros fell, would actually have to be put under siege. They would make a token resistance, then surrender. He hoped they would be in Hos-Bletha before winter arrived.

Kalvan was seated in the headquarters waiting for Prince Mnestros to arrive. He badly needed a better picture of the current political situation in the Kingdom of Hos-Agrys; it would be the remaining bastion of Styphon's House once Balph fell and he ran through Hos-Ktemnos like General Sherman through Georgia. The Prince knocked at the door and was escorted inside by one of Kalvan's Tymannian bodyguards.

"Your Majesty, how may I be of service?" Mnestros asked. The Prince had been a teenager when Kalvan had first laid eyes on him three or four years ago; now, he looked as though he were close to thirty. There were dark bags under his eyes, his forehead was furrowed and squint lines bracketed his eyes. He walked like an old man, as though he were carrying the sorrows of the world upon his shoulders. Maybe that was part of the baggage of being a prince-in-exile from a country you grew up in and where you knew every inch of its territory.

"I wanted to ask you some questions about the political and military situation in Hos-Agrys. After we take Balph and Hos-Ktemnos, it will be the last remaining Styphoni stronghold."

Mnestros nodded. "True, Your Majesty, but the Styphoni do not have a firm grasp on our Kingdom. They are strongest in those princedoms which make up the Friends of Styphon alliance; elsewhere, they hold power only by fear and intimidation. When Grand Master Soton left, after the fall of Agrys City, he took more than half of the Styphoni host with him. There are only some twenty-five to thirty thousand men under Styphon's colors spread thinly throughout the Kingdom, more than two-thirds of them garrisoned in Agrys City."

"That's good to know," he replied. "I was worried that Styphon's Voice might order his Agrysi forces to aid them in the defense of Balph."

"It depends upon how desperate the Inner Circle is, Sire. Styphon's House's major problem is that if too many of the troops holding Agrys City leave, the populace might rise up in rebellion. The Styphoni are hated for the atrocities and murders they committed when the city was sacked and occupied."

"I suspected as much from the dispatches I received from Captain-General Hestophes when he was in Hos-Agrys last year," Kalvan said. "Balph, as you know, is the heart of Styphon's House. The Innermost Circle would rather see their other interests in the Five Kingdoms collapse rather than face the loss of their Holy City."

Kalvan knew, from the venal upperpriests he had captured and killed, that self-preservation was the Temple's primary aim. So he fully expected Styphon's House to pull all of its fighting men out of Hos-Agrys and Hos-Bletha. The latter he could attempt to stop, but there was little he could do about reinforcements from Hos-Agrys unless he helped foment a rebellion there.

"First, is there enough dissatisfaction in Hos-Agrys to start an uprising?"

Prince Mnestros took a moment to light his pipe and draw in a pipeful of smoke. After he exhaled, he said, "Yes, but it would take some encouragement and help from the outside. The rebels would need arms and fireseed."

Kalvan nodded. "We have lots of battle-spoil weapons that are sitting in warehouses in Thagnor Town that we could send them."

"You would do that, Your Majesty?" Mnestros asked, suddenly perking up.

"Yes, and more. We can provide all the fireseed you need. However, we cannot spare any troops."

"I know many people in Eubros who would love to be able to take up arms against the tyrannical Prince Valdros. His father was a baron whose greatest accomplishment was to place his barony in hock to Styphon's House. Valdros has imprisoned or killed many worshippers of Dralm as well as those who supported my father, their legitimate Prince. There are other men, many former nobles before the war ended, who would love to redress old wounds. I could gather many of such men around my banner. I also know of important men in other princedoms who grow weary of Styphon's yoke upon their necks. Even more soldiers could be recruited if it became known that Your Majesty was behind the rebellion."

"Use my name freely, if it will aid your revolt. I suspect that if you're successful in defeating Valdros and his Styphoni-bought army, rebellion will spread to other princedoms that were formerly aligned with the League of Dralm."

"Oh, yes, Your Majesty!" Mnestros said excitedly. "Once you have brought down Grand Master Soton, word will spread like wildfire throughout the Five Kingdoms. This will give men throughout the realm the courage to throw off their chains."

"I'd like for you to leave for Thagnor at daybreak. I'll have a letter delivered before you leave, so that you will be able to obtain the arms, ships and other items you'll need for this insurgency from Prince Phrames. You'll need to set up a shipping depot where Prince Phrames can send you arms, fireseed and foodstuffs. I can give you everything but feet on the ground; that you will have to do yourself."

"That I can do, Your Majesty!" the Prince cried. He was standing straighter as if the weight on his back had been jettisoned. "You have my word. We will throw out the Styphoni scum and end their reign forever!"

FOURTEEN

The Great King's manservant led the two Hostigi delegates into Great King Phidestros' private audience chamber where he sat on a high-backed chair with his wife to his right.

"Your Majesties, I would like to present Duke Hestophes, an emissary from the court of Great King Kalvan of Nos-Hostigos, and Uncle Wolf Tharses."

"Please sit down," Great King Phidestros said.

As the Hostigi sat down, his manservant came forward with a plate of maple sugar candies, those being a famous delicacy of Hos-Zygros. After both Hestophes and Tharses took one, the servant put the plate down on a small table beside the two Hostigi.

Although he knew his manservant would love nothing more than to stick around and hear the proceedings, Phidestros dismissed him with a flick of his hand. This promised to be a very interesting conversation and certainly not one for public consumption; there would be rumors, of course, but only those inside this chamber would know the truth of these proceedings.

Uncle Wolf Tharses looked every inch the ex-soldier he had been; his hair and long beard were gray, his face lumpy and he walked with a limp. But the priest's steely blue eyes had no problem matching Phidestros' stare and Phidestros suspected there were a number of good reasons he was among Kalvan's inner circle of advisors. Duke Hestophes was even more impressive; he had the build of a blacksmith and brown eyes that were both deep and penetrating. From what Phidestros had learned about the Duke, he was a gifted leader and had an exceptional grasp of tactics and strategy. Hestophes was also one of Kalvan's paladins and most trusted advisors. Last year, he had acted as his king's stalking-horse during Styphon's

House's invasion of Hos-Agrys and acquitted himself well. Had Hestophes been given sufficient troops, he would have bet the outcome in that kingdom would have taken a completely different turn.

Duke Hestophes bowed, saying, "It is a pleasure, at long last, to meet Your Majesties. I have been acquainted with the Great King's prowess on the field of battle, and I suspect he will be no easier to defeat in the drawing room."

That brought a smile from the Great Queen Arminta's lips.

"Rather than continue in this manner, like a courtier, I will plain-speak since that is what I am best at."

Phidestros nodded, as he too preferred plain-speaking. He was tired to death of silver-tongued lackeys with slippery eyes. He had replaced as many courtiers as he could with his own trusted captains, although far fewer and slower than he would have liked at his wife's advice. With so many changes at head of state, the kingdom needed some stability and peace even at the expense of tolerating the fools and charlatans among its nobility. Most of the traitors and Styphon's House's bum boys had already been weeded out of his garden of state.

"I have been sent by His Royal Majesty Great King Kalvan to negotiate an alliance between our two kingdoms. A pact of friendship and support between Hostigos and Hos-Zygros."

Phidestros noted that Hestophes did not identify which Hostigos, Nos-Hostigos or the abandoned Hos-Hostigos, he was referring to. He raised his eyebrows. "I can see where such an alliance might be of value to Great King Kalvan, but I'm not sure of what advantage it would provide to Our Kingdom."

"As I understand, Your Majesty, you have recently presented Styphon's House with an offering that greatly displeased the Innermost Circle. Therefore, it might behoove you to join forces with Great King Kalvan who is mounting a campaign against them as we speak."

This was news, but not unexpected since word of events in the south traveled slowly northwards. It could be a serious problem if Kalvan was moving his army through the disputed lands of Hos-Hostigos that were now claimed by Great King Geblon. "Where is your King's army headed?"

he said, his voice growing heated.

"Right now," Hestophes answered with an even tone, "the Hostigi Army is fighting in the Upper Sastragath. My King has set out to besiege the Zarthani Knight's main fortress of Tarr-Ceros."

"Hmm," Phidestros muttered. Neutral territory, that was good. "That fortress will be a tough nut to crack."

"Not with the artillery the Royal Army has arrayed against it, Your Majesty."

"What are your Great King's plans once it has been taken?"

"Once Tarr-Ceros has fallen, my ruler will besiege each and every Order southern fortress to the end of the Mother River until they are all conquered. He will then winter in the Sastragath; in the spring, Great King Kalvan will gather his forces to prepare for the siege of Balph."

Kalvan is ambitious, Phidestros thought. "It appears that your Great King has matters well in hand, why then does he seek our help?"

Duke Hestophes nodded as if this were a fair question. "As you know, Balph is not only the heart of Styphon's House, but a depository of much of its wealth. Whoever takes Balph, will also gain millions of ounces of gold, silver—to say nothing of its other wealth, artworks, jewels, military supplies and so forth. If you join Great King Kalvan in this attack upon this heinous and blasphemous nest of traitors, he will give you equal shares of all of this bountiful booty. After all, Styphon is a false god and thus has no rights."

Phidestros paused to stroke his beard in thought. He looked over at his wife and she nodded, as though this proposition was worth further thought. "I agree with your latter statement. But just exactly what does Kalvan want in return for this great bounty?"

"That you intercede on his behalf with your good friend and fellow ruler, Great King Geblon, on his behalf."

"Ah, but first there is another matter that must be clarified. What about my own demesne of Great Beshta? Wasn't that once a part of Hos-Hostigos?"

"Yes, Your Majesty. However, Great King Kalvan, considering your current tenancy, as well as your value as friend and neighbor, will cede all claims to those lands to your house for now and in the future. Prince Phrames of Gytha, the most recent Prince of Beshta, agrees to these terms; as for former Prince Balthames of Beshta, he now occupies an unmarked grave and is in no position to complain."

Phidestros had to smile at that. He had wondered what had happened to the infamous Balthames; death, as he knew, solved most problems. "It is an interesting offer, but I hesitate to say generous, since I occupy that territory at present."

"Of course, sire, but my Great King wanted you to understand that whatever the future brings he will not dispute ownership or possession of your princedom."

That was smart of Kalvan, Phidestros decided. He had just taken a big bone of contention off the negotiating table. Now, all that was left was whether or not he would sell out his former subordinates' rights to the rest of Hos-Hostigos, his rightful territory, but an area no one appeared to be making use of. "And in return?"

"He would like your help in convincing Great King Geblon to relinquish his hold on territory that was once my Great King's demesne, other than your princedom, of course. At the moment, the land is worthless—war-torn, depleted, abandoned, of no value to anyone. My Great King is even prepared to make him a generous monetary settlement, if that will ease the transfer of possession."

All in all, Kalvan's requests seemed very reasonable. Were it not that Geblon was one of his best friends and paladins, he would have had no trouble agreeing. The time for this audience had come to an end; he needed to talk with Arminta and get her more neutral advice on this matter. There was a lot to gain; he was almost salivating over getting his hands on the fabled treasures of Balph....

"Finally, Your Majesty," Hestophes continued, after pausing to light his pipe, "even should you decide not to join in the sack of Balph, my Great King is prepared to give you one third of the proceeds if you can settle this property dispute with Great King Geblon."

That was more than generous. And, of course, a great savings in blood for Kalvan should he decide to go along with this proposition.

"Furthermore, should you agree, but not want to besiege Balph with Great King Kalvan, you can send one of your most trusted captains to see that the treasure is divided equally and fairly."

"What's in it for Great King Geblon?" Phidestros asked.

"He'll pay in gold for Geblon to drop his claim to Hos-Hostigos."

"How much?"

Hestophes shrugged. "The Great King mentioned to me a hundred thousand ounces of gold per princedom: Hostigos, Nostor, Sask, Nyklos, Ulthor and Kyblos. A handsome price for worthless land, in my estimation."

Over half a million ounces of gold! Phidestros thought. *Most generous.* "Thank you, Duke. You have given us much to mull over."

Both of the Hostigi bowed and left the room. When the chamber door had closed, he turned to his wife. "What do you think of Kalvan's offer, my love?"

"On the surface, it is extremely generous. On one hand, Kalvan wants to enlist you and our army in the invasion of Hos-Ktemnos, since Great King Lukthos will not idly sit by while Balph is sacked and the great treasures of Styphon's House are looted. With both armies, the outcome of that war is assured and at a smaller cost in casualties than if Kalvan invaded on his own. Plus, it would cement your alliance and put a wedge between you and Great King Geblon. His other offer of a third of the booty, should you decline to aid his siege, is even more generous; although, again it might pit you against your friend."

"So it all boils down to whether or not I want to sell out my old comrade?"

"Not quite, my dear. Geblon is only Great King of Hos-Harphax because you stepped away from the Iron Throne; he owes his throne to you and our army. He had no army of his own; it was your might and intercession that gave him his throne. Although, I doubt—knowing human nature—that he sees it that way. Still, were it not for Queen Lavena, you could easily talk him into abandoning his claims on Hos-Hostigos for Kalvan's price—which is more than fair, I might add."

"Aha," Phidestros said. "Now comes the sticking point."

"Yes," she smiled. "On the other hand, Great Queen Lavena is a spoiled child and will not look kindly on her husband giving away lands she believes are rightfully hers as the Great Queen of Hos-Harphax; even though her title was bought with her former husband's brother's blood."

"It is true," he said. "Great King Lysandros had his own brother murdered so he could claim the Iron Throne. He and Lavena were a good match. It's unfortunate that she outlived him."

"I know you suggested poisoning her, my husband."

"Yes, I did. But you talked me out of it because she was with child. Your kind heart is one of the reasons I love you."

Queen Arminta blushed.

"Didn't you tell me, love, that Duke Hestophes was once one of Lavena's swains back in Hostigos?"

"Yes," she said, "I learned a lot about Queen Lavena—much more than I ever wanted—during my stay in Tarr-Harphax. She and Duke Hestophes were a couple until her father broke them apart when he learned that Hestophes' father was a publican."

"Wasn't he a baron at that time?"

"Yes," she replied. "Hestophes was rewarded by Great King Kalvan with a small barony near Hyllos town; they were neighbors. Queen Lavena cast her spell over Hestophes, too. She told me proudly that he was quite heartbroken by their split. Lavena now views their association as a youthful indiscretion."

"I'm sure Duke Hestophes would not find that amusing, although it is said that he is married now. Is it true that Lavena is the spitting image of Great Queen Rylla?"

"Yes, but for their hair color, they could pass for twins. This I was told by one of her maidservants who has been with her for many winters. Lavena will not talk about it; she flies into a rage at the mere mention of Rylla's name."

"It sounds as if she is jealous," Phidestros said. "I understand Queen Rylla is not only comely, but a warrior of renown and a leader as well."

"Yes, that is what I've heard. However, the two women are complete opposites. Where Rylla is generous and loving, Lavena is avaricious and mean-spirited. She dotes on her father, Prince Sthentros, who now claims suzerainty over the Princedom of Hostigos and will not relinquish that claim except upon pain of death."

"Which he richly deserves," Phidestros added. He had only met the arrogant Sthentros a few times, but that was enough for a roomful of hatred. The man was a traitor and a fool; if it weren't for his daughter, he would be begging in the streets of Harphax City. "Queen Lavena is as pigheaded as a wineshop trollop. Unfortunately, she has cast some love spell upon Geblon and he worships the ground she walks upon."

"Yes, I fear Geblon is thoroughly browbeaten," Arminta said, shaking her head. "Lavena leads him around by the beak like a broken-winged goose."

"This means he will not be amenable to our alliance with Hostigos, which on the surface is quite generous," Phidestros replied.

"Yes, Kalvan was wise to be so magnanimous. It has given us a big problem, my husband. I believe Kalvan's offer is more than fair. You have a major decision to make."

Phidestros felt his head throb; he was beginning to suffer the kind of headache usually brought on by too many bottles of mulled wine. He knew his wife admired Kalvan and his administration of Hostigos. She often suggested that he should model his own rule after Kalvan's. "I take it, you think we should accept Kalvan's offer of friendship and alliance."

"Yes, I do, my love. Kalvan is many things, but one thing he is above all—is honest. If he makes a promise, he will keep it. And, as you know, I've approved of most of the innovations that he introduced in Hos-Hostigos. The two of you are the great captains of this era and it behooves us both that you work together. However, Geblon is your good friend, and the final decision is up to you as Great King."

"Thank you," he said, his head already pounding. "You've just made my decision twice as difficult! What I need to do next is talk with Duke Kyblannos and hear what he has to say."

FIFTEEN

I

Kalvan was fast asleep on their corn-shuck mattress when the pounding at the door woke him and Rylla up. "What is it?" he called out. "The Knights are breaking out of Tarr-Ceros!" someone hollered.

Kalvan rose up and used his tinderbox to set a splinter on fire, which gave him enough visibility to light a nearby candle. Cleon rushed into the room with another candle. In the flickering light, his manservant quickly found his breeches and helped Kalvan on with them. While Cleon was helping him put on his black leather jackboots, he heard Rylla struggling to get out of bed. "Darling, you stay here! Nothing short of a miracle could get them out of Tarr-Ceros alive. And I have a feeling Styphon's just about run out of those."

Rylla yawned. "Yes, husband. I'm too tired to argue…"

That was a blessing from Dralm, he decided, as Cleon tied up his arming doublet with mail sleeves and skirt. Next he put on his quilted helmet-coif followed by his throat-guard, plate cuirass and plate tassets down to his thighs. Lastly, Kalvan put on his morion helmet, then slipped his rapier and poignard into their scabbards. He wore practically the same outfit he had worn since taking command of the Hostigos Army: none of his armor was gilded or ornamented; that was how good commanders died. He wished he could convince Prince Sarrask, who still wore more silver plate than a dinner-service, of that.

Outside in the dark, illuminated by red bonfires, stood Colonel Leukestros with half a dozen armored men. "Your Majesty, the Knights are attempting a sortie. We thought you'd want to be there to see our response."

"Of course, man!" Kalvan cried. "Let's get a move on!"

He could hear musket and rifle fire in the distance in between salvos of cannon fire. A salvo went off roughly every thirty seconds from one of the dozen batteries around Wall-4. Already some of the bigger mortars were firing shells onto the roof of Tarr-Ceros adding to the cacophony. *It must be sheer Hell in there*, he decided. *No wonder some of the godforsaken bastards are trying to break out.*

The ground had been trodden by the troops, horses and big guns into a flat landscape devoid of plant or native animal life. Even at a fast pace, it took them almost five minutes to reach the first break out. The ground was littered with dead Knights in full armor splayed around the sally port. Some of the survivors were still firing muskets behind big shields and piles of their own dead. The crack of mass rifle fire sounded as the Hostigi First Royal Musketeers fired another volley.

As Kalvan watched, a Knight reared up to fire his musket when suddenly his breastplate—with about as much stopping power as aluminum foil—showed half a dozen bloody holes from the Musketeers' 8-bore rifled muskets. After that last volley, there were less than a score of the Knights still firing back, laying down cover-fire for the survivors or retreating into their portal.

Two volleys later and the last of the remaining Knights were down. Out of the more than two hundred bodies that littered the sally port entrance, Kalvan suspected there would be two score of enemy dead, twice that of mortally wounded men, most of whom would die of their injuries. He had truly escalated the low-impact warfare native to this area to total war. A part of him was still appalled at the waste of it all.

"Shall we follow them, Your Majesty?" Colonel Leukestros asked.

Kalvan shook his head. "It's not necessary. They're trapped inside Tarr-Ceros like rats in a drainpipe. Following them into their own sally port, is exactly what they want. It's probably mined and set to collapse. That's how I'd do it," Kalvan finished.

II

Grand Master Soton was seated in a special chair that had been provided for him in Galzar's new chapel. He bowed his head as he prayed for his men who had died trying to lure the Hostigi under the sally ports. Sadly, the ruse had not worked and two hundred Order soldiers had died in vain. *At least*, he thought, *they have earned a place in Galzar's Great Hall for their valor.*

A noise from behind brought his attention back to the chapel. *More bad news?*

A familiar face came into view. "Aristocles, what in Ormaz's name are you doing here? Did you bring an army with you?"

His old friend's face shuddered. "No, old friend. The fools at Balph refused to come to our aid. We are on our own, curse and blast them all to Regwarn's Caverns!"

"How did you get by Kalvan's sentries?"

"I've been waiting by the old farmhouse for the past moon-quarter for the Hostigi to break ranks. Your attack from the sally ports brought them running, so even the sentries left their posts. It's too bad it didn't work, but it was enough of a ruse for me to enter through one of the old tunnels."

"But why did you come back by yourself?" Soton said, his voice edged with anger. "I was trying to save your life."

"That's not your decision. What am I to do outside the Order? I cannot live without my comrades and my old master. Styphon's Voice even had the audacity to offer me command of the City's defenses. Would I be any better off in Balph, than here with my friends? No, if Tarr-Ceros falls, Balph will fall soon enough. So I refused. It's bad enough the Innermost Council refused us aid. I decided to return and I'm glad I did. Your sour face reminds me of home.

"But what is this?" Aristocles asked, his eyes widening as he looked around. "Where has Styphon's Idol gone? Now, I see Galzar...."

Soton couldn't face his old friend and looked down at the floor. "I finally saw the truth in our enemy's words. The Temple is a fraud and all Styphon's priests care for are gold and pleasures of the flesh. All the Styphoni priests fled the chapel as soon as they learned that Kalvan and his army were coming. Pshaw! Cowards and spineless jellyfish—all of them. May Galzar curse the House of Styphon and all his thieving priests!"

Aristocles drew back. "Is this truly Grand Master Soton? My, you have changed. What brought about this revelation?"

"The death of too many comrades and the lack of support from the Temple after all we have done."

"It's about time, my friend. Now, what are we going to do about this predicament?"

"What do you mean?" Soton asked.

"Has Great King Kalvan offered you terms?"

"Yes, but where would we go?"

"I've got an idea. It's time to set up a parley before they tear down another wall."

III

Great King Phidestros, with a small bodyguard, traveled incognito through the narrow cobblestone streets of Zygros City until he reached Duke Kyblannos' townhouse. The Duke had a large dukedom in the southern part of Mythrax, but preferred to live in town with his wife and many children. The townhouse was a four-story structure made of timber and white plaster. Phidestros was greeted at the door by one of Kyblannos' body servants and escorted through the chaos of the common rooms to the Duke's workshop at the back of the house.

About halfway across the great hall, the Duchess accosted him. "Your Majesty, may I speak with you for a moment?"

She was a large woman with breasts the size of pillows and legs like bedposts. "Yes, Lady Myrissa, what is the problem?" he asked; he could tell from the expression on her face that she was troubled.

"Your Majesty, my husband is always getting underfoot, and I think he's got wanderlust fever again. Is there any place you can send him to give us all some relief? I know he enjoys tinkering with his guns, but the rest of the time he's like a lost boy."

"I may have something for him," he replied.

She sighed heavily. "Thank you, Your Majesty. It would do us all a world of good. He's not used to staying cooped up, just as we're not used to having him around all the time."

Phidestros understood her problem very well, having been a mercenary on the move for most of his adulthood. Fortunately, he had found the right woman and was now comfortably settled down in Tarr-Zygros. Having a family was still a novelty, but he doubted it would ever grow stale with Arminta around to keep him busy and entertained. Her upbringing had given her a unique understanding of statecraft and diplomacy. Together they made a powerful couple. It didn't hurt that they were deeply in love, but that was just an unexpected bonus as far as he was concerned.

He found Kyblannos outside in a large outbuilding that looked like a former barn or stable. It was now the Duke's workroom. Inside he was tinkering with a massive wooden carriage, probably for one of the new thirty-two pound guns that were being cast at the Royal Foundry. When he spotted Phidestros, he said, "I've tried to make this carriage as small as possible, but it's still going to take four teams of horses to pull this monster once the gun is mounted."

Phidestros nodded. Pointing to the Duke's office, he said. "Let's have a quick drink."

Kyblannos led him inside and poured them both a goblet of winter wine. "What's on your mind, Cap'n?"

Phidestros lowered his cup, saying, "I've got a big problem and I need your advice. It may even involve a trip away from home."

A big grin broke out on his face. "I haven't spent this much time with the wife since our wedding. She and the kids are giving me battle fever."

"There are times when I long for those carefree days when all we had to worry about was whether or not we had enough silver for the paychest or enough fireseed for our muskets."

"Aye, Cap'n, those were the days…I even miss the battles."

"Yes, but there are advantages to our current positions."

Kyblannos nodded rather forlornly. “I suppose so, but I long for the wide open spaces and new towns and villages.” He opened his mouth, showing a gap-notched smile from missing teeth. “And firing my guns at soldiers, not at targets and sandbags.”

“You may get your wish. What have you heard lately about Geblon and Hos-Harphax?”

“I still get a short letter every moon or so from an old comrade in Harphax City. It seems Geblon is spending most of his time in the lap of his new wife. He dotes on Queen Lavena like a love-sick swain. It’s enough to turn my stomach.”

“What do you think of Lavena?”

“A she-devil, Cap’n. She treats our old comrade like dirt, and her servants even worse. We should have poisoned her when we had the chance. Your wife is too soft-hearted.”

Phidestros nodded, but it wasn’t something he wanted to change. “How are his subjects looking upon this weakness of his?”

“Not well. Geblon’s lost most of the respect of his princes and nobles; even the commoners snicker when his name is mentioned. He’s become a kingdom-wide joke.”

“How about his soldiers?”

“Well, they’re embarrassed, especially those who fought with him. As long as he pays them, he’ll have their support; after all, they know he’s your man. But he’s not a fit ruler—that’s for sure.”

“I made a big error enthroning him, but we were in a hurry and I needed someone on the Iron Throne I could trust. Well, he’s got a new problem now. King Kalvan is coming back to Hos-Hostigos.”

“Coming back! What do you mean, Cap’n?”

“He sent his envoy, Duke Hestophes—”

“My, hasn’t he risen, a ‘duke’ now. Just like the rest of us, that’s something war is good for. What does Great King Kalvan want from us?”

“Right now Kalvan’s besieging Tarr-Ceros, which is his first step in regaining Hos-Hostigos. At least that’s what Hestophes says.”

“Then that’s the straight word, Cap’n. Hestophes is a man of his word; I’ve never heard anything different. Tarr-Ceros is not going to go down easy, though."

Phidestros nodded, as Kyblannos' wife brought them a tray full of pastries. He took one and said, "I agree, but I believe Kalvan's got the big guns to do it. It could take a while, though."

Kyblannos asked, "I thought he had his own kingdom, another Hostigos, in the Upper Middle Kingdoms. What does he want from you?"

"Kalvan does have a new home in Thagnor, but now he wants his old home back. What he wants from me is our help. Either that, or stay out of his way when he's finished with Balph and returns to reclaim Old Hostigos."

"Phew! What's he offering to keep you out of the fray?"

"A lot. First, he's recognized my suzerainty of Greater Beshta. Next, I'm to receive a third of the booty he takes after sacking Balph and Ktemnos City. Or half, if we join him in Ktemnos."

Kyblannos whistled loudly. "By Styphon's Brass Bollocks! That's got to be the biggest treasure in the history of the Five Kingdoms. I hope you told Hestophes we'd meet him and Kalvan in Balph!"

Phidestros said, "I haven't told him anything, yet. I wanted to think about it, and run it by you first. What do you think Geblon's reaction is likely to be?"

"Ha! It all depends upon that she-devil he's married to. She's from Hostigos and now her father's Prince—though mostly Prince of Rack and Ruin. He's another crab apple, though. Still, I don't expect he wants to be run out of town by Kalvan. My guess is that she'll convince Geblon to oppose it."

"Without her interference, what do you think he would do?"

"It depends, Cap'n. What's Kalvan intending to offer him if he releases his claims on those princedoms?"

"A hundred thousand ounces of gold per princedom! That's half a million ounces in total."

Kyblannos mouth dropped. "That's more than a fair offer. Maybe the she-devil's greed will overcome her baser instincts."

Phidestros shook his head. "I wouldn't count on it, my friend."

"Then what're you gonna do, Cap'n?"

"That is a very good question, Kyblannos. First, I'm going to stall Duke Hestophes, while I send you to Harphax City to open a bag of talk with Geblon. If you can convince him to take Kalvan's offer, I might well join Kalvan in Hos-Ktemnos. It would do me good to slake my rage against Styphon's House by helping turn Balph into ruins."

"To say nothing about all that treasure," Kyblannos said with a big grin. "I'll do that. I'll leave for Harphax City in the morning. Anything to get away from here. Not that I don't love my wife and children, but they're much easier to love from a distance."

Phidestros laughed. "You've always had that problem."

"Aye, Cap'n. But there's another kingdom in play you haven't mentioned. What are you going to do about Hos-Agrys, since Great King Demistophon's death it's now ruled by Styphon's House?"

"If I cross their territory to join Kalvan, there's not much they can do about it. They have less than twenty thousand troops to control the entire kingdom, and half of those are in Agrys City. Besides, they rule in Hos-Agrys by proxy. The Regent Archpriest Grythos is still in charge, but his ward, Prince Dementros will be the ruler once he's of age."

Kyblannos smiled slyly, "Sure, if Styphon's House lets him live that long."

"True, there is evidence that a great wrong will be committed there in the future. One that maybe we should right. Anyway, it's something to think about."

"Yes, and help ourselves to the treasures of Styphon's House while we're going through Hos-Agrys like a wolf loose in a turkey pen." Kyblannos added with a wolfish grin.

They both laughed.

SIXTEEN

I

Kalvan was in his headquarters going over the next stage of the siege with Colonel Leukestros and Captain-General Alkides when a messenger entered the room. Now that Wall-4 was gutted, he was pointing out the areas on Wall-5 where they might best concentrate their firepower on the map of the fort's defensive walls.

"Your Majesty, the Knights are requesting a parley," the messenger announced.

Kalvan looked up from the map in surprise. "Really?"

"Yes," the messenger replied. "One of the Knights is Grand Commander Aristocles. He's accompanied by an Uncle Wolf."

"Then they're serious," Leukestros put in.

"Send for Uncle Wolf Xanthos. Have the emissaries brought here right away and give the order to cease fire."

"Yes, sir," the messenger snapped back.

In a few minutes the artillery guns stopped their firing and for the first time in months Kalvan could hear himself think. He couldn't even imagine what it must have been like in Tarr-Ceros for the past couple of months. Still, as stubborn as Grand Master Soton was, the last thing he'd expected was for him to sue for terms.

Grand Commander Aristocles, a tall man with a hawk nose and aristocratic face, entered the room at a quick pace. At his side was an older Uncle Wolf with a grizzled gray beard streaked with white.

Aristocles bowed, saying: "Great King Kalvan, I have been sent here by Grand Master Soton of the Order of Zarthani Knights to ask for your terms for surrender. As my witness, I've brought Uncle Wolf Olmnestes."

The presence of an Uncle Wolf highpriest instead of a Styphon's House upperpriest was a surprise, and boded well for the proceedings. "Greetings, Grand Commander Aristocles and Uncle Wolf Olmnestes. Commander, your reputation precedes you."

Since surrender of Tarr-Ceros had been just about the last thing on his mind, Kalvan needed to give himself time to think. He asked, "Gentlemen, before we get down to serious matters, would you like a drink of Ermut's Best?"

Both men nodded enthusiastically, leading Kalvan to suspect that alcohol was probably in low supply in the castle. While Colonel Leukestros hurried off to find Cleon, Kalvan showed everyone to a seat and passed around a full tobacco pouch to his guests. Both men quickly filled their pipe bowls and lit up. He noted that the Uncle Wolf's pipe was the typical corncob pipe, while Aristocles had a burl pipe carved into a likeness of Galzar's face, with tiny ruby eyes. The pipe was nicely done and Kalvan would have liked one for himself.

Colonel Leukestros returned with Uncle Wolf Xanthos and Cleon, holding a small barrel of spirits, in tow. Cleon brought out the good goblets and filled them with Ermut's Best.

Aristocles took a deep drink, sighed happily and said, "It's been a long time since I've had Ermut's Best to drink."

If this truce turns into a peaceful settlement, I'll send you a dozen barrels, Kalvan thought. *Now on to business.* "Since you have come to me asking for terms, I will present them: First, Grand Master Soton must publicly condemn Styphon and the Archpriests of the Inner Circle." Kalvan suspected this would be a sticking point so he brought it up first.

Aristocles nodded. "Done. We've already discussed this: Grand Master Soton is willing to renounce Styphon as his god and Styphon's House as his temple of worship in favor of Galzar Wolfhead. Oath to Galzar!"

Kalvan felt his jaw drop. The Order of Zarthani Knights played an important part in keeping the borders of the Southern Great Kingdoms free of nomads and other marauders. Its destruction would leave the western borders of both Hos-Ktemnos and Hos-Bletha open to intrusions by barbarians and bandits. Maybe a deal could be forged that would leave the Order intact....

"I would have never thought I'd hear the Grand Master renouncing Styphon. What happened?"

"The Order was betrayed by Styphon's Voice and the Innermost Circle," Aristocles replied. "Before the siege, when we learned of your imminent arrival, Soton sent me to Balph to ask for an army to break your siege. As I expected, they refused. This news, however, sorely tested the Grand Master's faith and he slowly came to the resolution that the god he had worshipped so faithfully was a fraud and a sham and that his priests were nothing but common thieves and sharpers, preying on the gullible and the weak. The death of his adjutant, whom he viewed like a son, was the match in the fireseed barrel that broke his allegiance to Styphon's House. He now feels the fool, having fought the Temple's battles for these frauds. The Grand Master now wants to rededicate the Order of Zarthani Knights to Galzar Wolfhead."

Kalvan turned to the two Uncle Wolfs. "Do you two have any thoughts on this matter?"

"I will speak first," Uncle Wolf Olmnestes said, "since I've already discussed this matter in detail with both Grand Master Soton and Grand Commander Aristocles—if that is acceptable to Your Majesty and Uncle Wolf Xanthos?"

Uncle Wolf Xanthos nodded, while Kalvan said, "It is acceptable, Praise Galzar."

"I believe it will be a great boon," Uncle Wolf Olmnestes said, "not only for the God of Judges but for the people living in the Sastragath, as well as their neighbors in Hos-Ktemnos and Hos-Bletha. While this proposition will have to be adjudicated by the High Temple in Hos-Harphax, I believe their final decision will be to accept. Do you agree, Xanthos?"

"Yes, I do. The Order has been doing Galzar's work all along; it's long overdue that the Order of Zarthani Knights passed into the Wargod's charge. It will also help with recruiting more men into the Order."

Aristocles nodded, as though that was something he had deduced himself.

"That is acceptable, then," Kalvan stated. "It also meets with my approval." Now all he had to worry about was a nomad army, at his invitation, arriving under Warlord Sargos. Fortunately, he wouldn't have to deal with it this campaign season. He wasn't sure how he would deal with Sargos in the future, but he would have to make it clear that the Warlord and his men would have to stay on their side of the Great River. This deal would help keep the peace after Styphon's House was destroyed and its temple grounds sown with bone and blood.

"Since my terms have been met," Kalvan said, "I will give orders to halt the siege and still the guns." He rose up, goblet in hand, saying, "To peace and good works."

Aristocles face broke out in a smile. "To Galzar. And Death to Styphon's House!"

"Aye, aye," came from the assembled voices. That was a proposition everyone could agree on.

II

A few minutes later, after everyone had left, Rylla came charging into headquarters. "My husband, why have the guns stopped firing?"

Kalvan smiled. "The siege has come to an end. It's over; we won."

"What?" she asked, thumping her breastplate with her fist. "How can it be, there are walls left to breach. Tarr-Ceros still stands unbroken!"

"The Order has sued for peace and accepted all our terms."

Rylla's eyes widened. "I cannot believe this. It's a trick, a ruse!"

Kalvan shook his head. "No, it's not. Grand Master Soton is a man of his word, is that not true?"

Reluctantly, she nodded.

"Besides, what would the Order have to gain by a ruse? A temporary halt to the bombardment, at most. There's no one coming to their rescue, and they know it. They also know that if it was a trick, we would be back and strike even harder."

"Yes, that makes sense. But will Soton renounce Styphon? He's a true believer, after all."

Kalvan grinned. "Not any longer. The rascals in charge have finally pushed him beyond endurance. He's not only willing to renounce Styphon, but he's going to announce it publicly. This will really damage the enemy's morale."

Rylla shook her head in disbelief. "I never thought it would come to this. Still, Grand Master Soton must pay for the depredations he and the Grand Host of Styphon's House committed during the siege of Tarr-Hostigos and in Hostigos Town."

Kalvan sighed; he had known it wasn't going to be easy to get Rylla to accept the new status quo. "From everything our agents have been able to uncover, it was Great King Lysandros who demanded that Tarr-Hostigos be captured, not Grand Master Soton or even Captain-General Phidestros. If Captain-General Phidestros and Soton had had their way, they would have followed us to the Great Seas, which might have ended badly. After all, we weren't a retreating army, but a folk migration. They had no interest in besieging Tarr-Hostigos; the siege was to fulfill Lysandros' revenge. And, as we both know, Lysandros has already paid the ultimate price for that and his many other sins."

Rylla blew out a deep breath of air.

He knew it was hard to let go of revenge, especially when the perpetrator was dead and far beyond earthly reach. The inclination was to strike out at anyone else who played a part. He needed to refocus Rylla's anger.

"The real perpetrators are still alive and living in luxury in Balph," he stated. "Soton, Phidestros—even Lysandros—were all nothing but the Inner Circle's tools. Is that not true?"

"Yes, the temple-rats are the ones who set the war in motion."

"Exactly, and they should be—no, they will be—the ones who will pay the price. And the end of this siege only brings that day closer."

That Rylla understood; finally she smiled.

III

It had only taken Duke Kyblannos a few days to sail from Zygros to Harphax City, but he was still cooling his heels after almost a moon, and he still didn't have an appointment to see Great King Geblon. He had a strong suspicion that it was Queen Lavena who was behind the delay. Every time he visited the palace, he got the run around from the Royal Chancellor; the man treated him as if he carried the plague. He wondered if Geblon even knew he was in town. When he talked to the chief Zygrosi intelligencer in Harphax, all the man could tell him was that the Queen Lavena had put out a blanket order that the Great King was not to be disturbed.

Fortunately, he had nice quarters at the Raven Inn where they had a wonderful tavern with everything drinkable on hand that one could want but Ermut's Best. Another reason, he decided, to favor an alliance with Great King Kalvan.

He knew the Cap'n hated delays and was certain his backside was as hot as a kitchen stove; nor was he sure how long Kalvan's envoys would wait patiently in Zygros City for his return. He was preparing to leave when a courtier, dressed in fancy red-and-yellow velvet apparel and wearing a neck ruff the size of a dinner plate, finally called upon him at the inn.

"His Majesty will see you now, Your Grace," he said with a sniff, as though he couldn't imagine why.

Kyblannos was tempted to rearrange the courtier's face, but decided against it. This fancy pants was probably some favorite of Geblon's wife and there would be Hadron to pay if anything happened to him. Now he was certain who wore the breeches in the family; in the old days Geblon would have never put up with such nonsense.

Great King Geblon saw him in a private presence room that was as luxuriously appointed as that of one of Styphon's House's archpriests. He didn't even greet him with a comradely pat on the shoulders, or the offer of a drink.

This is taking bad manners too far, Kyblannos thought to himself. *Probably expects me to address him as Your Majesty, too! Not in this lifetime....*

"May I ask what brought upon this visit to our kingdom?" Geblon asked, as if he didn't know him personally or as if his old comrade was some unfamiliar dignitary.

"I've come on the Cap'n's behalf."

"I assume you are referring to Great King Phidestros, my liegeman."

"Liegeman, my ass! The Cap'n put you on the Iron Throne, and he can throw you the Styphon off, if he wants. Now, you can start talkin' to me like an old comrade before I put my foot up your bung-hole!"

Geblon reared back as if he had been slapped. "I can call my bodyguards and have you clapped in irons with the snap of my fingers!"

"Do that and the Cap'n'll have your head. I came down here to see you on official business, not to be treated like some churl or Styphon's House temple-farm slave."

Geblon tugged at what was left of his short beard, cut into a V in the latest style. "You're right, we have started off on the wrong boot." He grabbed his bell pull and yanked.

Moments later a finely-dressed servant in the Harphaxi yellow-and-red colors appeared. "Your Majesty, what is your pleasure?"

"Some of our best winter wine for me and my friend."

"Yes, Sire."

While they waited, Kyblannos took out his pipe and fixings and filled the barrel with fresh tobacco, which he had noted wasn't scarce in Harphax City at all. By the time he had lit up, libations had arrived in golden goblets, Kyblannos took it upon himself to restart the conversation. "Good drink, I must say."

"We have it brought down from the mountains from a special vinery run by an order of priestesses of Yirtta. They seem to have a magic touch when it comes to fermenting. It's most expensive."

Kyblannos gulped down half a cupful and wiped his mouth with his sleeve. Geblon flinched but kept his mouth shut, proving that the old Geblon hadn't completely curled up and died.

"The Cap'n sent me down here to talk with you about something that's about to happen in your own backyard," Kyblannos said.

"You don't say. You wouldn't be referring to the invasion by the Usurper Kalvan, would you?"

Kyblannos shook his head. "I wouldn't be calling it an invasion. The man simply wants revenge on those that hurt him—and get his home back, too."

"Well, he's not going to get it. He took my territory in the first place, and I'm not about to give it up."

Kyblannos laughed. "What are you talkin' about? Your territory, my arse! You were a banner captain in the Iron Company when Lord Kalvan arrived and wrested Hos-Hostigos from Kaiphranos the Timid."

"It makes no matter. The territory, falsely and formerly known as Hos-Hostigos, is under my rule now and I'm not about to give it up without a fight. I might add, a fight in which I expect the full support of Prince Phidestros of Greater Beshta."

"You can't tell the Cap'n what to do, great king or not. He can make or break you anytime he wishes. He sent me down to see you as a favor to an old comrade and former subordinate. Kalvan has made him a good offer and he wanted me to run it by you before he came to a decision."

"What are you talking about?"

"Kalvan has asked the Cap'n to join him in the sack of Balph, and offered him half of Styphon's House's treasure if he does."

"If he joins the Hostigi army, he'll have to go through me first."

"Are you mad, Geblon? The Cap'n can bring thirty thousand men down on your head, and that's not countin' the ten or twelve thousand more he could raise in Greater Beshta. How long do you think the ten or twelve thousand poorly-trained troops you have garrisoned around Harphax City will fare against those odds? The Cap'n will eat your britches for first meal!"

For the first time, Geblon paled as he took this news in and digested it. "I couldn't help Phidestros if I wanted to. I've already contracted with Styphon's House to use my troops to protect Balph from the Usurper Kalvan."

Kyblannos shook his head in disbelief. "You've become a Styphoni?"

Geblon shook his head. “No, but they’re paying me a lot of gold to help them.”

“Well, so is Kalvan. He’s willing to pay you a hundred thousand ounces a princedom for the return of Old Hos-Hostigos, and it won’t cost you a single soldier. You’d better think this proposition over carefully, Geblon. The offer Kalvan made to the Cap’n is the kind that cleaves father from son and yanks brothers from their mother’s teats.”

“Are you telling me that Phidestros would side with Kalvan against me?”

Kyblannos shrugged. “Maybe not the old you. But, yeah, he might. Or he might just stay out of the fray and pick up the pieces.”

At this, Geblon turned as white as the robes of a Styphon’s House novitiate.

“Think about it,” Kyblannos threw over his shoulder, as he finished his drink, then turned to leave the audience chamber.

SEVENTEEN

I

"Whaaat?" Hestophes sputtered, as someone poked him in the side. He opened his eyes to find a candle over his face. A big drop of hot wax dripped off the candle and burned his cheek. "Ouch! Dralm-damnit, what in Ormaz's name—"

"Sorry, it's me, Tharses," the Uncle Wolf said, as he pulled back the candle. "We just received wonderful news from Great King Kalvan. Praise Galzar!"

That popped open his eyes. "Has Tarr-Ceros fallen?"

Uncle Wolf Tharses smiled. "Much better than even that. Grand Master Soton has surrendered the fortress to Kalvan and renounced Styphon's House!"

Hestophes rose up off his comfortable bed, pushing the heavy bearskin bedspread out of his way. He yawned, then started to shiver in the freezing air. He paused to wrap the bearskin around him, before saying, "That's great news! And unexpected…Soton renouncing Styphon is like hearing Rylla denounce Hos-Hostigos."

Tharses laughed uproariously. "I know; I was taken by surprise myself. What's even better, is that Grand Master Soton has rededicated the Order of Zarthani Knights to Galzar!"

"Praise Galzar and Allfather Dralm, how did you find out?" Hestophes asked, rubbing the sleep from his eyes.

The message just arrived by pigeon. The handler woke Aldos, who decoded it and brought it over personally. We may have to change our plans."

"Delay our departure?"

"Yes, Great King Kalvan wants you to brief Phidestros and stay here until he's made a decision about the invasion of Hos-Ktemnos."

"Curse and blast it! I was looking forward to leaving this wretched town before the weather turns nasty and it really gets cold."

"I don't blame you," the Uncle Wolf replied. "But Great King Phidestros' support—or neutrality—is crucial to the invasion. The difference between facing thirty thousand enemy soldiers or sixty thousand!"

"Well, when you put it that way, we don't have a choice. Does Kalvan think that Soton's surrender will help bring an end to Phidestros' fence-sitting?"

"He didn't say. However, as we surmised, when we learned that Captain-General Kyblannos boarded a boat bound for Harphax City shortly after our arrival, it's likely that Phidestros is still waiting to hear from his trusted subordinate. We don't have anyone close enough to Geblon's Court to tell us whether or not they've met. However, Klestreus' spies tell us that Archpriest Phyllos has been seen entering and leaving the new palace numerous times which—I don't have to tell you—is not a good sign."

"That turkey-pecked whoreson! Do you think Geblon could queer the deal with Phidestros?"

"By Galzar's Grace, it's possible, depending on how much he values his old comrade. If Great King Phidestros weighs in on the side of Styphon's House, the war could go against Hostigos very quickly. That's why your mission is so important."

"Is there anything else that I should tell Phidestros?" Hestophes asked.

"Yes, that Great King Kalvan says to inform him that he will be wintering in Hos-Bletha with his good friend and ally Great King Valthros."

"Ouch. That will get Phidestros' attention. I thought our alliance with Valthros was a secret."

Uncle Wolf Tharses nodded. "It was. But, now that Kalvan's going to be staying the winter in Hos-Bletha, it will soon be common knowledge. It might help sway Phidestros to learn that our Great King has an unexpected ally in his war against Styphon's House."

II

Geblon paced anxiously back and forth from the door to the bed of their bedchamber. He was caught in a bind and he didn't know how to extricate himself.

"What's bothering you, now?" Queen Lavena asked.

"I just had a talk with Duke Kyblannos—"

"Why was I not told of his visit!" she screeched. "He's always been a bad influence on you. Him and that mercenary, Phidestros."

"Did you have anything to do with why I was not informed of his arrival?" he asked, timidly.

"Of course, he's a bad influence on you. And that Phidestros is no better!"

"Darling, don't forget I worked with those men for many winters. Besides, Phidestros is no longer a mercenary, but a Great King now."

She threw up her hands. "How could I forget? You're always going on and on about the Iron Bandits, or whatever they were called."

He shook his head and winced; it felt as though someone were beating on it as if it were a drumhead. "I needed to talk to Duke Kyblannos before he finally departed for Zygros City. Otherwise, we wouldn't know what those two were up to."

"I doubt it's any good," she said, her face scrunching up in hatred. "Those two troublemakers could foul-up everything."

"You're right, my love. They've been approached by Duke Hestoph—"

"That base-born churl!" she cried. "I knew it. Hestophes is still in love with me and determined to hurt me in any way he can."

"I don't know about that, but he is representing the Usurper." He knew better than to say Kalvan or Rylla's name out loud in her presence.

Lavena's face screwed up into a hateful mask. "I knew it. Just when things were going so well. Those *people* have to come along to muck things up!"

"You're right about that. They want Phidestros and his army to meet them in Balph—"

"Ha! As if we'd let them cross our border."

"We might not have a choice. Phidestros has got over thirty thousand troops, twice what we can raise and better armed and trained. I told you we should have spent some of the money on rifling benches…."

"And waste it!" Lavena cried.

"Our musketeers won't stand a chance against Hostigi or Zygrosi riflemen. I know from experience."

"Then we'll just have to buy some," she declared.

Geblon threw up his hands. "Where? You can't buy rifles for love or gold crowns. However, there is a way out. The Usurper has offered up a hundred thousand ounces of gold for each of the princedoms in Old Hos-Hostigos."

"Ha! A pittance compared to what Styphon's House is paying us to defend Balph. And they've promised us much more!"

Geblon sighed. "What good are promises, if you're dead?"

"Now!" she cried. "Who's the defeatist. I wish you were strong like my first husband. He went out and defeated Kalvan, and then destroyed Tarr-Hostigos."

"Yes, and Lysandros was a regicide and murderer. If it hadn't been for his blockheaded desire to capture that old castle, the Grand Host would have caught up to Kalvan and dispatched him once and for all."

"Don't you ever say a bad word about my first husband!" she screamed, her hands lashing out like claws. "There was a man who had stones. When something needed to be done, Lysandros did it—no matter how messy. I wish you were half the man he was."

Geblon felt his heart sink. It was bad enough to know that his wife didn't love him, but it was even worse to learn that she still worshipped a bloodthirsty tyrant like former Great King Lysandros.

"And what about my father?" she continued. "Did you forget about him? He's Prince of Hostigos: what will those fiends do to him?"

Geblon just shook his head. *If there were any justice in the world, someone would tie up Prince Sthentros and drop him alive and squirming into a vat of molten lead—the traditional punishment for a traitorous dog.* However, he knew better than to say what he thought; it would bring about an eruption of bile, mostly directed his way. "We will honor our oath to Styphon's House and protect your father." Silently, he hoped that Phidestros had other devilment to occupy his time.

"You'd better do so, or this will be the last night we share our marriage bed."

III

When Duke Hestophes came into his private audience chamber, Phidestros could see that the Duke's patience was just about at an end.

"Your Majesty, we have enjoyed your hospitality for far too long. I would like to know, what conclusions you have reached regarding Great King Kalvan's generous offer?"

"I'm sorry to have tested your patience, Duke. However, since my friend and former comrade is involved, as ruler of Hos-Harphax, I decided to send Captain-General Kyblannos to Harphax City to ask him what his intentions are regarding Great King Kalvan's return to Hos-Hostigos."

Hestophes nodded. "I'll assume that your emissary will inform him of my Great King's offer to his coffers in regards to our return to Hos-Hostigos."

"Yes, I believe that might play an important part in his decision," Phidestros said. *It had better be*, he thought. *When it comes down to it, Geblon owes me far more than I owe him. Unfortunately, too much depends upon that feather-head he married to gain his throne.*

"How long before Duke Kyblannos returns?"

Phidestros shrugged. "He left by one of our fastest galleys over a moon ago. He arrived within a few days, but there has been a delay in meeting with Great King Geblon. Unfortunately, he will have to return by land. This late in the year one doesn't want to tempt the Weather Goddess."

Hestophes said, "Yes, Lytris can be very unpredictable, much like Great Queen Lavena."

Phidestros smiled wryly. "Very good, Duke. You have put your finger on the problem we both face. I need to know Geblon's intentions before I can make an informed decision."

"I understand," the Duke replied. "However, just this morning I received a missive from Great King Kalvan that might have some bearing upon your decision."

Why wasn't I informed about that? Phidestros wondered. *Apparently, my agents-inquisitory aren't as good as Great King Kalvan's.* "And what might that be?"

"Your Majesty, Tarr-Ceros has fallen. Grand Master Soton himself surrendered the castle to Great King Kalvan. He has also completely renounced Styphon as a true god and denounced Styphon's House as a fraud."

Phidestros fell back against his chair in shock. *Soton surrendered! I didn't know the word was in his vocabulary. I never believed that he would renounce Styphon! This means that Kalvan will not have to tackle each of the Order's forts, moving up his timetable for the invasion of Hos-Ktemnos.*

"That's unexpected. I thought he'd fight to the last Knight…?"

"So did Kalvan," Hestophes replied. "Soton has now rededicated the Order of the Zarthani Knights to Galzar Wolfhead."

"Phew, that's going to shakeup the Innermost Circle. But it makes sense, since most of the Knights are devout followers of the Wargod, not Styphon. I just never thought I would live long enough to see this day come."

"Neither did His Majesty. Still, it will save him many moons of besieging the Order's tarrs and tons of fireseed. Plus, it will leave the border of the Sastragath protected against the nomads and Ruthani."

"I agree that it's a good thing. Does this mean Great King Kalvan will be moving against Styphon's House immediately?" he asked.

Hestophes shook his head. "No, as you mentioned it is late in the season and the weather is unpredictable even in the southern kingdoms. My Great King did reiterate that his offer is still on the table for you to join him in the sack of Balph."

"Where will he be wintering? In Nos-Hostigos?"

"No," Hestophes said with a smile. "He will be going farther south. The Grand Master has promised him use of the Order's navy to help move his army to Xiphlon. From there they will travel to Hos-Bletha to join our ally Great King Valthros in his war against the False Great King Niclophon."

Phidestros' head reeled, one shock after another. *Who else knew that the Orphan Prince was Kalvan's ally? I doubt that anyone in the Innermost Circle knew. All of Balph will be in an uproar when they find out.*

"Will Great King Valthros be joining Great King Kalvan in his quest to destroy Styphon's House?"

"Oh, yes. It was Styphon's House's assassins who originally killed Great King Valthros' parents. He is most anxious to repay them in kind."

This changes everything, Phidestros thought. *Kalvan has more allies than I ever thought, and with Soton renouncing Styphon's House, the Temple is without their greatest general. I need Kyblannos counsel and quickly.*

IV

"I got your message," Arminta said, as she entered his private audience chamber.

Phidestros knew that she preferred to spend most of her day with little Soligon, and he hated to take her away from the nursery. He had never seen her happier, or more beautiful since the baby's birth. "I don't like disturbing you while you're with the baby, but I've just received some vital information from Duke Hestophes."

"Yes, the Hostigi envoy who has been waiting patiently for our decision," she said, as she sat down next to him. "What did he have to say?"

"As our agent-inquisitory told us, he was making preparations to leave. I believe I convinced him to stay; that is, at least, until Kyblannos returns."

"What's keeping him in Harphax City, I wonder?"

"Kyblannos in his last letter said that he is still waiting for an audience with Great King Geblon. It seems he's unable to get an appointment to meet with Geblon."

"It's probably his wife again," Arminta noted. "She's trouble, that one. Lavena is probably afraid that Kyblannos will be a bad influence on her husband."

"Yes, maybe remind him of a time when he had a mind of his own."

Arminta laughed. "My mother used the same technique. She would isolate my father from his old friends and advisors so that he was forced to listen to her. When she died of the pox, it left him bereft and depressed. That's why he depended so much upon my advice."

"Don't disparage yourself, I depend on your counsel, as well," Phidestros said, "because it's sound advice and often warranted."

Arminta smiled. "I love you, too."

Phidestros reached over and took her hand. "Duke Hestophes passed on some very important news. It appears that Grand Master Soton has surrendered Tarr-Ceros and has publicly abandoned Styphon's House. He's gone so far as to label Styphon a fraud and his priests' thieving hypocrites."

"What took him so long, is the real question?" she said. "They've used him up like an old nag."

"You wouldn't bother to ask if you knew Soton as well as I do. The Soton I knew was a true-believer down to his core. Kalvan must have shaken more than the foundations of Tarr-Ceros with his attack. One thing is certain, Soton's renunciation of Styphon will hurt the Temple in many ways."

"Obviously, it will make it easier for Kalvan to besiege Balph, but how will it help us?" She asked.

"Good question. A lot, if we join Kalvan and help overthrow Styphon's House. Hestophes also let it slip out that Kalvan plans to winter in Hos-Bletha with his ally Great King Valthros—"

"Valthros is Kalvan's ally?!" Arminta interrupted. "That will give the Hostigi army additional weight. This means that Great King Niclophon's days are numbered, too. I suspect that once the Innermost Circle learns of this alliance, they will be forced to order Archpriest Grythos to bring his army back from Agrys City, leaving a power void in Hos-Agrys. I wonder if Kalvan intends to liberate the Agrysi from Styphon's tyranny and add those lands to Hos-Hostigos?"

Phidestros gave a wolfish grin. "Not if we take them first, my love. This 'power void' means that all of Hos-Agrys will be ours for the picking."

"I sense your excitement, but we must think this action through. Your father already added one former Agrysi princedom to our Kingdom, and it's been difficult to win their allegiance. A whole kingdom would be a lot to digest. We could spend all our time putting down Agrysi rebellions, fighting revolts and dealing with recalcitrant princes and nobles. All the while we're still building the foundation of Our House here in Hos-Zygros; after all, you've only been Great King for less than a year. If we're not careful, we might find ourselves in the position of a rat snake swallowing a calf."

Phidestros tugged at his beard thoughtfully. "That's a very good point. This is why I wanted to run this by you, my love. Sometimes my ambitions are longer than my sword arm. You're right, I've already got more headaches here, than I have time to deal with them. It was never my goal to be Great King of Great Kings."

"I believe we have enough here in Hos-Zygros to keep us busy for the rest of our lives, lives that will be a lot longer if we can refrain from sticking our fingers into every honey-cake that beckons along the road of life."

EIGHTEEN

I

Great King Kalvan, with Rylla at his side, stood on the banks of the Lydistros River watching the flurry of activity in and around Kythar Town as its inhabitants returned and life began to return to normal. With the siege over, the streets were clogged with pedestrians, horses, buggies, hand-carts and wagons, while the river below was dotted with boats, including Hostigi warships and transports as well as the Order's galleys and Hostigi transports arriving to take the army downstream on the Great River to Xiphlon City. Now that he had changed sides, Soton was anxious to make up for past mistakes; he'd all but offered to join Kalvan in the attack on Balph.

Kalvan was glad to have wrapped up the Siege of Tarr-Ceros without having to destroy the old fortress and the Order of the Zarthani Knights. They served a valuable service and now that the Order had rededicated itself to Galzar, he felt good about leaving them in Soton's capable hands. Styphon's Own Voice would probably blow a gasket when he got the news. Not only was Styphon's House losing over half its military might, but also its greatest captain-general. Of course, if the Innermost Circle had really valued Soton they would have made some kind of attempt to break the siege. He suspected they were looking ahead and more worried about their own necks.

Meanwhile, he wanted to spend as much time with Rylla as possible since last night she had mentioned returning to Thagnor Town to be with the children. There was no need for her to winter in Hos-Bletha. There would be plenty of time for her to catch up with the army next spring.

Frankly, he wished she'd stay in Thagnor for all of next year's campaign season, but that was like wishing for wings on pigs.

Rylla rested her hand on his shoulder. "Kalvan, I know you want me to join you in Hos-Bletha next spring, but I've been thinking it over. I think I can do more good by taking a small force and traveling through Old Hos-Hostigos than I can by joining you."

He felt his heart catch in his throat. "But that could be extremely dangerous, my love. The only inhabitants are derelicts and bandits. Something might happen to you—"

She punched him in the shoulder. "Stop that! I wouldn't miss our triumphal return to Hostigos for all the gold in Balph. Besides, it will give me the opportunity to see the lay of the land as well as settle a few old scores."

It was the latter that worried Kalvan. He suspected that predominant among those "old scores" would be ending the reign of Sthentros the Traitor, who now wore the official chain of the Prince of Hostigos. "You do realize that most of our former homeland is in ruins and the rest has reverted to wilderness."

"Yes, I've read the dispatches and talked to the scouts. So far this fall has been mild and I should be able to set up some food depots inside Ulthor along the Akyros Road, which will make our job next spring much easier. I don't intend to bring a large army—just a few thousand men—and remember Hestophes will have returned from Zygros City; he'll be there to help."

Praise Dralm for small miracles, he thought. He wasn't sure how favorably Captain-General Hestophes would consider his new assignment, knowing he'd rather be with the Royal Army in Hos-Ktemnos settling old scores with Styphon's House, than babysitting a great queen. Still, Hestophes was the ultimate professional and would do his best no matter what the job. It was Rylla who worried him most; she had a tendency to shoot first and ask questions later, which could foul-up any possible settlement with Great King Geblon.

Certainly, Geblon wouldn't look favorably upon Kalvan and the Hostigi Army when he learned that a separate force commanded by Rylla was raising hell in his provinces. To say nothing about how Great Queen Lavena might take such an adventure—badly, he suspected. She was a loose cannon at best; this might well set her to blowing up all her fireseed at once. She was known to have Hadron's Own temper.

On top of that, Lavena was a Daddy's Girl with a few loose screws.

Finally, he realized there was nothing he could do to keep Rylla home, unless he wanted to ruin their leave-taking. At least there was an end in sight to the Fireseed Wars; afterwards they would resume a normal life—whatever that meant with Rylla as his life partner. One thing he did know, it wouldn't be dull.

"Fine," he said. "But I want you to be extra careful. No leading the troops from the front." That tactic had gotten better generals than Rylla killed back in otherwhen, like Epaminodas, the great Theban general who died at the Battle of Mantinea, or King Harold who died with an arrow in the eye at the Battle of Hastings or Richard III who died ignobly at Bosworth Field.

"I won't take any chances. I'm a mother now, and don't want to leave our children motherless; or worse yet, leave you with the first strumpet who bats her eyelashes at you!"

Kalvan guffawed, then Rylla quickly joined in.

"Seriously, my husband, I promise to lead the army from the rear."

Kalvan wasn't sure he believed her, but there wasn't much he could do to stop her short of staying home himself. Now that events had been set in motion that was all but impossible.

II

This was Archpriest Danthor's third visit to Anaxthenes' private audience chamber in less than a ten-day. He was going to have to be on the outlook for assassins as some of the old guard were beginning to resent his apparent closeness to the current Styphon's Voice. Of course, paranoia was de rigeur for a hotbed of intrigue like Balph where the slightest slip could cost one his life, or his place in the Temple hierarchy.

As the bodyguard opened the door, he caught the smell of incense burning on a brazier, probably to cover up the lingering stench of burning flesh which permeated the City's air. There had been a big public auto-da-fé in the Great Plazos, which faced Styphon's Great Temple, this morning and four former highpriests and nine underpriests had been burned alive. All had been convicted of trying to flee Balph with personal possessions and treasure, the definition of which—as in the case of one black-robed underpriest—included pocket change. It was the fifth public burning in the last three days.

One more sign of the growing fear that had hit the Holy City like a jolt of electricity when it was learned that Grand Master Soton of the Order of Zarthani Knights had not only surrendered to Great King Kalvan, but had recanted his belief in Styphon. Then he had publicly rededicated the Order to Galzar Wolfhead. Many of the City's inhabitants could already see the Hostigi wolves at the city gates in their imaginations. Not even Styphon's Golden Idol's pronouncements had been able to calm the City's fears.

Anaxthenes looked up from the table where he was pouring over a scroll. Probably the latest intelligence report from one of the Temple's spies in the Sastragath.

"Please come in, Danthor," he said, pointing to a stuffed armchair covered in gold brocade.

Danthor took the proffered seat and took out his pipe.

Anaxthenes dropped the scroll. "That's a good idea. I could use a good smoke about now. Would you like some of the Hostigi drink called Ermut's Best?"

"Yes, Your Divinity. That is, if drinking one of the Daemon Kalvan's creations is not a heretical act."

Anaxthenes chuckled. "I like you, Danthor. Most of these bed-sheeted fools around here are so afraid of me their voices tremble when they speak. Besides, when the time comes that good potables are considered heretical, no matter who makes them, it'll be time for me to step down as Styphon's Voice."

A servant suddenly appeared out of a curtained area carrying a tray with two gold goblets, a large glass flask filled with drink, an ornately carved clay pipe and a porcelain dish overflowing with tobacco. *There must be a hearing tube for the servants,* Danthor concluded.

When the servant had finished serving them, Styphon's Voice said, "Gasthos, you can return to your room, but shut off the listening tube. Is that understood?"

The servant nodded fearfully, then quickly exited the chamber.

Danthor suspected that, like most of Styphon's Voice's servants, his tongue had been cut out.

"Good," Anaxthenes said, then turned to face Danthor. "As I'm sure you've surmised, morale here in Balph is at an all-time low. We had prepared the populace for the fall of Tarr-Ceros, but no one in the Inner Circle, myself included, had expected this fireseed blast from Grand Master Soton. He has done the Temple a great disservice."

Danthor nodded. Actually, in his opinion, when faced with overwhelming odds, Soton had made a good choice. He had simply forsaken the Temple, which had already abandoned him to Kalvan's guns. Now, he was still Grand Master and servant of a new god, Galzar, whose hierarchy was much less demanding than Styphon's rapacious priesthood.

"If we opened the gates of Balph tomorrow and allowed everyone leaving to take a cartful of possessions, the Holy City would be deserted by the following day; that's how much faith in our future these hypocrites have."

"True, but it appears your punishments are not delivering good results."

"What do you mean?" Anaxthenes asked, with a scowl.

"The public burnings are not attracting the populace any more. Instead, all they are doing is polluting the city air."

"Hmm, I agree. I grow weary of the stench myself. Do you have a suggestion?"

"Yes, one that will provide both spectacle and entertainment to the populace. Instead of burning the thieves, I suggest we put them into the Balph Arena with hungry panthers."

"Oh, I like that!" Anaxthenes cried out. "And so will the people of Balph. I shall order it done."

Danthor preferred this solution. He could avoid the games, but not the smell of burning flesh. At the very least, the poor devils condemned to the area would have some slight chance of saving themselves. A friend might toss them a dagger or club to fend off the predators.

Anaxthenes continued, "We need to move up your trip to Harphax City. Our agents-inquisitory in Harphax City have informed us that Geblon has granted several audiences with his former comrade, Captain-General Kyblannos. Kyblannos, of course, comes as an emissary of Great King Phidestros, who is no friend of the Temple's."

"No he's not, but do you believe Phidestros poses a possible threat?" Danthor asked. He already knew the answer to that question, but one always deferred to superiors as egotistical as Styphon's Own Voice.

Anaxthenes shrugged. "We know Phidestros is ambitious. He's gone from a mercenary captain to great king in less than six winters. He has a large standing army with nothing to do at the moment, and he hates the Temple. The question is: is his fear of Archpriest Grythos' army enough to keep him out of the war?"

"That's a good question, Your Divinity. From our intelligence reports, Phidestros could leave a quarter of his army back in Hos-Zygros and still field twenty-five thousand veterans of the Fireseed Wars. Archpriest Grythos has fifteen thousand men in Agrys City; if he took more than half away from the city, it would break out in open rebellion. He has not been a popular ruler." An understatement if there ever was one. Grythos had terrorized the city folk of Agrys City and demonized himself in the name of security and his own enrichment.

Anaxthenes brought his fist down upon the table in a loud boom. "Unfortunately, you are right! No one else among my staff has dared to voice the truth as you have. Once again, Danthor, you have done me good service."

Danthor made what he thought might pass as a humble nod.

"As we discussed earlier, I want you to leave tomorrow for the Court of Hos-Harphax and guarantee our relationship with Great King Geblon."

Danthor was taken aback by how swiftly events were unfolding.

"One of my personal galleys is waiting for you at the docks. I am placing a great deal of trust in your hands. Is this understood?"

"Yes, Your Divinity. I will follow your orders to the last rune."

"Good reply. When you see Geblon, tell him that upon the defeat of Kalvan's army we will pay him one million ounces of gold."

"Yes, Your Divinity," Danthor replied. "I understand."

"Since the Temple's word is no longer trusted, as it once was, you will issue him one hundred banknotes, each worth ten thousand ounces of gold. They will only be redeemable upon the death of Kalvan."

"That much gold will purchase a lot of loyalty, Your Divinity."

"Exactly. Then, after you have shored up our accord with Great King Geblon, I want you to travel to Zygros City and make the same offer to Great King Phidestros."

"After what he's done," Danthor said, omitting that Anaxthenes had ordered the kidnapping of Phidestros' wife, "can we trust him?" He knew the answer to that question—"no." That was one order he was not about to obey. Arriving in Hos-Zygros in one of Styphon's Own Voice's personal galleys would likely be a death sentence. After he finished his business in Harphax City, it would be a good idea to disappear.

Anaxthenes smiled. "I suspect that much gold can buy an unlimited amount of forgiveness. And, if we can buy Phidestros that cheaply, we can destroy Kalvan and his army. Gold we can always get, our blood is much dearer."

III

Great King Phidestros greeted Kyblannos personally as he entered his private audience chamber. After Mynos, his manservant, had filled their goblets with ale and left, Phidestros asked, "Did you have any trouble crossing Hos-Agrys?"

Kyblannos said with a snort, "No, Cap'n. I had a Styphon's House high-priest as an escort. He wasn't happy about it, but did what he was told."

"How did you rate that?"

"It seems that our old friend is an important personage as far as Styphon's House is concerned. And, as we Zygrosi aren't too popular in Hos-Agrys, it probably saved my hide."

"Then a toast to absent friends."

"Aye, aye!"

"So how did your meeting with Geblon go?" Phidestros asked. He suspected not well; otherwise the usually garrulous Kyblannos would be talking it up.

"Not good, Cap'n. First of all, he kept me waitin' for almost a full moon before he *granted* me an audience. A slap in the face to both of us!"

"I suspected your long absence was not a good omen," Phidestros noted.

"No, it appears that Styphon's House has bought his loyalty. These days our old comrade lives in a palace that would put this one to shame."

"That doesn't sound right," Phidestros said. "The Geblon I knew was never much concerned with personal comfort or luxurious surroundings."

"You're right, Cap'n. It's that she-devil he married. She's bollixed up his mind, like some witch, and got him confused about his loyalties."

Phidestros sighed. "It's sad. Geblon was never one with the ladies, and now this shrew has him in tangles. Is there any hope he'll come out of her spell?"

Kyblannos shook his head. "When a man avoids his old comrades, you know all is not right. The Queen's got everyone in that entire palace walkin' on tippy toes. I swear to Galzar, I never saw anything like it."

"So I take it he's not interested in Great King Kalvan's offer."

"Oh, no! Geblon wouldn't touch it with a trooper's lance. My guess is he's already cut a deal with the Temple to fight Kalvan in Hos-Ktemnos."

"Well, that makes more sense than fighting him in Hos-Harphax," Phidestros allowed. "Still, I thought Kalvan's offer was a good one. And, unlike any deal with the liars at Balph, there are no strings attached."

"Talk about strings, our Geblon's become a regular puppet. And she who is pulling his strings isn't about to let them go. I believe, Cap'n, the best deal on the table is Kalvan's. You won't have to lift a hand against your old banner bearer. Plus, you can get a third of Balph's treasure without spending the life of a single soldier; deals like that only come once in a hundred winters."

IV

Prince Mnestros waited patiently inside the burnt-out tarr for the rest of the rebel commanders to gather. The stone walls of the Great Hall were laid bare, only a few tattered and smoke-blackened wall-hangings survived. The chairs and stools—those that hadn't burned in the fire—had been removed by the local peasants for firewood; only the great table remained. There were hack marks where someone had taken an ax blade to the table, but the scavenger had probably succumbed to the fire stench and left empty-handed.

The room was still rank with old smoke and burnt things that Mnestros would rather not think about. The baron, a noted follower of the Allfather, who had inhabited the tarr had been killed, along with his family. It had been abandoned for over a year now and the fields were all filled with weeds and nettles. A few of the peasant farms remained and were still being worked. Eventually, some minor nobleman's second son would claim the land and, if he had the Temple's blessing, would be proclaimed as the new baron.

His men, except for his aide Captain Phylos, were guarding the perimeter of the barony to ensure they were not caught in a trap by the local guardsmen. Mnestros believed the men he had contacted were reliable, but during war loyalties could not be guaranteed. As Kalvan always said, "better safe than sorry." It was sound advice.

Baron Othron had lost a lot of weight and had aged a decade since their parting. They clasped hands. "Prince, it is good to see you. We had wondered if you had survived."

"I have been building support in Nos-Hostigos. Great King Kalvan is now committed to overthrowing the Styphoni. But more on that, when the others have gathered."

It took a candle-half before nine of the ten men he had contacted secretly were gathered inside the drafty hall. Only two of the men retained their former holdings, the rest were living off the land and resembled vagabonds more than the former nobility of Eubros. One of the minor barons did not show up. They debated for a short time and decided to hold the meeting anyway. It would take too long as well as arouse suspicions if they attempted to gather again.

It was cold in the open hall and Mnestros passed around a flagon of Ermut's Best to the assembled rebels. One of the lords' men had lit a fire in the great hearth, using what was left of the chairs as kindling wood. Someone else dragged in a scorched tree limb and began hacking off branches.

"By Dralm, that's good drink!" espoused one of the lords.

"It's Ermut's Best, provided by our ally, Great King Kalvan."

"Aha," Duke Marthames said. "Now, at long last, we are worthy of his support? Where are his troops, then?"

The Prince shook his head. "King Kalvan is off besieging Tarr-Ceros with his entire army. Thus, he is unable to lend us any of his troops. However, the siege means that the Grand Master will be too preoccupied with his own troubles to aid Arch-Devil Grythos in our realm."

"That is good news," Baron Othron stated. "The first I've heard in a long time."

"Hear, hear," several others said.

"Bah!" replied the Duke. "How are we to throw off Styphon's yoke without outside support? Tell us, Prince?"

"By our own wits and strength," Mnestros replied. "And using the weapons that Kalvan has supplied us with."

"Weapons!" the Duke cried. "Where are they?"

"I have them hidden in a deserted tarr near the border. Plus, Kalvan has promised to resupply us with both arms and victuals."

"Excellent news," another baron said. "What kind and how many?"

"So far we have over a hundred hogsheads of Hostigi fireseed and five thousand arquebuses and two thousand muskets, with more on the way. Maybe four thousand pikes and twice that number of swords. And armor, tons of it. Enough to outfit an entire army!"

"Great King Kalvan has been most generous," Baron Othron said. "What's in it for him?"

"Our success in Eubros and elsewhere will tie up Styphon's Houses forces, leaving Kalvan free to besiege Balph."

"Balph!"

"Yes, Great King Kalvan plans to end Styphon's House for once and for all."

That was something they could all agree upon. The hall quickly rang with the cries of "Down Styphon!" echoing through the empty room.

NINETEEN

I

As the galley made its way downriver on the Mississippi, Kalvan studied the pure blue river and its untouched banks; it was like going back to the time of Huck Finn. Every once in a while, they encountered a small town or village, but for the most part the banks showed no evidence of human settlement. Birds and waterfowl proliferated and he found himself enjoying the trip. For once, everything was out of his hands. The army was being ferried downriver by Order of Zarthani Knights' galleys on barges and by their own transports. Their guns, weapons and supplies were on barges.

He saw a big semi-submerged log floating near the galley's hull, near enough that the overseer had to use a pole to push it away. He watched to see if it moved; they had run across dozens of large alligators, some as long as fifteen feet, which was unusual in the Mississippi on otherwhen. He wondered if they'd been introduced by trappers, but when he'd asked Grand Commander Aristocles, who was overseeing their journey, about the alligators; he'd told Kalvan that the river dragons, their name here-and-now, had been introduced by the Zarthani Knights several centuries earlier to help keep the Sea of Grass nomads on the other side of the banks.

The beating drum of the overseer was almost hypnotic in its repetition. Unlike the Styphoni ocean galleys, the Orders' boats were rowed by free men and their own soldiers. He had outlawed slavery in both Hos-Hostigos and Nos-Hostigos. Now, Great King Phidestros had done likewise in Hos-Zygros at the urging of his wife, it was said. Regardless, it was a big step and would have repercussions throughout the Great Kingdoms.

Baron Halmoth, one of his generals, broke him out of his reverie. "Your Majesty, how long will we be staying in Xiphlon?"

"It's hard to say. I want to leave as soon as possible. But we'll have to stay long enough for me to meet with High King Roldolf and hire enough sea transport to get to Pytha where we'll join up with Democriphon and Duke Skranga."

II

Having finished the salutation, Danthor Dras began the meat of his letter to Styphon's Voice, dipping quill pen into ink, he marked:

I arrived a moon-half ago in Harphax City. My first action was to arrange an inspection of the Harphaxi Royal Army. The state of their equipment was appalling, musket firelocks and armor rusted (some beyond repair), pikes and halberds seated on rotting staves, horses with the mange and underfed, and a host of other problems. Among the lower ranks, morale is almost non-existent and some hadn't received their pay in several moons.

My next action was to investigate the office of the Royal Pay Master, which is in charge of military pay and finances. The office was riddled with corruption: the Pay Marshal in charge had siphoned off substantial funds for himself, enough to build a palatial townhouse and support a small company of trollops and their offspring. My response was to have the Marshal beheaded, along with the other dozen or so underlings who were involved in theft of military monies and the selling of ordnance and supplies. After much digging, I found the most honest officer in the Royal Army and appointed him to the thankless job of his predecessor.

I also instituted accelerated training and re-training exercises for the Harphaxi Royal Army. I have used some of the funds you supplied to reward those who have shown initiative and improvement. By next spring, the Royal Army of Hos-Harphax will be able to take the field without embarrassing itself. As to how they will hold up against the regulars of the Usurper Kalvan's army, that is an answer only Styphon can supply.

I have met several times with Great King Geblon who has shown very little interest in the state or maintenance of his army, which is typical of his misrule of Hos-Harphax. It appears that most of his attention is directed to Queen Lavena, who keeps making demands for more gold from the Temple. The King is browbeaten to the point that he lives in a constant state of anxiety. He even went so far as to make Great King Phidestros' envoy wait over two moons for a short audience, after his wife ordered Geblon not to meet with him until Duke Kyblannos had been "shown his place." It is clear, due to his financial woes and fiscal irresponsibility, that the Harphaxi Great King is totally dependent upon the Temple for the Iron Throne's financial support.

Unfortunately, it will be impossible for me to travel to Hos-Zygros and meet with Great King Phidestros. I fear I will have to remain in Harphax City, or nearby, until the army leaves for Balph next spring; otherwise, my reforms will be abandoned upon my leave-taking. I should have sufficient gold to maintain the army and purchase the services of those free companies from Hos-Agrys I mentioned in my previous dispatch.

Instead, I have made plans to travel to Agrys City, which is close enough to Harphax City that I will be in close contact with our agents-inquisitory, so that I will be able to keep tabs on the progress of the reforms of the Harphaxi Army I have initiated. There I will meet with Prince Regent Grythos about his providing us with reinforcements. It would be best if Grythos sent half of his army garrisoned in Agrys City to aid in the defense of Balph and our other—

"Who is it?" Danthor asked, in response to a light tapping upon his door.

"May I come in?" asked a whispered voice of the female persuasion. He wondered if the King had sent him a bedwarmer to share his bed. Another attempt to refocus his attentions, he suspected.

He cracked open the door to see a face he recognized. It took only a moment for his total recall to place the female who was now dressed in Zarthani garb. It was a Dhergabar student he had seen at his introductory lecture to the Kalvan Time-Line study teams a number of years ago; his total recall brought forth her name: "Danar Sirna, what are you doing here? Why aren't you with the Harphaxi Study Team?"

"Can I please come in?" she whispered.

He nodded, opening the door. "Now, tell me what is this all about?"

"That's what I want to ask you, Scholar Danthor. I haven't been able to reach anyone at the Harphaxi Study Team HQ. The place is abandoned and you're the first Home Timeliner I've seen."

"I ran into the same problem in Balph," he replied, his forehead furrowed. "It appears everyone has bugged out except for the two of us." It was hard for him to admit that he had been abandoned; he could understand that happening in the case of a young student—but *me!*

"I haven't been able to reach anyone from the Harphaxi Study Team on my communicator, either," she said. "Do you have any idea of why we were left behind?"

"No, I do not, young lady. I suspect some kind of emergency on First Level, but of what nature I do not know. Nor do I care to guess."

"Are we stranded here for good, then?" she asked.

That was a question he hadn't dared ask himself. "I don't know. I certainly hope not. We can form some kind of liaison so that we support each other."

She pointed to his yellow-robes with the red borders. "That doesn't make you too popular here or anywhere else outside of Balph, sir. My existence is fragile enough as it is, depending upon Great Queen Lavena's whims." She started to tear up.

Danthor had spent enough time in the Queen's presence that he could well understand her trepidation; Great Queen Lavena was mercurial to say the least. He put his arm awkwardly around Sirna and let her weep onto his chest. "We will find some way to get through this. I promise," knowing full well that was a promise that might be difficult for him to keep. If Kalvan managed to sack Balph, it might be impossible. Maybe staying in Harphax City was not only the necessary thing to do, but the smart thing as well.

I need to start looking for a bolthole and another identity. Fortunately, Anaxthenes provided me with enough gold to do both. I'll have to include Sirna in that equation before the poor girl is executed for slighting the Queen. Who knows what will happen in Harphax City if Kalvan is successful and defeats the Harphaxi and Ktemnoi armies. Certainly, total chaos here in Harphax City. The Queen is quite unpopular—if not outright hated—so she and her attendants will be the first to die in any citywide insurrection. I will need a safe place for both of us to live until contact is reestablished with the Paratime Police or the University.

III

From about half a mile away, Kalvan could make out the towering walls of Xiphlon, which reared up out of the swamps and bayous surrounding the city. They must have had the stone blocks that made up the walls brought in barges downstream from hundreds of miles away. He turned to the local pilot, "Hroyld, where does the City get their blocks?"

"From the Zarthani Knights, Your Majesty. The Order has ownership of several large quarries and they provide the stones in return for gold and silver."

Another good reason for not toppling the Order, he decided. They were an integral part of the Middle Kingdoms' economic and defensive structure.

When they reached the harbor entrance, Kalvan noted that it was protected by sunken logs, some of them whole trunks. They were linked together by heavy chains and protected the entrance to Xiphlon's man-made harbor. At either side of the entrance were huge gates, easily ten stories high with bombards covering the small harbor entryway.

By the King's orders, Kalvan's galley was the only ship being allowed past the log barrier. He could understand why High King Roldolf wasn't eager to allow Kalvan's thirty thousand soldiers the run of Xiphlon City. However, Roldolf had better provide the ships he promised, and quickly, because Kalvan was running low on patience. He did not have enough transports to ship more than half his army, so it was necessary to hire more and soon. It was hurricane season and the last thing he needed was to have his army out to sea off the coast of Florida when a hurricane blew in.

Fortunately, it was cool enough in autumn that there wasn't much of a mosquito problem, but, regardless, he wouldn't be satisfied until his entire army was safely encamped in Hos-Bletha.

Kalvan's party was met at the docks by a large group of dignitaries distinguished by their rich fur cloaks. Those cloaks may have made sense to their Urgothi ancestors, when they were living in the upper Great Lakes area, but they were an anachronism here at the sweltering mouth of the Great River. As they passed through busy city thoroughfares on the way to the palace, Kalvan noted that his bodyguard, led by Vanar Halgoth, was getting more stares than even himself and his retinue. He was surprised to see what appeared to be Mexicotal—by their feathery costumes—walking unattended down the crowded streets.

He turned to the plenipotentiary who had met them as they disembarked from the galley. "When will we be meeting with His Majesty, High King Roldolf?"

The dignitary seemed shocked that Kalvan would ask such a question without the usual verbal puffery.

"His Majesty, Sire, is not in the habit of confiding in me," he replied in an oily tone of voice. "You will have to address your questions to the palace seneschal,"

From that point on, Kalvan saw no reason to discuss matters with Roldolf's underlings. For a king seated upon a kingdom set at the edge of nowhere, Roldolf appeared to have an inflated sense of his own importance in the larger scheme of things. Since Kalvan was in a hurry to get his men to safety, he saw no reason to pussyfoot around with the king or his minions. *If Roldolf wants my help in establishing fireseed mills, by Galzar, he'd damn well better be cooperative!*

They were met at the foot of the palace stairs by a tall man with a shaved face and head. For a moment, Kalvan thought he might be a Styphon's House highpriest until he welcomed them, introducing himself as the palace seneschal. His strong Urgothi accent proved his local antecedents. Besides, if the Styphoni had made inroads here, the King wouldn't be so interested in obtaining his own fireseed mills and gun foundry.

"Your Majesty, I have a room for you to refresh yourself after your long journey."

"Thank you. My bodyguard will accompany me, but the rest of my party will need accommodations."

"They will be well taken care of, Your Majesty," the Seneschal said.

"Good," he replied. "I would like to have an audience with High King Roldolf as soon as possible."

The Seneschal looked shocked, as if he wasn't used to visitors making demands upon his king.

Kalvan hardened his face. "Right now, sitting in boats, I have thirty-thousand soldiers to feed and find accommodations for. Unless your King would like me to have them enter the City and have them billeted here, I suggest you tell him we need to meet shortly."

Now, pale as a sheet, the Seneschal said, "I will inform His Majesty of your requests at once." He left Kalvan in the central entryway as he darted up the marble stairs toward what Kalvan assumed were Roldolf's quarters.

Another servant led him to his downstairs rooms which were large and palatial—no attempt at a snub here, he concluded. Kalvan changed out of his britches, doublet and underthings, slipping into a large warm pool of water, reminiscent of a Roman bath. He wasn't surprised when two young and very comely women appeared out of nowhere, removed everything but their undergarments and eased into the pool with him. The girls used scrapers and washcloths to clean his body. He did his best to ignore their obvious physical assets which could lead to waters far more dangerous than those of this tepid bathwater, regardless of local customs. Rylla was not understanding at all when it came to such matters—to say the least.

When he was finished with his bath, the girls dried him off with large fluffy cotton towels. Then they helped dress him in a white linen toga with golden trim.

When he asked them, in passable Urgothi, whether or not to wear his crown, they appeared shocked that he could speak their language. From the expressions on their faces, despite his stature as Great King, he was considered a mere barbarian by the more cosmopolitan Xyphloni. If the High King felt the same way, he feared that might not bode well for the upcoming audience with Roldolf.

TWENTY

I

High King Roldolf sat behind a large table piled with manuscripts and scrolls in his private audience chamber. The shelves behind him were filled with scrolls and leather-bound volumes. It was not the sort of place Kalvan had expected. There were a couple of wall hangings of historical events, mostly sieges against the city walls, but they appeared faded by age and the ravages of time. Roldolf himself appeared to be in his late seventies, although Kalvan found it difficult to determine ages here-and-now. The King's head was mostly bald, with a few wisps of white hair around his ears and at the back of his skull. He used a large square of glass as a magnifying piece; there were no glasses here. His nose was beaked and his ears overly large, probably from age.

"Please have a seat, Your Majesty," Roldolf intoned.

Kalvan bowed and then sat down. "Your Majesty, it's a pleasure to finally meet with you."

Roldolf, looked chagrined, then nodded his head as though just reminded that he was a king not a Great King. "Likewise, Your Majesty."

Smiling, Kalvan said, "Enough with the formality, we're not at court."

Roldolf visibly relaxed, doing everything but emitting a sigh of relief.

Kalvan brushed the sides of his crown with both hands. "No, I don't have horns."

The King reddened, then smiled wryly. "By the gods, we've heard so many stories about you, Your Majesty, we weren't sure if you were even mortal."

Kalvan shook his head. "Yes, and I trim my nails, and even bleed when cut."

"Fine, I deserved that, but you must know your reputation precedes you. Everyone has been talking about you ever since you arrived, turning the tiny backward Princedom of Hostigos into a Great Kingdom. You have singlehandedly given Styphon's House its worst defeats in centuries. You have introduced a dozen innovations, including fast-moving gun carriages and those far-shooting muskets you call *rifles*. On top of all that, somehow, you have convinced Grand Master Soton to renounce his lifelong faith in Styphon and rededicate the Order of Zarthani Knights to your Wargod. This is unprecedented!"

After all that buildup, Kalvan felt as if he should take a bow. Instead he said, "Yes, I've managed to introduce some improvements that have made warfare more deadly and destructive. I'm not proud of some of them, but they were necessary at the time. If Styphon's House had not been so determined to destroy Hostigos and its rulers, I would not have acted as I have."

Roldolf nodded. "That may be true, but the fact is they were made and introduced. And they have had repercussions far beyond the borders of your kingdoms. Our problems with the Sea of Grass and Sastragathi nomads have increased tenfold since you've provided them with fireseed and arquebuses. Now, it will be only a matter of a few years before they show up with big guns, maybe big enough to bring down our walls as your guns threatened to do at Tarr-Ceros. You can see how your deeds have upset a balance that has been in place for hundreds of years."

Kalvan shrugged. "It wasn't my intention to undermine your defenses; however, it was inevitable that at some point in time the tribesmen would get their hands on fireseed weapons; whether directly from Styphon's House, or through third-parties. My appearance has only accelerated the process."

The King frowned. "Yes, and brought the problems to my reign instead of to my grandchildren's."

"Maybe it is better this way," he said. "You strike me as a learned and sagacious leader, one who is willing to make the changes necessary to keep his kingdom safe. Those who follow in your footsteps may not be as perceptive or adaptable. I can loan you one of my engineering staff officers, who can provide you with a more modern design for your walls and bastions, one that will make it very difficult for the barbarians to breach—even with big guns."

"You would do this?" Roldolf asked.

"Yes, I have no enmity against Xiphlon or its rulers. One of my best friends, King Verkan of Greffa, has relatives within these very walls."

"Yes, we have heard of the House of Verkan. It was a minor trading house until your friend gave it new leadership and energy. They have even imported some of your Hostigi products."

"Good. Then it will be done. Now, can we discuss the terms and conditions of shipping my army up the coast of Hos-Bletha to Pytha."

"There is a problem there," Roldolf said, smiling through clenched teeth. "The Styphoni might send a fleet to intercept my vessels and we could lose many boats and their crews."

Kalvan sighed. "Yes, their fleet does pose a problem. However, I have brought a small fleet of my own warships and transports; they should be sufficient to spare your ships from any difficulties with the Temple's boats."

"The Styphoni have a large coastal fleet that patrols the Great Eastern Ocean, maybe two hundred galleys or more. My advisors tell me you brought only thirty or so warships when you arrived at our harbor. Are more on the way?"

"No, that is my entire squadron," Kalvan said. These were his best three-masted schooners, half of them armed with Greek fire and cannon; the others bearing only guns. He would have liked more, but these were all that he could assemble without leaving Thagnor unprotected. "I believe they will be sufficient for the battle ahead."

"How could that be?" Roldolf asked, drawing back.

"As I understand it, the galleys do not carry a full complement of guns—only small bow and stern chasers capable of shooting five or six pound cannonballs."

Roldolf nodded. "Yes, that is their standard armament. They do have boarding boards and rams, as well as catapults."

"I don't believe any of them will get close enough to our boats to use either their rams or boarding boards."

"How can you stop them?"

"First, our ships are equipped with twenty-four guns, twelve sixteen-pounders on both the port and starboard sides. Plus, we have machines that shoot out fire."

The King drew back. "I've heard rumors...."

"They are true. These devices, which we call Greek fire, shoot out plumes of fire up to a hundred paces."

"Fire shooters—what a terrible weapon. They must wreak terrible damage on wooden ships."

"Yes, especially wooden galleys where there are so many open spaces for the slaves and their oars. They light up like kindling wood."

"I should like to see these in operation before I grant permission for you to rent our vessels."

"Of course. Where would you like to see one in operation?"

"Away from the city. It would not be good for our enemies to learn that we harbor such vessels, or that our allies do."

II

Aspasthar was in the small chamber designated as his study room for his daily lessons from his tutor, a dusty old man of some seventy winters. Today they were studying the reign of Erasthames the Great, the ruler who had broken the reign of the Ruthani tribes in Hos-Harphax and Hos-Ktemnos some four centuries ago. It was dusty old history, and his tutor made it sound as dry as the crinkly parchment he was copying from. Erasthames had avoided big battles and had instead slowly overrun or isolated the Ruthani settlements until they were bleeding from a thousand wounds. There was little valor in killing broken men, women and children or starving them out of their holdings, but it had proved an effective way to destroy and eliminate the Ruthani inhabitants who had ruled the land long before the Zarthani tribes had arrived.

It wouldn't work today, Aspasthar concluded. The Ruthani had been poorly organized and led; the different clans and tribes did not trust each other or work together. The great kings of the Five Kingdoms were well organized, although poorly led in the case of Hos-Harphax. He doubted that Great King Geblon's forces could resist Kalvan's army for long. The latest word was that Kalvan had defeated Grand Master Soton, although that was hard to believe. It was also rumored that Soton had renounced Styphon and put the Order of Zarthani Knights under the aegis of Galzar the Wargod. That was news that he filed under the heading, "too good to believe." However, credence was added when the Prince-Regent put out word that anyone repeating that rumor would be labeled a traitor and put to death.

He was starting to daydream about leading a charge against a Temple Band of Styphon's Own Guard, when his tutor broke in—

"Prince Dementros, it appears your mind is straying from the text. It is important to learn from the past. Someday—may the gods help us—you will become great king and have to fight wars."

The old man held up the long stick that he often used to rap Aspasthar's knuckles when he wasn't paying attention. That was happening a lot recently. Sometimes he daydreamed of the day he became great king and ordered that his tutor's fingers be removed a joint at a time.

"Yes, Master Tysog." He bent over to show the proper concentration to the old text, when there was a banging at the door.

"Who dares intrude upon the young Prince's studies?" barked Master Tysog.

"It is I, Governess Tymolara, you old toad. The young master is wanted in the Prince-Regent's private chamber. If you delay, he will have your head mounted on a pole outside the city gates!"

Master Tysog shook his head. "No respect for the learned anymore," he mumbled into his long white beard.

Tysog opened the door and Lady Tymolara bounded in. "Off you go, boy. The Prince-Regent is in a sour mood today. Be sure and answer his guest's questions with all due respect."

As they walked down the long passageway to the private audience chamber, she whispered, "Be careful. His guest is an archpriest of the

Inner Circle. I don't know what he wants or what news he's delivering, since Rythor hasn't reported in today, but I expect bad news. That means arch-devil Grythos will be in a foul mood, so don't do anything to upset him," she finished.

He nodded, wondering why the Prince-Regent wanted to see him.

The door to the Prince-Regent's private audience chamber was flanked by two of Styphon's Own Guard, wearing polished silver-plated burgonets and full-armor. Both were wearing red cloaks. One of them grabbed his upper arm and knocked on the door with the other hand.

The door opened to the scowling face of Prince-Regent Grythos, now wearing his Styphoni yellow robe with the red trim which denoted him as an archpriest. "Come in, boy. And quickly."

"Yes, Your Sanctity."

There was another archpriest, a strange older one with silver hair. Aspasthar couldn't ever remember meeting a Styphon's House upperpriest with hair before. *He must be important*, he thought.

Grythos took his seat behind a long trestle table, made of highly polished hardwood. The other archpriest was sitting on the only other chair in the chamber, facing the Prince-Regent. Aspasthar stood quietly at attention.

"You're right, Grythos," the silver-haired Archpriest said, after he turned and studied Aspasthar closely. "The lad is close to his majority."

He felt like a slave on an auction stage and began to understand Kalvan's animosity toward slavery on a personal level.

The Prince-Regent made a shark-like grin. "Prince, how would you like to lead men in battle?"

Aspasthar perked up. "Very much, Your Sanctity."

"Are you certain he's ready?" the silver-haired Archpriest asked.

Grythos looked directly into Aspasthar's eyes. "This is Archpriest Danthor straight from Balph. He has come to ask for our aid in defending the Holy City against an invasion force to be led by the Usurper Kalvan."

It took all of Aspasthar's self-control not to give out a cry of triumph. Instead, he remained steely-eyed and said, "I am ready, Your Sanctity."

"Has the boy been tested in battle?" Archpriest Danthor asked. "He may yet be useful in other ways."

"No," Grythos replied. "The Prince has spent more time at the tiltyard than with his tutor. My blade master gives him accolades. He is ready."

"Good, then he can help lead the Agrysi contingent."

"Yes, the King's Guard. Do you know what that means, Prince?"

"Yes, Your Sanctity. More time at the tiltyard, less time with my studies."

Grythos made a thin-lipped smile. "Yes, you will do well, boy. If you practice hard enough, I will let you lead the King's Guard."

Aspasthar's chest swelled with pride. *Finally, my patience has been rewarded. Somehow some way, I will find a way to help our Great King in his battle against the manure-eating Styphoni!*

III

"Truly, husband, it is long past time that you gave that poor man from Hostigos an answer," Great Queen Arminta said. "He's anxious to return to Nos-Hostigos and link up with his Great King."

"Hmm. You're right, as usual," Phidestros said with a yawn. "I keep hoping that another day will bring a courier from Hos-Harphax and all will be right with the world."

"Well, it hasn't come, and it probably won't. Geblon is firmly in the grasp of that shew he's married to. The way he treated your friend and our emissary was a direct insult to us and the Ivory Throne."

"I know. I just find the whole thing sad and upsetting. Geblon is one of the bravest men I know; after all, he was the Iron Company's banner-captain for five winters. He was always in the thick of any fight, and watched my back numerous times. It's hard to imagine that same man now cowering behind a woman's petticoats." He made a face. "It sickens me to think of it."

"People change, my love, oftentimes not for the better. You raised Geblon far above his station and now you're going to have to allow him to rise or fall accordingly. It was his decision to back Styphon's House, knowing full well how they insulted and defamed us."

"I know, I know. I feel like it's my fault because I used him to fill a role I didn't want for us. And, now, he's caught tight in a vise: in one jaw, his wife; in the other, Styphon's House."

"What you did was not all your fault," Arminta said. "He could have refused the Iron Throne. Once Geblon laid his eyes on Lavena, his brains leaked out his ears. Even I underestimated the Queen's cupidity and cruelty. The time has come to roll the bones—be it for Geblon, which is indirectly for Styphon's House, your great enemy; or for Kalvan, who offers you a great reward for little or no effort. What's your call, my love?"

"Mynos, bring my pen and ink. I have a dispatch to Great Kalvan to write."

"Good. You're doing the right thing."

"By Galzar, I hope so. Unfortunately, I don't believe Great King Geblon will agree."

TWENTY-ONE

I

As soon as the lad left, the Prince-Regent looked deeply into Danthor's eyes. "What do you think?"

"I saw the lad's eyes light up at the prospect of leading his troops," Danthor said. He had a pretty good idea of what Grythos was getting at. He wanted his tacit permission to have the boy put in a place where he might get killed. Thanks to inside information from Chief Verkan he was aware that Aspasthar was former Captain-General Harmakros' only son and the ward of Great King Kalvan. Kalvan was using him as a mole in an attempt to wrest control over Hos-Agrys; not for imperial reasons, but to eliminate it as a threat. Not that anyone in Styphon's House or Hos-Agrys would see it that way.

The truth was Kalvan had put the young man in a very tenuous position. The slightest error or wrong move on Aspasthar's part would result in his death. So far the boy had been doing an excellent job of walking that tightrope, not giving the Prince-Regent an excuse to have him deposed or executed. Grythos, besides being a sadist and an out-and-out flint-hearted bastard, was a power monger. As Prince-Regent he had tasted absolute power, now he did not want to relinquish it. Only this lad stood in his way of gaining the Throne of Light for himself.

"Yes, the lad is quite willing to play the dupe," he said.

"Like most young men, he sees the honor and valor of warfare, not the darker side," Grythos observed.

"Prince Dementros appears to be entering manhood," Danthor observed. "He is near man-height and his limbs are strong. I even saw a slight outline of facial hair."

Grythos nodded. "He's even sired a couple of bastards with two of the more comely kitchen wenches."

"Hmm. Does he know of this?"

Grythos shook his head. "As soon as the Kitchen Mistress discovered their condition, it was reported to me. The girls were immediately sent away."

"Do they know they're carrying the Prince's offspring?"

"They're both buried in unmarked graves; there's nothing to know. They were cute little wisps, but not to my taste. I like my women full-bodied, if you know what I mean?"

Danthor had to assert First Level mental disciplines to keep the distaste he felt from showing on his face. He nodded and changed the subject: "How long before the Prince's sixteenth name day and ascension to the Throne of Light?"

Grythos' face darkened and his eyebrows furrowed. "Soon, too soon. Less than a year."

"What happens if he survives the attack against the Hostigi?" he asked.

Grythos made a slicing motion across his throat. "I will have one of my best men in the rear ranks. If the boy survives the battle, he will ensure his death in the confusion that follows. It will appear to be an honorable death so that all of Hos-Agrys can mourn his demise. A great tragedy. I will declare a plague upon the Usurper Kalvan and Hostigos in the boy's name."

Danthor nodded. "Very good, it will make you appear to be his advocate—even in death."

"Yes, shortly thereafter I will declare myself as Lord Protector of the Realm. Later, when my rule is firmly established, I will orchestrate the Electors so that I am elected Great King of Hos-Agrys."

"Of course, that is based on the assumption that Kalvan's army is defeated," Danthor said, laying the untenable out on the table. He wanted to gauge Grythos' grasp of the big picture.

"Hmm," Grythos paused. He picked up his long clay pipe and began to fill the bowl with tobacco. "Such traitorous thoughts might cost you your head in Balph," he poised, as he lit his pipe. "However, like yourself, I try to examine all possible outcomes of any critical action, before committing myself to action. The Usurper has some thirty thousand men under his command, according to our intelligencers. He will probably add another ten thousand after the conquest of Hos-Bletha. Balph will be protected by ten thousand of Styphon's Own Guard and another fifteen thousand of the Hos-Ktemnoi royal troops. Plus, another ten thousand Harphaxi that Great King Geblon has promised Styphon's Own Voice. I plan to bring ten thousand soldiers with me, although it will leave the kingdom vulnerable to malcontents, Dralmists and rebels. However, if Kalvan succeeds in destroying Balph, my reign here will be a short one."

Danthor was surprised at Grythos' grasp of the real military situation.

"What about Great King Phidestros?" Danthor asked. "I have heard rumors that Kalvan has offered him a rich reward if he helps him attack Balph."

"A very good question and one that has kept me awake for more than a few nights. Great King Geblon is Phidestros' vassal—in all but name—and, for all his faults and grasping ways, Phidestros is an honorable man." Grythos paused to shake his head in wonderment at such folly. "I cannot foresee him forsaking Geblon who has already cast his bones with Styphon's House in this game of chance. He will most likely sit out the war."

That of course begs the real question, Danthor thought. What if Phidestros had eyes for Hos-Agrys? With Grythos and most of Styphon's loyal troops off in Balph, what was to stop Phidestros from conquering all of Hos-Agrys, or even just sacking Agrys City?

"So you will reinforce Balph in the spring?"

"Yes, I've already rotated some troops from the outer princedoms, those with princes in the Temples' debt. I will leave some five thousand men, many of them militia, behind to garrison Agrys City. There has been increased rebellion in some of the former League of Dralm princedoms, but I will deal with them harshly once Kalvan has been defeated."

"Styphon's Voice Anaxthenes will be pleased to learn of your faithfulness and loyalty. He has told me you will be well rewarded for aiding Balph in its hour of need."

II

Aspasthar and Lady Tymolara waited impatiently for almost a candle before Rythor joined them in their secret meeting chamber. He had Athos with him. Both boys looked worried and lacked their usual care-free expressions.

"Your Highness!" Rythor blurted out.

Aspasthar knew it was serious since Rythor only used his honorific titles when they were in public.

"What is it?" he demanded.

Lady Tymolara rested her hand upon his shoulder. "Calm down, let the boy speak."

"The Devil, who goes by the name Grythos, wants you dead. He and that silver-haired Archpriest were plotting your demise."

He was taken aback by the seriousness of Rythor's voice, as well as the charges. "But why? He rules in my name without my say-so, regardless."

"You are almost of age, now, Sire. On your sixteenth name day, you will be enthroned upon the Throne of Light and become Great King of Hos-Agrys. The Arch-Devil means to ensure that outcome never happens."

"But how?" Aspasthar asked, his heart jumping in his chest like a drumhead.

Rythor barked out an evil-sounding laugh. "He's offered you the chance to lead the King's Guard into battle, am I right?"

"Yes," Aspasthar said proudly. "I will be at their head."

"Yes, and you will die there," Rythor added.

"War is a dangerous business, but can Grythos predict the future, too?"

"He doesn't mean to predict it, sire. Just ensure it. One of his men will be in the ranks to murder you, if you survive the battle."

Aspasthar, who was rarely afraid, felt the blood in his veins chill. "Then you and Athos will have to be there to protect me."

Rythor drew back. "But they're bigger, stronger and better at arms than we are. What can we do?"

"The two of you can watch my back for treachery and find others you feel you can trust in the King's Guard, then let them know the game is afoot. We can do it. I will entrust you with my life."

The three boys hugged.

Then Rythor looked down at the ground, refusing to meet Aspasthar's eyes. "What else did the Styphoni say?"

"You know those scullery maids you were seeing?"

"Sure, Amna and Stylla. Did you find out where they disappeared to?"

The boy nodded, his eyes moist. "They were carrying *your* children. The Arch-Devil had them murdered!"

Aspasthar felt his heart freeze. He couldn't believe Rythor's words. Yes, they had bundled many times, but neither girl had told him they were with child. *And, if they had: what would I have done about it?*

If he knew anything, he could not allow this to happen again. Even if it meant an end to his bundling. *I will avenge their deaths,* he decided. *One day the Arch-fiend will have to answer to me for my dead babies....*

III

After knocking and receiving permission to enter, Chancellor Archimanes stepped cautiously into Great King Niclophon's private audience room. The Great King had been in a foul mood ever since his realm had been split in twain by the so-called Orphan Prince and his supporters. It had made his own life difficult, especially now, since recent developments were adding up in a very frightening manner. Unfortunately, the Great King was inclined to blame bad news on the bearer, not the cause. For around the thousandth time, he wondered why he had not joined up with Styphon's House and become an upperpriest. The highpriests made far more money than he did; they certainly got more respect.

He had Niclophon's body-servant announce his arrival. "How's his mood," he asked sotto voce as he passed by him, and warily entered the chamber.

"Not good, Your Excellence." The man had the expression of a cur, one which had taken one too many lashes.

Chancellor Archimanes bowed as low as his stiff back would allow, then tip-toed into the room.

"What do you want this time?" Niclophon bellowed.

"A courier from Xiphlon just arrived with the morning tide, Your Majesty."

"Yes?"

"He has word that Great King Kalvan arrived in Xiphlon at the head of a great army—"

"What!?" exploded Niclophon. "Last I heard he was busy besieging Tarr-Ceros."

Archimanes drew back in fear. "Sire, the courier says that Tarr-Ceros surrendered to the Hostigi. Grand Master Soton has now sworn the Order to Galzar Wolfhead."

"What madness is this?"

Archimanes shrugged. "He had no details, only news that Soton surrendered the great fort to the Usurper Kalvan and renounced Styphon's House and Styphon as his god."

Niclophon turned as white as an alabaster sarcophagus. "Grand Master Soton renouncing Styphon; it must be the end of days."

He may be more right than he suspects, thought Archimanes.

"There's more news, Your Majesty."

"What, more? What else, damn your tongue! I'll order it yanked out with hot pliers if you don't answer swiftly."

Archimanes expelled the rest of the news like an explosion from the bottom of his gut. "Kalvan only stopped in Xiphlon to obtain a fleet of boats. He is on his way to Hos-Bletha, if the courier is to be believed."

"Here?!" Niclophon exclaimed, leaning forward. "How old is this news?"

"Over a moon-half, Sire."

"Then Kalvan could already be on his way?"

He shrunk down. "Yes, Sire. It is possible."

The Great King fell back upon his seat as though he had been struck. "Why is Kalvan coming here?"

"I do not know. The courier claimed that Kalvan was coming here to attack Styphon's House."

"Then why is he stopping here and not in Hos-Ktemnos? If it's Balph he wants, he should be going there."

"There is another possibility, Sire."

"Yes, out with it!"

"He may be joining forces with the Usurper Valthros."

Niclophon fell back upon his chair. He began to tremble as though he were suffering from the ague or a great chill. Then he began to hyperventilate. Between breathes, he ordered, "Bring me Archpriest Lesthros. We will need Styphon's Voice to order another crusade against the Usurper Kalvan."

"Yes, Your Majesty," Archimanes said, as he walked backwards out of the audience chamber, bowing and scraping all the way. He doubted there would be any succor from Styphon's House, not with the Usurper this close to the Holy City. However, he would let Archpriest Lesthros be the bearer of that bad news. He had more than given his share. *Let someone else have their tongue ripped out!*

IV

Governess Tymolara walked as casually as she could manage through the crowded byways of Agrys City to the bakery which she frequented every few days. At first, she had been followed by the arch-tyrant's spies, but those tails had become less and less frequent over the years. Now, it was rare when she noted an observer. Arlos' bakery was a good place to meet; it was a popular shop and frequented by city dwellers of all stripes, from wealthy nobles to beggars. Arlos often gave away older baked goods to those who could not afford to buy their own bread.

As she entered the shop, she saw her contact sitting at a small table. She knew very little about her spymaster other than that she was from Eubros and a secret worshipper of Allfather Dralm. At the counter she ordered her usual honey-cake, with raisins and walnuts, and a mug of hot sassafras tea.

"Good morn," her contact said, as she took her usual seat.

"Good day to you, sister Verla," she replied. Verla was a woman of middle age, but the permanent scowl she wore on her face made her look much older. It also directed attention away from her, since few wanted to deal with such a scold. She often wondered how much was camouflage and how much was her true nature, since Verla was the only Hostigi contact she had in the city.

"I see you have no followers, again," Verla noted.

"Great things are afoot in the palace and as a result smaller things are being overlooked," she answered. "It is certain now, Archpriest Grythos plans to bring most of his army to Balph. Plus, who would notice a field mouse such as myself?"

Verla nodded, then said with a smile. "Only a fool, that is who. But you bring good news, and there is also news from the provinces."

A smile on that sour face was so unusual that it took Tymolara aback for a few moments. "I take it you have good news, as well?"

Verla looked around carefully to see if they were being noticed, then said under her breath, "Yes, Prince Mnestros is back on his seat and the Styphoni have been vanquished from Eubros. Two other princedoms are also in rebellion!"

"That is good news, indeed!" Lady Tymolara quickly put her hand over her mouth, realizing she had spoken too loud. She covertly glanced around and her pulse dropped when she saw that no one was paying them any attention; she had quickly learned to dress drably and wear a frowning demeanor, as it kept men at a good distance.

"Yes, as soon as *our friend* destroys that snake pit in Balph, we will be free of our own tyrants," Verla hissed back.

"However, the Arch-fiend has plans for our lad," she replied.

"What do you mean? What deviltry is he up to now?"

"He plans for Aspasthar to lead the King's Guard, then die in the defense of Balph. His men will have orders to kill the boy if he survives the battle."

Verla gasped. "Truly, he's a daemon in human guise come up through the earth from the Caverns of Regwarn."

She nodded. Verla didn't know the half of it. She still wept silently for the young girls Archpriest Grythos had murdered. "You must pass the word. Maybe *our friend* will be able to protect him."

"I will do my best. When will the arch-devil be departing?"

"In the spring with most of his troops."

Verla smiled openly, revealing gaps between her teeth. "Then the blood-bath will begin."

TWENTY-TWO

I

The fleet was just off the Florida Keys when the lookout announced, "Ships, ahoy!"

The ocean was glassy with only some small swells rocking the caravel Kalvan was using as his transport. After the last two nights of constant rocking, he was pleased that he'd been able to keep his breakfast down. He had been suffering from seasickness ever since the boat had left Xiphlon harbor.

He preferred the caravels, which were similar to the ships Columbus sailed across the Atlantic, to the triremes. The Xyphloni galleys were too noisy and stank to Styphon's Sky-Palace! Plus it made Kalvan sick to see the rows of slaves chained to their oars. He had attempted to explain the economic realities of owning slaves to High King Roldolf of Xiphlon, but it had been a complete waste of time.

Overhead, the sky was gunmetal gray and there was a light rain splattering the deck.

Kalvan had been expecting a Styphoni attack farther up the coast, but here was as good as anywhere. Thirty of the Hostigi naval schooners were at the forefront of the eighty or so galleys and caravels carrying the first part of the Hostigi army, horses and armaments. High King Roldolf of Xiphlon had refused to send any of his warships for fear of alienating the Styphoni.

The Hostigi-designed caravel Kalvan was sailing on was well in the front third of the fleet and he made his way cautiously up the mast to the crow's nest—over the captain's objections—so that he could watch the upcoming battle. He hated the movement of the crow's nest, but more importantly he needed to see how the battle fared.

The schooners held several surprises for the oncoming Styphoni fleet of galleys, most of them large triremes and biremes. Naval warfare here-and-now wasn't much advanced over the Roman era of Marc Anthony and Julius Caesar. The galleys all had rams and carried boards, or crows as the Romans called them, for boarding parties. A few of them carried small guns at either the bow or the stern, a relatively new innovation. The Styphoni-built galleys weren't built sturdily enough for mounting guns on the port and starboard sides.

Kalvan's schooners had no such problem. The safest course of action would have been to fire their cannons from a distance and destroy the leading galleys. Unfortunately, that would warn the others and most would escape. Instead he wanted to draw the Styphoni fleet into a fire trap few would evade.

He watched with great interest as the first galleys, three big triremes, closed in on the lead schooner. Suddenly a lance of Greek fire shot out and the lead galley's sail caught fire. Within a minute, the entire boat was engulfed with flames. The forward galleys tried to turn and run, but instead their oars intermingled with a crashing sound while the higher Hostigi ships sent plumes of fire to their decks and sails. Already Kalvan could smell the burning canvas and flesh of screaming men, many of them chained to the boats.

He felt his stomach roil, and fought it back down. It wouldn't look good for the Hostigi commander to lose his lunch in the middle of a battle a half mile away.

Some of the forward galleys were firing their bow chasers and the Hostigi schooners were taking a few minor hits. A four or six pound cannonball wasn't going to do a whole lot of damage, except to any soldier or marine who got in its way.

Suddenly the schooners in the main group began to fire their guns. It reached their boat like distant thunder. Several of the sailors whispered prayers to the weather goddess.

"Pray to Galzar!" cried one of his men on deck. "He's the one who will save you from slavery, not Lytris!"

Some of the galleys had taken direct hits, and two of them were sinking. Others were floundering. Most of the ones in the rear were trying to change course, causing more collisions. The butcher's bill for this battle was going to be high. The lead schooners were now among the main fleet, causing the rest of the galleys to try and flee. Many crashed into other galleys or began to sink when their bottoms were shot out by the Hostigi artillery.

Now more than thirty or forty of the Styphoni galleys were on fire, and were causing collisions as they veered off and in one case spun around in circles. One of the Hostigi schooners came too close to a burning galley and suddenly went up in flames. More broadsides thundered out, smashing and sinking the fragile galleys. The air was rent with the screams of galley slaves being burnt to death or pulled under the ocean by sinking boats.

The Styphoni fleet was now in a complete rout. All they could think of was escaping the Greek fire and broadsides of the schooners. The schooners trailed the now fleeing galley fleet like hounds after a wounded bear, picking off the weak, galleys or those with damaged oars. By the time the battle drew out of eyesight, he estimated the Styphoni losses at a hundred sixty to a hundred and seventy boats.

Admiral Herad boarded Kalvan's boat just before dark with his action report. His usually perfectly groomed hair and beard were in disarray and there was soot on his face, which made the toothy smile on his face stand out in stark relief. "Your Majesty, this has to be the greatest sea victory in history!"

"I believe it," Kalvan replied. "What were our losses?"

The Admiral shrugged. "Very small, two ships sunk with minimal loss of crew. Another damaged by fire, but still afloat. A few sailors were lost to musket fire. All together we lost less than two hundred and eighty men, while the Styphoni lost thousands, not counting slaves chained to their oars. We tallied over a hundred and fifty boats sunk or burned to the waterline, Your Majesty!"

Kalvan shook his head. There were typically four men chained to each oar; therefore, each ship had to have had two or three hundred slaves, which meant more than thirty thousand slaves went down with the doomed galleys. Well, if he had his way, this would be the last great naval battle here-and-now using slave rowers.

"It's all clear sailing ahead, Sire. We chased them until our crews were exhausted. They won't leave port again unless Styphon's Own Voice orders them to. Even then, many of them will desert. They've never tasted defeat like this before, I promise you!"

II

From Kalvan's latest message, Hestophes knew his Great King was now on his way to Hos-Bletha, there to join up with Duke Skranga and Democriphon, who was now a great king. *We do live in strange times*, he decided. *I should be with them, though. And would have been if the Great King of Fencesitters would ever make up his mind.*

Now, his orders were to return to Thagnor Town and join up with Great Queen Rylla, instead of joining Great King Kalvan and the Army of Styphon's Destruction. The message had come over a moon ago and he'd had plenty of time to mull it over. *What is Queen Rylla up to?* he wondered. The faster he got away from Zygros City and back to Nos-Hostigos, the sooner he'd get his answer.

Finally, after endless delays, Hestophes had been granted another private audience with Great King Phidestros. *This time I hope he's made up his mind.* Kalvan had been emphatic that he remain in Zygros City until he had a firm reply from Phidestros. He knew it was an important job, for if Phidestros were to bring his troops into Hos-Harphax to back Great King Geblon, the Hostigos Army of Styphon's Destruction could be in jeopardy.

As Phidestros' page led him into the king's private audience chamber, Hestophes noticed that a desk had been added to the room. A familiar looking piece of furniture. It looked almost identical to the one that had been in Great King Kalvan's study in the summer palace in Hostigos Town.

Without thinking, he blurted out, "By Dralm, is that King Kalvan's old desk? How did you ever get it out of Tarr-Hostigos in one piece?"

Phidestros looked up shyly. "No, it's a new one. I built it myself based on Kalvan's design."

Hestophes ran his right hand along the desktop. "Very nice work, Your Majesty. Where did you learn working skills like this?"

Phidestros' face flushed with pleasure. "When I was a boy, I was apprenticed to a cabinet-maker. Back then, I hated every candle of the time I spent woodworking." He shook his head in wonderment. "Sometimes we don't know when we're well off."

Hestophes nodded in agreement. "My father was a publican. I was his only son and he wanted me to take over his tavern. There are times I wish I had stayed with him. Still, there is much to be said for being a nobleman or great king."

Phidestros laughed. "Very true, Duke. I must apologize for keeping you here in Zygros City for so long, but I have had a difficult decision to make." He paused to take a maple-candy and offer one to Hestophes. "In the end, after much thought, I have decided to take Great King Kalvan up on his offer. My army and I will stay here and keep out of the upcoming war; in exchange, I will receive a third of the battle-spoils and treasure from the Styphon's House Temple's Treasury, its temples and Great Banking House. Those were his terms, am I correct?"

Hestophes bowed. "Yes, Your Majesty, those were Great King Kalvan's terms." He paused to pull out two parchment documents he had kept in a leather satchel. "And thank you, Your Majesty."

He waited while Phidestros finished his candy and slowly read over the terms of the agreement. When he was satisfied, he wrote his signature in runes on both documents. Kalvan's signature and Royal Seal were already on both. After his signature was finished, he heated some red wax and fixed it to each of the documents, then used his signet ring, with the Zygrosi Royal Device, to seal one copy.

Phidestros waited a short while for the wax to dry, then handed the sealed document back to Hestophes who put it back in the satchel.

"My Great King will see that your shares are delivered once he has returned to Old Hostigos. Have you selected an emissary to keep track of your shares?"

"Yes, Duke Kyblannos will act as my eyes and ears. Is that acceptable?"

Hestophes bowed his head. "Of course, Your Majesty. After his return from Harphax City, the Duke and I shared a cold evening together. He is a wonderful storyteller and a good trencherman and drinker. I had trouble matching him cup for cup."

Phidestros smiled. "He is that, and much more." He paused, then added, "I suspect he is looking forward to this journey. I got the feeling that he has some difficulty in adjusting to civilian life."

"Yes, he's a born wanderer and soldier. I will miss his good company. I wish I could join him, but I was ordered to return to Thagnor Town."

Hestophes got the feeling that Phidestros had a bit of wanderlust himself and an ache to get back up on his charger. *It must be tough to hang up your spurs after a lifetime of warfare and soldiering. If this war goes well, I may have an opportunity to find out for myself.*

TWENTY-THREE

The boat ride from Xiphlon had been at its worst when they had swung around the peninsula of Florida. The Florida Keys had been as deserted as they were when Ponce de Leon had visited them in the Sixteenth Century. Massive untouched mangroves hugged the coast, making him wonder if there was anyone living there. The profusion of garish wildlife, especially the birds, had to be seen to be believed. If it hadn't been for the occasional fishing ship, he would have believed the entire coastline was uninhabited.

Kalvan was thrilled beyond belief when the broad-beamed caravel finally arrived at Dalthax Port's harbor, which was in the same spot as Savannah, Georgia back on otherwhen. Despite the lack of storms the last two days of his voyage had been very unpleasant, as the boat rolled like a pig in mud, creaking and groaning as it pushed its way through the Atlantic Ocean swells. He had suffered the worst case of sea-sickness in his life. As he was lowered off the side in a bosun's cradle to the wharf, Kalvan swore that he would never board another boat. If it wasn't for his royal dignity, he would have kissed the ground when his feet landed on the wharf's planks.

If he had to, he would walk back to Nos-Hostigos. Halgoth and his bodyguards weaved back and forth along the dock like a bunch of drunken sailors as they tried to get their land legs. The Great King's party was met dockside by a large party of dignitaries. He spotted some of the princes dressed in white togas and wearing golden crowns. Kalvan's jerkin was already soaked; he realized he was going to have to start wearing togas himself if he was going to stay in this muggy climate for long. Thank the gods that winter was on its way.

Duke Skranga was the first to arrive, his scraggly red beard as long as a billy goat's. Next was a broad-shouldered man wearing the gold circlet of a prince. *More names to remember….*

"Welcome, Great King Kalvan," a prince he didn't recognize said in stentorian tones.

"Thank you, Prince—"

Duke Skranga interrupted, "Your Majesty, I would like to introduce you to our loyal ally and First Prince of Hos-Bletha, Prince Vythron of Taurnos."

Kalvan made a slight bow in the prince's direction, who fell to his knees and all but kissed the ground.

"Prince Vythron, please rise. I suggest we meet tomorrow for a real talk, but right now I need some rest. It was a long journey from Xiphlon and I need to get my legs and body accustomed to being back on land."

"Of course, Your Majesty. We can meet at the Dalthax Guildhall. Would midday be good?"

"Yes," he replied, turning to Skranga. "Do you have a room for me?"

"Yes, Your Majesty. We've reserved an entire floor at the Seaman's Inn." He waved his hand in dismissal, and the crowd began to scatter. "I will accompany you there, Your Majesty."

"Thank you," Kalvan replied, as they made their way down the street. The streets were lined with rubberneckers and he wondered if half the city was out to see him.

Inside his spacious bedchamber, Kalvan told his advisors he'd speak to them later in the evening after he caught up on his sleep. Cleon helped him strip off his jerkin, removed his doublet and britches. Kalvan fell onto the bed and promptly fell asleep. He woke up the next morning to a lighted room, suddenly noticing he still had his boots on.

Kalvan grabbed the nearby bell pull and Cleon, followed by a page, came into the room with candles to help him get dressed again. He washed his face in a bowl of scented water and let his manservant put on fresh clothes. "Thanks, Cleon."

His manservant blushed, even after all this time with Kalvan he still wasn't used to being thanked.

"I know there's a roomful of dignitaries downstairs waiting on me."

Cleon nodded.

"Have they picked a meeting room?"

"Yes, Your Majesty."

As I suspected, he thought. He turned to his page and said, "Tell them I'll be right down."

As the Royal Page rushed off, Kalvan tried to sort through his thoughts. When he had a reasonable plan of action, he left the room where he was joined by Halgoth and two massive bodyguards.

Duke Skranga was waiting at the bottom of the stairs. "Your Majesty, it is good to see you again." He even managed to sound sincere.

Kalvan smiled, as he noted the heavy gold chain around the Duke's neck and the massive bejeweled rings on every finger. "I can see you've done well here. So you're Chancellor now?"

"Yes, Great King Valthros highly respects my confidences."

Kalvan smiled.

"I thank you from the bottom of my heart, Sire, for including me in this mission. I've never had such a wonderful time, although it was dangerous on occasion. I got to play a Styphon's House highpriest! It was the role of a lifetime. I'd never realized I had the bent for acting, but I may have missed my calling...."

"Maybe, maybe not. I can see that your rank has done you well."

Skranga laughed embarrassedly. 'Well, Your Majesty, I will admit my time here has been profitably spent. The Royal Treasury has done well, too. I'll leave Democriphon to fill you in on that."

"Before you take me inside, what's the inside information on the major players?"

"Of course, Your Majesty. I wouldn't let you enter the great hall without a briefing. I've obtained a small room off the hall where we can talk in private."

Kalvan followed his Chief of Intelligence through a warren of hallways and small rooms to a back room full of barrels that had been hastily cleaned. Skranga sat down on an upended barrel and he did likewise. His bodyguard stayed outside guarding the thick wooden door.

"As you know from our letters, it wasn't until after our arrival in Hos-Bletha that we decided to use the Orphan Prince gambit. The letters were infrequent and in code so there's a lot you don't know."

Kalvan nodded. "True."

"It all started out innocently enough. We played highwaymen for a while, attacking rich merchants and Styphon's House priests. Captain Ranthar made a wonderful Robinos and is still featured in many songs and legends. We were quite successful for a time, but then our quarry got spooked and we ran low on targets. Then it was decided that I would don the robes of a Styphon's House upperpriest so that I could gain entrance to some of the local temples and reconnoiter them for raids." Skranga paused to wipe his beaded forehead with a linen handkerchief. "It took more preparation to pass for a Styphoni upperpriest than I had expected."

Kalvan forced back a guffaw, and ended up choking. He knew that one of Styphon's requirements for its priesthood was circumcision. He suspected that Skranga had not found it a pleasant procedure.

"You must be thirsty, Sire," Skranga said, jumping off the barrel. "I set aside some tankards and a small cask of good ale." He pointed to the barrels that surrounded them on three sides. "Swill, for the most part."

Kalvan nodded, burying his face in his hands to keep from laughing out loud. "Please, I could use a drink," he sputtered. He could only imagine the pain his Intelligence Chief suffered to pass as a Temple highpriest.

Skranga took out two leather tankards from a shelf and filled them with ale from a small barrel with a spout. "Here, Your Majesty."

Kalvan took a small sip, which was as much as he dared to drink. At least, until his urge to laugh died away.

"Anyway, getting back to my tale. I passed myself off as a Styphon's House highpriest and we were able to sack two handfuls of Temples. All of them rich in booty and gold tiles. Meanwhile, we were being chased by Great King Niclophon's Royal Guardsmen and the Red Hand. We had some heady adventures, but we could see it wasn't going to keep Niclophon from contributing to Styphon's Grand Host—or whatever they were calling their army that year—so we decided to expand on the Orphan Prince dodge."

Kalvan was impressed by the matter-of-fact presentation.

"Democriphon volunteered to play the Orphan Prince," Skranga continued, "which made sense for among us he had the most *princely* aspect and manner. Plus, he's fair-haired and resembles the supposed appearance of the young princeling. We even established our own outpost at Mallegast; unfortunately, we picked the territory of the one Prince who knew that the tales of the Orphan Prince were sheer fabrication."

"How's that?" Kalvan asked.

"Prince Mythros was one of the first on the scene, after the death of Great King Marocles and Queen Delra, and he helped rescue the *real* Orphan Prince. When confronted with his knowledge, we were forced to take Mythros into our confidence. It was pure good fortune that he despised Great King Niclophon and agreed to support Democriphon's impersonation of Prince Valthros. Otherwise, we would have been as bad off as a pack of treed polecats."

"Why had Mythros kept the identity of the real Valthros secret all these years?" Kalvan asked.

"The real prince was nearly strangled from the birth cord while birthing and grew up to be an idiot. The Prince has protected him and given him a home, but the real prince's identity can never be revealed. Mythros feared that even though the boy was dimwitted, Great King Niclophon—were he to learn of his identity—would have him killed or imprisoned. From what we've learned of Niclophon, Mythros' fears were well-founded."

Kalvan nodded in agreement. From all the intelligence reports he had received about Niclophon, he wouldn't show the man his back within pistol fire range.

"Once Prince Mythros learned of our identity and mission, he decided to join forces with us. He went so far as to call a meeting with the other princes of the realm and put his support behind Democriphon, even providing evidence to *prove* he was the Orphan Prince."

"What kind of evidence?"

"The Prince's nurse and some missing jewels. It helped convince the anti-Niclophon crowd, but was rejected by the King's ardent supporters."

Kalvan didn't bother to ask why Niclophon, despite his failings as a ruler, had supporters among his princes: some undoubtedly because of the Great King's incompetence, others because of blood relations or promises of future gain at someone else's expense. Many princes saw a strong leader, like Valthros or Phidestros, as a threat or nuisance. To Styphon's House,

Niclophon's weaknesses as a ruler were virtues, while his princes—even those who used him—despised him for the same reasons.

"Once the bird escaped the quicklime," Skranga said, "we had to act quickly before Niclophon organized an army and put us out of business." He paused to remove a large scroll from a leather tube. The scroll contained a lambskin map of Hos-Bletha, which he carefully unrolled and set on the table. He took a handful of gold coins out of his purse to secure the corners.

Kalvan nodded. "That will be helpful, Duke. I'm not very familiar with the geography of Hos-Bletha."

Skranga said, "That's why we had this map drawn by the Royal Cartographers. They have also made detailed maps of each princedom, as well as the capital."

"I can see that the new kingdom has been in good hands," Kalvan noted.

Skranga shrugged. "Valthros and I only tried to do as Your Majesty would have done were you here instead of us."

"You all have done well, and will be properly rewarded once we return to Hos-Hostigos."

Skranga nodded, then continued, "After Mythros produced convincing evidence that Democriphon was the real Prince Valthros, several of the princes vowed to join him against Great King Niclophon and Styphon's House. Prince Kosklos of Artigos was the first to swear fealty to Valthros, he was followed by Prince Vythron of Taurnos and Prince Xandros of Zynophon. Of these princes, Kosklos is the most valued; he is a fighter of great renown and has proven himself as a steadfast supporter, despite the fact that his realm borders upon Hos-Ktemnos. Prince Vythron of Taurnos has also proven his loyalty and steadfastness, but suffers from a bleeding disease that makes him unable to lead his men. The slightest wound and he bleeds profusely."

"I have heard of such an illness in my former homeland. Few men survive their childhood, Prince Vythron must have a good head on his shoulders."

"He does. He is good at strategy, too. On the other hand, Prince Xandros of Zynophon is an opportunist and, as we suspected, a backstabber as well. We kept him in the dark in regards to our real plans."

"Wise move," Kalvan said.

"Our plan was to draw our enemies, Prince Basilron of Syragon and

Prince Carthames of Drathor, into an attack upon Tarr-Pytha. They are both avaricious blackguards and would battle more for land and treasure than any loyalty to the throne. We created earthworks around the town and fort, as well as set traps and dig deep ditches to keep the enemy guns from reaching our walls. Meanwhile, knowing that Tarr-Drathor would be stripped of men, we sent Prince Kosklos there to strike while Prince Carthames was attacking Pytha Town."

"An ambitious plan," Kalvan said, pausing to take out his pipe and tobacco pouch. "What happened next?"

"The combined armies of Basilron and Carthames ran into trouble trying to besiege Pytha Town. Democriphon set up a number of traps: moats, hidden musketeers, a bomb field and falling timbers, that cost our opponents dearly. They lost thousands of men in the first moon-half. Finally, as he predicted, they made a direct attack upon the gates when a relief force sent by Great King Niclophon arrived. That was when the traitor Prince Xandros changed sides and joined the enemy. When their military forces were fully committed, Democriphon attacked with our full force."

Skranga paused to shake his head. "Your Majesty, it was a slaughter. Half of the enemy soldiers were killed either by the bomb field or Democriphon's troops. We took over two thousand mercenary prisoners and killed three times that many enemy soldiers. A glorious victory. Afterwards, we captured Prince Carthames and recovered the body of former Prince Basilron. Xandros fled the field in ignominy. Such a victory celebration!"

"What happened next?" Kalvan asked.

"There was a parley with Prince Carthames where he swore an oath of fealty to Great King Valthros, who that day took the title of Prince of Syragon as well as Great King of Hos-Bletha. A glorious, glorious day. Everyone was hot to gather our forces and descend upon Bletha Town and depose Great King Niclophon, the false king. This is where it got very sticky...."

"Yes," Kalvan said, entranced by the story as it was unfolding. He had gotten a few reports from Hos-Bletha since the expedition to Bletha had departed, but they had been short on detail and very sporadic.

Skranga grinned. "I had to knock some sense into their thick heads; otherwise we were going to have the full might of Styphon's House bearing down upon us. First, I took Democriphon aside and gave him a talking to. I explained that our mission had not been to gain him the Silver Throne, but to prevent Hos-Bletha from aiding the Grand Host of Styphon's House. He agreed, but asserted that by removing Niclophon from the throne we would have accomplished our mission and then some."

He paused to shake his head in wonderment. "Next, I explained that if we overthrew Great King Niclophon, we would force Styphon's House to send a real army to restore either Niclophon or some other lackey to the Silver Throne. However, if we just consolidated our gains, they would leave us alone until there were less pressing matters at hand. And so far it has worked!

"Then I took Princes Mythros and Kosklos into my confidence, telling them the same story I had already given Democriphon. They didn't like it, but were unable to counter it with anything but false hopes. In the end, they agreed to hold off on attacking Niclophon until Styphon's House was weakened. Since then we've been involved in a delicate dance with Great King Niclophon. He's moved around our holdings, while we've stayed away from his. I'm sure that not attacking him has been driving Niclophon crazy, since we have more and better soldiers and could easily defeat his army any time we please."

Kalvan smiled and patted Skranga's boney shoulder. "You did well, Duke. I couldn't have done it better myself. For the past few years the Temple's armies have been bogged down in Nos-Hostigos and then Hos-Agrys. Now that we have put Grand Master Soton out of business, it's time to strike and strike hard!"

Skranga's mouth broke open with a wide smile. "They all will love you for it, Your Majesty. Let loose the dogs of war, as you put it!"

TWENTY-FOUR

I

Boats were still arriving from Xiphlon with more soldiers when Kalvan left Dalthrax Port for Prince Mythros' palace in Pytha Town. He was given a cordial welcome by the Prince and provided with a series of interconnected rooms fit for a great king. His first act after resting and having a dinner of roasted flamingo and baked potatoes was to invite Democriphon to a private meeting.

Democriphon entered the chamber with all the bearing and dignity of a great king. *He looks more like a great king than I ever have*, Kalvan decided. His only non-regal aspect was the big smile plastered all over his face. Kalvan assumed that Skranga had told him of his plans to invade Bletha Town and depose Niclophon from the Silver Throne.

"Have a seat," Kalvan said.

Democriphon sat down on a large chair upholstered with soft black leather. "Thank you, Your Majesty. It's good to see you again. We've been here so long I was afraid I'd forgotten what you looked like."

"You and the Duke have done a great job here, far better than I had ever anticipated. You two not only kept Hos-Bletha out of our wars, but put added pressure on Styphon's House. You both are to be congratulated. After Styphon's House has been destroyed, I will see that you are both properly rewarded with lands and titles. Either here in Hos-Bletha, or back in Hos-Hostigos."

"Thank you, Your Majesty. We had very strong support from the rest of our party, particularly Colonel Ranthar and Grand-Captain Myklon, who died fighting the Styphoni. However, we have both profited greatly from our time here. I, as Great King, and Duke Skranga as the Royal Chancellor of the realm. Your return is reward enough."

Kalvan waved his hand as though to banish all false modesty. "I mean it. First, I want your thoughts on the Silver Throne."

Democriphon's brow furrowed. "What do you mean, Your Majesty?"

"After Great King Niclophon is deposed—and that's going to happen soon, I promise you. I need to know if you want the Seat of Hos-Bletha for yourself?"

"Ahh. I'm not sure, Your Majesty—"

"Enough formalities, we're not at court; just two old friends talking."

Democriphon shook his head grinning. "Yes, yes. To be honest, I have enjoyed acting as great king. I had not expected it to be so rewarding, but I have been able to enact a number of reforms throughout our allied princedoms that have pleased me. And, yes, there is something to be said for great wealth and the adoration of one's subjects. Is that not true?"

Kalvan agreed. "I also understand you have married a princess."

"Yes, Princess Eryka of Pytha. She is her father's oldest daughter, and the prettiest I might add. She's almost as beautiful as Great Queen Rylla, but—may the Gods be blessed!—she has no desire to spend time upon the battlefield."

Kalvan broke out into laughter. "Then you are doubly-blessed! May you have many children and both live long lives."

Democriphon bowed his head. "Thank you. I do want to continue as Great King of Hos-Bletha, but only with Your Majesty's permission and blessing."

"You have both," Kalvan said. "You will have my full support, and I suspect the support of your five princes.

"I have their support," he replied.

"Then, henceforth, you will be known for all time as Great King Valthros of Hos-Bletha."

"Thank you, Your Majesty."

"Now, what are your thoughts on the best way to hit Great King Niclophon?"

"How many soldiers did you bring with you?" Democriphon asked.

"Roughly, about thirty thousand men, including gunners and light cavalry."

Democriphon smiled dashingly. "I've got another five thousand Royal Guard, mostly cavalry. Plus we can count on another four thousand good men from Prince Mythros. Prince Kosklos is good for another three thousand and we can expect two thousand apiece from Princes Carthames and Vythron, for roughly another sixteen thousand men."

Kalvan whistled. "No wonder Niclophon has been shitting his bed at night!"

It was Democriphon's turn to burst out in laughter. When he had finished laughing, he said, "Poor Niclophon can't figure out why we haven't invaded Bletha and thrown him into his own dungeon. As far as Styphon's House is concerned, they haven't been paying attention. They've been too busy chasing you and other problems in Hos-Agrys so that we've been mostly ignored. Your advice to Skranga to postpone the invasion of Bletha was a wise one."

"Actually, I never gave him that advice; he just used good judgment. Your accomplishments here far exceeded my most optimistic hopes. It was only later, when I learned of your enthronement, that I told the Duke that it was wisest to let the sleeping panther stay asleep."

"Well, now that I think about it. He never 'said' it was your order; he just presented it as the kind of strategy that you would adopt. After a little thought, we all agreed that it was the smart thing to do. Since we held the larger portion of Hos-Bletha, we certainly weren't worried about Great King Niclophon invading any of our princedoms. At least, not without Styphon's House sending a major army behind a tested captain-general, such as Grand Master Soton or Captain-General Phidestros."

Kalvan nodded. "Phidestros has cut all ties with Styphon's House so we don't have to worry about him carrying Styphon's boots. I don't know if you've heard the news here, since Styphon's House is doing its best to suppress it, but a few moons ago Phidestros sent a boat filled with the heads of all of the Temple's highpriests in Hos-Zygros to Balph. I've tried to enlist Phidestros' support in the invasion of Hos-Ktemnos, but Captain-General Hestophes, my emissary, has not yet gotten a firm answer. Well, he may have by now, but word hasn't reached us. We've been out of touch with Nos-Hostigos since I left Tarr-Ceros. I don't know when I'll be back in contact with Queen Rylla."

"We hadn't heard a word about a boatload of heads! Styphon's House couriers pass through two of our princedoms, but Skranga advised that we leave them unmolested."

"That was good advice. If you hadn't permitted their couriers access to Bletha Town, the Temple might have retaliated against Artigos or Taurnos, which would have forced you to fight both Niclophon and Styphon's House."

"That's what Skranga thought. We've also let their priests and merchants travel freely along the Silos Road and other major thoroughfares. Even a few bands of Styphon's Own Guard."

"Yes, they were probably testing you. If you had attacked them, you would have gone from nuisance to big trouble in a heartbeat with predictable results. But that song is changing. Soon the Styphoni will be dancing to our tune; you can bet your life on that."

II

Great King Niclophon was sporting with his newest "friend" when Chancellor Archimanes burst into his private chamber. "What are you doing here! How dare you, the insolence!"

"Excuse me," cried the Chancellor, dropping to his knees, squeezing his eyes tightly shut and resting his chin on the floor. "It's most urgent that I speak with you, Your Majesty."

Niclophon dismissed his new young "friend" with a snap of his fingers, straightened his robe and rose to his feet. "Archimanes, you know I'm not to be bothered when I'm entertaining! What if my wife were to accompany you? Whose head would roll, then?"

"Mine, Your Majesty. I apologize, I didn't mean—"

"Damn your eyes! Stop your groveling. What is so urgent that it brought you bursting into my private chamber like some berserk

Sastragathi barbarian?"

"One of our agents-inquisitory from Dalthrax just reported in, Your Majesty. He brings bad news, very bad news."

"What tale does he tell? Out with it, man!"

Archimanes paused to rise up on his haunches. It was hard for a man his age to grovel on marble floors—to say nothing about the loss of one's dignity. "He says that the Usurper Kalvan arrived at Dalthrax Port over a moon-quarter ago."

"What in Hadron's name is Kalvan doing there! Does your agent have any word on the Usurper's plans?" Niclophon demanded.

"Not directly. My intelligencer is not known to the Pretender Valthros' intimates so he has to take his information third-hand from barkeeps, serving wenches and whores. He did say that many other boats were arriving on a daily basis, all of them ferrying Hostigi soldiers, horses, armor, supplies, fireseed, weapons and armaments. Thousands upon thousands of men. He's heard talk in the wineshops that Kalvan is joining forces with the Pretender Valthros."

He could hear the noise of grinding teeth as Great King Niclophon mulled over this latest news.

"Damn that loathsome pile of rat droppings Valthros! Somebody should have strangled him in his cradle. How many soldiers has the Usurper brought with him?"

"Our man counted some fifteen thousand before he departed. He said they were still unloading ships when he left and that rumors were told that the Usurper Kalvan had brought over forty thousand men with him."

"Bah! I don't believe it—still, even if he only brought ten thousand men, it will be enough, when combined with the Pretender's forces, to send us straight to Regwarn!"

Archimanes was wringing his hands. "What shall we do, Your Majesty? Kalvan is known for firing his enemies out of cannons, especially those allied with Styphon's House!"

"You had to bring that up! Where is that damnable Archpriest?"

"Archpriest Lesthros left for Balph yesterday, Your Majesty. He claimed that he had to attend an important conclave in the Holy City."

"Like a rat running out of a burning building! His own agents probably got word of Kalvan's arrival and he left town without even telling us."

A wise man, thought Archimanes. *He knew that if he told Niclophon about Kalvan, he would never leave the palace alive. I only wish I had some place to flee to myself.*

"How many men can we raise to defend Bletha Town?"

"I don't know, Your Majesty. You need to ask Captain-General Theodoros."

"Then, you cack-handed bastard, bring him to me at once!"

III

Captain-General Theodoros made his way to the Great King's private audience chamber as fast as dignity would allow. He was greatly worried by the rumors circulating through the wineshops and taverns that Great King Kalvan had arrived in Dalthrax Port. The two guardsmen at the King's door were standing arms akimbo and he noted their dress was sloppy. The captain of the guard was one of the Great King's favorites, a bootlicker who probably knew about as much about soldiering as Theodoros knew about inn-keeping.

Inside the chamber, Great King Niclophon rose up as he entered, with a scowl prominent upon his face. "What took you so long?" he demanded.

"I was in the barracks doing an inspection, Your Majesty," Theodoros explained.

"Have you heard the latest news?"

The Captain-General shook his head; he wasn't about to repeat barroom gossip as news.

"One of our agents-inquisitory just returned from Dalthrax with terrible news. The Usurper Kalvan has arrived at the port at the head of a large army. His first act upon arriving was to meet with the traitorous Pretender Valthros. Our agent reports that it appears that the Usurper Kalvan is going to join forces with Valthros and besiege Bletha Town."

Theodoros fought to keep his face from falling. *My worst fear realized.*

"If this is true, we will have to call up the princely levy and make preparations for a siege. We'll need lots of foodstuffs, fireseed and—"

"Enough! Do you think I am a fool? Do you think that I don't know what a siege requires?"

"Of course, Your Majesty," he said. "I was just stating what I believed we should focus our attentions on."

Niclophon shook his head in exasperation. "What we need to focus on is how to best keep our Kingdom and our heads upon our shoulders. Will the Usurper's forces be enough to take Tarr-Bletha and Bletha Town?"

"More than enough, Your Majesty. If Kalvan's guns were enough to bring down the walls of Tarr-Ceros, they will certainly blow away the pitifully thin walls surrounding Bletha Town. They might halt his advance by a few days, nothing more."

"I had hoped he would stay in the Sastragath after bringing Soton to heel. What about Tarr-Bletha?" asked Niclophon, who had suddenly turned pale.

"Those walls are much stouter and will fare better under cannon fire. They should hold up for maybe as long as a moon-quarter; should Kalvan refrain from a direct attack and try to starve us out.... Well, there isn't enough food stored to feed the town's populace for more than a moon-half. Nor do we have enough soldiers in the entire Kingdom to halt his advance."

"Then what is your advice?"

"Run—run like the wind!"

WINTER

TWENTY-FIVE

I

Kalvan had gotten a message from Uncle Wolf Xanthos that there were problems at the army bivouac. He arrived with his bodyguard to find Xanthos at the edge of the clearing with several other priests. "Your Majesty," he said. "More of the men are coming down with the disease you called *cholera*. They're vomiting and suffering from the flux."

"Is it the bloody flux?" Kalvan asked, a symptom of dysentery which was much more serious than cholera.

"No," the Uncle Wolf replied.

"Let me see some of your patients," Kalvan ordered.

Xanthos hesitated and he held up his hand. "Your Majesty, I would never forgive myself if you were to come down with this dreaded disease."

Kalvan was pleased by his response; it meant that his lectures about communicable diseases were beginning to be taken seriously. "In this case it is not a problem. Most hot-climate diseases are either carried by mosquitos or bad drinking water. Have some of the men been drinking directly from the streams again?"

An elderly Uncle Wolf with white hair and a straggly beard came forward. "Your Majesty, some of the younger men do not listen and drink freely from the pools and streams. Many of them are among the stricken."

"Be sure and tell the rest of the men why they are ill. Now, take me to the infirmary."

Xanthos led the way. The first of four infirmary buildings, built to Kalvan's specifications, was a large open building with big open windows and canvas wings to allow fresh air to circulate. Kalvan carefully examined the first victim: he was a younger man with deeply sunken eyes, cold skin and wrinkled hands and feet. All classic symptoms of cholera.

He was relieved; he'd feared it might be something much worse. At least some of the men had a chance of recovery from cholera. Napoleon's army in Haiti had grown ill with Yellow Fever, and most of them had died there. If he remembered correctly, Yellow Fever was another mosquito-borne disease, like malaria, that came from Africa so it was very unlikely it had made it to the North American continent here-and-now. Still, he was relieved that it was late in the year; men unaccustomed to the tropics did not do well in the heat and humidity when mosquitos were at their peak.

"Xanthos, these men are suffering from cholera. If they had listened to your warning, they wouldn't be sick. Use them as examples: have those who survive talk to their comrades and tell them why they got sick."

Uncle Wolf Xanthos shrugged. "Your Majesty, you don't understand. I could talk to the men until I run out of breath, and some will still not listen or hear a word I've spoken. They'll listen even less to this lot. We need something to tell them better than the name of a disease they've never heard of. They need to be frightened of drinking fresh water."

Kalvan paused to light up his pipe, trying to think of a way to reach the common soldiers. Then it came to him. "Aha! Tell them that the rivers and streams in Hos-Bletha are ripe with Swamp Devils who will give them fevers and the flux. They are too small to be seen by the naked eye, and only boiling the water will kill the Swamp Devils. Will that do it?"

Xanthos smiled, showing a mouthful of broken and darkened teeth. "Yes, Your Majesty. Yes, Swamp Devils. Now, that's something a soldier can believe in."

II

Danar Sirna looked around the corridor warily as she arrived at the archpriest's private chamber. There were a lot of spies in the Harphaxi Royal Palace, many of them under Great Queen Lavena's wing. A midnight visit to Archpriest Danthor's private rooms would require more explaining than she was prepared to do.

The two guards, both Temple Guards with red capes, ignored her presence as she tapped at the door. A moment later Danthor opened the door into the anteroom. "Come in, girl. Make it quick or there'll be rumors running through the palace that we're bundling."

She repressed a shudder at the thought. Scholar Danthor was ten times her age and as bossy as her father had been. There was no attraction here, at least on her part.

Sirna nodded her head back at the doorway. "What about them?"

"Those two work for me; they know how to keep their mouths shut."

Despite having lived at the palace for over a year, even she was impressed by the richness of Danthor's quarters. *One of the perks of going undercover as a Styphon's House archpriest*, she surmised. Sirna was even more surprised to see a familiar face waiting inside. It was Aranth Saln, the former Hostigos Study Team military expert, who had been presumed dead after the destruction of the Hostigos Royal Foundry.

"Aranth!" she cried. "I thought you were dead…" She had to fight back the tears that threatened to well up in her eyes.

Aranth nodded and gave her a wry smile. "No, I managed to escape from the Red Hand. I decided it was time for an outtime sabbatical, so I left the area and joined up with some other deserters."

"You could have told me! I thought we were friends."

"We are, Sirna. I didn't want to burden you with my secrets. Later, you were shacked up with that Phidestros fellow and I didn't want to be anywhere around him. He can smell a rat a mile away. I figured you had your own fiddle. Then, after he married Princess Arminta and you hooked up with Great Queen Lavena, I thought you had it made being the new queen's confidante and all."

If he hadn't been wearing a steel breastplate, she would have beaten her fists on his chest. "Had it made: I've been living a nightmare existence with a she-wolf capable of having my head chopped off because I curtsied at the wrong time!"

Aranth shrugged and looked, for him, apologetic. "Sorry, I didn't know the full extent of your situation. From afar, it looked damn good."

"Well it wasn't, and it isn't!"

"Enough bickering, children," Danthor interjected. "You both have bigger problems than reliving the past. I just got word from Balph that Great King Kalvan has arrived at Dalthrax Port with his army, some thirty thousand strong. If I know our man, shortly he will be invading Bletha and deposing Great King Niclophon."

"What's that have to do with us?" Aranth asked.

"Plenty. Things have been hopping in the Five Kingdoms ever since Tarr-Ceros fell to Kalvan's army. I just got back from Agrys City where I learned that Prince-Regent Grythos intends to strip Agrys City of most of its military garrison—some ten thousand men—to come to the aid of the Holy City. He'll be joined by five thousand men sent by Agrysi princes who, while not loyal to the Temple, well understand that if Balph falls, Hos-Agrys will be the next target."

Aranth whistled. "That news isn't even in the wind."

"Not yet," Danthor added. "You just got here, Aranth, so there's a lot you don't know. It gets worse. Great King Geblon has started to feel the pinch and has beefed up the Royal Army of Hos-Harphax. He'll be sending twelve thousand men or more to Balph himself. And he's not the only one. Most of the Harphaxi princes who have supported Styphon's House have been sending in their own 'contributions'—to the number of ten thousand or more men. With promises of more by the time spring arrives."

"That's not good for Kalvan," Sirna said out loud.

"No, it's not. He's going to have over seventy to eighty thousand men arrayed against him when he reaches Hos-Ktemnos. True, his men are veterans and have better weapons, but he's going to be seriously outnumbered."

"So what does that have to do with us?" Aranth Saln asked.

"Saln, if Kalvan should win, your position here might become untenable. If he loses, there will be little need for artillery officers and you'll find yourself out of work. Sirna, on the other hand, is in a much more vulnerable position."

Sirna nodded. "Lately, Queen Lavena's been mistreating her maidservants worse than ever before. Geblon, for the first time, is acting like a Great King and taking charge, and she doesn't like it. She has to accept it because it's their heads on the chopping block. She knows that if Kalvan wins, he will have her killed. So she's been taking out her anger and anxiety on the palace staff!"

"Exactly," Danthor said. "That's why you both need to leave Harphax City."

"But how?" Sirna asked.

"Quickly and surreptitiously," Danthor said. "You'll need a place far enough and isolated enough to be out of the Queen's reach. There's a small village in Phaxos that's a perfect hiding place. The headman in charge 'rents' hideouts to people on the run. A number of wealthy Hostigi stayed there after the fall of Hos-Hostigos. Lately business has been slow, so I'm sure Headman Dagnar will appreciate your business. I will send an envoy to ensure his cooperation. He doesn't know me as an archpriest; if things get any worse here I may be joining you."

III

Finally, after the better part of a moon-half, all the princes of the "new" realm were gathered within the walls of Tarr-Pytha. Rather than waiting for them to arrive, Kalvan would have preferred moving directly against Bletha Town before the King's army had time to prepare for their assault. However, Democriphon and Skranga had argued that it was best to involve all the princes and make it a joint decision to rise up against Great King Niclophon. Reluctantly, Kalvan had agreed; if Democriphon was going to continue on as great king, this would give him an opportunity to display his leadership skills among his princes.

All the allied princes, Prince Calthros of Drathor, Prince Kosklos of Artigos, Prince Vythron of Taurnos and Prince Mythros, gathered in the Great Hall. Great King Valthros, flanked by Great King Kalvan and Chancellor Skranga, sat at the head of the hall. Valthros opened with, "We have invited you all here to join in with us in the invasion of the Princedom of Bletha, where the Pretender Niclophon sits upon the Silver Throne. We invite you to join us as observers. The troops we have already gathered should be more than sufficient for our purpose."

This had been at Kalvan's suggestion. If the princes were allowed to bring additional soldiers, there would be too much jockeying for position and backroom politics. Plus, they would have to wait another moon for all their forces to come together in Pytha. Kalvan wanted to get the invasion underway and over with as quickly as possible.

Valthros rose to his feet, looking every inch a Great King. "The moment we have all been waiting for has finally arrived. Great King Kalvan of Hostigos has arrived to help us vanquish the False King who now occupies the Silver Throne. His army will be joining Our own in the invasion of Bletha. It is Our desire to move quickly, before Styphon's House can come to the False King's aid."

The assembled princes nodded their agreement.

"Once the False King's army has been defeated and he has been taken prisoner, he will be tried by the Council of Princes. I will recuse myself from the trial; you will be the ones to determine his sentence."

It had been Kalvan's idea that instead of immediately beheading Niclophon, they leave his fate up to his former princes. From the smiles on their faces, he knew Kalvan had made the right call.

"All of the False God Styphon's temples," Valthros continued, "will be sacked; their treasures to be shared equally among all the princes who have loyally supported their true Great King."

That pronouncement got more than smiles, several of the princes rose to their feet with calls of "Down Styphon!" and "Long Live Great King Valthros!"

Democriphon, who had already accumulated a mass of gold and treasure from a year's worth of sacking Styphon's House temples, had told Kalvan before the council that he thought this division of spoils would help cement his vassals to his new realm. Kalvan thoroughly agreed.

When the hall had quieted, Valthros continued, "We shall be leaving for Bletha Town in two days. Any of you who wish to join as observers are welcome to come along."

That brought out a few more cheers.

"Now, let me introduce you to Great King Kalvan of Hostigos who has been fighting the False Temple for over five winters now." Valthros sat down.

All cheered and applauded when Kalvan stood up and paused, surveying the Blethan nobility seated along both sides of the table. "As you all know, Styphon's House has been falsely selling fireseed as a temple miracle for hundreds of years. This has allowed them to gain dominance over nobles, princes and even great kings. However, their 'miracle' has been nothing but a Big Lie, a scam designed to extort your gold and compliance. In my homeland in the Cold Country, fireseed is as common as flour. When I first arrived in the Five Kingdoms, I shared my knowledge with former Prince Ptosphes of Hostigos and in response Styphon's House gathered a great host to kill us and bury the secret of the Fireseed Trinity.

"Gathering the largest force ever assembled in the Great Kingdoms, the Grand Host of Styphon's House overran Hos-Hostigos and destroyed Tarr-Hostigos with a month-long siege. However, thanks to the heroic Last Stand by Prince Ptosphes and Captain-General Harmakros, We, along with the better part of Our army, were able to retreat to the Middle Kingdoms and found the new Great Kingdom of Nos-Hostigos.

"However, our relocation was not enough to placate the Temple. Styphon's House wanted me, my wife and my children dead as well as our subjects and all knowledge of the Fireseed Trinity. To that effect, they besieged Thagnor Town, our new capital, and attempted to starve us out. In this they were unsuccessful and eventually forced to return to their lairs. The Regicide Lysandros, who had faithfully followed the Temple's orders, was killed by his own men during his return to Harphax City. The turmoil he left behind encouraged his Queen to marry a mercenary and use his army to support their false claim to the Iron Throne.

"Since Styphon's House has declared me anathema and will stop at nothing to kill me and my family, I have decided to bring the Temple down. To this end, I have assembled a great army and will be invading Hos-Ktemnos in the spring. All those who wish to join in this crusade will be welcome and have a share in the treasures that Balph holds."

That got their undivided attention.

The huge form of Prince Kosklos of Artigos rose up. "Your Majesty,

I will pledge my army and my services to you and your quest to end Styphon's House's stranglehold on our lands." He bowed, then sat back down.

"I welcome your pledge, Prince Kosklos."

Suddenly all the other princes were clamoring to join the fight against Styphon's House, while Kalvan breathed a sigh of relief.

TWENTY-SIX

I

Styphon's Voice Anaxthenes was awakened from his nap by a light tapping on his chamber door. "Who is it?" he called out.

"Your Divinity, it is I," Archpriest Euriphocles replied.

"Come in," he ordered. His head felt groggy from too little sleep and too much humidity. "What gives you leave to break up my afternoon repose?"

"Urgent news, Your Divinity. Archpriest Lesthros has just arrived from Hos-Bletha with news of great importance."

Anaxthenes forced himself to refrain from raining down curses on Euriphocles' head. The position of Supreme Priest he had worked so hard to achieve was beginning to seem as if it were cursed by demons or evil spirits. *It is no wonder now*, he thought, *why Old Sesklos was eager to die in bed. Besides, what news of importance ever came out of Hos-Bletha?*

"Take him to my private audience chamber. I will meet with him in a quarter-candle."

Euriphocles left his bedchamber and Anaxthenes went over to the sink, turned a knob and splashed cold water on his face. A large cache of ice was kept in the temple basement in a huge wooden-box bound in iron. The ice was cut into blocks, swaddled in sawdust, with straw placed between the layers of ice. It was used to cool his wine and to keep his piped in water cool. *I would hate to have to live life without such luxuries*, he decided. *Curse and blast this Daemon Kalvan who threatens the very foundations of Styphon's House!*

Followed by two of his giant guardsmen, he made his way to his private audience chamber. Archpriests Euriphocles and Lesthros were there waiting for his entrance.

Anaxthenes sat down upon his padded chair. "What is so important that I need to be roused from my sleep like the landlord of some flea-bitten tavern?"

"It is news of the utmost in importance, Your Divinity," Archpriest Lesthros stuttered, obviously shaken by Anaxthenes' stern visage.

"Then spit it out!"

"Yes, Your Divinity. The Daemon Kalvan has arrived in Dalthrax Port with a great army. There he has joined up with the Pretender Valthros. It appears they are gathering a large host to advance upon Bletha Town."

Anaxthenes smiled through tight lips. "So, you departed with utmost haste to keep from getting captured by the Hostigi?"

Lesthros fell to the floor and all but kissed the marble floor. "No, Your Divinity. I came as soon as my intelligencer arrived with the news. I believed it was news of the greatest importance and too important to entrust to some courier."

"What did Great King Niclophon have to say about this report?" he asked.

"I suspect he was shaken, Your Divinity, although I did not wait to give him the news myself. I believed my first duty was to return to Balph bearing this important news for you."

No, he'd left to save his own skin from Niclophon's flaying knife. Anaxthenes knew, were he in the Great King's position, that he would blame the Daemon's arrival on the Temple. After all, had not Styphon's House spent the last six winters trying unsuccessfully to kill the Usurper and destroy the Hostigi people.

"You know Great King Niclophon best. What will he do now?"

Archpriest Lesthros rose to his knees. "What choice does he have, Your Divinity? He will either have to fight or flee. I cannot see him leaving his palace without a fight. His vices alone would make it difficult for him to live in exile."

Anaxthenes nodded. Maybe the Great King of Hos-Bletha was made of stronger material than we previously had believed. Maybe he and his men would die to some purpose, that of blunting Kalvan's sword and winnowing his troops.

"Leave me, both of you. I have much to ponder."

II

After what seemed like moons, the walls of Thagnor Town were finally in sight. A light snow was falling and the temperature was well below freezing. Soon winter would rush in with full force, although to Captain-General Hestophes it felt as though it had already truly arrived. Wearing a bearskin coat and several layers of wool clothing, he was as well insulated against the chill wind as possible.

The first part of his journey from Hos-Zygros had been aboard a trading vessel, but the weather had turned and the Sea of Skirlos had become too rough and unpredictable. His party had been forced to make landfall in Hos-Agrys. They had stayed clear of the major port towns and were a large enough party that any bandits—brave enough to disregard the weather—had left them alone.

Beside him, Uncle Wolf Tharses was breathing heavily. Tharses was an old man and the rigors of the overland journey had taken their toll. "Are we there yet?" he asked.

"I just spotted the walls, Uncle Wolf. We should be there before the sun sets."

Uncle Wolf Tharses came out with a laugh that quickly turned into a cough. "How can you tell? It's already as dark as night."

The old man's eyesight had started failing while they were waiting in Zygros City. It was a good thing they were almost home.

Soon they were at the gatehouse and several of the guards recognized him and Tharses. "Welcome, Captain-General. Her Majesty will be pleased to learn you've finally returned," said the Guard Captain.

"Captain, tell Her Majesty that I am returning home for a bath and change of garments. As soon as I'm presentable, I'll make my way to the palace."

"Yes, sir."

"And, take care that Uncle Wolf arrives home with a proper escort." He took the captain aside to whisper, "Tharses' eyesight is failing, but he doesn't want anyone to know. Let his escort know so they don't embarrass him."

The Guard Captain nodded. "Of course, sir."

It took Hestophes several candles to scrape and bathe away the dirt of the moon's-long journey and he was tempted to stay in the tepid water even longer. He forced himself, like a bear ending its hibernation, to step out of the marble basin and have his manservant spill pails of recently-heated warm water over his head until the last of the soap was gone. He then got dressed in hose, britches and doublet before making his way to the palace.

Great Queen Rylla was waiting in her private audience chamber. Upon his entrance, she rose up and hugged him tightly. "Old friend, we were beginning to wonder if you'd been taken prisoner by the Zygrosi or had run into pirates on the way home."

"Neither, Your Majesty. We were detained because Great King Phidestros was torn between his greed and his loyalty to his former underling. I'm not sure whether it was greed that won out, or his disgust at Geblon for being so turkey-pecked. Eventually, reason won and he decided to stay at home with his army. In the spring, he will be sending Captain-General Kyblannos to join Great King Kalvan in Hos-Bletha to see that he receives his fair share of the Styphoni plunder."

Rylla sighed. "That is very good news, Duke. My husband will have enough enemies to fight without adding the only one he fears to the fray."

"Yes, and with good reason. Phidestros has his own rifles and is making more every day. Plus, his men are veterans and well-disciplined. He also has the next best artillery in the Great Kingdoms; only ours is better. I must admit I was very impressed by what I observed; Phidestros trains his men year-round. And pays them, too!"

"A man to be respected as well as feared," she observed.

"Yes, he will make a good ally. Nor does he have any love for Styphon's

House. He had all the upperpriests in Hos-Zygros beheaded and sent their heads to Balph!"

"Yes, we heard about that when we were besieging Tarr-Ceros."

"Of course. Such news must have shaken the walls at Balph to their very foundation."

"I'm sure it did. Great King Phidestros was the best military ally and strategist the Temple had. It's good to know that he is out of the fight."

"I understand the siege went well."

"Much better than we had ever prayed for," Rylla said, shaking her head in wonder. "Who would have predicted that the hard-headed Grand Master would repudiate Styphon and swear to Galzar? Lyklos the Trickster must have been at work."

Hestophes smiled. "Praise Galzar, it sure appears that way. The gods are always happy to mock us mortals. And it took Great King Phidestros by surprise as well. He knows Soton as well as any man who himself is not a member of the Order of Zarthani Knights. I believe it helped win his allegiance to our side. Plus, like most mercenaries, Phidestros is a believer in Galzar. He was overtly pleased to see Soton change allegiance to the Wargod's camp. As I, myself, am."

"True," Rylla admitted. "Grand Master Soton was a worthy opponent, and now shall be a righteous friend."

"Yes, the Order helps keep the peace in the Sastragath. Without them, the Southern Kingdoms would be at constant war. What about Warlord Ranjar Sargos?"

Rylla frowned. "He deserted us in our time of need. My husband may feel some loyalty to that barbarian, but as far as I'm concerned, the debt has been wiped clean. Sargos will receive no more weapons from us, nor shall we help him against the Order. If he is smart, he'll stick to his side of the Great River."

Hestophes kept quiet; no one carried a grudge longer than his Great Queen. Unknowingly, Sargos had made a huge strategic error. Kalvan might forgive his lack of loyalty, but Rylla would cradle it like an infant and take it to her grave.

"Where is the Great King now?" he asked. His unsaid question was:

When and where am I going to join up with him?

"He left Xiphlon several moons ago for Hos-Bletha where he plans to meet up with Democriphon—or Great King Valthros as he is now called—and Duke Skranga."

"Are we going to join them in the spring?" Hestophes asked.

An enigmatic smile played upon Rylla's lips.

His stomach sank.

"No, Captain-General, I have other plans."

III

Kalvan seated himself on the butt of a large log and made himself comfortable in front of the rosy campfire. Gasphros was telling stories about the expedition to Hos-Bletha and how they tricked the Styphoni into allowing them egress into their temples.

"Duke Skranga often rode with us as Highpriest Sangar, but he was very reluctant to take the title."

A series of laughs and guffaws broke out around the fire ring.

"Why not?" Kalvan asked, playing the straight man for his audience. Skranga he imagined would enjoy playing any part that gave him pomp and authority over others quite well.

"As you know, Your Majesty," Gasphros said, after taking a drink from his tankard, "there is one specific requirement for becoming a Styphon's House priest. A most painful and embarrassing one."

Kalvan smiled. Of course, he'd heard it before. Still, not a pleasant operation for a grown man with local medical equipment; he even felt sorry for the Duke.

"So he undertook the circumcision," Gasphros said, failing to hide a wry smile. "It left the Duke in a foul temper for the entire half-moon his incision took to heal. I've seen a bear lose a cache of honeycombs with more aplomb."

As everyone laughed, one of the maidservants came over with a cup of hot chocolate and presented it to him. "Thank you," Kalvan said, as he took the hot beverage into his hand. It wasn't coffee and it didn't taste like any chocolate back home, but it was better than nothing.

She blushed and scooted away. It made him glad that Lady Eldra had left with First Captain Ranthar for Xiphlon to aid King Verkan in his search for Dalla some time ago. Eldra was a real temptress and he didn't need or want that kind of distraction.

"Would you like a shot of Ermut's Best to keep your chocolate warm?" Gasphros asked.

"Sure," he replied, between puffs on his pipe. In a few days they'd be marching off to Bletha Town to fight a battle; he was enjoying the down time.

Gasphros leaned over and poured a generous dollop into his cup. As he returned to his makeshift seat, the troubadour said, "I don't believe you've meet Gycules yet, have you, sire?"

He shook his head. He'd heard a number of stories about the huge petty-captain, but they had yet to meet.

Gycules stepped forward; he was one of largest men he'd seen here-and-now; in the same league as Xykos, Queen Rylla's chief bodyguard.

They clasped hands.

"I've heard so much about Your Majesty that I thought most of it was codswallop."

Everyone laughed.

He bowed his head. "Now, I can see that you are a man of your word, Your Majesty. I look forward to fighting with you and your men."

Kalvan smiled. "I look forward to welcoming you to our side. Maybe you can bash the walls of Balph with your fists!"

Everyone smiled.

"I wish it were that easy," Gycules said.

"So do I," Kalvan replied.

IV

Kalvan was sitting at a table in the War Room in Tarr-Pytha poring over the local maps, which left a lot to be desired in terms of detail. Valthros had done his best, but he hadn't had any real mapmakers in his expedition. Kalvan had his own Royal Cartographers working on better maps, but they wouldn't have anything useful until long after the war was over. From what he could remember from school, since he had never traveled through the southeast, was that Bletha Town was located approximately in the same spot as Atlanta, Georgia. The maps placed Balph, the Holy City of Styphon's House, at roughly Wilmington, North Carolina. From the lack of interior roads, other than the back roads used by Styphon's House's couriers, which crossed swamps, rivers, streams and hills, the best route from Bletha Town to Balph appeared to be along old US Route 17, the coastal highway called the Balthros Road.

While the Hostigi schooners had badly damaged the Styphoni coastal ocean fleet, he was going to need more ships. The Styphoni still had scores of galleys and he needed more ships to address their sea advantage. He sent a courier to bring in Admiral Herad.

He had barely finished smoking a fresh bowl of tobacco when the Admiral came into the room.

"Your Majesty," the Admiral said with a nod.

Kalvan indicated a seat situated next to him. He pointed to the Balthros Road, which was delineated with red ink and ran north up the coastline. "That's the best road to reach Balph from Dalthrax Port. Unless you can get enough boats and transports to ship the entire army up the coast."

The Admiral shook his head. "Not possible, Your Majesty. We only brought fourteen transports with us from Xiphlon. Even if we pressed all the local shipping, we wouldn't have enough boats to transport a quarter of the army. Nor would we have any boats to transport arms, armor, powder, horses, victuals and other necessary supplies." He shook his head wearily. "I wish I could do more."

Kalvan nodded. "That's what I was afraid of. If we sent a courier to Thagnor Town and had Rylla send all the available ships, would that make a difference?"

"Well, they'd have to wait until spring to make the journey. The canals between Thagnor and Greffa are sufficient for the schooners and some of the smaller transports; if they haven't iced over. This time of year the ocean is too stormy for safe passage. In truth, there aren't enough ships in the entire Hostigos Fleet to ship the entire army, much less our allies and supplies. However, it's still a good idea. The Styphoni still have a formidable fleet of galleys and we're going to need all the warships we can get to guard the transports with the army's supplies."

"So, Admiral, what you're saying is that we're going to need most of the fleet to both protect and transport our supplies."

He shrugged, "I wouldn't say that, Sire. But having the rest of the fleet would make our position much stronger. With all fifty-six of our warships, we can hold the Styphoni galleys at bay forever. However, with the twenty-eight schooners we do have, the Styphoni fleet won't dare close because of our superior firepower. I would hate to delay the siege of Balph for the two or three moons—with the Weather Goddess' blessing—it would take for the rest of the fleet to navigate their way here from Thagnor. We still have enough ships based at Dalthrax Port to protect the convoys going between Dalthrax and Balph. We could even make some attacks on their coastal towns to keep them off balance."

Kalvan smiled. "I like that idea. Plus, it will hurt morale. The Styphoni have become accustomed to owning the oceanfront, and have grown fat and happy here. Nor will their allies in Hos-Ktemnos be pleased by our incursions. However, the fleet's primary goal will be to transport supplies, reinforcements and foodstuffs to the army, not engage the enemy."

"I agree, Your Majesty. If we are going to win this war, we're going to need a well-protected supply line."

Kalvan said, "Yes, as a famous general in my homeland once said, "'An army marches on its stomach.' And our army will have a very big stomach, indeed!"

TWENTY-SEVEN

I

The cavalry in the army's van had halted to give the rearguard time to catch up and water their horses. Kalvan was drinking from his canteen when one of the outriders rode up. He identified him as Roaring Panther, one of the Ruthani scouts who'd worked with Democriphon's expeditionary party. Kalvan wondered what part the Indian had played in their Robin Hood ruse. Gasphros, the troubadour, had been regaling them with stories about waylaying Styphon's House treasure trains and sacking Styphoni temples for the past three nights. The big man told some great tales of daring-do and hand-to-hand combat that Kalvan wished he could have been a part of.

"Great King Kalvan," Roaring Panther said, in heavily accented Zarthani. "No sign of scouts or guards close to Bletha Town. Come close to the gate. No see guards manning walls or at gate."

"How about the local farmers, what do they have to say?" Kalvan asked.

"They say that town deserted. All left."

Kalvan wasn't sure what that meant. Was it an elaborate trap set up by Great King Niclophon, or was the capital truly abandoned?

Gasphros, who was riding alongside, said, "Your Majesty, let me reconnoiter the town. I spent many an afternoon and evening in the Blethan inns and taverns when I was working undercover."

"Do you need any support, Baron?" Kalvan asked. Democriphon had rewarded most of the members of the expedition with titles of nobility, all of them well-deserved, he had claimed. They had accomplished far more than he had dreamed possible, so Kalvan wasn't about to argue the point.

The troubadour shook his head. "Something's wrong, Your Majesty. We've been traveling the Silos Road for three days and for the last two, we haven't run into anyone—not even a farmer riding his cart, or a peddler and his pack-mule. The scouts will stick out; and if it's some sort of trick or ruse, we'll— If I'm not back by sundown, you'll know something's up."

Gasphros was an important intelligence asset as well as good company. Kalvan would hate to see him fall into a trap, but it was better to risk one man's life, than possibly lose a squad or more.

Kalvan nodded, and Gasphros rode off on his big mare.

II

As he approached the town walls, Gasphros wondered how the town would hold out against the four batteries of guns Alkides had sent with the Hostigi army. Captain-General Alkides had the rest of the guns back at Prythos Town, claiming that those four would be more than enough to take down any stone wall in Hos-Bletha. Having seen them at close range many times, Gasphros knew that they were not heavy walls—even the walls of Hostigos Town had been taller and thicker. Kalvan had said that might be because the stone had to be hauled a long distance and was therefore quite expensive. Democriphon brought up the point that few of the princes in Hos-Bletha had cannons they could easily move around so there was little need for stout walls of stone.

Gasphros was surprised to note that Roaring Panther had been right: the city gates were open and there were no visible guards. He had been to Bletha Town over fifty times and never once had he seen the gates unguarded or standing open—like an invitation. He felt the hackles rise on his neck and shoulders.

Nearing the gates, he called out, "Anyone here? I come in peace."

There was no reply. There had been a squall earlier in the morning and the berm of the cobblestone road was too muddy and treacherous to ride on. Gasphros wished he could keep the noise down as his horse's hooves made a loud clamor striking the cobblestone pavement, one which he supposed could be heard all the way to the center of town.

He was surprised when no one came out of the nearby buildings to see who was coming to visit. *By the gods*, he thought, *a war party of Swamp Ruthani could ride through town and no one would be the wiser*.

A few blocks down Bletha Road Gasphros saw an old familiar haunt, The Ram's Horn Tavern. The sign was tilted and it was awfully quiet. He dismounted and tied his bay mare to a hitching post. As he opened the door, he was hit with the familiar smell of stale beer and unwashed bodies. The common room was almost pitch black expect for a single oil lamp over the bar. As his eyes grew accustomed to the dark he saw that the inside of the tavern looked as if a herd of bulls had stampeded through the middle of it; tables were knocked over, barrels askew and most of the stools and chairs broken into pieces.

At the bar slouched a middle-aged man, his jerkin stretched out over a gut as big as if he were about to give birth, sitting on a stool drinking a flagon of ale.

"Barkeep?" he asked.

"Noo shur," the man slurred. "Juss old Jess.... Ev'r one else ish gowne."

Realizing he wasn't going to get any useful information from the drunk, he went back to the street. He saw a couple of heads looking out windows to see who was about. A young man, braver than the rest, wearily stepped out of an abandoned boot shop. "Sir, this is not a safe place for a stranger."

Gasphros said, "I'm a troubadour, every place is safe for me."

The young man shook his head. "A great army is on its way here. We are the worthless trash that got left behind. Their Great King will not be happy to learn that all the nobles worth ransoming have already fled with their jewels and money."

"What happened to Great King Niclophon and his Royal Army?" he asked.

"They were the first to leave." He paused to spit on the wooden sidewalk. "Cowards, blackguards and lickspittles, all of them gone."

"Where have all the townspeople gone?" Gasphros asked.

"Those with family outside Bletha Town left to stay with their relatives. Others, with money, fled to nearby villages and towns. Only the pfennig-less and those with nowhere else to flee remain. We are at the Daemon Kalvan's mercy."

Gasphros could see that Styphon's House's lies about Kalvan had left the populace fearing for their lives. However, he couldn't see any way to rectify it without giving himself away.

The youngster pointed a ways down the street. "See those men down there?"

He nodded. A dozen men or so were milling outside a butcher's shop, some of them waving their swords, others shouting.

"They're building up courage to attack. You have the only horse in town and they're probably arguing over who's going to be the new owner."

"Thank you, young man," Gasphros said, as he quickly mounted his horse. He flipped him a silver crown by way of thanks. "Try and tell those fools that Great King Kalvan comes in peace. If they'll let him…."

III

Kalvan was halfway through his lunch when Gasphros galloped up. The troubadour dismounted agilely and he noted that he was in much better shape than when he'd left Hostigos almost five years ago. The roll of fat around his waist was gone and he had a new nimbleness that he hadn't displayed before.

"Your Majesty, they're all gone! Great King Niclophon and all his nobles have left their lair. The entire town is deserted except for a few townsmen too poor to leave."

Great King Valthros looked nonplussed.

Kalvan had wondered if that might be the case, but hadn't said anything. He hadn't wanted to raise their hopes. Niclophon was not a fighter or warrior king; he was used to Styphon's House fighting his battles for him. Something they were no longer able to do.

He raised the turkey wing he'd been nibbling and used it to point in the direction of Bletha Town. "That just makes our job that much easier. No enemy to fight, no casualties." He turned to Democriphon. "Your Majesty, it appears that Niclophon just ceded the Silver Throne to you."

"Aye, aye!" Prince Mythros said.

The new Great King rubbed his chin. "Well, it'll be nice not to have to clean the blood off of everything for a change. It's just so…unexpected."

Prince Kosklos looked visibly disappointed. Kalvan suspected he'd been looking forward to a good fight.

Kalvan nodded. "Let's mount up and see your new capital."

The army passed only a few townspeople on the road, most of whom looked like typical refugees. When they caught sight of his troops' maroon and green colors, they ran off the road to hide. Kalvan considered rounding a few of them up for questioning. After mulling it over, he decided against it; they probably didn't know any more than he did. Anyone important enough to know what was going on had already fled the premises.

The Blethan town gates were still partially open, although it looked as if a person or persons unknown had tried ineffectually to close them. The army halted while a team of engineers and scouts winched the gates all the way open. Kalvan turned to Democriphon, the three princes (Prince Vythron, the hemophiliac, had elected to stay home), Gasphros, Colonel Leukestros and the captain of his bodyguard. "If we're going to do this right, I want all of you to accompany me and my bodyguard."

"Yes, sir," snapped Captain Vanar Halgoth, who looked as if he was spoiling for a good fight.

Other than the clamor of hooves on cobblestones, the town was completely silent; no hammers striking anvils, no snorting horses, no shouting vendors or trollops. The place reminded him of a Wild West ghost town. The streets were completely empty except for a few half-hearted barricades—turned-over carts, old furniture, cast iron stoves and miscellaneous junk—which his bodyguards made short work of. When they reached the town square, or plazos as it was known here-and-now, they dismounted. The palace doors were hanging askew and it looked as if their woodwork had taken more than a few ax strokes.

Inside, the first floor of the palace was a mess. The only statues that remained were broken or in fragments; the tapestries and wall-hangings were gone except for a few older ones which had split into pieces when someone had tried to rip them down. They followed the huge form of Vanar Halgoth and several of the Tymannian Guard into the Royal Presence Chamber. The room had been completely stripped bare; the Silver Throne was gone. The only evidence it had ever been there were the broken marble tiles on the dais where it had been bolted to the floor.

"By the gods, what a mess!" Prince Kosklos cried. "Curse and blast Niclophon!"

The other princes looked around in amazement.

"Well, you've got your work cut out for you, Valthros," Kalvan told Great King Valthros.

He nodded. "We have a good silversmith. I'll put him to work recreating the original Silver Throne."

"Good idea. Your subjects will be happier if you stick to tradition."

"If they ever come back," Democriphon said wistfully.

"They will, once they learn we Hostigi aren't demons and that you're not going to punish them for their allegiance to their former great king. By spring, this town will be bustling again; especially if you come up with some WPA projects."

"WPA?"

Kalvan laughed. "Sorry, a slip of the tongue. Work projects. Hire the locals to fix the damaged buildings and build new ones. It's probably a good thing most of the locals fled; we're going to need housing for the army and there isn't much here in the way of barracks. How many people were living here?"

Democriphon called Gasphros over. "He spent more time here than any of us, reconnoitering and spreading the song of the "Orphan Prince."

"I've heard all about that song, but I haven't heard it sung."

Gasphros bowed, taking his lyre from its shoulder belt. "Then let me sing it for you, Your Majesty:

When the Orphan Prince comes marching home,

Hurrah! Hurrah!
We'll give him a hearty welcome then,
Hurrah! Hurrah!

We'll hoist Old Nic upon a stick,
Then use our swords to cut him quick,
And we'll all be dancing when the Prince comes marching home!

Niclophon will lose his crown,
Hurrah! Hurrah!
And Styphon's House will tumble down,
Hurrah! Hurrah!

Rejoicing we will light our fires,
While drowning in our own desires,
And we'll all be dancing when the Prince comes marching home!

Kalvan suddenly noticed everyone in the chamber had drawn around the troubadour. He knew the catchy melody; he must have sung "When Johnny Comes Marching Home" on more than one occasion around the palace when Gasphros was around. *It's no wonder this song helped bring down Niclophon's regime*, he thought.

King Marocles' son and heir,
Hurrah! Hurrah!
Will restore justice ev'rywhere,
Hurrah! Hurrah!

Let's drink a jar and sing a song,
We'll all get drunk and get along,
And we'll all be dancing when the Prince comes marching home!

He'll take the crown and buy a round,
Hurrah! Hurrah!

Now that the true king has been found,
Hurrah! Hurrah!

Not only will he bring us peace,
But we will also be released,
And we'll all be dancing when the Prince comes marching home!

The Styphon's House priests will all die.
Hurrah! Hurrah!
From giant cannon they will fly,
Hurrah! Hurrah!

Sparks and embers will abound,
And bloody parts lay on the ground,
And we'll all be dancing when the Prince comes marching home!

The regicide will be denied,
Hurrah! Hurrah!
Down in Regwarn he'll abide,
Hurrah! Hurrah!

He'll beg and plead upon his knees,
His carcass burns while we hear his screams,
And we'll all be dancing when the Prince comes marching home!

Everyone clapped and hooted when the song came to an end.

"Very good," Kalvan said. "Niclophon wasn't just outnumbered, he was out-classed."

They liked that, too, and gave another round of cheers.

He turned to Gasphros, "But back to my original question. How many people were living in this town?"

Gasphros tugged at his brown beard, now tinged with hoarfrost at the edges. "Your Majesty, Bletha Town is smaller than Hostigos Town was before your arrival from the Cold Lands."

After Kalvan had been enthroned as Great King of Hos-Hostigos, he'd taken a census of the population. At that time, Hostigos Town had held some fifty thousand people. By the time the Grand Host of Styphon's House had arrived, the population had swelled to over eighty thousand. Bletha Town's population was probably closer to twenty-five thousand inhabitants. It was the rare Zarthani town or city not located on a sea or navigable river, which severely limited its size and explained why it had remained a town rather become a city like the other great kingdom capitals.

"We should have plenty of room to bivouac the Hostigi army here in town," Kalvan said. "The townspeople that left; well, that's their problem. They'll just have to make do in the countryside. Princes, you can return home with your armies; we won't need them again until spring."

They all seemed pleased with that. And why not: what had looked to be a bloody battle, although, certainly a one-sided one, had been averted without a single drop of blood shed. Kalvan knew just the thing to seal his reputation as a gods-fearing man and follower of the Wargod.

"First, Uncle Wolf Xanthos, I want you to lead us all in a prayer of celebration and thanks to Galzar the Wargod. I am sure that he interceded in this affair to see that the proper Great King will be enthroned in Hos-Bletha. Galzar be Praised!"

All their voices joined in with several rounds of "Galzar be Praised!"

III

Styphon's Voice Anaxthenes paced back and forth in his private chambers. As if he didn't have enough problems, now he had Niclophon begging for sanctuary. Instead of staying put and defending his capital, Great King Niclophon had instead forsaken it, then had come running to Balph, like a whipped cur, dragging his privy parts. *That diseased whoreson*, Anaxthenes fumed, *he deserves to be horse-whipped!*

He turned to Archpriests Euriphocles and said, "I ought to have Niclophon's hide ripped from his back and mounted on my wall! Instead of staying put and sacrificing his army and his life, he had the unmitigated gall to come crying to me. What a loathsome pile of rat droppings!"

Euriphocles nodded his agreement. "The man is certainly a base coward, but he might prove useful, Your Divinity."

"How do you mean?" he asked.

"He did bring the better part of his army with him."

"You mean the ones too stupid to desert?"

"It is true, the former king did lose over a third of his men on his way to Balph. Still, there are some good troops among the remaining soldiers. And certainly we will need every man jack of them in the battle to come."

Anaxthenes was forced to agree. There was no longer any doubt; the Daemon Kalvan and his army would be coming in the spring. "I see where you're going. We can use the Blethan Army as cannon fodder."

"Even better, we can put their former king at their head."

Anaxthenes smiled. "Yes, let us see how well the coward fares in the front lines. Of course, he will try to run away at the first opportunity."

Archpriests Euriphocles' lips twisted into an evil smile, "Not if he has a bodyguard comprised of Styphon's Own Guard with orders to kill him if he attempts to retreat."

"Good. I will see that your plan is put into motion. However, we did get some good news. A messenger from Great King Lukthos said that he will be sending his High Marshal Symnos to lead the Sacred Squares to protect the Holy City. There will be six Sacred Squares and the Royal Square, all almost up to full muster, plus eight thousand cavalry. That will give us another eighteen thousand men committed to our defense, three thousand more than we counted on."

Euriphocles whistled. "What crawled up Lukthos' tunic?"

"After learning about Kalvan's victorious takeover of Bletha Town without a shot fired, it appears our ally is worried that if Balph falls, Ktemnos City will follow right behind. He fears that Kalvan may already have a replacement waiting to occupy the Golden Throne, as he did in Hos-Bletha with the Orphan Prince."

Euriphocles shook his head. "I doubt even the Usurper has planned that far ahead."

Styphon's Voice laughed. "Neither do I, but I sent a message to

Archpriest Theomenes in Ktemnos City and he planted the suggestion in the Great King's ear. Lukthos is a candle with a short wick, and I knew he would buy the story."

"Yes, he's still not firmly seated on the Golden Throne. There are many among the Ktemnoi nobility who would like to see him slip."

"Not as long as we prop him up," Anaxthenes replied. "And he knows it."

SPRING

TWENTY-EIGHT

I

Captain-General Hestophes took a deep breath and waited for the fireworks to begin: Great Queen Rylla's audience chamber was filled to bursting with hotheads and even hotter tempers. Besides himself, Prince Phrames was the only cool head in the room. King Chartiphon was insisting that he was not going to stay behind again while Queen Rylla and Prince Sarrask went jaunting off to Old Hostigos and had all the fun. Rylla was insisting that Prince Phrames had done a great job managing the Kingdom's affairs while they were off besieging Tarr-Ceros, but that he couldn't guard the Kingdom all by himself—not with King Chartiphon gone.

Chartiphon insisted that Phrames could protect their thrones, and that his Chancellor could manage his own Kingdom's affairs just fine without him. "Your Majesty, I'm not going to allow you to travel through the wilderness to Hostigos without my—"

"Allow!" Rylla exploded. "As I recall, I stopped allowing you or anyone else to manage my affairs when I became of age, including my father!"

Chartiphon shrugged. "You're all that's left of Old Hostigos. I left Tarr-Hostigos, at Kalvan's request, and what happened? Your father and Harmakros died. Xentos left for Agrys City a long time ago, and no one knows whether he's alive or dead. If I lose you, I've lost everyone and everything."

Chartiphon's voice was filled with such a plaintive note that even Rylla noticed and shook off her anger. She reached over and put her hand on top of his. "I know you're only trying to protect me, Uncle. But I need to help fight this war, too. Kalvan would prefer that I stay home with our babies, but I need to see our land, that is, what's left of it. This land is too rocky and cold. I want to return to Hostigos. It's my duty."

"I understand, Your Majesty. I still intend to bring part of my army and accompany you. Is my lifetime of soldiering not enough for you?"

Rylla sighed. "You can come. But I will never forgive myself if anything happens to you...."

The old soldier straightened up. "I've learned from the Great King how to lead from behind. I'm not about to leave a widow with three children to rule in my stead!"

Hestophes was shocked. *The old dog must have had another child while I was in Hos-Zygros.*

"Fine," Rylla huffed. "You can join us. How many troops will you be bringing?"

"I can bring six thousand men, four thousand horse and two thousand foot, without compromising the safety of Rathon," Chartiphon said proudly.

Maybe the time has come for Kalvan to enthrone Chartiphon as Great King of Hos-Rathon, Hestophes thought. He would have to bring that up the next time their paths crossed. One of the character traits he most admired in his Great King was Kalvan's ability to take pleasure in his subordinates accomplishments and enjoy rewarding their successes. No other king or noble in the Five Kingdoms would have ever elevated him, a publican's son, to the nobility, much less made him a royal captain-general, no matter how great his military exploits.

"Prince Phrames, how many men will you need for the proper defense of Thagnor and Our Kingdom?" the Great Queen asked.

"With six thousand men and the city militia, I can hold the city for a year. The Kingdom's princes have enough troops to hold their lands. Since peace has been declared with Grefftscharr, there has been no hint of war from any of our neighbors. I might worry about King Hyrum of Dorg, except the nomads from the Sea of Grass hit him very hard last year. Several towns were sacked and burned; he's got too much rebuilding work to do in his realm to trespass on anyone's lands. Furthermore, now that Grand Master Soton no longer poses a threat to us, most of our neighbors want to ally themselves with Nos-Hostigos. I believe I can say with certainty, never has there been less chance of war in the Middle Kingdoms than at the present time."

Rylla nodded. "I agree. Captain Halgoth, my husband's envoy to Warlord Sargos, whom he was trying to enlist in the war against the Order of Zarthani Knights, returned with a refusal. Sargos claimed that the headmen and sachems of the various clans and tribes in the Sea of Grass refused to join under his banner. Many of the chiefs are still recovering from the previous summer's losses, while those who were successful are busy enjoying their spoils. So there should be no trouble from the southwest."

That was the first Hestophes had heard of Ranjar Sargos and the Great King's request. Rylla liked to keep information tight to her bodice, which was a problem for her top underlings. Sarrask didn't mind as long as he got an opportunity to wield his sword. Hestophes, on the other hand, found it problematic. He was supposed to be Captain-General of the Army of Old Hostigos, but far too often found himself lacking essential information. If he hadn't owed Her Majesty so much, he might have balked at returning to Hostigos without Kalvan. He knew that if he didn't go and something bad happened to the Great Queen, he would never be able to forgive himself. Much less explain his reasons for staying behind to Kalvan.

"When will we be leaving?" Sarrask, Prince of Ragyath, asked. "I can bring six thousand cavalry to add to the army."

"Soon," Rylla replied. "I'm only waiting for the depot teams to return."

As winter had wrapped up, Great Queen Rylla had sent out large teams of quartermasters to set up depots along the Nyklos Trail so that the army wouldn't have to bring so many victuals for them and hay for the livestock during their trek.

"As soon as the first team returns, we will leave. With King Chartiphon's army, we will be taking over eighteen thousand troops, twelve thousand of them cavalry."

With that number of men, Hestophes thought, *we should be able to march right into Harphax City, much less retake Old Hostigos which these days probably didn't have more than a thousand soldiers in all of the former princedoms combined. I wonder what Rylla is really up to?*

II

Governess Tymolara indicated with a hand signal that the boys were to follow her to one of their secret chambers where they could speak in private without fear of being overheard. They followed her like puppies, running ahead, then falling behind. They had sword practice scheduled in another half candle and were excited. When they reached the fourth intersecting passageway, she had them turn left and then walked to a battered wooden door that was deeply recessed into the stone wall. According to palace rumors, the chamber had once been where former Great King Demistophon's father had kept his concubines hidden from his wife. Now, the room was filled with discarded furniture and decaying tapestries. She burrowed her way through the clutter and the boys followed her to a small alcove in the back of the chamber.

Once they were seated, she put the candle on a small sconce on the back wall. The candle sputtered, then burned strongly again, illuminating the small chamber filled with broken stools and other junk.

"What is it, Lady?" asked Dementros.

Rythor and Altos both nodded.

"I have learned more about the Prince-Regent's plans for you, Dementros."

The young man's eyes lit up. "Is he going to put me in the front lines?"

She shrugged. "I fear his plans do not include you reaching Balph alive."

"What do you mean?" he asked, his voice trembling.

She had no idea exactly what the archpriest had planned, other than the planned battle assassination for Dementros; but, he was in her charge, and she knew that if she let him leave with Archpriest Grythos, he would never return. "His plans have changed. He's going to drown you at sea."

"What, that's not an honorable death!" the boy squawked.

"No, nor is the Arch-butcher Grythos in any way an honorable man. Their plan, once the transport is underway, is to wake you in the middle of the night and tell you to put on your armor. Then they'll take you up to the main deck and throw you overboard where you will sink to the bottom like a stone."

To the boys, the image was so real that they all turned white as virgin snow.

"B…b…but," sputtered Dementros. "That's murder!"

"Yes, Grythos wants you gone so that when he returns to Agrys City he can mount the Golden Throne himself. If the Styphoni are successful and defeat Great King Kalvan, who can stop him?"

The boys shook their heads.

"No one," whispered Althos.

"Right," she said.

"What can we do?" Dementros asked.

"I have a plan," she replied. "I have already spoken with an apothecary, one who lives in hiding and is unrecognized."

The boys understood that. Ever since the Styphoni had taken the capital city, many followers of the former king, as well as worshippers of Dralm and Yirtta, had gone underground, living in the city's nooks and crannies.

"This apothecary has given me a potion that, when taken in small quantities, mimics a deadly illness. I will administer this potion to you a few days before the army is scheduled to depart for Balph so that you will be too ill to leave with them."

"But," sputtered Dementros, "this is not honorable—"

"Shut your mouth, boy! You know nothing of honor. This will save your life. Tell me, what honor is there in drowning in the ocean depths or having your neck slit open?"

Dementros shook his head in confusion.

"You have responsibilities, Dementros. To your Great King, to your subjects and to the Throne."

"But I'm not really—"

"Don't ever say that out loud, don't even *think* it! You are the true prince of Hos-Agrys and your people need you. Think of how proud of you this would have made your father."

He gulped. "Yes, Governess. I will take the potion."

"Good," she replied. She looked pointedly at the other two boys. "Do you understand what we are going to do and why?"

"Yes," they both replied quickly. They weren't stupid and knew full well that they too would share their prince's fate should Grythos get his hands on them.

"Now let us pray to the Allfather. First, that our Great King Kalvan defeats the godless Styphoni and destroys Balph. Next that Archpriest Grythos is killed during the siege. And, finally, that Hos-Hostigos is once again restored to its former glory."

TWENTY-NINE

I

Kalvan pored over the deerskin maps of the Southern Kingdoms, trying to compare them to familiar maps he'd grown up with. Bletha Town was located near Atlanta, Georgia, while Dalthrax Port was in the same spot as Savannah. The Sylos Road ran directly from Dalthrax, where a good part of his army had wintered, to Bletha Town. The best path to Wilmington, or Balph here-and-now, was the old coastal road, Route 17. Here-and-now it was called the Balthros Road. Ktemnos City was located about where Norfolk, Virginia was in otherwhen. The successor great king to Cleitharses was Great King Lukthos, who, from all indications, was deep into Styphon's pockets. After Balph fell, he would take his army there just to finish off the last of the Styphoni.

With the addition of several Blethan princely armies, his force had grown to number over forty-five thousand men, and he wanted to get them to Balph by the most direct route. He wasn't at all eager to tackle all the swamps and streams of central Georgia and South Carolina. The mosquitos were bad enough as it was....

At least, now that most of the soldiers were bivouacked in Bletha Town they had conquered the cholera problem. He knew from his study of history that one of biggest killers of pre-industrial armies was not fighting, but disease. God help them all if there was an outbreak of the plague. Another reason to transport as many soldiers as possible by sea travel. Plus, they could transport much of their supplies and foodstuffs via the ocean and wouldn't have to bring everything in the baggage train. After their initial loss, the Styphoni warships had left them alone.

Still, Kalvan needed his warships riding herd over the transports, providing protection. During the winter, he had sent Rylla a dispatch telling her to send all the ships she could spare to Dalthrax Port. As soon as the ice melted, she'd sent the entire fleet, except for the gunboats: sixteen armed schooners and twenty-two transports had arrived within the last week. The boats from the Saltless Seas weren't designed for ocean travel, but the schooners' guns and Greek fire made them the most dangerous warships here-and-now.

He felt his stomach rumble and smelled the fresh odor of baking bread; it permeated everywhere in town. Every bakery in Blethan Town was baking bread for the army. He hadn't had time to introduce yeast, and wasn't sure where to get it. *Mental note: Have Brother Mytron look into brewer's yeast.* He suspected that unleavened bread had a longer shelf life, but the local loaves quickly got tough, probably as bad as the seabiscuit the British Navy lived on in the Age of Sail. Fortunately—and thanks to his wife's foresight—the incoming ships had their holds filled with fireseed, weapons, parched corn, dried beans, squash and sausages—not necessarily in that order. This campaign they weren't going to be caught short on either foodstuffs or gunpowder.

He heard a discreet knock on his chamber door and Cleon stuck his head in. "Great King Valthros to see you, sire."

"Send him in."

"Your Majesty," Democriphon said, as he bowed with a flourish. "You called?"

"Yes, Colonel—I mean Valthros."

Great King Valthros smiled openly. "I still have a hard time believing all the events of the past few winters myself. I'd always dreamed of being a great soldier, but never royalty. My family were barons in Old Hostigos, but not overly wealthy. They did provide me with a good tutor, which turned out to be their most important legacy considering all the parchments I have to read and sign."

Kalvan nodded his agreement. "I know you went into this great king business reluctantly, but you've done a good job. Your princes admire and look up to you, and you have the loyalty of our soldiers and subjects. There is one problem that we need to address."

Valthros looked puzzled. "What's that, Your Majesty?"

"Prince Mythros told me that if the real Prince Valthros had a child, you would step down when he reached his majority. Is that true?"

"Yes, at the time I was reluctant to take the throne, and that seemed like a convenient escape clause. Now, I'm sorry I ever agreed."

"I know the Prince is a valued vassal; we would hate to lose his trust and loyalty. What are the chances of the true prince ever having issue?"

At this, Valthros smiled. "Slim to none. He's made sport with more milkmaids than Duke Skranga, and has yet to produce an offspring."

Skranga was a notorious cocksman and if the real prince hadn't produced an heir yet, the chances were good that he would never do so. "That's good to know," Kalvan said. "But it is a good lesson: Don't make promises you cannot guarantee to keep."

Valthros blushed and looked uncomfortable. "I won't make that mistake again, Sire."

"Good," Kalvan replied. It appeared that Democriphon's years in Hos-Bletha had done him a lot of good. Gone was the cocky and arrogant young Colonel in the mold of General Custer. "Now, I have some bad news for you."

He paled. "What, Your Majesty?"

"We're going to have to leave you behind. I need someone here I can trust to make sure any Styphoni sympathizers don't start causing trouble. We need our supply line to be as secure as possible." Kalvan could read the hurt on Valthros' face. He held up his hands, palms out. "I know it's asking a lot, but I need you here."

Valthros did his best to keep a stiff upper lip. "Yes, Your Majesty. Are you sure? Prince Mythros could do just as good job as I can of holding Bletha Town and our supply line."

"Maybe. But, if the army were to suffer some kind of reverse, I want someone I can trust with my life holding the reins of power."

That seemed to mollify Valthros. "Yes, Your Majesty. I will do my best to keep Hos-Bletha firmly in your camp. It will give me a good opportunity to work with the militia as well."

"Have you introduced all the elements of the Hostigos Great Charter?"

Valthros shook his head. "I wasn't secure enough in my powers to announce it and make it stick. I was able to outlaw slavery in the princedoms I ruled, but not serfdom. The right to declare war upon their neighbors is going to be a tough one to enforce, but after Balph falls I don't believe anyone will challenge it."

"Good," Kalvan replied. "I'll look forward to your progress. Do understand, I value you and your loyalty to Hostigos. When this war is over, we will frame an alliance that will bind our two houses together for all time."

II

Prince-Regent Grythos came charging into Prince Dementros' bedchamber as though he was assaulting an enemy fortress—all he needed was a sword in hand to finish off the image. "What is wrong with you, boy?" he demanded. "We're leaving for Balph at first light tomorrow morning. The Prince is supposed to be coming with us."

The boy attempted to speak, but his words were jumbled and barely discernable.

"Young Dementros is deathly ill, Your Highness," Lady Tymolara answered. She knew, after two years of living in the same palace, that the Archpriest didn't like to see his plans thwarted, and reacted accordingly.

Grythos leaned over the sickbed, peering into the boy's face. Then he took one of his large calloused hands and put it on Dementros' forehead. "He's very hot. What's wrong with him, wench?"

"Some sort of flux with a high fever. Uncle Wolf Fynog has been treating him. He can tell you more than I can."

"That doddering old fool, what does he know? Most of his patients don't survive his care. Another charlatan. I wouldn't trust him to put cobwebs on a fresh wound."

"If you have someone you trust more, Your Highness—"

He smiled viciously. "The only competent healers I have are leaving with me in the morning. They will be plenty busy once we arrive in Balph,

I promise you that."

"The Prince will be heartbroken when he learns that he missed the boat."

"If he survives this illness," Grythos said, as though he were expecting that he would not live to see many more days.

"I will see that he gets the best care, Your Highness."

"Do that, and I will see that you are rewarded upon my return."

The implication behind those words chilled her to the bone.

Grythos spun around and tromped out of the bedchamber.

She looked down at the sick boy and said. "Only another day of this, my love. Then a miracle recovery. I fear we have ill-tarnished Uncle Wolf Fynog's reputation."

III

After spending a handful of ten-days in the same lodging, Danar Sirna was beginning to get cabin fever. The three timeliners were living in the manor house whose former owner had died somewhere in Hos-Hostigos on the Trail of Death—as the Harphaxi called "it," during former Great King Lysandros' return from Thagnor to Harphax City. The place was palatial, but there was nothing for her to do; the servants took care of all the cooking and housework. She'd grown tired of listening to Danthor Dras pontificate about his past exploits and how his experience as a Styphon's House archpriest would elevate his status into legend. She almost missed Queen Lavena; at least, in the Harphaxi royal palace she'd never been bored—although on more than one occasion she had feared for her life.

Sirna was discussing tonight's dinner with the cook, lamb was to be the main course, when Aranth Saln entered the room. He had been spending his afternoons at the White Horse Tavern, supposedly gathering intelligence. However, by the state of his growing belly, she figured he was mostly quaffing tankards of ale.

"Hi, Sirna, where's Danthor?" he asked.

"He's in his private chamber dictating more notes."

"Good," he replied. "Come with me, I have news that everyone will want to hear."

Danthor, who was talking into what looked to be an idol of Tranth, but was really a voco-recorder, was sitting at a large table covered with parchments and scrolls. He looked up when the two of them entered the chamber.

"I've some good news," Aranth said.

"Oh, good," Danthor said. "What have you learned?"

"According to my source, the Harphaxi army left for Balph by ship two days ago."

"Who was your source?" Danthor asked skeptically.

Sirna suspected he thought it might be one of the White Horse Tavern drunks.

Aranth appeared oblivious to the slight. "A merchant newly returned from Harphax City. He claims he saw them boarding transports and big sailing boats. He claimed there were thousands of soldiers lining up along the harbor quay."

"That is good news. That means we can leave for Agrys City tomorrow morning. Start packing. Oh, did you get anything from him about Lady Sirna?"

Aranth barked out a laugh. "The Queen is offering a thousand ounces of gold for her return. The story they're telling is that Hostigi agents abducted her for her knowledge of the Royal Family."

Danthor nodded. "That's as good a story as I could have come up with on my own. Plus, it means the Queen's agents-inquisitory will be looking in all the wrong places."

Sirna wasn't sure whether to be flattered or angered.

"So, what's the plan, Danthor?" Aranth asked.

"I'm going to continue representing myself as a wealthy Greffan merchant, Sirna will continue to act as my daughter, while you'll continue on as the captain of my guard."

"How many of my men should we bring?"

Before leaving Harphax City, Aranth had sold his guns for a good price and disbanded his mercenary company, only retaining the services of twenty of his best and most reliable soldiers. The soldiers had guarded them and their carriage from the city to the town of Lasgrath. Since Lysandros had left for Hostigos, the roads and byways of Hos-Harphax had not been safe for merchants or travelers. Only armed parties dared travel these days and commerce had suffered as a result, creating more resentment against the rule of Great King Geblon. Not that his tariffs and taxes had helped, either. Geblon was a very unpopular ruler, and Sirna doubted he would stay seated upon the Iron Throne for long, even if he managed to survive his encounter with Kalvan and the Hostigi army.

"Bring them all. We're going to be traveling a few hundred marches along poorly guarded roads and trails. The breakdown in law and order has affected both Hos-Agrys and Hos-Harphax. However, there aren't many outlaw bands willing to take on such a large group of armed guards. They prefer smaller parties and lone travelers. Once we get to Agrys City, I'll hire a boat to take us all the way to Xiphlon. The guards will earn their salary by keeping the captain and crew honest."

Sirna knew it wasn't uncommon for ship's captains on Aryan-Transpacific to hold their wealthy passengers for ransom if they thought they could get away with it. Especially foreigners, such as Grefftscharrers, far from home. Regardless, the Grefftscharri disguise had a lot of advantages.

"How long will it take us to get from here to Greffa?" Aranth asked.

"We'll be lucky if we arrive before fall's end," Danthor answered.

"Ouch!" Aranth cried. "That's a lot of sea travel and downtime. Do you have any seasickness pills?"

Danthor smiled. "Wouldn't leave home without a full medkit. We'll be fine once we get to Xiphlon, assuming any of the Xiphlon Study Team are there. If not, we'll just continue upriver to Greffa. According to everything we've heard, Kostran Garth is now Prince Regent in-charge of Greffa during our Paratime Chief's absence. He should know what in Xarphta's mandibles is going on."

"It must be something big," Aranth said, "for Verkan to leave like he did. And that story about Dalla being kidnapped by the Mexicotal—did you ever hear a bigger pile of codswallop?"

"No," Danthor said. "That story was for his buddies in Hostigos, specifically for Kalvan and Rylla. You are right about one thing, though—something 'Big' is going on."

THIRTY

I

Kalvan watched in horror as three of Styphon's Own Guard attacked Rylla with their blades. Their red capes swirled as they slashed out with their swords. They were fighting in the inner courtyard of Tarr-Hostigos. The flagstone tiles were littered with fallen bodies, many wearing Hostigi red sashes. He tried to warn her, but his voice was drowned out by the sound of rolling thunder outside—or was it gunfire? She managed to stab one guard in the armpit where the chainmail was at its weakest. There was a gush of arterial red blood and the guardsman collapsed. Another used the distraction to strike her helm with his sword.

Rylla fell down like a marionette with its strings cut. Kalvan tried to pull his sword out of its scabbard, but he was frozen, as though he were encased in amber. Lying next to Rylla on the flagstones was her father, Prince Ptosphes. He had taken a terrible blow to the neck that had almost decapitated him. The remaining guardsmen grabbed Rylla by the arms and started to drag her away, but she kicked back, striking one in the knee.

He dropped her and grabbed his knee. Rylla pulled out a poignard and stabbed at the other guardsman. The guardsman released her hand and raised his sword, then brought it down on her lovely neck—

Kalvan closed his eyes. He couldn't watch anymore. His screamed out in rage, "RYLLA!"

"Your Majesty, wake up!" cried a familiar voice.

Somebody was shaking him. He reached for his blade, but suddenly realized he was in bed. Something in the corn husk mattress stabbed him as he sat up. He cursed and rubbed his backside.

"Are you all right?" Cleon asked.

Outside he could hear thunderclaps and the sound of rain pelting his tent.

"Yes, yes. Just a dream."

Cleon suddenly made the sign of a star on his chest with his right hand.

Realizing that his dream might be taken as a portent, he quickly dissembled. "I was in a great fight in the Golden Temple of Styphon and saw the Great Idol of Styphon fall to the ground."

In the candlelight he could see his manservant's eyes widen. "Praise Dralm! It is an omen from the gods of our coming victory over the godless Styphoni."

Kalvan nodded. Soon word of his victory vision would spread all through the camp. As his dream dissipated, Kalvan realized that his nightmare was not of today, or tomorrow, but of what might have been had he not arrived in Hostigos before the Styphoni offensive against Hostigos. Or, sometime in the future, if Styphon's House was not decisively defeated and put out of business.

"What time is it, Cleon?" he asked.

"Dawn, Your Majesty."

"Time to get up. Please, pack my mattress and sleeping roll."

He could smell the odor of frying bacon and onions, and his stomach rumbled. The weather had been good for the past three days and the Hostigi army had covered some forty to fifty miles along the Balthros Road, a coastal feeder road. Their speed was hampered by the oxen pulling wagon loads of provisions, fireseed, artillery and ordnance. They still had a ways to go, but he believed they were finally closing in on the cesspool that was Styphon's House. Once Balph fell, the rest of the war would consist of mopping-up operations in Hos-Ktemnos, Hos-Harphax and Hos-Agrys.

He noticed Duke Skranga and Admiral Herad were hurrying toward his tent. Skranga's flowing midnight-blue cloak and long legs gave him the appearance of a stork preparing to take flight. Skranga had volunteered to accompany the Navy so that he could provide Kalvan with firsthand intelligence.

"Your Majesty," his Intelligence Chief gasped. "Our fleet made contact with the enemy fleet as it entered the mouth of the Maltos River."

Kalvan nodded. The Maltos River was called the Cape Fear River back in otherwhen, and led directly to Balph. "I was hoping that Styphon's Voice would call in all his forces."

The thick-bodied Admiral Herad was winded, and took a minute or two before he caught his breath. "Your Majesty, our fleet waited outside the Aklos Bay, waiting for the Styphoni transports, as you suggested."

Kalvan thought hard for a moment, trying to visualize a map of the North Carolina coastline which was getting more difficult as time passed since his arrival here-and-now. *Yeah, that was the Onslow Bay back home.*

"The enemy arrived shortly before nightfall. The transports, mostly caravels and large cogs, were accompanied by what appeared to be the entire Styphoni Navy, two or three fleets, some three hundred and fifty to four hundred galleys and support ships. We were outnumbered six to one, but our Greek fire and cannons ripped the heart out of their fleets. Unfortunately, their suicide attack allowed most of the enemy transports to enter the Malthros River unscathed. The Styphoni galleys attacked us in waves. We had to focus almost all of our firepower on them."

Kalvan grimaced. He had hoped to sink most of the Hos-Agrys army transports before they entered the river mouth. He looked into the Admiral's gunmetal blue eyes and asked, "How many ships did we lose?"

"Twelve, Your Majesty." The Admiral gulped. "But the Styphoni lost well over two hundred galleys and seven transports, holding maybe two thousand soldiers. But most of the transports made it into the mouth of the river safely. I fear they have already reached Balph."

"What was different about this attack?" Kalvan asked. "When we fought their Navy earlier, the Styphoni retreated quickly once they realized they were outgunned."

The Admiral shrugged. "It was as if we were fighting a different navy and—"

Skranga interjected. "My spies reported that there was a squad of Styphon's Own Guard posted to each craft. I saw them myself; their red uniforms and silvered armor made them very visible. I suspect their orders were to kill any captain or mate who attempted to retreat."

Kalvan nodded. That made sense, with the Red Hand squads on board each galley, only the foolhardy or suicidal would attempt to hold back or retreat. He had to give Styphon's House credit for fixing a major problem. True, they had defeated the Styphoni armada, but it would have little effect on the outcome of the war. However, those soldiers from Hos-Agrys very well might make a crucial difference in the final outcome.

"How many transports escaped our attack?" he asked.

"My spies counted over a hundred," Skranga posted. "But you have to give Admiral Herad and the Hostigi Navy credit. The Styphoni galleys arrived in waves, well in advance of the transports. The Styphoni came at our ships with everything they had, many of them trying to ram into them. Knowingly, the Styphoni sailed straight into our trap; all this despite continuing salvos of heavy gunfire and Greek fire. Hundreds of their ships burned or were sunk. The ocean was filled with dying and drowning men."

The Admiral looked abashed. "We should have been better prepared—"

Kalvan shook his head. "We were overconfident. And it wasn't just you, Admiral. The enemy made adjustments to our previous attack; we're lucky they didn't have more time to build better boats with more guns. How many of the Agrysi soldiers escaped?"

"At least twelve to fifteen thousand enemy soldiers," Skranga interjected. "Do we have enough men to counter their army, including the Agrysi contingent?"

"I hope so," Kalvan said. He would not have been so noncommittal if he were talking to his princes and allies. He believed it was best to play it straight with his core advisors. "We're already facing the Styphon's Own Guard, the Ktemnoi Sacred Squares, the Harphaxi contingent and now the Agrysi army all together in one place. If we defeat this host, we can bring a complete end to Styphon's House in the Five Kingdoms."

"If we don't?" Skranga asked.

"Then we will have hurt them bad enough that they will die soon anyway. Now that the Fireseed Mystery is common knowledge, it's just a matter of time before their house of straw collapses. Meanwhile, Rylla will have her army coming from the west. Now that both Hos-Agrys and

Hos-Harphax have been bled dry of soldiers, I'm certain she will extract revenge upon Balph should our attack fail. Rylla will be in a perfect position to finish them off, if we can't. So they lose either way."

Somehow that outcome didn't appear to satisfy Skranga. "I want to live long enough to savor the Temple's death."

"I will do my best to see that you do," Kalvan finished, as he took out his pipe and began to fill it with fresh leaf. To himself he added, *but I'm not making any promises.*

II

Rylla was appalled by the needless destruction they kept encountering during their journey. The army had followed the Akyros Road through Kyblos and now into Sask. It was one thing to read reports and hear the words from scouts, but another thing entirely to have to witness the wreckage of her beloved Kingdom firsthand. As they had traveled through Kyblos, the only living people her scouts had encountered were a few hunters, farmers and trappers. There were only a few farmsteads where peasants were still attempting to wrest a living from the land, most had been abandoned. The few who prevailed were hardy souls who welcomed their sovereign's passing with great joy.

It had broken Rylla's heart to see her subjects, scarecrow-thin and dressed in rags, with little children with big eyes and small frames. Most of the farms and cottages they passed had been razed or burned to their foundations. Skeletons and desiccated corpses of all ages were scattered among the ruins. At each farmstead where there were survivors, she had ordered her men to leave behind foodstuffs and a few livestock to help them recover from winter's losses.

After their journey through the ruins of Sask Town, Sarrask was moved to gibbering anger. His former palace had been completely demolished, with only a few scarred and blackened walls remaining. After sputtering oaths and cursing their enemies, he had sworn: "We will pay Styphon's House back for their cruelty to our people!"

Rylla agreed: How many of her people had died on the long Trail of Tears leading from Tarr-Hostigos to Thagnor Town? Ten thousand, twenty thousand, maybe more. It had been even worse for those who had stayed behind. Rylla swore to herself right then and there that ten of the enemy would die for each Hostigi casualty.

Her thoughts were interrupted by the arrival of one of the outriders. It was old Hectides, the wolf hunter, who had helped Kalvan many years before. Despite his white beard and weathered face, the captain was as vigorous as men half his age.

"Your Majesty, our advance party approached the Alathor Heights. As you suspected, the old castle is in ruins."

"Captain, did you run across any guards?" she asked.

He nodded. "Yes, Your Majesty. They have a small watch post in the ruins. We watched them for three or four candles. It's poorly guarded. We only counted a handful of guardsmen."

"Any guns?"

Hectides laughed. "That tightpurse Sthentros would never waste money on guns. Not so far from Hostigos Town."

"Good. Can you and your party outflank them? I'd like to ensure that none of them escape to sound a warning."

He shrugged. "It can be done, Your Majesty. However, it might be more profitable to let at least one man escape."

She raised her eyebrows and Hectides went on: "I believe the news that an army is advancing upon Hostigos Town will provide interesting results. I suspect that Sthentros the Traitor will find that most of his soldiers and subjects will flee at the first opportunity. I believe his support among his subjects is as thin as his peasants' winter gruel. By Galzar, I cannot envision there are many stout men who will risk their lives in support of such a badly bent branch."

"Your words are wise, Hectides. I want you and your men to secure the gap. Meanwhile, I will order the army to move out in the morning."

"It might be best, Your Majesty, if we wait to let the watch guard see the army approach before we overrun their post."

"Yes, you can wait until sunrise. That will give the survivor much to crow about upon his arrival in Hostigos Town."

III

Now that the Arch-Devil had left Agrys City with his troops, Lady Tymolara no longer had to worry so much about security and was meeting with her fellow rebels in a basement underneath a large inn. More than twenty of them had gathered to discuss undermining Styphoni rule of the city.

"How many troops did the Arch-Devil leave behind to guard Agrys City?" She asked her advisors, those few nobles, captains and former counselors of Great King Democriphon who had managed to survive the Styphoni occupation.

"From what we've been able to find out, only about two or three thousand garrison troops, many of them older soldiers and out of shape," Count Wexlor replied. "Archpriest Grythos took his best men with him to Balph, where I pray to Galzar they all die en masse."

There was a chorus of "Down Styphon!" following that pronouncement.

She waited until the shouting was over to add, "I have heard that Great Queen Rylla and a second Hostigi army are on their way to Harphax City."

The Count shook his head. "Praise Galzar! My Lady, how did you learn of this good news?"

She smiled mysteriously. "I have friends in Nos-Hostigos. Now, even if—by way of some pox-addled disaster—the Styphoni manage to defeat the armies of Nos-Hostigos and Hos-Bletha, they will suffer great losses. Plus, they will then have to marshal their forces to strike Queen Rylla and her army. Now if, by some miracle, the Styphoni curs manage to defeat both Hostigos armies, their forces will be severely depleted and most of the men who left with the Arch-Butcher Grythos will be battlefield leavings."

"That is true," Baron Balmoth replied. "If we can secure the city, it will almost be impossible for the Prince-Elect to retake it without a lengthy siege—"

"Which he will be in no position to enforce," a former captain of the guard offered.

"Exactly," she finished. "Now, it is up to us to marshal whatever anti-Styphoni forces remain in the city and strike soon!"

IV

Kalvan was in the middle of a quick lunch consisting of a ham, squash and potatoes, when Duke Skranga arrived with a large soldier he'd never met wearing the colors of Hos-Zygros.

Skranga bowed. "I apologize, Your Majesty, but Duke Kyblannos just arrived by boat from Zygros City."

Kyblannos was a big bear of a man, with a broad chest, wide hips, short bowed legs and a lumbering gait. Kalvan knew that Kyblannos was a captain-general of artillery in the Royal Army of Hos-Zygros and one of Great King Phidestros' few confidants.

Kyblannos bowed, saying, "Your Majesty, I've long looked forward to meeting you. My liege lord, Great King Phidestros, wishes you all success in your battle against the viper's nest that calls itself Styphon's House. Last spring, he sent them a cargo containing the heads of all the Styphoni high-priests formerly residing in Hos-Zygros."

Kalvan laughed. "That must have caused Styphon's Own Voice some discomfort."

"Yes, I daresay Anaxthenes' return letter was flaming hot." He paused to blow on his fingers. "My Great King would have loved to have joined you personally in this great quest, but his duties in Zygros City made that impossible. He is new to the Ivory Throne and there are fences that need to be mended and others to be built."

Kalvan nodded. He turned to Cleon and said, "Tell the kitchen staff to bring another meal for our visitor."

"Thank you, Your Majesty," Kyblannos replied. "I haven't eaten a decent meal in days. That shipboard fare isn't fit for man or sailor."

"As soon as we finish lunch, I'll arrange for you to meet with our Royal Treasurer. He can give you an exact accounting of the Styphoni pillage we've taken so far."

Kyblannos nodded distractedly. “That’s fine, Sire. Your reputation for fair dealing precedes you. I trust your accounts will all be in order. Who I’d like to meet is Captain-General Alkides of the Royal Artillery.” He paused and rubbed his hands.

The Zygrosi Duke practically inhaled the lunch that Cleon delivered and finished about the same time as Kalvan. He must have been starving, Kalvan thought.

As Kalvan lit his pipe, he said, “I will arrange a meeting with Alkides. Now, I understand that you served as a mercenary in Hos-Ktemnos before joining the Iron Company.”

Kyblannos nodded. “That was about fourteen or fifteen winters ago. I fear that my knowledge of Hos-Ktemnos is out-of-date and not of much use.”

Kalvan agreed. “Chief Skranga, find Colonel Leukestros and see that he introduces our new ally to Captain-General Alkides.”

Skranga looked put out, but kept his mouth shut.

He returned a few minutes later, asking, “Do you believe it was wise to let our former enemy see our guns, especially the rifled cannon?”

“Chief, there’s an old saying in the Cold Lands: ‘Keep your friends close and your enemies even closer.’ I believe, for now, that Great King Phidestros is our friend, and by association his representative, Captain-General Kyblannos.”

“How can you say that?” Skranga asked, clearly outraged. “It was Captain-General Phidestros who led the successful Siege of Tarr-Hostigos that cost us our homeland.”

It was a good thing that Rylla was occupied in Hos-Harphax. There was no doubt that she would have agreed with Skranga, and maybe done something about it. “Yes, but Phidestros was the sworn captain of Great King Lysandros, not Styphon’s House. He only did a job he was paid for; that he did it damn well leaves no rust on his escutcheon. By sacking all the Styphoni temples in Hos-Zygros, and beheading their priests, Phidestros has made his sentiments known throughout the Six Kingdoms. For now, we can trust him and his confederates.”

“I pray to Galzar that you are right,” Skranga said, still miffed.

THIRTY-ONE

I

Prince Sthentros of Hostigos was talking with his daughter's envoy from Harphax City when several guardsmen approached his throne. He waved them aside: he hated being interrupted, especially when he was angry. The new subjects his daughter had promised had still not arrived.

"I'm telling you, Valthamos, I was promised two thousand artisans and farmers by Her Majesty. Not a coach full of ne'er-do-wells." He rose up waving his hands. "How am I supposed to rebuild this princedom with no subjects?"

"I fear that Her Majesty's subjects would rather remain in Hos-Harphax than relocate to Hostigos," Baron Valthamos replied. "There are rumors running through the capital that Great Queen Rylla has raised a large army to reclaim her former lands. The people are frightened." He shrugged. "I don't blame them. Besides, there is little here for them."

"That's because they won't come. I can't rebuild this kingdom by myself! I need artisans, guildsmen, farmers and people! Do I have to go to the capital myself—"

There was a sudden commotion at the archway leading into the palace presence hall. The captain of his guard entered with a bedraggled soldier, the dust and sweat of travel soiling his britches.

The guard captain cried out, "Your Highness, I have grave news!"

Sthentros turned savagely, "Lykthros, how dare you interrupt me, you swine!"

The grizzled captain looked the Prince right in the eye. "You'd better listen to me, Your Highness. I have with me a soldier from the Alathor

Heights watch. He claims that a large Hostigi army overran his position and is now on its way to Hostigos Town."

"Speak up, man!" Sthentros yelled, turning to the unkempt soldier who looked as if he had crawled all the way from the heights.

"Your Highness, our watch post at Alathor was overrun by Hostigi outriders. They killed the rest of the watch, every last man jack but myself. I was kept a prisoner until I saw the Army of Hos-Hostigos arrive at the pass!" he said, his eyes bulging. "Tens of thousands of cavalry and infantry. They cover the land like a plague of locusts. I was released with orders to warn Your Highness that Great Queen Rylla is on her way. And that she has special plans for you."

Sthentros felt a chill run right down his spine. "Get out of here! And don't spread this nonsense around. Captain Lykthros, prepare your command to defend the palace."

The Captain looked at him as if he had spoken in a foreign language. "My two hundred men can't defend this place. Not even two thousand men could, or even ten times that number."

"Do your job!" he commanded.

He turned and noticed that the Baron had departed. "Where is Baron Valthamos?"

The Captain looked him straight in the eye. "He's already left. I suspect he'll be at the border by nightfall."

They'll all be gone by the time the Great Queen's army arrives, he decided. *I have no friends or true allies. Just lickspittles and false friends. What am I to do?*

II

Great Queen Rylla was waiting with the army about ten marches outside of Hostigos Town when Captain-General Chartiphon returned with his advance party. She had just relit her pipe when he rode up and reported, "Your Majesty, the town is deserted."

She smiled. "The rats have all fled the burning barn, I take it?"

"Something like that, Your Highness," Chartiphon replied. "It appears that few of his subjects are fond of the Traitor Sthentros, even those who have eaten at his table have abandoned him."

"Leaving him behind?"

"So it appears. We won't know for sure until we secure the palace."

"Do you expect any resistance?"

He shook his head. "It appears that all his soldiers, down to his personal bodyguard fled, the moment word arrived we had crossed the Sask border."

"What about those who remained behind?"

"I have with me their representative, Talsog. He's the putative publican of the Black Boar. You might remember it as the Red Halberd Grog Shop."

She nodded. "Wasn't that shop owned by old Vymanes?"

"Yes," Chartiphon said. "He died during the siege. This Talsog appears to be an opportunist. He changed the name of the bar to match the Traitor Sthentros' personal device, a black boar."

Rylla bit down on her pipe stem. "Another *Quisling*, as Kalvan calls them."

"Yes, but he's now one of the town fathers. He's been selected by the others as their representative. I suspect he's the only one brave enough to personally face Your Majesty."

"Bring him to me." Her first impulse was to have him put in chains, but she knew that her husband would have advised otherwise. The remaining shopkeepers and merchants in Hostigos Town were all survivors who had managed to make accommodations, first with the invading Great Host of Styphon's House, then later with their new overlord, Sthentros. Not everyone had had the opportunity, or desire, to flee with her and Kalvan after the Siege of Tarr-Hostigos.

Talsog was dressed in a black doublet with matching britches. His face resembled that of a rodent, and his gray-streaked black hair was slicked back with bear grease or some other foul smelling pomade.

"You...Your Majesty," he stammered.

"How and when did you become publican of the Red Halberd?" she asked.

"Ah, when my master, old Vymanes, was murdered by a drunken

mercenary during the siege, I took charge of the bar. The mercenaries were thirsty and someone had to take over; otherwise, the soldiers would have rioted and burned the place to the ground—like they did to the Silver Stag."

Rylla couldn't fault his logic, although she suspected the greater part of the story was left untold; she suspected that he may have played a part in Vymanes' demise. However, nothing could be proved at this late date, as much as she would like to find a reason to put him in irons.

"What do these so-called *town fathers* want?" she asked in a no-nonsense voice.

Talsog pulled back, his shoulders rising. "We want to plead for Your Majesty's forgiveness and clemency."

Rylla paused to knock the dottle out of her redstone pipe bowl. Her initial response was to hang them all and let the gods sort them out, but that would reduce the population of Hostigos Town to herself and the returnees with the baggage train. Some four to five hundred former merchants, shopkeepers, guildsmen, carpenters, stone masons and tanners had accompanied the army through the wastelands. More would have come, but there weren't enough rations for all those who'd wanted to accompany her.

"Here's what you can tell them," she began. "The occupants can stay in their current locations until the former owners return. Then they will have to leave. Once the proper owner has been determined, all goods and properties will be returned. No exceptions. If, however, the former owners and their descendants have died, the current occupants can petition the Royal Court to determine ownership and adjudicate any disputes. Is that understood?"

The publican turned white. "Yes, Your Majesty. We had assumed that since we've been in possession for over three winters that the properties we hold would remain in our possession. Especially, since repairs and improvements have been made to both the structures and their contents."

"That's the cost of doing business with traitors and enemies of the throne!" Rylla snapped back.

Talsog jerked back as if she'd slapped him. "By Allfather Dralm, most of us are loyal subjects, whose only crime was attempting to survive the Styphoni conquest of Hos-Hostigos."

"Yes, you survived by taking possession of abandoned businesses and properties," she returned. "You're fortunate that the Traitor Sthentros did not attempt to raise his arms against our army."

He grinned. "I don't believe he had enough loyal men to resist your scouts."

"Enough. Take my words back to your cronies. If they have any further complaints, they can direct them to me personally."

III

As the Hostigi army approached Hostigos Town, Rylla noted that the Great King's Highway had not been taken care of since their departure. Rain and mudslides had washed out several sections and the roadbed itself had been undermined in a number of places. Most of the trees had been cut for firewood or burned; all that remained were stumps and blackened tree trunks with skeletal branches alongside the road. There was some second growth as nature attempted to reclaim the territory, but it was sparse as though the land itself had been cursed by the gods.

When they reached the town border, they took the Old Tigos Road. The town didn't look much better than the outer areas of the princedom. Most of the outlying cottages had been burned to their foundations. A few had been rebuilt with scavenged wood, reused stones and other materials.

Rylla felt a severe pain in her stomach, as if she had been kicked. It was even worse than she had imagined.

"It looks bad," Captain-General Hestophes noted.

As they approached the center of town, the destruction was even worse. Many shops and buildings showed blackened faces or had completely collapsed into piles of rubble. Even those few stores which remained were completely deserted. Other than a few scrawny dogs and cats, the streets were empty of life. Hostigos Town was a mere shadow of its former bustling self.

Sthentros and the Styphoni will pay for this! she promised.

As they approached the junction of Old Tigos and High Street, Old Hectides and another scout rode down from High Street and approached the van.

"Your Majesty," he called out. "The town is deserted. All the soldiers are gone, as are most of the townsmen."

"What about the palace?" she asked. "And the Traitor Sthentros?"

His face scrunched up. "I fear Your Majesty will not be pleased by my report. The Traitor is dead."

"How?" Rylla asked, her voice rising.

"By his own hand, it appears. But not as he desired, I believe."

"Hectides, do not try my patience with riddles!" she demanded.

"By the force with which he died, I would say he took a strong dose of Wolf Bane."

"Was he that frightened of Our justice?" Rylla asked.

Hectides shrugged. "I believe that when he sought out a poison from an apothecary or witch woman, he was given the Wolf Bane. He was not well-liked. No one—no matter their distress—would take such a compound willingly."

Rylla remembered Kalvan had another name for the poison; he called it *strychnine*. In Hostigos Wolf Bane was used primarily as a poison to kill wolves.

"I want to see his body," she demanded. If she could not kill him herself, at least she could view the remains and satisfy herself that Sthentros was truly dead and gone from this world.

"He died in severe agony, Your Majesty. You really don't want to view his corpse."

"Take me to the palace, now! It wasn't bad enough that Sthentros betrayed Hostigos; now he has stolen my vengeance."

"Yes, Your Majesty," Hectides replied.

Chartiphon took hold of her upper arm. "Do you really have to see the body?"

"Yes, or he will steal my dreams for years to come."

The closer they got to the center of town the better preserved things were. She noted that most of the wine and grog shops had been repaired. The High Temple of Dralm had been completely demolished. Nothing remained, but a small Styphon's House temple.

She turned to one of her bodyguards. "Have that godsforsaken abomination torn down and burned!"

"Yes, Your Majesty!"

"Hectides, are there any more Styphoni temples in our town?"

The old wolf hunter shook his head. "There weren't enough townsfolk to warrant even one, I believe."

"Good," she replied. "Now, take me to the palace."

The outside of the summer palace appeared unscathed. They walked into the presence chamber, their footsteps echoing in the empty hallway. She remembered walking these same passages as a child when her father was still alive. For a few moments, despondency battled the anger flowing through her veins.

It appeared that Sthentros had not stinted when it had come to repairing the damage to the palace. There were a number of rich hangings and tapestries she had never seen before.

There were marble statues of the gods, but fortunately Styphon was not among them.

The stench of death and ordure met her nostrils when they reached the presence chamber. Sthentros himself was stretched out in a most unnatural way before the throne; his back was arched as if he were trying to escape his bodily form. As she drew closer, she could see that several of his limbs were broken and his teeth were bared in a fierce rictus.

"A most terrible and painful death, Your Majesty," Hectides offered. "I've used it many times on wolves, but only when I had no other choice. Not even a beast should suffer so."

Rylla smiled. "It's only a piece of what the traitor deserved. He will get the balance when he is called before Galzar, the Judge of Princes."

"Praise Galzar!" Hectides cried.

She turned to one of her bodyguards. "Have this despicable piece of offal dragged out and put into the nearest lime pit. He deserves no burial."

"Yes, Your Majesty."

As King Chartiphon and Captain-General Hestophes entered the chamber, the stomp of their boots echoed throughout the empty room. They paused for a moment to watch as two of the Queen's Bodyguards took the body of Sthentros by the feet and drug him out of the chamber.

"Your Majesty, it appears that the Traitor will no longer haunt our land," Chartiphon noted.

"No," she replied. "I only wish that he had died at my hand."

"He might have found it preferable to the death he chose for himself," Hestophes said, shaking his head. "I can think of many more pleasant ways to die than from Wolf Bane. I have bivouacked the army, Your Majesty. Where do we go next?"

"To Harphax City! We have more debts to settle. Now that the heart of the Harphaxi army is in Balph fighting to preserve Styphon's House, there is little there to oppose us."

"We are growing low on rations," Hestophes said. "We don't have nearly enough to make it all the way to Harphax City."

"We'll forage on the way. There are lots of fat merchants and nobles in the princedoms of Arklos and Harphax to feast upon!"

THIRTY-TWO

I

As a flurry of rain pelted his tent roof, Kalvan cursed the weather and the muddy roads that had stalled the Hostigi Army's advance. They had been laid up for five days waiting for the weather to break. It was almost impossible to drive the oxen- and horse-drawn wagons over ankle-deep muddy roads. It was a seasonal problem, he noted. Still, it was delaying their advance on Balph.

Before they had pitched camp, two of the wagons carrying the big thirty-two pounders, had tipped over, spilling the guns onto the muddy roadway—or "path" as Kalvan would have called it back home. It had taken an A-frame and block and tackle to get the big guns back on their mounts, but by that time the mud was ankle deep. That was when he realized that they were stalled and weren't going to get anywhere until the weather improved and the rain stopped.

He was mulling over the state of their provisions, when one of his bodyguards stuck his head through the tent flap, saying, "Your Majesty, Chief Skranga begs entrance."

"Let him in," he replied.

"Your Majesty," Skranga said, accompanied by a nod which sprayed water around the tent. "One of my intelligencers has returned from Balph with fresh news."

"Good," he replied. It was about time.

"He says that Styphon's Voice has demanded that all the non-essential civilians in Balph exit the city. Tens of thousands have been streaming out of the city for the past three days. Most of them are women and children who are non-essential to the war effort. Also the elderly, disabled and infirm, many of them slaves. In a few days, there won't be anyone left in Balph who isn't a priest or soldier."

"It looks like they're clearing the decks for the siege."

"That would be my guess, sire. We know the Styphoni have enough provisions stashed away to feed the city for two or three years; although with over eighty thousand soldiers to feed, it might cut that time in half. Still, more than enough foodstuffs to keep them fed for longer than we want to stay in this godsforsaken land."

"I'll agree with you on that, Skranga. Any word from inside the city?"

"From what my intelligencers have been able to pick up by questioning some of the temple workers who are evacuating Balph, feelings are mixed. Many are terrified that the Daemon Kalvan might call down the wrath of the True Gods against Styphon. The kings and princes are more worried about who will get the credit for destroying our army and turning you over to the Innermost Circle. The rank-and-file soldiers are bored and tired of waiting. Styphon's Voice ordered the whores and camp wives to vacate Balph, leaving the city filled with rioting. The order was quickly rescinded and double rations of beer were given out for the next moon-quarter."

"That's about what I expected. Things are about to get a lot worse. I'm just glad they're getting rid of most the non-combatants. I have no desire to harm innocents. This way we can kill everyone remaining in the city with a clear conscience."

"I don't know about that, Your Majesty. As far as I'm concerned, anyone living in Balph who's not in gaol or in a dungeon is an enemy."

"You're probably right, Skranga. Still, I do not want to earn the reputation of being a man who slaughters women and children—even if they are the enemy's spawn."

Skranga shrugged as if it were another one of his king's peculiarities. "There was another attack by the enemies' irregulars, mostly Sastragathi and Ruthani horsemen, this morning. They didn't get very far. Our own Sastragathi troopers and the Mounted Rifles made quick work of them. Captain-General Halmoth reported that the enemy irregulars took over three hundred casualties—and that's just the bodies they counted."

"Excellent, Halmoth has done a good job with the Rifles. Another thing, he didn't run up the casualty list." Kalvan didn't like inflated body counts. He'd seen enough of that in Korea. "So, the Styphoni haven't gotten desperate enough to give rifles to the light cavalry?"

His Intelligence Chief shook his head emphatically. "No! They don't trust them, nor should they. If any of the Sastragathi tribesmen were to get a rifle, they would run away at the first opportunity. Owning a rifle would buy any one of them a chieftainship in the Sastragath, or across the Great River. Plus, the Styphoni don't have any rifles to spare. There are probably less than two or three hundred rifles in the entire host."

"Well, that's good news. If Great King Phidestros had come, it might have been a horse of a different color."

"Yes, Praise Dralm and Galzar, that Captain-General Hestophes was so successful in his negotiations. Regardless, we are still badly outnumbered."

Kalvan nodded. That spoke for itself. The Hostigi force had better troops, better weapons and better morale. That had to count for something. Other than pray to Galzar, there wasn't anything more that he could do about it.

"How is the Admiral doing with the blockade of the Malthros River?"

Skranga smiled. "Very well, sire. Not a dinghy or rowboat has gotten past his ships since they were stationed there a moon-quarter ago. They've captured enough provisions to keep the Navy fed until year's end. The Styphoni will get no relief from that quarter, not with their own fleets in shambles and disarray."

"Good. I understand that much of the city's provisions are stored in warehouses near the waterfront. Correct?"

"Yes, Your Majesty. Over half of their provisions and supplies are kept there, most likely for fast shipment."

Kalvan smiled widely. "Maybe we can do something about that."

II

Even at his table in the Supreme Priest's private sanctuary, Anaxthenes could hear the distant thunder as more rain fell upon the city. It almost sounded like gunfire. He knew that no matter what he did soon the thunder would be replaced by the roar of Hostigi guns. It was unfortunate that he didn't have a bolt hole he could use if the enemy entered the city and things went bad. His future was inextricably intertwined with that of Balph; either the Great Host of Styphon defeated the Hostigi, or the Innermost Circle of Styphon's House was doomed.

There was a knock at the door and one of his servants informed him that Grand Commander Grythos, head of the Great Host, wanted to speak with him.

"Bid him enter."

The burly archpriest came into the room like a charging bull. Throwing out his arms, he said, "Your Divinity, the Hostigi naval ships have destroyed the docks!"

"Aha! I thought I heard gunfire," Anaxthenes said. "They can be repaired."

"True," Grand Commander Grythos replied. "But the Hostigi ships have also destroyed most of the harbor warehouses, which contain over a third of our provisions and supplies."

"Why didn't our guns stop them?" he asked.

Grythos shrugged. "The Hostigi warships have whole banks of guns on each side. It didn't take them long to dispatch our old bombards. For too long, the Temple has been complacent. We have let our past success blind us."

Anaxthenes nodded. "True. And, now we are paying for it. If the Usurper's ships have the river blockaded, the docks are worthless. Do we not have more than enough foodstuffs and ordnance in the temple storage bins to feed the army and keep them supplied?"

"Yes, unless the siege drags on for over three or four seasons," Grythos replied.

"Then I don't foresee a problem. If we don't defeat the Hostigi before then, it won't matter."

"True, Your Divinity. The men's morale is high and we outnumber the Hostigi almost two to one."

"Then it is up to you to bring the battle to the Usurper and defeat him. There are great honors for you, Grythos, if you can defeat the Daemon Kalvan. Your name will go down in history as one of the great captain-generals, such as Erasthames and Simocles the Great. If not, we will all perish."

Grand Commander Grythos all but preened.

"How are our allies faring?" he asked.

"Great King Geblon is always complaining. Ever since word has arrived that a second Hostigi army has entered Hos-Harphax he has badgered me to return home. He fears that Great Queen Rylla will take revenge upon his wife."

"I hope you have not encouraged his request," Anaxthenes replied. The last thing they needed was to lose one of their allies, even one as feckless as Geblon.

Grythos shook his head. "I pointed out that no one is leaving Balph without your permission, Your Divinity. Furthermore, now that the Hostigi control the river, there is no way for him to return to Harphax City by sea. Even Geblon is not fool enough to try and take his army overland. However, should he attempt such a stunt, it might help relieve the siege by drawing off some of Kalvan's forces."

Anaxthenes rubbed his chin. "Hmm. If Geblon attempts to leave Balph, let him go."

Grythos smiled. "It may well be to our advantage, although I wouldn't expect too much from the Harphaxi army."

"Understood, but what about the Ktemnoi contingent?" Anaxthenes asked.

"Great King Lukthos put Lord Marshal Malthros in charge of the Hos-Ktemnoi army. He has fought Kalvan before and understands what defeat will mean to both him and his overlord."

Anaxthenes smiled. "It is nice to know that not all of our allies are fools. Unless they depart, we will use Geblon and his Harphaxi army as cannon fodder. I had anticipated using Great King Niclophon and the Blethan army in that role, but Geblon has won the prize. Back them up with Styphon's Own Guard so that they will not be able to recoil or retreat. Then, let Kalvan's guns chew them to pieces!"

III

Kalvan had established his headquarters in what had formerly been the Cryd mayor's office. The town of Cryd was a small harbor port on Mythros River and ideal for use as a collection depot for provisions and armaments coming from Hos-Bletha. Plus, from here he and Admiral Herad could coordinate further bombardments of Balph. The Admiral had already accomplished his primary goal, the destruction of the Balph wharfs and docks, as well as the harbor warehouses. While it was not a crippling blow, it served to remind the Styphoni that worse was on the way.

Captain-General Halmoth knocked the dottle out of his pipe on his boot heel, then paused to relight his pipe with a burning splinter from the fireplace. After drawing in some smoke and exhaling, he said, "We're only two days march from Balph. Is it wise to stay here for so long, Your Majesty?"

Chief Skranga nodded in agreement.

"I want to give the troops a chance to rest up. Finally, the rain has stopped and they need to dry out. Plus, I'm hoping to draw the Styphoni host out of Balph. I've had more than enough sieges for one campaign season."

Halmoth snorted. "So have I. I only hope this siege will wrap up as nicely as the siege of Tarr-Ceros."

Kalvan nodded. "That won't happen, Halmoth. Having Grand Master Soton publicly renounce Styphon was a big win for us. Another thing to be thankful for is that Soton's not in Balph riding herd over the Great Host of Styphon's Deliverance. As he's proved before, he's the best Temple commander Styphon's House had; I believe they're going to miss him."

"True," Halmoth replied. "We have another problem: Our scouts to the south have reported that over two hands of villages and small towns there are suffering from the Great Pox. We need to warn Great King Valthros in case some of them flee over the border into Hos-Bletha."

The Great Pox was what here-and-now they called smallpox. From what he'd learned, it was even worse than the version of the disease they'd eradicated—probably because it hadn't been tamed. "Good point. We also need to be careful that any scouts we send into that area have pox scars."

"Why, sire?" Skranga asked, his forehead furrowed.

"Once a person survives the pox, the body builds up—" Kalvan paused for a moment to try and frame immunity to someone who was ignorant of modern theories of disease. "The body fights diseases much like we fight Styphoni propaganda. Once we explained that the fireseed devils were not real; the people accepted that, because no devils ever appeared when they used our fireseed. Therefore, in the future they were less susceptible to future lies by Styphon's House. The human body works in a similar manner."

Skranga nodded. "Then the body, having already fought the pox devils and survived, is safe from future attacks."

"Exactly, Chief," he said, pleased to see that Skranga had grasped the concept so quickly. "Therefore, we need to find those soldiers who have survived the Great Pox and use them to guard our southern arm."

"Very wise, Your Majesty," Halmoth said, nodding his head. "I'll have all my captains go through their muster lists and have them send me all the soldiers who have survived the pox. That way if the sick villagers decide to flee north, we can contain them without getting the plague."

IV

From the corner of her eye, Great Queen Lavena noticed as Chancellor Lyphannes entered her private chamber. Baby Sirna was flailing about on her lap and yelling at the top of her lungs. Lavena had a headache so bad it felt as though her head were the battlefield of writhing fireseed demons.

She screamed at her nursemaid, "Take the baby to the nursery! I can't take this crying anymore!"

The nursemaid grabbed little Sirna and ran from the room, her face as pale as a nearby alabaster statue of Yirtta Allmother.

"What do you want?" she demanded, turning to face Lyphannes.

"I have news," the Chancellor said reluctantly.

"Yes, about what?"

"The Hostigi Army is now within a day's journey of the city walls, Your Majesty."

She sucked in a deep breath, forcing herself to remain calm. "Has there been any word from Great King Geblon?"

The Chancellor shook his head.

Well, she thought, *he's deserted me, too. It figures: men, you can't trust any of them.* "How many Hostigi should we expect?"

"Fifteen to twenty thousand, Your Majesty," he said, obviously shaken. Lyphannes was obviously aware that Rylla would have plans made for him, as well the Great Queen. Nobody nursed a grudge better than Great Queen Rylla, unless it was Lavena's late father. Maybe it ran in the family.

"Go get Captain-General Wilkros and bring him to my chamber," she ordered.

"Yes, Your Majesty."

She was smoking her second pipeful of tobacco when Captain-General Wilkros entered the chamber, trailed by the Chancellor. He was an old man, bent and crooked, but he had a stiff spine compared to the other captains her husband had left behind.

"How bad is it, Captain-General?"

His slender hand shook as he tugged at his long white beard. "Very bad, Your Majesty. The Great King took much of the city watch as well as the Royal Army and his own bodyguard. We have less than five thousand men guarding the walls."

"What about the City Bands?" Lavena asked.

He actually spat on the marble tiles. "Pshaw! Styphon's Own refuse! I've already had them mustered out—less than half of them showed up, maybe forty bands—four to five thousand men. I fear that Your Majesty's recent budget cuts have left many of the militia bands with weapons and armor their fathers would have considered old and decrepit. We do have lots of fireseed, but even that's of dubious quality."

It was all coming back to her. She should have spent more on arms and training, rather than galas and rich furnishings for the palace. But who had ever predicted that the Great Queen Rylla would dare to attack Harphax from the west, while Kalvan was busy investing Balph?

"Can we stop them?" she asked, her voice shaking.

"For a few days, Your Majesty. Once their guns go to work on the gates, nothing we have will keep them out. I suggest you open the gates and parley with their commander."

Lavena shuddered, as she imagined what kind of welcome she would receive from her cousin Rylla. "Will your men fight?"

Captain-General Wilkros shrugged. "Maybe, for a few days. Most will surrender the moment the gates are sundered. I heartily suggest you meet and offer terms before the enemy's blood is heated up. By then it may be too late."

She nodded wearily.

THIRTY-THREE

I

Chancellor Lyphannes, wearing his silver chain of office, looked up and down the corridor before he opened the door to the private chamber deep in the bowels of the castle. Seated at the long table were the Master-at-Arms of Tarr-Harphax, the Lord High Mayor and a dozen or more of the most important merchants and officials in Harphax City. Behind them, a large fire was roaring in the stone hearth, throwing shadows on the wall hangings and tapestries.

Lyphannes took a seat at the head of the table, pushing his chair as close as his large belly would allow.

The Lord Mayor spoke first: "Chancellor, we have to do something! The Hostigi are almost at the city gates."

Lyphannes nodded, turning to the Master-at-Arms, he said, "How long can we keep them out of the city?"

The grizzled Master-at-Arms shook his head. "A few days, at best. Great King Geblon left only a token garrison, and most of those were the dregs of the Harphaxi Army." He paused to spit on the stone floor. "The City Militia aren't worth the fireseed it'll take to blow them to Regwarn! Curse Geblon and the she-bitch he left behind!"

"What do you think will happen when the Hostigi bust through the gates?" Lyphannes asked.

"Pure mayhem! They'll sack this city like it hasn't been done in a hundred and fifty winters. No man will be safe, no woman will retain her virtue and no house will escape unscathed. It'll be a disaster!"

"We must stop them somehow!" the Lord Mayor cried out. "We've all got too much to lose, to allow this Hostigi plague loose upon our city."

"I agree," the Chancellor said. "However, the Great Queen demands that we prepare for a long siege and keep the Hostigi Army out of the city."

"Will she be fighting atop the walls?" a fat merchant asked.

"No," the Master-at-Arms replied, spitting on the floor again. "She'll be hiding in the safety of our private chamber with her nursemaids. Nor, will all of Lavena's words keep the city walls from tumbling down! We all know that Great Queen Rylla despises Lavena and blames her and her bastard father for the Hostigi defeat at the hands of the Grand Host of Styphon, leading to the fall of Tarr-Hostigos and her father's death. Rylla won't be placated until Lavena's head decorates the city gates."

"Then let's give the Hostigi spitfire what she wants," one of the Barons said.

Lyphannes smiled to himself, careful to keep it off his face. The meeting was going even better than he had expected. After a year of being humiliated and kowtowing to that she-devil Lavena, he was about to get his revenge.

"Great Queen Rylla and Great King Kalvan have no personal stake in sacking our city," the Lord Mayor opined. "If we can give Rylla what she wants, maybe she'll leave us in peace."

The Chancellor doubted that, but it would give them a bargaining point—as well as keep their own heads from being cut off. Rylla was known to be a devilish opponent and not one to forgive a slight. "If many Hostigi soldiers die breaking through our city walls, Great Queen Rylla might well take her ire out on those she holds responsible—that is, the people in this room."

Everyone at the table nodded.

"What can we do to prevent this miscarriage?" the fat merchant asked, sweat now dripping off his nose.

Lyphannes turned to the Master-at-Arms and nodded.

As prearranged, the battered old veteran stood up over the table and its occupants. "We give Great Queen Rylla what she really wants."

"And what is that?" someone asked.

"Queen Lavena's head!"

II

Kalvan watched from a gentle rise as the Hostigi army wheeled into position. Next to him rode Duke Skranga, his Chief of Intelligence, and Vanar Halgoth.

They were positioned over four miles away from the gates of the Holy City of Balph. Captain-General Alkides, commander of the Hostigi Artillery, was busy setting his batteries in position. Kalvan could hear the squeal of turning axles, the thud of heavy guns dropped into position and snorting horses. From this distance, only the battery of rifled guns could actually reach the positon outside the gates where the Styphoni Army had arrayed itself, some sixty thousand strong.

The rest of the artillery would be held in reserve. His plan was to pound the Styphoni forces into submission or force them to retreat back behind the city walls. It was going to be a lot like shooting fish in a barrel.

The poor bastards would think Galzar was raining cannonballs down upon their heads when the first salvo reached them from such a distance. Styphoni smoothbore gunfire was good for about two and a half miles—if that, since the fireseed they used was Styphon's Best—they would either have to remain in position and take it, or charge directly into the face of the Hostigi army. If they were smart, they'd retreat behind the city gates.

Colonel Leukestros rode up to his position with two mounted riflemen. "Your Majesty!"

"What now?" he asked.

"There's another force of Styphoni cavalry to the west."

"How large, Colonel?"

"About twenty thousand horse, maybe more. Captain-General Halmoth of the Mobile Force begs your permission to set up a field of fire."

The Hostigi army was deployed with the right flank along the river and the rest of the Hostigi aligned along an east-west axis facing Balph's main gates. As Kalvan saw it, the Styphoni plan was to hit the Hostigi rear with their cavalry while the infantry struck from the front. Considering their numerical superiority, the terrain and lack of cover, it wasn't a bad plan.

"Tell Halmoth to take to the ground with the Mobile Force. I'll send Colonel Leukestros and four thousand dragoons in support." About two-thirds of the dragoons were armed with rifles, the rest pikes and pistols. That would give the Baron almost eight thousand men, the majority of them armed with rifles.

"Yes, Your Majesty."

"Also, and I want you to be quite clear on this point, I want Halmoth to order his men to fire on the horses, *not* their riders."

Leukestros blanched. Like most cavalrymen, he had more affection for horses than the men who rode them. "But why, sire?"

"When a cavalry horse goes down, Colonel, it not only dismounts its rider, causing him grievous injuries, but it may take down two or three horses behind or around him as they attempt to jump or stumble over its body. I've seen cases where a few downed horses took out an entire troop."

"Yes, Your Majesty," Leukestros said somewhat stiffly. Obviously he agreed, even if he didn't like the message.

Kalvan didn't mind ruffling a few feathers as long as it got the job done.

III

Grand Commander Grythos stayed at the rear of Styphon's Host along with the other commanders, Great King Niclophon, Lord Marshal Malthros of Hos-Ktemnos and half a dozen captain-generals and princes.

"What in Galzar's name are the Usurper's men doing?" Niclophon asked.

Marshal Malthros shrugged, while Grand Commander Grythos—looking through one of the Hostigi farseers captured during the Siege of Tarr-Hostigos—said, "They only have a single battery of guns guarding their center. It appears the Hostigi have gone to ground. They want us to charge them."

"Look at all those guns they have in reserve!" Malthros exclaimed. "It would be suicide. They have over a hundred cannon, some of them big thirty-pounders or more!"

So it appears. Then why are they using their main body of guns as a reserve? Grythos wondered. *Are they trying to lure us into a charge?* He looked closely at their own small artillery force now arrayed before the Grand Host; he doubted they numbered more than twenty guns. A formidable force, only if Kalvan were stupid enough to charge them in a direct advance. Having fought the Hostigi Great King on several occasions, he could not foresee such a thing happening.

From the center of the Hostigi artillery force, the two batteries of guns fired and a thunderclap struck their ears. He was shocked when most of the cannonballs not only hit the army, killing a score of men and dismembering others, but a few actually struck the city walls behind them.

"What in Ormaz's Caverns was that?" Great King Niclophon demanded.

"Flying death!" Malthros shouted. "The Hostigi are almost ten marches away. What kind of demon fireseed are they using?"

"It can't be!" exclaimed one of the artillery captains, a mercenary from Hos-Zygros.

"Can't be what?" Grythos demanded. "What are you talking about?"

"Rifled cannon. Captain-General Kyblannos of the Zygrosi Royal Army has been talking about those for years. He claimed that if one could figure out how to rifle gun barrels, it would change siegecraft forever."

Another Hostigi salvo went off. This time several of the lead companies fell back, as though they could back away from the flying death about to smash into their ranks. Moments later the iron balls struck their midst spraying blood and body parts. The entire front began to recoil.

"We'd better retreat back behind the city walls, or we'll be crushed!" Niclophon cried out.

"By Styphon's Bollocks!" Grythos cursed. "Captain-General Syros, give the horns the order to retreat and get those Dralm-damned gates open!"

As the gates slowly opened and the Great Host wheeled, another salvo of cannonballs struck them, disordering the ranks and causing some to panic—horses riding over infantry, infantry running like turkeys with their heads cut off. Soon the entire Host was scrambling to fight their way through the gates of Balph and into the city.

IV

Kalvan was amazed when he saw the effect the new rifled cannon batteries had on the Grand Host of Styphon's House. Even in his wildest dreams, he had not expected such results. Men were riding their horses over those behind them in their hurry to get back inside the walls for protection, while others were scrambling away from the gates in a mad panic. It was like kicking over an ant hill.

Chief of Hostigos Intelligence Skranga, cackled in delight. "They do not like your new guns, Your Majesty!"

Kalvan nodded. "I know. They'll keep them penned in behind their walls."

"What about the cavalry force?" Skranga asked.

"They will either have to advance or retreat. I'm sure their commanders would rather die in their saddles than retreat ignobly."

"Praise Galzar!" Skranga exclaimed, clapping his hands. "By tonight, Ormaz's Caverns will be stuffed to overflowing with Styphoni dead."

V

Captain-General Halmoth levered himself up to a higher branch on the longleaf pine tree. The upper trunk swayed, as he rubbed the sticky gum off on his blue trousers. From his new position, he could see the main Styphoni force retreating back into Balph. Kalvan's new rifled guns had put the fear of Regwarn in those whoredogs!

Halmoth turned to watch the cavalry force about two marches away. They were beginning to mount up, but he still wasn't sure if that meant they were going to return to Balph or charge his detachment. Then he saw one of the commanders pointing in their direction. He dropped down from the pine tree as fast as dignity and safety would allow. Since the longleaf pine trees naturally pruned their lower branches, his major concern was not impaling his privy parts.

"Colonel Leukestros!" he called out, as he hit the ground.

"Yes, Captain General."

"It looks like those whoresons are going to advance. Prepare the men."

"Yes, sir."

When the enemy horse reached the mark Halmoth had set in his mind, he gave the order, "FIRE!"

A loud volley of rifle fire cracked the air, and he watched as five score or more of horses jerked and dropped, many of them severely wounded and dying. With the second volley, twice as many horses dropped, completely disordering the front ranks. Horses were tripping over fallen animals and men, falling sideways and on top of dismounted riders and dying horses.

The screams of wounded horses were now competing with the sound of gunfire. He watched as the succeeding ranks ran into the fallen and milling horses, breaking up and disordering their charge. Many were stomping their riders into the ground. The next volley took the fire right out of the charge and the rear ranks began to recoil and redress themselves.

"Open fire!" Halmoth ordered. "Now, take out the men!" He was certain that their next move would be to retreat and he was determined to inflict as many casualties as possible before the Styphoni cavalry returned to the safety of their walls.

THIRTY-FOUR

I

As they watched the distant Styphoni cavalry fall into a disordered retreat, Captain-General Hestophes turned to Kalvan. "Your Majesty, it looks like that bunch is headed back to the city, too."

Kalvan nodded. "The fighting is over for today. I was hoping for a few more casualties."

Hestophes laughed. "Now you're sounding like Rylla! It's not even noon yet, and I suspect the Styphoni lost a few thousand men, at no cost to us. It was almost too easy. They'll be like turtles from now on; I don't expect they'll leave the safety of the city walls again."

Kalvan agreed. "Now, we're going to have to besiege the city," he said as he studied the layout of the Holy City. Balph was perched right on the waterfront of the Mythros River while the rest of the city formed a large oval with the Golden Temple of Styphon's House at the center. There was an uneven ditch running around the entire city; Kalvan suspected that at one time it had been a moat, fed by the Mythros River. It had been abandoned long ago and partially filled in.

"Where are we going to hit them?" Hestophes asked. "The city gates?"

Kalvan shook his head. "They've been reinforcing the gates for several moons." He pointed to where the moat was almost completely filled in. "That's where we'll hit them. Our big thirty-twos will make short work of that wall."

"Then what?"

Kalvan spat on the ground disgustedly. "Then we'll take the city block by block. Dralm damn-it!"

"That's going to be expensive," Hestophes noted.

"City warfare is the most costly fighting of all," he replied. "But I don't see any other alternative."

II

"What happened out there?" Styphon's Voice screeched. "Why did the entire Host retreat?"

Grand Commander Grythos threw out his hands in disgust. "We were out-gunned and out-maneuvered. Kalvan has some new-fangled cannon that shoots twice as far as any gun I've ever seen. It would have been suicide to stay in our position any longer."

"What do we do now?"

"We wait for him to attack the walls. Then we throw everything we have at him."

"Will that work?" Anaxthenes asked, puffing like a long-distance runner.

"It better, because it's all we've got."

"What about our bolt hole?"

"Too late. Kalvan's men have encircled the entire city. His Sastragathi outriders are pillaging the countryside and taking prisoners. Anyone they find outside Balph who's been circumcised, they're slitting their throats—low priest, underpriest, or highpriest. There's no way out. We either stop the Usurper inside these walls, or we all die."

"What about Great King Lukthos? Can we get word to him?"

Grythos shook his head sadly. "Lukthos has already sent us his best men and they're penned up inside Balph like lambs ready for the slaughter house. Any men he has left will be busy protecting him in the event Balph falls."

III

Prince Sarrask watched with bated breath as the small group of nobles and wealthy merchants slowly rode out of the Harphax City gates. Most were wearing their finest garments and fur cloaks, despite the heat. Their upside-down flag indicated it was a parley. One of the men held up two poles, which was topped by what appeared to be a head with long black hair.

He heard Great Queen Rylla's intake of breath when she realized that it was Lavena's head that graced one of the poles. Then she grabbed Sarrask's vambrace with her gauntlet so hard that her grip would have fractured his arm had he not been wearing armor.

There was a tiny head on the other pole, a baby's. *It must be Princess Sirna!* "Stab me!" Sarrask cried out.

"Dralm-damnit, Sarrask!" Rylla cursed. "I'll have all their heads!"

"Hush, Your Majesty," Uncle Wolf Tharses said in a harsh whisper. "These pox-ridden fools only think they are doing your will. If you insult them now, we may have to take the city by force. It won't be hard, but hundreds of Hostigi lives will be needlessly spent."

"But they killed her baby!" she whispered in a tone that almost turned into a screech. Nearby eyes were searching her out. Fortunately, the city notables were not close enough to overhear her words.

"Remember Phaxos, Your Majesty," Sarrask said.

"How could I forget," she replied.

"After we sacked Phaxos Town, you had the Prince and his entire family executed, including the children."

Her face blanched.

"Well, these Harphaxi whey-faced varlets haven't forgotten!" Sarrask exclaimed, banging the pommel of his saddle for emphasis. "These fools believe they are doing your will. With Lavena and her daughter dead, there will be no chance that in years to come a pretender to the Iron Throne will arise, claiming to be the husband of Princess Sirna, the rightful claimant by birth. And, as you know, there is some truth to their fears."

Rylla released his arm, then nodded.

"They believe they have done you a great honor, Your Majesty. Now, it is up to you to accept their offerings with the same grace in which they are presented."

She smiled through gritted teeth.

"Now, which one of these knaves do you plan to make the next Great

King of Hos-Harphax?" he asked.

"None of them. How about you, Sarrask?"

His face turned ashen, then he shook his head mightily. "No, no, no…. Stab me, Your Majesty! It's a thankless job. I prefer to be a big turtle in a small lagoon. I've seen all the headaches running the great kingdoms of Hostigos have given you and Great King Kalvan. Such is not for me!"

"That's why you'd be the best man for the job," Rylla replied, her eyes twinkling. "Great King Sarrask has a nice ring to it."

"Not to these ears!" he cried out.

"I'm sorry, but there are not a lot of choices. Prince Soligon of Argros and Prince Valthames of Xanx are dead. The only surviving prince from the League of Dralm, is the man who succeeded Valthames, Prince Davtor. And one has to wonder how he kept his position after Lysandros' enthronement, then during Geblon's reign."

"Better him than me. I'm not known to the Harphaxi and there will be problems if I ascend to the Iron Throne, Your Majesty."

"There will *not* be a problem, Sarrask. I promise. I plan to remove all the Styphoni princes and replace them with our own men. It will be a wholesale housecleaning, as Kalvan would put it, of the entire Kingdom of Hos-Harphax. Anyone who has a problem with your ascension will have to answer to me personally!"

"How about Duke Hestophes? Your Majesty—a wonderful choice for great king! Or Prince Phrames. Or maybe King Chartiphon. Duke Skranga? Anyone but *me!*"

IV

It was early morning, but shots still rang out in the streets of Agrys City. Prince Mnestros had done as promised, launching an attack on the city the night before, drawing the garrison troops to the city walls. Then the rebels had struck from behind, killing many of the Styphoni even before they knew what was happening. Baron Balthron had been true to his word, using his men to clear the palace of Prince-Regent Grythos' guardsmen and Styphoni priests.

The Styphoni had not died easily, and the presence chamber still stank of death and voided bowels.

Lady Tymolara ordered Prince Dementros to seat himself upon the Throne.

"But why?" Dementros asked.

"Because we need to establish precedent. While you are still too young to be enthroned, such rules are often ignored or changed in times of great upheaval. With Archpriest Grythos in Balph and his allies and representatives in Agrys City all dead, there is no one to challenge your claim to the Throne of Lights."

"But I'm not really Dementros," he put forth. "I'm Aspasthar, a citizen and noble of Hos-Hostigos, and the son of Harmakros the Great."

She whispered, "Keep your voice down! You are all of that, Aspasthar—and more. Your Great King has given you the opportunity to raise yourself far above your station, while aiding him in creating a better and more peaceful world."

"But that means I won't be able to return to my friends and homeland—"

"True," she interrupted. "But is that so terrible? Here you will be able to rule an entire kingdom and you can bring any of your Hostigi friends that want to join you here."

The boy brightened up.

Several soldiers came in and began dragging the Styphoni dead out of the presence chamber by their boot heels, while servants and maids began to clean the walls and floors. In another couple of hours, no one would know that two score of men died violently in this chamber.

She turned to the door, when Baron Balthron entered the chamber followed by a small retinue of soldiers. Their boots clomped loudly as they approached the Throne of Lights.

This was the critical moment, she realized. If the Baron accepted Dementros' enthronement, then there would be little opposition. On the other hand, he could easily—by virtue of being in command of the rebel soldiers—take the seat for himself.

She did not know the Baron well, nor how he had survived during the

Styphoni occupation. He was a big man with a rough-hewn face that displayed little of what went on behind his skull.

Balthron looked her in the eyes, then turned to the throne. "So, I see you've made your choice."

Lady Tymolara pointed to the still blood-splattered floor and said, "Your Lordship, I believe that we need to coronate our new great king as quickly as possible. Otherwise, a succession struggle will only enable the Styphoni opposition, which would leave us weak and indecisive should the Hostigi be defeated in Hos-Ktemnos."

"Yes, My Lady, that makes sense. We need to be united in the face of the former Prince-Regent's return. However, I had thought you might have wanted the position of Prince-Regent for yourself."

She shook her head. "Lord Balthron, I know my bloodline and my limitations. I'm a good governess, but I know little about governing."

The Baron guffawed. "I doubt that, Your Ladyship, having seen you at work. However, I believe you are correct. Hos-Agrys needs to be united against the Styphoni so that we can throw off their shackles once and for all. Prince Mnestros might be a better choice for great king, but he has his work cut out for him liberating the rest of Hos-Agrys. It would be a disservice to the Kingdom to distract him from his work."

"Then we should do the official enthronement as soon as possible," she replied. "Did any of the upperpriests of Dralm survive the culling?"

The Baron nodded. "Several of them have been in hiding. I will bring the ranking priest to the palace tomorrow morning for the official enthronement. It will also give the people something else to celebrate, as well as help take their minds off the losses we have suffered today and during the Styphoni occupation."

V

Great King Phidestros entered his bedchamber with a scowl on his face. Queen Arminta sat up in bed, fluffed her goose down pillows, asking, "What's the matter, my love?"

Phidestros put down the oil lamp he'd been holding. "I just received word from Harphax that Queen Rylla and a Hostigi Army are at the outskirts of Harphax City. With most of the Harphaxi Army in Balph, this could cost Geblon the Iron Throne."

Arminta sighed. "A throne he should never have been seated upon in the first place. While Geblon is an old comrade, he is no more qualified to be great king than a butcher. Just because a soldier knows how to wield a sword doesn't mean he knows how to carve a carcass of beef. Look at how Geblon has misruled Hos-Harphax, letting that she-devil Lavena run roughshod over the kingdom. It's a wonder that their subjects haven't revolted in protest against their high taxes and capricious enforcement of laws."

Phidestros knocked on his head repeatedly with his knuckles. "I know, I know! I didn't think his appointment through, nor did I confer with you about it. My mistake. The last thing I expected was Geblon to become lovesick over that she-wolf Lavena."

"Well, it's going to cost him his throne. That is, if he returns from Balph alive."

He nodded. "It's still too early for news about the siege, but I would put my wager on Great King Kalvan."

"You already have, my dear," Arminta replied with a smile. "And we stand to earn a good return on our investment."

He rolled his shoulders uncomfortably. "I still don't feel good about not backing my old comrade."

"Let's not go there, my love. It was Geblon who snubbed you when he kept our envoy and his old friend Kyblannos waiting in Harphax City for three moons for a simple audience. And we know who was behind that stall. No, it is your old comrade, the man you elevated, who let *us* down. Nor did you encourage him to take his army to Balph in support of our enemy!"

"That is true," Phidestros said, as he picked up his pipe. "He had to have known that I would never support such a move. Not after the Styphoni curs kidnapped you, my love. Geblon must be truly addled to have made such a foolhardy mistake."

"No, he's just a man who doesn't know how to swim, who suddenly found himself drowning in a deep well. Any news from Hos-Agrys?"

Phidestros paused to light his pipe, before speaking: "Prince Mnestros continues to make progress against the Styphoni forces in Kryphlon. At last report, Mnestros and his men were on the outskirts of Kryphlon City. Prince Atron is untested in war and will not hold his capital for long. There is also unrest in Agrys City since Prince-Regent Grythos left the city for Balph. It wouldn't take much to upset the entire Styphoni applecart."

Arminta smiled. "Yes, I know, you long for some action. This is the first war where you have had to sit on the sidelines and miss all the fighting. But you have nothing to prove, my love. Along with Kalvan and Grand Master Soton, you are held throughout the Five Kingdoms to be one of the three greatest commanders of this age. No one can deny that, and Styphon's House would give you all their golden temples to win your support. Great King Kalvan went to great lengths to win your favor and it was a wise decision. Nor will he forget you when peace comes, as it inevitably will do."

Phidestros began chuffing his pipe, throwing out smoke rings. Then he pulled out the pipe stem, saying, "I'm a man of action. It's no fun waiting idly by when so many opportunities are within ones grasp."

Arminta giggled. "You're like a big kid! We don't need any more 'opportunities,' my love. We have enough on our plate ruling Hos-Zygros. Sure we could go south and add the Agrysi princedoms of Orchon and Meligos to the kingdom with minimal losses, but we're still busy swallowing the Princedom of Kelos. There isn't enough gold in either princedom to pay for the headaches that incorporating them into Hos-Zygros would cost us."

Phidestros put down his pipe and dropped his head. "As usual, you are right, my love." He grabbed the bell pull. "I'm going to request a flask of Ermut's Best. Would you like some, too?"

"Yes," she replied playfully.

THIRTY-FIVE

I

As Prince Mnestros rode through the gates of Agrys City, he was shocked by the blasted buildings, burnt stores and the ruins that looked as if they'd been untouched for years. He hadn't been inside the city for over five winters and many of the sights and places he remembered were gone or in disrepair. It appeared that Prince-Regent Grythos had done little to repair the damage the Styphoni siege had brought upon the city. Once, the wealthiest city in the Five Kingdoms, Agrys City was now a place of desolation and poverty.

Baron Balthron, who had met him outside and provided an escort, turned to him and said, "It makes me sick every time I look upon the damage those manure-eating priests have cast upon our home."

As they approached the center of town, the damage was less apparent and people began to appear, some of them waving and throwing flowers at their small procession. A few held up idols of Dralm and Yirtta Allmother. Before Archpriest Grythos left, simple ownership of those images would have cost these followers their very lives.

"The people of Agrys City appreciate your sacrifice, Prince Mnestros. Praise Galzar! Without your attack upon the walls to draw the Styphoni soldiers' attention, our counterattack might well have failed."

"We've been fortunate, Baron. Archpriest Grythos stripped too many soldiers from the southern princedoms to take with him to Balph. Our forces have been able to liberate the Princedoms of Glarth, Eubros, Varthon, Kryphlon, Cythor and soon all of Hos-Agrys, north of the city. When our army entered Cythor, the people rose up against their rulers and hung them from the nearest tree limbs. The Styphoni soldiers and their allies fled into Arbelon without firing a shot! We now have over twenty thousand soldiers to fight against the Styphoni occupiers and their collaborators—with more joining every day."

Baron Balthron spit on the ground. "A pox on all the Styphoni blasphemers! I'm overjoyed at your success. However, this news will not be greeted with joy when it reaches Balph."

"I doubt they'll even notice," Mnestros said, laughing. "They've got the Army of Hos-Hostigos to worry about. The Hostigi are already at the gates of Balph!"

"This is wonderful news!" Balthron cried.

"Furthermore, we have just learned that Great Queen Rylla and her army have taken Harphax City without firing a shot!"

"What about Great Queen Lavena?"

"She was beheaded by her own subjects. If Geblon the Usurper should survive the attack on Balph, he'll find no support or joy upon his return to Hos-Harphax. The Styphoni reign of terror in the Northern Great Kingdoms has come to an end!"

"Praise Galzar and Allfather Dralm!" Balthron cried out. Then he turned serious. "I need to warn you that Prince Dementros was enthroned this morning as the Great King of Hos-Agrys." As the Baron waited for Mnestros' response, he drew back as if he expected a blow.

"Praise Dralm and Galzar!" Prince Mnestros cried out.

"Praise the True Gods! Some advisors here were worried that you might desire the throne. Not that you don't deserve it. We didn't want to slight you, after helping us to rid the city of Styphon's minions, but Dementros has the bloodline of the Agrysi great kings."

"I know," he said. "I met him several winters ago, before he was captured. I was impressed by the boy. I was worried that Grythos would never ever allow him to live long enough to take his rightful place."

"Yes, there was a rumor that the Arch-Devil wanted to take the lad to Balph where he intended to have him murdered."

"I believe it," Prince Mnestros said. "I'm sure the swine would have then enthroned himself. I pray to the gods that he dies in the Siege of

Balph."

"May the gods will it!" Balthron echoed.

As they reached the central plazos, Mnestros noted that the high temples of Yirtta, Dralm and Tranth had been leveled, as well as the newer temple to Styphon.

The Prince pointed to the ruins, saying, "It doesn't appear that the people wasted any time tearing that abomination down!"

"No," Balthron replied. "We stripped the golden tiles from the dome first, then we allowed the people to pull it down. Grythos took most of the Kingdom's treasury with him when he left, so the gold we looted from the Styphoni temples will help restore the city's coffers."

"It will be a start," Mnestros said.

They dismounted and tied up their horses before the palace. Mnestros noted several trails of blood leading from the stairs to the Presence Chamber, where the newly enthroned king sat with Lady Tymolara at his side.

Great King Dementros stood up as soon as he spotted Mnestros, jumping off the dais and running to the Prince with a big hug.

Balthron stood like a statue, his mouth hanging open.

"Prince, we thank you for your attack upon the city walls. They drew the Styphoni like flies to a fresh corpse."

"Thank you, Your Majesty. It's good to see you again; you look healthy, and much bigger!" Mnestros replied.

"It's been a tough couple of years, living under the Arch-Devil's thumb, but we managed with some help," he ended pointing to Lady Tymolara.

"You mean Duchess Lysia," he returned.

"What do you mean duchess?" she asked.

Balthron now looked totally confused. Mnestros turned to the Baron, saying, "When we located the heir, with Grand Master Soton on our trail, we feared the real Lady Tymolara would have a difficult time appeasing Archpriest Grythos and Grand Master Soton. We needed a woman who would not bend under great pressure, so the Duchess Lysia was chosen by Great Queen Rylla to impersonate the governess."

"But who is she?" the Baron asked.

"The Duchess is Captain-General Hestophes' wife."

Mnestros couldn't have dropped one of Kalvan's shells in the center of the room without greater effect.

"The Hostigi Great Captain-General's wife!" Balthron cried.

"Yes, she is his wife."

"What I want to know is where does this duchess nonsense come from?" Lysia demanded.

"Oh, you wouldn't know. Great King Kalvan has elevated your husband to Duke. After the war, sufficient property and monies appropriate to your new status will be provided."

Dementros danced around Lysia. "This is wonderful news." Then he quickly sobered. "Does this mean you'll be leaving Us?"

Mnestros noted that boy was already using the royal we. *He learns fast!*

Lysia shook her head. "Not for some time, Your Majesty. My husband will be busy cleaning the Styphoni stables for quite some time."

II

Kalvan watched from a nearby copse of pine trees as the attack opened. The dark green and maroon colors of Hos-Hostigos were flying in the breeze at his back. It was early morning and there was a light fog that clung to the ground enveloping the artillery. Captain-General Alkides was using three batteries, two batteries of ten eighteen-pound guns and one battery of the thirty-two pounders, against the walls of Balph. From behind, his position was supported by some twelve thousand infantry with two sleeves of cavalry to either side, in case there was an unexpected breakout. The Mobile Force Sharpshooters were charged with the job of keeping the palisades clear of enemy riflemen and musketeers; so far they had swept the battlements free of snipers and observers.

The Styphoni had a big old bombard in the nearest tower and were trying to lever it to where it could fire on the Hostigi batteries, when the battery of eighteen-pounders went off. Half a dozen shots hit the stone tower, knocking the gun backwards, pinning a few men, and wounding the rest of the artillerymen with flying shards of stone. Their screams were audible from Kalvan's position next to the artillery batteries.

"They won't try that again, Your Majesty," Chief Skranga noted.

"No, that was the closest tower to our target area."

A round of explosions, just behind the batteries went off, resulting in loud bangs and geysers of smoke pouring out of the buildings crouched behind the wall.

"What in Galzar's Name was that?" Skranga asked.

"The two mortar batteries I convinced Alkides to bring along. We've got them firing shells over the wall. A couple of days of firing and they'll knock down every building and structure within three blocks to their foundations."

The battery of thirty-two pounders fired, shaking the ground as far away as Kalvan's position. The thick wall shuddered, as stones splattered and cracked along a wide front about twenty yards wide.

"How thick is the wall at the base?" Skranga asked.

"Alkides estimates that the wall here is two to three rods deep," or twelve to eighteen feet thick by otherwhen measurements, Kalvan reckoned. "It's about a third of the width at the wall walk. A hundred and fifty years ago, Balph was the heaviest fortified city in the Five Kingdoms. We're fortunate that they never got around to upgrading it."

The guns fired again, shaking the earth and splattering the wall with loose stones. Several of the cannonballs fractured upon impact, ricocheting shards of hot iron.

"I wouldn't want to be too close to that Dralm-damned wall," Skranga noted.

Kalvan read his lips more than heard him; he'd stuffed his ears with cotton to protect them from the gun blasts. He noted that Skranga, Captain-General Alkides and most of the other artillery men had adopted his idea.

"What are we going to do when the wall comes down?" Skranga asked as the smoke was clearing.

"Achoo!" Kalvan sneezed. The stench of brimstone this close to the artillery batteries was overpowering. When he'd recovered, he said, "We're going to work our way into the city and take it a block at a time, if that's what it takes."

III

"What are they doing to my city?" Styphon's Voice cried. He was half mad from the artillery blasts that had kept him up for the past three nights.

"Tearing it down, a block at a time," Grand Commander Grythos answered. "When their breach is big enough, the Daemon Kalvan's Army will enter Balph and fight us for each and every block."

"Can we stop them?" Anaxthenes implored.

Grythos shrugged. "I have an idea, Your Divinity. One of our couriers just brought a message from Harphax City. It may be the last one."

"What does it say?"

"Upon the approach of Great Queen Rylla and the Army of Hostigos, the Harphax City fathers had Queen Lavena's head chopped off, then surrendered her head and the city to the Hostigi. The Usurper Rylla is already inside Harphax City sacking our temples and killing our priests."

"What good is this news?" Anaxthenes asked.

"No one knows of this disaster, but the two of us."

"What about the courier?"

"I strangled him myself. Dead men carry no tales."

"Good," Anaxthenes said, removing his tobacco pouch from his belt and filling the bowl of his pipe. "What do you plan to do with this news?"

"The last thing we want is King Geblon learning about his wife's death. He's a corroded enough tool as it is."

"And what do you suggest?" Anaxthenes asked, as he fired up his pipe.

"As his commander," Grythos said, "I am going to order him to attack the Hostigi when their breach is wide enough to allow passage of his army."

"What will that accomplish?" he asked.

"It might catch the Hostigi off guard and allow us to break out of this death trap."

"Hmm. That would be a miracle, and I don't believe in them."

Grythos shrugged. "In warfare, an unexpected move can created chaos as well as opportunity. Besides, what do we have to lose?"

Anaxthenes laughed. "What if Geblon refuses? Such a counterattack would be suicidal."

Grythos leaned in. "He will have no choice. Behind him I will muster several bands of Styphon's Own Guard. He will either go forward or die."

"What's to keep him from retreating?"

"The guardsmen will form up behind the Harphaxi Army. If they recoil or falter, they will die where they stand."

IV

After five days of artillery barrages, Kalvan's ears were numb and he had to take the cotton out of them before he could understand what Captain-General Halmoth was trying to tell him.

"It looks like the Styphoni are preparing a counterattack."

"Against our artillery? That's sheer madness!"

"The lead units are wearing the red and yellow colors of Hos-Harphax, Your Majesty."

"What would cause the Harphaxi such distress that they would make a frontal assault upon our big guns?"

Halmoth shook his head.

"Colonel Leukestros, tell Captain-General Alkides to load his guns with case shot and to hold his fire until the attackers reach the gap."

After the Colonel rode off, Kalvan said, "Maybe I'll talk to him myself; I want to see this up-close."

"It could be a trap, Your Majesty," Chief Skranga said worriedly. "It would be best if you waited here in safety."

"What kind of a ruse could it possibly be, Skranga? I'm tired of sitting here, twiddling my thumbs and doing nothing. Let's go talk with Alkides and see what he thinks."

Vanar Halgoth and the Great King's Bodyguard, with their black and white raven banner held high, followed Kalvan to the battlefront. Halmoth shrugged impotently to Skranga, then followed.

"What do you think they're doing, Alkides?" Kalvan asked.

The brown-bearded Captain-General said, "Maybe they're running low on food in Balph and Styphon's Voice decided to decimate their numbers. A full frontal attack on our guns and riflemen is pure death."

Kalvan watched as the Harphaxi force began to move forward. They were still a good thirty feet or so from the breach, but he could make out their red and yellow colors.

"Let them reach the gap before you fire," he ordered.

"Are you sure, Your Majesty? That will barely give us time to reload."

"I'm sure. After your batteries fire, their entire front will be in such a state of shock that they'll be picking themselves up off the ground. I swear by Galzar's Mace, I doubt the few still alive'll have the courage to advance again."

The Harphaxi army was in full movement, cavalry at the fore and the infantry massed behind. Great King Geblon, wearing black armor chased with silver and gold, led the pack with his bannerman beside him. When they were about ten feet from the opening, the Harphaxi banner bearer lowered his flag of Hos-Harphax and the lead horsemen removed their helmets, hoisting them on their swords.

"Are they giving up, or covering up a surprise attack?" Skranga asked.

Kalvan shrugged, shaking his head. "I don't know?"

Captain-General Alkides looked at him questioningly.

"Hold your fire!" Kalvan ordered. Even if it was a ruse, there was little to be gained. A few salvos of the Hostigi guns would clear the field.

The artillery men stood stock-still.

Suddenly, from the rear of the Harphaxi Army, a volley of shots rang out.

"The Styphoni curs in the rear have finally figured out what they're up against," Baron Halmoth noted.

As the Harphax moved across the broken wall, they dropped their pistols and knives, continuing to hold up their helmets. The Hostigi cavalry had moved up to the gap and were busy leading the Harphaxi cavalrymen away from the walls. Great King Geblon and several of his commanders dismounted and advanced, ignoring the gunfire from behind their position. The rest of the Harphaxi followed their lead.

"I think it's time for a parley," Kalvan said.

Chief Skranga was too busy shaking his head in amazement to say anything.

V

They met in Kalvan's temporary headquarters, a hastily built one-room shack with pyrographed deerskin maps of Hos-Ktemnos and Balph covering all four walls. In the middle sat a trestle table with six chairs and candles at both ends, lighting the room. Kalvan sat at the head of the table, with Chief Skranga and Captain-General Halmoth on either side; Great King Geblon sat at the foot by himself.

Kalvan sat silently, waiting for the Harphaxi ruler to explain what had just happened.

Geblon splayed his hands on the table. "First, Your Majesty, I want to apologize for being in the Styphoni camp. I had my reasons, but they are not good ones. I foolishly borrowed a great deal of gold from Styphon's House; in the end, I fear I have sold them my kingdom and good name for next to nothing in return. I am not a worshipper of Styphon, nor have I ever been." He spat on the floor. "In truth, I despise Styphon's House and their false god. I'm just a fool who took their crowns without thinking about what they were buying. After your attack on the gates, I realized that to Styphon's Voice we represented nothing more than cannon fodder and that we would all die inside the city, whether you took it or not.

"At that time, I promised myself I would find a way to save my men; even if it cost me my life. So, here I am beseeching Your Majesty for terms; not for myself, but for my soldiers."

Kalvan nodded. "What you have done in surrendering your men is honorable. Although I doubt Styphon's Voice will see it that way."

They all laughed but Great King Geblon.

"What would you have me do, Your Majesty?"

"First, I would like to have your word of honor that you have renounced Styphon's Voice and will honor your parole and that of your men."

"By Galzar's Great Mace, you have my word of honor, Great King Kalvan. I not only renounce my former allegiance to Styphon's House, but promise to obey your commands until we are released at your will."

He nodded. "I will send Highpriest Kythamos and his Uncle Wolfs to take oaths from all of your soldiers. For now, we'll relocate you and your men to the small town of Dytha."

Kalvan rose and went to the map showing the environs of Balph. He pointed to the circle, south of Balph, representing Dytha. "You will stay there until the siege is ended."

"Thank you, Your Majesty. We were badly treated by the Styphoni, Great King Kalvan. My men would be happy to join yours in an attack upon the ungodly priests of Styphon's House."

Kalvan shrugged. "I believe we have more than enough men to finish the job. However, I will keep your offer in mind."

He turned to Halmoth, saying, "Escort Great King Geblon and Highpriest Kythamos to Dytha Town and take along a proper escort. Return when they are settled in."

"Chief Skranga, you will accompany them. I want you to question them and find out everything you can about what's going on inside Balph: morale, food stocks, gossip—anything that might help."

"With all dispatch, Your Majesty," Skranga said.

Captain-General Hestophes and Chief Skranga led the Harphaxi Great King out the door.

THIRTY-SIX

I

Chief Skranga returned to Hostigi HQ several hours later. He looked thoroughly wrung out. "Sire, I thought I'd give you a preliminary report. I have my agents questioning all the Harphaxi commanders and petty officers. We'll have a complete report ready at first light."

"Good," Kalvan replied. He knew from past experience the report would be thorough and inclusive.

After the headquarters door closed, Chief Skranga asked, "Do you think that's wise to leave them with so few guards, Your Majesty? I thought you would send two or three regiments to guarantee the Harphaxi Army's parole."

"I'm not worried, Skranga. Dytha Town is south of Balph; so there's no place for them to escape. If they go any farther south, they'll run into the Great Pox. Any that survive the pox will have to fight their way through Great King Valthros and the Blethan Army. They have no boats so they can't go east and use the Mythros River to reach the Great Ocean. If they go west, they'll have to face Great King Lukthos and the Ktemnoi Army. Truly, there is no haven for the Harphaxi here. Besides, I believe that Great King Geblon is a man of his word."

"I agree, a foolish man, but one who takes his oaths seriously. This brings me to another matter, Your Majesty."

"Yes?" Kalvan said, sensing Skranga's reluctance.

"I just received a dispatch from my head operative in Harphax City. It appears that the city has capitulated."

"How do you mean?"

"Before Great Queen Rylla reached the walls of Harphax City, the city elders took matters into their own hands and surrendered the city to Rylla without Queen Lavena's permission."

"Well, that's a good thing, Right?"

"Usually, I'd say, yes. However, the elders may have overreached themselves. To placate your wife, they had both the Great Queen and her infant daughter beheaded."

Kalvan's face blanched. "What? I can almost understand why, in view of her arrogant and asinine behavior, they had Great Queen Lavena beheaded. But why her baby daughter?" His voice rose, "Dralm-damnit, was this one of Rylla's terms?"

"No, absolutely not. From what those around her had to say, she was appalled by baby Sirna's beheading. It appears the elders were mistakenly trying to appease your wife."

"I can't understand why they would have thought that killing that infant would help gain her favor."

"From what my agent gathered, they didn't think she would want a child, be it a baby boy or girl with the birthright to the Iron Throne to stay alive, causing future problems. Either by herself, or by those who would use the baby for their own advancement."

Kalvan nodded. Otherwhen history was replete with stories of claimants with royal blood seeking to overthrow the current ruler and regain their thrones. Or manipulated by others using their bloodline to cast doubt on the legitimacy of the current ruler. In this light, he could understand why the Harphaxi representatives may have thought they were doing Rylla and him a good turn. Plus, it kept the blood off their gowns. Still, there must be more to it…. "Is that all?"

"Well, the Harphaxi were well-acquainted with your wife's action in Phaxos, when she removed the ruling prince's entire bloodline, so in their minds there was a precedent." Skranga's face scrunched up. "Not a very good reason, but one can see why they might have come to that conclusion…."

"Ah, Rylla—what have you done?"

"Please, Your Majesty, do not blame your wife. By all accounts, Rylla was as horrified by baby Sirna's execution as yourself. It took a lot of persuasion by Prince Sarrask, Captain-General Hestophes and King Chartiphon to keep her from sacking the city."

"Oh, that would have been a real disaster!"

"I agree. Cooler heads prevailed; a tragedy was averted."

Kalvan still felt as if he were about to lose his lunch. "As you point out, it could have been worse. Poor Rylla. Anything more?"

Skranga's face twisted. "Well, she appointed a new Great King to rule over Hos-Harphax."

"How? Who? Why? By what right?"

Skranga threw his hands out. "She had her reasons, Your Majesty. It appears that every Harphaxi prince who supported either Hos-Hostigos or the League of Dralm either died in battle or was murdered by Styphon's House, leaving only a few Styphoni-supported princes and those Styphon's House elevated to replace those princes who died. A real mare's nest. After all, it's not like Your Majesty is going to allow Geblon to return to Harphax City and remount the Iron Throne."

"True. That's not going to happen."

"In the face of such a power void and not trusting any of the surviving Harphaxi princes, the Great Queen took it upon herself to advance one of her own."

"Her own? Do you mean King Chartiphon?"

"No, he would not want to leave Rathon and his family. Instead she elevated Prince Sarrask of Sask as the new Great King of Hos-Harphax."

"PRINCE SARRASK!!!" Kalvan shouted.

"Please, Your Majesty, think this through," Skranga cried out. "While true, that after your arrival, Prince Sarrask was one of Hostigos' most implacable foes. It is also true that once you defeated his army, he became a valued ally. In fact, there are few among your princes who are more loyal and trustworthy. Is that not the case?"

"Well, there's Chartiphon and Prince Phrames, but Sarrask does dote on Rylla and he's proven his loyalty many times over. But my dog Whiskers is as loyal as the day is long, but that doesn't mean I'd enthrone him as great king."

"Of course, not. Still, Sarrask has done a good job in Ragyath. Is this not true, Your Majesty?"

"Well, Sarrask has followed most of my policies. And his subjects appear to be content under his hand. He seems to have built-up a lot of goodwill, but then the prince he replaced was a thoroughgoing scoundrel. Still, you're right, Sarrask has changed his ways."

"Sarrask greatly admires Your Majesty, and strives to follow in your footsteps. He's not always temperate with his drink nor his tongue, but he does mean well."

"I would have never thought of elevating him to such a lofty position, but he is a completely different person than the Sarrask who ruled over Sask when I first arrived in Hostigos. But ruling a great kingdom is a big job. Do you believe he's up for it?"

Skranga shrugged. "I don't know, but then I don't know anyone else whom Your Majesties would approve of that is more worthy than Sarrask, or could do a better job."

That stumped Kalvan for a moment. "How about yourself?"

"Oh, no! I'm too much of a gadfly to want those shackles around my ankles, Your Majesty. I would be a very poor choice indeed."

Kalvan laughed. "You're wiser than I am, Skranga. I wouldn't wish this job on my worst enemy. Maybe Rylla didn't make such a bad choice after all."

"I'll be off then, Your Majesty, to see to the questioning of the Harphaxi officers. What about Great King Geblon?"

Kalvan paused, stroking his goatee. "Good question. I'm afraid Geblon's going to cause us some problems when he learns he's been deposed. That'll put Great King Phidestros in a bind as well. Why don't you sound him out and see where he's at?"

Skranga nodded. "Yes, Your Majesty."

II

Chief Skranga left headquarters with a heavy load of worries on his mind, first among them was what to do with Great King Geblon. Outside Hostigi HQ he untied his horse, a black stallion, from the hitching post and called over Chief Petty-Captain Gycules, who was waiting outside. "Gycules, come with me."

"Yes, sir," the big man replied. They had to wait half a candle, until a horse large enough to carry Gycules was found in the stable, before he got up on his horse.

Several of Skranga's guardsmen started to mount up, but he ordered them to stay put. He wanted to talk with Gycules in private.

As soon as they reached the open road, he said, "I have a delicate mission for you to undertake."

The big man nodded.

He was one of the few men Skranga trusted to not only keep his mouth shut, but do exactly as ordered. And one of the few men big enough to do the job. Halgoth was another, but he tended to talk too much when he had a snoot full.

"Where are we going, Chief?"

"To Vyklos farm, outside of Dytha Town, where we're holding the Harphaxi officers."

"What are we going to do there?" he asked.

"I'm going to question some of the officers, but I have a special assignment for you."

The big man nodded again.

"It looks like Great King Geblon did us no favor by surrendering and it appears that his continued existence threatens the delicate balance between the various great kingdoms."

Gycules was no fool. "You mean he might be angry when he finds out he's been dethroned and his wife and her baby were beheaded."

This was top secret news but he wasn't surprised that the Chief Petty-Officer was acquainted with it. There was little that went on in the camp that Gycules did not know about.

"Exactly," Skranga replied.

"You want me to terminate the problem, Chief?"

"Right. However, I want you to make it look like a suicide. We've been keeping Geblon inside a room in the barn to isolate him from his bodyguards and commanders who are billeted in the farmhouse."

Gycules nodded.

"I want you to hang him in the barn from a timber with his own belt, but leave no marks."

"Can do," the big man said.

"Good," Skranga replied.

At the barn, Skranga ordered his men to bring Geblon into the back room. He wasn't surprised to see that the former Great King was disheveled in appearance and in an unhappy frame of mind. However, he was pleased to note that he was unmarked; some of his agents could be a bit overzealous at times in following their duties.

"Who are you?" Geblon demanded.

"I'm Duke Skranga, Chief of Hostigi Intelligence. I have a few questions to ask."

"Ask away," he threw out, with a look of disdain marring his countenance.

Skranga got right up in his face. "First of all, you're the one who surrendered, not me. So quit with the act. I'm in charge, you're not! Understood?"

Geblon nodded.

"Good. Now, I've got a few questions to ask. First, what is the general state of morale inside Balph?"

"Poor," Geblon replied. "The constant bombardment is taking a toll. However, most of those inside are determined to fight to the death. They know there is no alternative to death at Kalvan's hands and they plan to take as many Hostigi to Regwarn with them as they can."

That was not unexpected. "How are the city's stores holding out?"

"Good. There's plenty to eat, even though the warehouses at the docks were destroyed. The walls will be down long before the city's foodstuffs run out."

Kalvan wasn't going to be happy with that bit of intelligence.

"What about the Innermost Circle?"

Geblon barked out a laugh. "They're soiling their yellow robes in fear. If there was a safe place they could go, they all would have fled Balph long ago."

"Is there anything else you can tell me?" Skranga asked.

Geblon shook his head. "I have a question. How are my wife and daughter?"

Skranga shook his head. "They are both dead. The Harphax City fathers had them both beheaded when they spotted Great Queen Rylla and her army."

The Great King let out an inhuman howl. Then started to pull out his hair until Skranga ordered his men to stop him. He needed the corpse in good condition if they were going to sell the suicide story to Kalvan. Besides, from the look on Geblon's face he'd be doing him a favor, as well as Great King Kalvan. The last thing Kalvan needed was an angry, vengeance seeking Phidestros coming south to avenge his old friend.

III

Styphon's Voice Anaxthenes sat in his chair staring down at his red robe of primacy. *I wonder how much longer I'll be wearing this?* This was the first time he'd actually considered that he might lose his seat and his life. Even here, deep within the Golden Temple of Styphon's House, he could hear the infernal thunder of the Hostigi guns. Already, they had blasted a gap large enough to give entrance to their army. Why were they still blasting away?

He looked up at Grand Commander Grythos with a sneer. Not for the first time, he actually missed Grand Master Soton. "Please explain to me how some six thousand Harphaxi soldiers evacuated the city right before your eyes?"

Grythos looked thoroughly cowed. "Your Divinity, I hadn't expected the Harphaxi to surrender to Kalvan! Maybe we should have told Geblon about his wife's decapitation. It might have put some starch into his breeches."

"It's too late for that. I thought Styphon's Own Guard was there to ensure the Harphaxi stayed in line?"

The Grand Commander held out his hands and shook them angrily. "I thought the boil-brained Harphaxi would attempt to retreat, not surrender in front of Kalvan's cannons! I didn't think they had that much courage. Once the guardsmen realized they were surrendering, they attacked, but it was already too late. They only killed twelve hundred or so."

"Will Kalvan be able to use them?"

"I don't believe so, Your Divinity. The Harphaxi Army is made-up of the worst-trained bunch of soldiers I've ever encountered. From their training and demeanor, you would never guess that their commander had worked under Captain-General Phidestros, one of the greatest captains of our time. Unless Kalvan uses them as fresh fish, they will probably remain under guard."

"They have hurt us in other ways. Many of the Ktemnoi soldiers are asking to retire."

"Ha!" Grythos laughed. "Kalvan will not be so gentle with the Ktemnoi. His Uncle Wolf sent us a message this morning stating that anyone who leaves the city walls will be killed. The Daemon plans to bring Styphon's House down for all time."

"Was that smart?"

"I don't believe so; it forces our allies to realize they are fighting to the death and that there will be no escape through surrender."

"Why would Kalvan encourage our soldiers not to yield?"

"Because he doesn't want any of us to escape. It's a war to the death."

IV

Chief Skranga arrived at headquarters shortly after the rising sun. Kalvan was surprised to note the deep look of concern that showed on his face as he came through the door. "Has there been a breakout?" he asked.

"No, Your Majesty. The Styphoni curs are still trapped within the walls of Balph. But I do carry bad news."

"Out with it, man!" Kalvan demanded.

"I was halfway here, when a courier came with news that Great King Geblon took his own life sometime during the night."

"Geblon's dead! Did you see for yourself?"

"Yes, Your Majesty. I turned around and returned to Vyklos Farm immediately. Geblon had been held inside the barn alone in order to keep him from conspiring with the other ranking Harphaxi princes and nobles. It appears that during the night he used his belt to hang himself from one of the joists."

"But why? How did he appear when you questioned him?"

"Great King Geblon was despondent, Your Majesty, very upset. After questioning him about conditions inside Balph, I took the liberty to tell him about the death of his wife and daughter—that may have been my mistake...."

"Don't beat yourself up about it, Skranga," Kalvan said, he knew that Geblon would have found out soon enough; gossip was the only thing faster than the speed of light. "You couldn't have known that he would kill himself. Besides, he had to learn about it sooner or later. Better coming from you than from barroom gossip."

"True, but he took the news badly, breaking down and sobbing. I should have ordered one of my men to hold watch over him."

"No," Kalvan said, shaking his head. "Maybe it's better this way. He'll no longer be a wedge between Great King Phidestros and myself. I fear Geblon might have blamed me or Rylla for his family's demise and wanted revenge."

Skranga nodded, thinking, *which is why I had him killed.* "Sire, what do you want me to do with the body?"

Kalvan paused to fire up his pipe. After he had it drawing well, he said, "First, notify Duke Kyblannos. He will want to examine the body personally; they were good friends and comrades. When he's finished, have it pickled. I'm sure his old commander will want to examine his body for himself. We'll send it back with Kyblannos to Zygros City with the first of the treasure ships."

"It shall be done, Your Majesty."

"If Kyblannos has any questions, bring him to me."

"Yes, Sire."

"Now, what did you learn from the Harphaxi you questioned about conditions inside Balph?"

"As we expected, Your Majesty, morale is bad. The night and day bombardment has taken its toll. Both low- and high-born are suffering. The archpriests are as squirrely as rats trapped in a chamber pot! The soldiers promise to sell their lives dearly. They know there is no escape."

THIRTY-SEVEN

I

The gap in the walls of Balph was now wide enough they could run several companies through it side by side. Kalvan looked over at Captain-General Halmoth. "It's time to take the war to the enemy."

Halmoth agreed, but with one caveat. "You must stay here, Your Majesty. It's going to be a building to building, house to house fight, the worst kind. Too dangerous for senior commanders, like us. Instead, we'll have to send in the youngsters."

"Dralm-damnit!" Kalvan said in response. Despite his disappointment, he knew that Halmoth was right. As much as he was bored with the siege, he could no longer throw himself into the thick of the fight; not with all his responsibilities. Another problem with being the indispensable man.

"Besides, Your Majesty, it's not going to be much fun rooting out the Styphoni troops." He pointed to the crumbled and fallen nearby buildings. Every once in a while a shot rang out and Alkides would return fire with one of the eight-pounders.

To Kalvan this section of the city looked similar to pictures he'd seen of Berlin after the German surrender. "It's unfortunate that most of Balph's buildings are made of stone rather than wood."

Halmoth snorted. "That would have been too easy. We could have burnt them out a moon-half ago. This was the richest city in the Five Kingdoms; although, no one would make that claim now."

They had seized a king's ransom of loot and valuable treasures in the outskirts of Balph where the upperpriests had lived in their summer mansions. They'd even taken tens of thousands of prisoners, mostly the elderly, along with women and children. Many were former residents of Balph who'd been evicted before their arrival, when Styphon's Voice had evacuated the city of all nonessential personnel; the rest were former servants and their families. Kalvan had everyone but the men of military age released and sent on their way to Ktemnos City as displaced persons. *Let Great King Lukthos support them*, Kalvan had decided. He hoped they ate him out of house and home; it might make Lukthos think twice about coming to Balph's rescue.

"Colonel Leukestros is going to lead the attack," Halmoth said. "He'll have ten companies of infantry."

"What happens if they run into a large force?" Kalvan asked.

"They'll pull back immediately and attempt to draw them within range of our guns."

"Not much of a plan," Kalvan said. Still, he'd always known that at some point they were going to have to take the fight to the enemy.

Halmoth shrugged. "Short of starving them out over the next five or six seasons, this is as good as anything I can come up with, Sire."

II

Colonel Leukestros hunched down behind a chimney stub, knocked down to the height of a man. A score or more of Styphoni marksmen were holed up in the upper stories of a nearby building, which was pockmarked with bullet holes but otherwise structurally sound. The company's riflemen had the Styphoni pinned down, but hadn't been able to eliminate the marksmen, even though they were using muskets. Despite the disadvantages of accurately aiming a smoothbore, some of them were pretty deadly shooters. The six men he'd lost to their fire could attest to that.

He raised his rifle to cover one of the windows where most of the shots were coming from, then turned to the sergeant in charge of the sappers. "Can your men get a few bombs inside that building? Enough to bring it down?"

The Sergeant replied, "Sure, sir, if you can give us adequate cover."

"I'll do my best."

"Fire by squads," he ordered. The first volley blasted the windows while the sappers ran with their leather-cased bombs to the opening that had once been a doorway. Despite the Hostigi fire, several of the Styphoni got off shots and two of the sappers went down. Leukestros fired at one marksman who was dangling down from one of the windows trying for a better shot. His bullet struck the gunman right between the shoulder blades; he slumped down, almost falling out the window.

By the time the third squad volleyed, the sappers were inside the building lighting their fuses. The tricky part would come when they left the building.

"I think we stung 'em," his sergeant said.

"Good. Now, let's keep them inside while our men return."

Suddenly the remaining six sappers ran out of the building. At the same time, his men opened fire on all the exposed building positions. Their volleys kept most of the Styphoni inside the building, but they lost another sapper.

WHOOMP!

The bottom story collapsed and in slow-motion the entire building fell in on itself in a billow of smoke, killing most of those still inside. As soon as the gray and white cloud cleared, Leukestros ordered his men forward. *There's got to be a better way to take this Dralm-damned city than this*, he thought to himself.

III

Her herald announced King Chartiphon, and Great Queen Rylla ordered, "Bid him enter."

She was using one of the many large chambers in the Harphaxi palace as her own presence room, trying not to upstage Great King Sarrask who was busy establishing himself as the new great king of Hos-Harphax.

Chartiphon entered, holding a scroll and an I-told-you-so look on his face. She felt her stomach drop; it had to be a letter from Kalvan. She noticed the seal was unbroken and hoped that boded well. She was still uneasy about how her husband would take her enthronement of Sarrask as great king of Hos-Harphax.

“Your Majesty, this dispatch from Great King Kalvan just arrived from Balph.”

In her last missive, she had offered her army in aid of crushing the Styphoni Holy City. Not that Kalvan needed her help, but so they could spend time together. It had been over two seasons since they’d parted and she missed him terribly.

Chartiphon passed her the scroll and she used her small blade to break the seal.

My Darling Wife,

I was surprised by your elevation of Prince Sarrask to the Iron Throne of Hos-Harphax and immediately thought of a dozen objections. Then I attempted to view the chaotic situation in Harphax from your view, and realized that you have made a sound selection since there is no Harphaxi house in that kingdom we can trust or depend upon. Most have either sold out to Styphon’s House or have been coerced into cooperation with that most heinous of temples. So, upon further reflection, I realized that you had made an excellent choice since no one is more loyal and faithful to our reign than Sarrask, formerly Prince of Sask.

Rylla exhaled deeply. She had been holding her breath since Kalvan’s letter had arrived, but hadn’t realized it. She looked up at Chartiphon and saw a puzzled expression on his face. She read him the appropriate passage and watched as his face went through several changes.

“Ah, ah,” he sputtered.

She promised herself not to gloat and began to read the rest of the letter.

While I would very much enjoy your company and miss you more than words can deliver, we have more than enough soldiers here in Hos-Ktemnos to put Styphon's House out of business—for good. A better use of your time and resources, in my opinion, would be for you and Great King Sarrask to visit each of the Harphaxi princedoms and find replacements for all of the current princes. In this way, the two of you will guarantee their loyalty to both the Harphaxi and Hostigi thrones as well as find the best men for the job. Plus, it will give you both the opportunity to learn about Sarrask's future subjects, both the good and the bad. He has not always been a good judge of character; so, if you see him making an error of judgment, please correct him gently and patiently.

The siege here at Balph is moving slowly, since our initial success. We have been forced to take the city a block at a time. As the remaining Styphoni in Balph know there is no mercy to be found at our hands, they are fighting tenaciously to keep us out. Unfortunately, we cannot afford to allow any of them to escape. Styphon's House has to be crushed once and for all and its Holy City leveled and sown with salt. In the end, we may have to starve them out. However, we will prevail, but at a cost.

She looked up at Chartiphon who was fiddling with his tinderbox in an attempt to hide his curiosity.

"Yes," she asked.

"How is the siege coming along?"

"Slowly, I fear. The Styphoni are like rats trapped in a cellar and are fighting for their lives. It may be several seasons before the city capitulates."

IV

Kalvan and Captain-General Halmoth sat in the HQ's building waiting for Colonel Leukestros. The siege of Balph was turning into a nightmare of block by block fighting. He'd already lost more soldiers in Balph in the past two weeks than they'd lost taking Tarr-Ceros. It was time for a change of strategy.

There was a knock at the door.

"Come in," he said.

Colonel Leukestros entered. His morion helmet was dinged and battered and he was covered in ash and charcoal. "Your Majesty, Captain-General."

"Have a seat, Colonel. You look like you could use a good drink."

He passed over a flagon and a small cask of Ermut's Best. The Colonel quickly filled the vessel and took a deep drink, sputtering and coughing. In between coughs, he said, "I needed that."

"At this rate, how long do you believe it will take to own the city?" Kalvan asked.

The Colonel shook his head wearily. "I don't know, sire. A season or two…maybe more. We'd do better to use our guns to blast the entire place to Regwarn!"

Kalvan nodded. "I agree, but the problem is that we can't get our artillery very far beyond the city walls because of the mountains of rubble and broken stone they've created. We'd have to haul it away, and we don't have enough prisoners to do that—even if the Styphoni didn't end up shooting them like hogs in a pigpen. We just may have to starve the bastards out."

"That could take a long time," Halmoth interjected.

"I know. There must be another way…, but what?" Kalvan took out his pipe and began to fill it. Then he recalled how the early American colonists dealt with the Indians. It was fortuitous that the Styphoni had evacuated all the women and children, except for a few whores, before their arrival. He wouldn't have been able to do this otherwise.

He turned to Captain-General Halmoth. "How many pox survivors do we have?"

"Six companies worth, sire. I've used them as a line of defense against the south, not that many of the varlets living there have come north. Our scouts report that many of villages in the Princedom of Cythlos are filled with the dead and dying."

"It's unfortunate, but the pox may be something we can use to our advantage."

Both Halmoth and Colonel Leukestros perked up. "What do you mean?"

"First, I want to isolate all of our pox survivors from the rest of the army. This corps will need a special uniform; maybe an all-black one, one that can't be missed and will let it stand out from the rest of the army. Halmoth, I'll leave it to you to talk to our quartermasters and see that the new uniforms are turned out. Once that's done, I'm going to send them south on a mission to go to the pox-ridden villages and gather up all the bedding and clothing they can find."

"Why?" Halmoth asked.

"The Great Pox is spread by either close contact with those who have it, or proximity to their clothes and bedding. I want to spread this plague throughout Balph. I'll need our engineers to start building catapults so that we can toss bundles of clothing and bedding over the walls into Balph proper."

"But won't they just ignore them?" Leukestros asked.

"Not if we hide a few silver crowns in each bundle."

"That will work for a while, sire. But won't they catch on?"

"By then," Kalvan replied, "it'll be too late. The entire city will be infected with the Great Pox."

"Won't we have to be careful, too?" Halmoth asked, his voice trembling.

"Certainly," Kalvan said. "Only our pox survivors will handle the infected material and it will be up to them to catapult it over the city walls. Anyone leaving Balph will have to be shot dead on sight. Styphon's Voice did us a favor when he evacuated all the non-priests and soldiers. We won't have to worry about non-combatant casualties."

Plus, I won't have the deaths of thousands of women and children on my conscience, Kalvan thought. He might have had to come up with another way to break the siege, if Anaxthenes hadn't unwittingly helped out. One of the biggest problems with siege warfare was the high incidence of civilian casualties. Starvation, in the long run, was almost as bad as the primitive form of biological warfare they were about to release on Styphon's House's last bastion.

"Also," he continued, "I need to talk to Uncle Wolf Kythamos and the other healers. We need to be ready to contain any breakouts that come over the wall."

"Yes, sir."

"Halmoth, who's in charge of the pox scouts?"

"Captain Mythames, Your Majesty."

"Have him brought to headquarters. I want to speak with him and explain our mission."

V

Styphon's Voice looked up questioningly as Grand Commander Grythos entered his private chamber. The Commander was finely outfitted in silver and gold chased armor, but his face looked pinched. *More bad news*, he decided.

"Your Divinity, the Daemon Kalvan has come up with a new tactic."

"What are the damned Hostigi doing now?"

"They are using catapults to throw bundles of old clothes and bedding over our walls." Grythos shrugged. "It makes no sense...."

"From everything we know about the Usurper, he never does anything without a good cause. But why send old clothing and blankets over our walls? There has to be a reason."

"I agree. I have ordered my soldiers to collect everything the Hostigi catapult over the walls and burn them."

"A wise decision until we learn why the Hostigi are sending them over our walls," Anaxthenes said.

"However, there is a problem with that, Your Divinity. The Hostigi have hidden silver crowns within the bundles and when the commoners come across them they hide them. Plus, my soldiers—despite my orders—are rummaging through them as well." He shrugged. "There aren't many soldiers who can resist the lure of easy gain."

"This is the craziest thing I've ever heard of," Styphon's Voice said, shaking his head. "Why would the Usurper put silver coins in amongst old clothes and bedding? It has to be some sort of a ruse. Are you certain there is nothing else secreted amongst the trash?"

"I've watched my men rip the bundles apart. They're always the same, torn and used clothing and ripped bedding. By Styphon's Own Beard, I can't figure out what they're hiding."

SUMMER

THIRTY-EIGHT

I

Grand Commander Grythos did not look like himself as he made his way into Anaxthenes' audience chamber. He looked feverish and Anaxthenes noticed a red rash on his face, starting just above his beard. He was carrying a bundle of rags in one of his arms.

"What have you there?" Anaxthenes asked.

"One of Kalvan's gifts, Your Divinity."

"Why?"

"I wanted you to see one close-up. All over the city thousands of priests and soldiers are coming down with the Great Pox."

Anaxthenes shuddered. He remembered as a child when the plague had run through their small town, killing a third of the population including two of his sisters. "Now we know why Kalvan placed pieces of gold and silver inside the bundles. What an insidious trick! A curse on his house and children! To Regwarn with the lot of them!"

Grythos dropped the bundle and took out his sword. "I believe the pox devils live inside the blankets!"

Styphon's Voice drew back in horror. He knew there were devils, malignant spirits of the netherworld; everybody knew that. He cringed, imagining them infesting the bedding—scrawny bodies, bat-wings, with claws and fangs fighting to be released.

The Commander began stabbing at the bedding as though it were a living thing. "Depart, you pox devils and fever demons."

He ripped the bedding apart, but no devils or demons flew out.

Anaxthenes sighed in relief. "They have departed. Styphon be praised!"

Grythos let his blade rest on the marble floor. "I fear they are still here, invisible, hiding within the cloth. Only late at night, when darkness is complete, do they make their presence known."

"Then get this pig flop out of my chamber!" His heart was beating like a drum.

One of the servants ran over and went down on his hands and knees, picking up every piece of cloth—even the shredded bits.

"What can we do to stop this abomination?" he demanded.

Grythos shrugged. "I have gathered all the healers in the city together and they are taking care of some of the sick, as many as they can manage. Soldiers are dying in their barracks by the hundreds. We could try to fight our way out of the city, but I fear Kalvan's guns would make short work of any escape."

"There must be something we can do…."

For the first time since he had known the burly archpriest, Grythos looked defeated. "I feel feverish and weak. I need to lie down, Your Divinity."

Not you! he thought. He needed the Grand Commander to command the forces of Styphon's House. He didn't trust any of the other military leaders; they were either fools or incompetent witlings. "You can stay here in the Golden Temple."

He pointed to one of his servants. "You, go prepare a bed chamber for the Grand Commander." He turned to another servant, "Find my personal healer. Bring him here at once. Do you understand?"

The man ran out of the chamber as though one of the pox devils were writhing within the backside of his breeches.

II

Kalvan watched as the big thirty-twos fired at a new section of the wall. The cannonballs slammed into the wall with little to show for it, other than a few falling slabs of stone and clouds of white and gray dust. It was slow and methodical work, but the city walls of Balph were slowly coming down. Colonel Leukestros had suggested undermining the wall and emplacing big charges of fireseed, but Kalvan had nixed that idea. The walls were too thick for mere gunpowder: what they needed was dynamite, if truth be told.

He looked up and saw Halmoth riding toward him, hell-bent for leather. The Captain-General quickly dismounted and ran to where Kalvan was perched.

"Your Majesty, shots were heard from inside Balph. A lot of them. Is it possible they're fighting amongst themselves?"

He nodded. The Zarthani did not know of the germ theory of disease and instead blamed illnesses and plagues on fester devils and demons or other supernatural phenomenon. When the plague struck, they were likely to lash out at the sick and blame them for the infection.

"We need to be prepared," Kalvan told Hestophes. There were nearly a quarter of a million soldiers and priests inhabiting Balph when they had started the siege. Giving the city the plague was like shaking up a warm bottle of Pepsi. At some point, the lid was going to fly off and all Regwarn was going to break loose; they needed to have a plan.

"What do you have in mind, Your Majesty?"

"Tell Alkides I want to have both of the main gates covered with guns. Three batteries stationed at each gate. The rest will cover the gap. And tell him to load the guns with case shot."

"That will mean an end to bombarding the walls," Hestophes noted.

"At this point, they're the least of our problems."

III

Highpriest Mytron entered the presence room in the Thagnor palace and saw Prince Phrames, seated on the Fireseed Throne, deep in thought. "What is it, Your Highness?" he asked.

"I just received a dispatch from Great Queen Rylla. It's full of surprises."

"Is Her Majesty all right?" Mytron asked. He had been praying to

Dralm every night for her safe return. On more than one occasion he had counseled Rylla to remain here in Thagnor with her young children who needed her more than the army did. Being Rylla, of course, she ignored his advice.

"Yes, she's fine," Phrames responded.

He made the sign of a star on his chest, crying out, "Praise Allfather Dralm! My prayers have been answered. Has she been successful in her efforts to retake Hostigos?"

"Yes, she has recaptured Hostigos Town and all of Hos-Hostigos is now in her hands. In fact, one of her requests is that we start sending parties of former refugees back to Hos-Hostigos. She is especially interested in tradesmen, artificers, joiners and carpenters, stone masons and other artisans."

"Praise Dralm, Galzar and Yirtta, too! Soon we shall be able to return home."

Prince Phrames frowned. "Not everyone who was displaced by the Fireseed War will be as anxious as you are to return."

"Many will, you'll see," Mytron said.

"Now, Her Majesty's gone and taken her army into Hos-Harphax."

"Have they been successful?" Mytron asked.

"Very. Harphax City surrendered without a shot being fired. They opened the gates of the city and presented her with the head of Great Queen Lavena and her baby daughter."

Mytron shrugged. "Better the death of that she-devil and her spawn than the loss of one Hostigi soldier."

"Aye. But you won't believe this! Rylla has elevated Prince Sarrask to the Iron Throne as the new Great King of Hos-Harphax!"

Highpriest Mytron froze as though struck with a mace in the forehead. "Sarr...ask," he stammered. "Great King!?"

Phrames frowned. "Yes, he is now the Great King of Hos-Harphax. What would cause her to make such a calamitous choice."

Prince Phrames had never warmed-up to Prince Sarrask, even after Sarrask had become one of Rylla's trusted advisors. *Was he jealous?* Mytron wondered. Before Dralm-sent Kalvan had arrived, Phrames had been promised Rylla's hand in marriage by former Prince Ptosphes. After Kalvan's arrival, all that had changed. At the time, he'd thought that Phrames had been relieved. Rylla was a handful and a half, and probably more than an ordinary man—like Phrames—could handle. Maybe he still had feelings for Rylla and harbored a grudge against Kalvan.

It was also true, at one time Sarrask had been Rylla's and Hostigos' enemy, but he had changed after Sask had been conquered. He was now one of the most ardent supporters of Kalvan and the Hostigi regime.

"Who would you have suggested, Your Highness?" he asked. "Yourself, perhaps?"

Phrames face scrunched up as if he'd just bitten into a crab apple. "No, I like it here in the Middle Kingdoms. I do not plan to return to Hostigos proper. Nor would I ever want to be a great king."

"Then who do you suggest as worthy of that honor?"

"King Chartiphon would be my first choice."

"Really?" Mytron said. "Do you actually believe that Her Majesty did not ask him if he wanted the office before approaching Sarrask?"

"I suppose so," Phrames said, taken aback.

"If she did," Mytron said, "I'm certain he turned her down. He is content as King of Rathon with his loyal subjects and new family. Why would Chartiphon want the bolts and arrows of the Iron Throne? The entire kingdom has been in an uproar ever since Great King Kaiphranos' death. I know that I wouldn't want the office, nor would anyone else I can think of but Prince Pheblon—and for that reason I wouldn't trust him on the Iron Throne."

"True, Pheblon is too ambitious and treats his subjects harshly. I've had numerous complaints from his subjects ever since Their Majesties left Nos-Hostigos. I fear Prince Pheblon is taking advantage of their absence. I have made a list of all his wrongdoings prepared for Their Majesties' return."

"Now," Mytron added, "I'm not saying that Sarrask will be a great king, but he will be a loyal one. And he will whip any of the Harphaxi princes who get out of line back into shape. They may not love him, but they will fear him. Sarrask's a lot tougher than Kalvan about his subjects following his orders as well as dishing out punishments."

Phrames laughed. "Maybe he's not such a terrible choice, after all. I, for one, won't miss his poor jokes, crude yarns and non-stop cursing. Let Sarrask exercise his bad humor on the Harphaxi! Better them than us!"

THIRTY-NINE

I

Kalvan waited anxiously as the huge gates to the main entrance to Balph slowly started to vibrate, then move. He turned to Captain-General Halmoth and said, "This is going to be something you've never seen the likes of before."

Halmoth, who appeared in shock, just nodded.

"Halt!" Kalvan cried when one of the soldiers fired prematurely. "Wait until the gates are fully open, damn your eyes!"

Everyone settled down. Stretched before him were five batteries of guns and behind them stood newly elevated Colonel Mythames' Black Guard, as they were now called. The six companies had expanded to nine once the army realized that there was status and better pay in being among the Black Guard. Five of the companies, armed with muskets, were covering the main gate; the rest stood at the west gate. All of these new recruits were soldiers who had natural immunity to small pox, having survived the plague when it struck their homes and villages. They were now the second line of defense, after the artillery, against the horde threatening to squeeze its way out of Balph.

As the gates slowly moved open, he could hear the roar of the tens of thousands of Balph's residents who would rather face dismemberment and death than the Great Pox. It was up to the Army of Hostigos to see that none left the killing field alive.

Suddenly one of the gates slumped to the side and the other jerked free as tens of thousands of panic-stricken Styphoni tried to leave the city at once. Most of them were unarmed; in their panic even the soldiers had left their muskets and swords behind. Captain-General Alkides turned to look him in the eye, then turned back and gave the order to fire.

The roar of thirty guns, loaded with case shot, was as loud as if a train had derailed and hit a stone embankment.

Kalvan went momentarily struck deaf.

For a few moments, there was a bloody red splatter that reached the top of the walls, followed by flying body parts. But the crowd inside Balph didn't appear to have noticed and was pushing their way through the gates when the second salvo struck. When the smoke and red haze had cleared, Kalvan could see dismembered bodies blocking the road like cord wood. Those still behind the gates were forced to push the dead out of their way, making it easier for the Black Guard marksmen to pick them off.

A red fog now surrounded the gates and the nearby area.

The surge continued as the panic-stricken inhabitants of Balph tried to fight their way out of the city and certain death. The artillery batteries continued firing as Alkides put the guns through their paces. Finally, the mountain of dead was too high for those trapped behind the gates to maneuver over and the exodus came to a stuttering halt.

Kalvan had to take a stiff drink of Ermut's Best to still the roiling of his stomach. He'd seen some horrible things since his arrival here-and-now, but this was worse by whole orders of magnitude.

"By the Wargod's Mace, I've never seen anything like this," Halmoth cried out. "I almost feel sorry for the pox-ridden buggers. There's no glory to this kind of war."

Kalvan shook his head. "There never is, especially in a religious war. They forced this upon us, remember that. Styphon's House is like a cancer; it has to be rooted out and destroyed, no matter what the cost."

Suddenly, in the distance, they could hear the mass fire of guns as the citizens of Balph attempted to fight their way out of the other gate. Kalvan shook his head wearily; it was going to be a long day.

The crowd attempted two more assaults before they retired. Kalvan had the Black Guard douse the dead bodies with turpentine and light them on fire. No one inside the city was fool enough to attempt another breakout. Orange and red flames danced across the hills of corpses; the resulting stench was bad enough to make grown men run away crying.

II

Over the next moon-quarter there were four more half-hearted attempts by the inhabitants of Balph to break out of their prison. The numbers of those trying to flee were in the low thousands by now, and most were weakened by illness. They were halted at the gateways and the artillery made quick work of them. The big thirty-twos went back to pounding the walls into rubble.

The guns rumbled and thundered without pause. Kalvan did not want to imagine the hell that life had become inside those walls, buildings were burning and gunshots were fired off intermittently. The Balph corpse factory was working day and night.

The question that kept him awake at nights was: When did he send his soldiers into the city? Too soon, and many would catch the pox. Summer had arrived with a vengeance and it was getting hotter. This part of the south was known for its humidity and heat. He was determined to wrap up the siege as soon as possible.

Over the next few days things began to wind down. Fewer and fewer shots were fired inside Balph and most of the fires were out, either from lack of combustibles or those willing to light them. Not all of them had died of the Great Pox; many would survive. Still, there were no more suicidal attempts to storm the gates. He decided to wait another two days before sending the Black Guard inside to do a reconnaissance.

Kalvan was inside his headquarters when there was a knock at the door. "Colonel Mythames is here to report in," one of the sentries called out.

"Send him in."

Mythames' face was lined and smudged with charcoal, and there was a twitch in his left eyelid; he looked a decade older than the man who had entered Balph only this morning.

"How did it go?" Kalvan asked.

"Your Majesty, it was as if we were cast into the Caverns of Regwarn. Dead and rotting bodies fill the streets, along with huge rats feasting on their flesh. We only ran into a few hundred stragglers; it was merciful to shoot them and end their miserable lives. Most were starving. Those fires we saw, some of them were set at the depots filled with provisions." He paused to shake his head. "They must have been mad with terror to burn them. We found a few Styphoni highpriests nailed to the sides of buildings. And other sights that I will never banish from my eyes."

"Was there any resistance?"

"No, Your Majesty. Most of the barracks were burned to the ground with armor and weapons scattered like leaves after an autumn thunderstorm. There was no organized resistance. Most of the surviving soldiers died trying to get out of the gates."

"How long will it take for you and your men to do a complete reconnaissance of the city?"

"A moon-quarter, but longer if we set charges and knock all the buildings down. Plus we'll have to set up work parties to remove the gold tiles and pillage the primary temples in the Great Hos-Plaza."

"That will do, Colonel. I wish I could offer you more men, but I don't want to expose the rest of the army to the plague. We've had less than a few handfuls of men coming down with symptoms of the pox and we've managed to quickly isolate them and anyone they've come in contact with."

"I understand, sire. Now that we can work inside the city, we should have Balph looted and blasted to the ground within a moon or two."

III

Kalvan looked out the window at the wrecked and blasted city that had once been the most majestic and richest city in the Five Kingdoms. Now it looked like Dresden after it was firebombed. Like the Nazis back home, Styphon's House was officially out of business. *I should be feeling great right now; we took this city without losing more than a regiment's worth of soldiers—and most of those to smallpox.* Instead he felt down in the dumps. Was it because Balph fell too easily, or because he hadn't fought fair? If fighting fair was losing tens of thousands of good men to gunshots, sword slashes and horrible wounds, then he'd rather fight by slick tricks or duplicity.

Still, Kalvan couldn't shake the despondency that had gripped him for the past several days while he waited for the Black Guard to finish their mopping-up operation. They had stripped enough loot from Styphon's Golden Temple, the Great Council Hall of Styphon and the Supreme Priest's Palace to pay for the entire war, with enough left over to do it again—even after paying Phidestros his share.

Kalvan knew he should be planning the march on Ktemnos City with Skranga and Hestophes, not moping around. He wondered how Rylla was doing. In her last dispatch, she had written that she was returning to Hostigos Town with a large detachment. He wasn't sure that was a good idea; but, typically, she hadn't asked for his permission. Rylla had been full of praise about his diabolical attack on Balph and his success in ending the Styphoni menace.

Maybe it had all been too easy, he wondered. *Could it be I'm waiting for the other shoe to drop? Or was it just a letdown from bringing a successful end to the Styphoni threat that has been hanging over our heads since my arrival and cost us so much?*

He was wrenched from his musings by a knock at the door.

"Chief Skranga to see you, Your Majesty," the sentry cried out.

"Let him in," Kalvan replied.

Skranga's eyes were sparkling and he was breathing hard. "Your Majesty!" he cried. "It looks like all of Hos-Ktemnos is headed our way!"

"An army?"

"No, sire. It's a bleeding procession and treasure train. It must include every prince in Hos-Ktemnos, a wagon train over a hundred strong and a coffle of slaves over two marches long."

"Any soldiers?" he asked.

"Only ceremonial soldiers and the usual princely bodyguards. Less than a thousand men. Shall I approach the party?"

"Yes, and have them send their representatives to my Headquarters."

"Shall I send for your Bodyguard?"

"Yes, but just Vanar Halgoth and two of his men in their finest armor. That should be more than sufficient; otherwise there won't be room to breathe."

"Yes, Your Majesty," Skranga replied as he skipped out of the room.

IV

It took about half an hour for his guests to arrive, but arrive they did; all the princes of Hos-Ktemnos save two. No advisors or guards were allowed in the room. They appeared sufficiently cowed by his presence and that of his massive bodyguards that he had no worries about an assassination attempt. While Kalvan didn't know any of the princes by sight, his spies had purchased or commissioned pictures of them all and he had committed them to memory.

"Where are Prince Mydronos of Imbraz and Prince Prysigon of Chaliphax?" he asked.

The delegates appeared surprised that he knew the missing princes by name. Their spokesman, Prince Balros of the Princedom of Zacryth, said, "Your Majesty. They refused to recant their belief in the false god Styphon upon pain of death. So they were reunited with their ancestors."

"A wise decision. What about Great King Lukthos?"

"We have him in shackles," Balros said. "We will transfer him into your custody as soon as this meeting is over."

"So exactly what is it that you require from Us?" Kalvan asked, although he had a good idea of what they wanted.

"We have a Declaration of Peace we have all signed. We would like Your Majesty to sign it."

Prince Balros handed him a thick roll of parchment. He quickly perused the document. Essentially, the Ktemnoi princes were asking—no, begging—for peace and to make an alliance with Hos-Hostigos, renouncing all ties to Styphon's House and the former ruling family.

"What about Styphon's priests?"

"We have captured every priest in Hos-Ktemnos that has not slipped over the border into the Sastragath—where they will not fare well—and put shackles on them. Those that resisted were killed. We had thought of beheading them, but reserved that pleasure for Your Majesty. They are outside in chains awaiting your judgement."

Kalvan noticed that the assembled princes looked upon him as if he held their lives in the palm of his hand, which he supposed he did. Nervous glances went back and forth and several were as pale as alabaster.

He had grown weary of killing after the sack of Balph. The worst thing he could think of other than death was putting all the former priests in the mines with the slaves they had oppressed. He paused to speak *sotto voce* to Halgoth, who then left the room.

"I will have my men brand each one of them with an X upon their forehead so all will know they are the worshippers of the demon Styphon who dares to masquerade as a god."

The Princes all nodded as if they agreed with his judgment.

"Rather than kill them all, let us use them to good purpose. Put all the priests to work in the lead mines."

"It will be done," Prince Balros said.

Kalvan knew that working in the lead mines was as good as a death sentence. "What about the Styphoni temples?" Kalvan asked.

Prince Balron looked him straight in the eyes. "Your Majesty, all the false temples have been torn down and stripped of valuable ornaments and their golden tiles. We have brought all the treasure we recovered in a wagon train as a sign of our good faith."

"Good," he replied. With all the gold coming into Hos-Hostigos he was going to have to be careful about how they used it, or runaway inflation would be the result.

"Is there anything else you want from me?" Kalvan asked.

"We want you to select our next great king," Prince Balron said, "as Her Majesty did in Hos-Harphax. All the members of the previous dynasty are dead. We willingly submit to your will."

Picking the next Ktemnoi great king was an obligation he did not want. Nor did he have anyone to propose. Skranga would take the job if he ordered him to, but in the end he would prove to be a disaster. He was not cut out to be ruling material, and had even admitted it. No one else, of sufficient stature among the surviving Hostigi, wanted the job. "I will not select your new ruler; instead I want the princes of the realm to elect their own ruler."

There were startled looks and a few smiles among the assembled princes. This was not the answer they had expected, and already they were making plans.

"I look forward to uniting Our realms in peace and cooperation. As soon as our job here is done We will be returning home." *Home*, he thought. *I'm not sure where that is anymore. Is it Thagnor Town or Hostigos Town?*

"Are you sure that it was smart letting them off so easily?" Halmoth asked after the princes had left their headquarters."

"What was I supposed to do? They came to us voluntarily, and saved us from a long campaign fighting our way through Hos-Ktemnos, defeating each prince and destroying Styphon's House's temples. By my lights, they did us a big favor. Now, once Balph is cleared of survivors, we can depart from this godsforsaken place. Unless you're interested in being the next great king of Hos-Ktemnos."

"What me!?" Halmoth said. "No, sire; not for all the gold in those wagons. All I want to do is go back home.'

"Which one?" Kalvan asked.

"Now, that's a damn good question."

FORTY

I

It took another moon-half before all the smallpox survivors in Balph were hunted down and killed. Most of them were already weakened by the disease and were not hard to kill. The difficult part was finding them all. Skranga came up with the idea of torching different quadrants of the city to drive the survivors to the center where they could quickly be dispatched. About a third of Balph had already been fired so those areas were the most difficult to clear. This was the Black Guard's responsibility and they cleared them block by block.

Finally, it was done and Colonel Mythames made his final report to Kalvan and the rest of the high command about the state of the former Holy City of Balph. He still looked bushed but the spark was back in his eyes now that he knew the operation was finally wrapped up.

"Your Majesty, Balph is officially sacked and destroyed."

"Are there any survivors you might have missed?" he asked.

"If there are, they're in bad shape. I'm sure there are a few holdouts, but we could spend from now until next winter digging them out. We found most of the Archpriests inside the Golden Temple dead from the Great Pox."

"How about Styphon's Voice Anaxthenes?" Chief Skranga asked.

"He was found in his bed in the Supreme Priest's Palace, covered from head-to-toe with huge red pustules. It appears he died in great agony."

Kalvan blew out a deep breath. "The web spinner is dead! Styphon's House is really finished."

Cheers of "Down Styphon!" broke out among the assembled

commanders.

It was almost too good to be true. "What about Archpriest Grythos?"

Mythames shrugged. "We weren't able to locate his body, Your Majesty. A lot of the corpses were badly deteriorated. Other bodies had been purposely mutilated, some so badly not even their mothers could have identified them. Commander Grythos probably died in one of the attempts to break through the gates."

Kalvan nodded. That made sense, Grythos was more a soldier than a priest and probably would have died with his command. If by some twisted miracle he survived, he was in no shape to return to Agrys City and make a claim on the Throne of Lights. Still, he didn't like loose ends. On the other hand, he couldn't wait to get away from this dreary site of death and corruption.

He turned to Admiral Herad. "How many soldiers will your transports hold for the return journey to Thagnor?"

"Twenty thousand, easily, Your Majesty. More, if we have to."

"Fine. You can start loading them tomorrow morning."

"Good," Herad replied. "I'd like to get away from here before the hurricane season peaks."

"What about the rest of the troops?" Skranga asked.

"They'll come with me. I've decided to return to Hostigos Town." He didn't mention the letter he had just received from Rylla asking him to meet her there. He missed her terribly and there was no one to stop them from being together now that the Fireseed Wars were finally over.

II

"What does it say, what does it say?" Great Queen Arminta asked her husband as he carefully handled the parchment that had just arrived from Hos-Ktemnos. All she knew was that it was a letter from Great King Kalvan. The other boats had been filled with gold and other treasures, but were of little interest to her. Although she knew their contents would set the mouth of their Royal Treasurer salivating.

Great King Phidestros looked up at her, but he was not smiling.

"What is it, my love?"

"Geblon is dead." Phidestros looked down in the face, almost ready to cry. She'd never seen him display so much emotion before, except when viewing their newborn child.

"How?" she asked, her voice trembling. *Please, by all the true gods, let it be in battle, or accidental. We do not need another war….*

"By his own hand, or so it appears. Great King Kalvan pickled the corpse and sent it with the ships. I'll have our chief healer look it over."

"I'm sure he died by his own hand, if Kalvan says it is so. I thought he was inside Balph, so how did he get captured by the Hostigi?"

"The Styphoni attempted to use Geblon and the Harphaxi army as cannon fodder to cover a counterattack against the Hostigi. However, instead of charging the enemy, the Harphaxi surrendered en masse. Styphon's House retaliated by killing those they could reach in the rear ranks. Kalvan says it was quite a slaughter."

"What happened to Great King Geblon?" she asked.

"According to Kalvan, he was taken prisoner and held overnight in a barn at the outskirts of Balph. There he used his belt to hang himself from one of the rafters."

Arminta shuddered. "How horrible! Does he say why?"

"He was inconsolable when informed of the fate of his wife and her daughter. It appears, according to Kalvan, that he wanted to join them in the Sky-Palaces of the gods."

"May All-Mother Yirtta's will be done," she intoned. "Maybe it was for the best. Geblon is now at finally at peace."

Phidestros shook his head. "I need to talk with Kyblannos and see what he believes."

"Has he returned, too?"

"Yes, he came back with the treasure fleet. Unfortunately, they hit a bad storm and three boats were lost."

"Send for him."

"I will." He turned to his manservant Mynos. "Have someone locate Duke Kyblannos and have him brought to our private chamber."

"Yes, Sire."

In less than a candle, Duke Kyblannos was escorted into their presence. He bowed, saying, "Your Majesties, I should have visited sooner, but I wanted to get a drink and see my wife and children first."

Phidestros waved his hand, as though swatting a fly. "It is of no matter, my friend. I understand your desire to reunite with family. However, I have some questions for you about the death of our old comrade."

Kyblannos shook his head wearily, then threw out his hands. "A bad business, for sure, Your Majesty. Great King Kalvan informed me of his death shortly after the body was discovered and provided me with immediate access. "

"How did it look to you?"

"Geblon's body had already been cut down from the rafter, but was still lying on the hay inside the Vyklos barn. I examined the body carefully. There were no marks or unexpected bruises, except around the throat where the belt had resided. Everything appeared consistent with suicide. I fear our old comrade could not face life without that she-devil he called his wife."

"Do you believe he was that smitten with her?"

Kyblannos nodded. "To the point of madness, Cap'n. I doubt he wanted to face life without her at his side."

Phidestros nodded. "Geblon changed so much since our time together, I fear I no longer knew him. You are probably right. Let us bury the body with all honors. The truth be known, I'm glad it was done by his own hand and not by the machinations of Kalvan."

Arminta let go of the breath she hadn't realized she'd been holding. *Maybe we'll see true peace for the first time in our lives. Praise the gods!*

III

"Your Majesty, King Kalvan and his escort have been sighted about five marches from Hostigos Town."

Rylla felt her stomach flutter, as though it were full of butterflies. She hoped her husband liked the renovations she had made to the palace; not that he would know what they were since he hadn't seen the place since they'd fled from the Grand Host of Styphon's House years before. She had been working hard on this victory celebration for over a moon-quarter, ever since Great King Sarrask had informed her that Kalvan and his companions had arrived in Harphax City. She had invited people from near and far who deserved to be included.

"Are the streets lined with well-wishers?" she asked.

"Yes, Your Majesty," King Chartiphon said. "All of them with Hostigi flags and banners. There'll be a lot of babies come next spring!"

Rylla laughed, with Yirtta's help she and Kalvan might have another one of their own.

The presence chamber was filled with lords and nobles all dressed in their finest: Uncle Wolf Tharses, Highpriest of Galzar, Chancellor Mytron, Captain-General Hestophes, Dean Ermut, King Chartiphon and many of the lower nobility and merchant classes. All ready to welcome Great King Kalvan after his dramatic sacking of Balph and the utter destruction of Styphon's House.

It was another three-quarters of a candle before a dusty Kalvan, followed by Duke Skranga, Prince Mythros, Captain-General Halmoth, Baron Gasphros, lute in hand, and Captain-General Alkides, entered the chamber. Her husband looked around with complete surprise. "What's this all about?" he asked.

Servants with drinks and appetizers were circulating through the room.

"It's a party!" Skranga cried. "A welcome home party!"

"That's just what it is!" Chartiphon yelled. "A victory party! Down Styphon!"

This started a chant of "Down Styphon!" that went on for a few minutes.

It was brought to an end when Skranga called out: "For all time!"

"HUZZAH!" Halmoth cried out.

This was followed by the sound of music as Gasphros began strumming his lute.

Rylla had a hard time making her way to her husband as he was surrounded by well-wishers and friends, all congratulating him.

Prince Mythros waylaid her before she reached his side, saying, "I've always want to meet Your Majesty. Your beauty is noted throughout the Six Kingdoms!"

"Thank you," she said, trying not to blush. She had heard that the Blethan Prince was not the kind of man to offer false compliments and blandishments.

"I believe in time our two kingdoms will become close friends."

Rylla liked the sound of that and smiled.

She saw Baron Halmoth standing by himself drinking from one of the new glass goblets.

"Congratulations, Baron, upon your victory," she said.

"It was Kalvan's victory," he replied. "I would have never thought of using the plague to bring down Balph. It was a nasty end to an ugly war, but those godless Styphoni deserved it."

Rylla wasn't sure if he was trying to convince her or himself. He didn't look very happy. She suspected that few who had participated in the downfall of Balph felt any pride in their accomplishment. In time that would change as the results of that victory flowered within the Great Kingdoms.

She smiled and went over to Duke Hestophes who looked down in the mouth. She knew he missed the siege of Balph and in part blamed her for it. However, she had a surprise that would change that dour look.

"Come with me, Duke. I have someone I want you to meet." She led him to the far side of the chamber where a well-dressed lady awaited.

Hestophes' mouth dropped open. "Is that who I think it is?"

Rylla nodded, smiling. "Yes, it's your wife, Duchess Lysia."

Hestophes took his wife into his arms, tears of joy leaking from his eyes. They talked privately for a few moments, then he turned to Rylla. "Thank you, Your Majesty. This is the best gift you could have given me!"

"You wife has done a great job in protecting Aspasthar and aiding him in becoming enthroned upon the Throne of Light. He still needs her guidance, but it occurred to us that we needed an official representative at the Court of Hos-Agrys. Of course, you would be the ideal person. What do you think, Duke?"

"I think I'm the happiest man in this room; that is what I think!" he said, smiling and raising his goblet to make a toast. "To Great Queen Rylla who has kept the home fires burning!"

"Aye, aye," several voices cried out.

Kalvan, when she finally reached him, didn't look all that pleased, and she knew why. He probably wasn't happy about all the casualties the siege had cost, even though most of the dead were the priests, soldiers and sycophants of Styphon's House. She knew how to rectify that and brought him a full goblet of Ermut's Best.

"Why the long face, my dear," she asked, as people made way for her.

Kalvan took the goblet and drank deeply. "I had to use some underhanded tactics to end the siege of Balph, and I'm not happy about it. It was the plague that won the siege; not my genius. We left behind tens of thousands of dead bodies in Balph."

"True, darling. But, the good news is they were all Styphoni priests, bodyguards, sycophants and their allies. The Army of Hos-Hostigos took less than two thousand casualties during the entire siege."

"True. How did you know?" he asked.

"Duke Kyblannos told me in a letter. He also believes that you and Phidestros will become allies."

"If true, that's a very good thing. A war between the two of our kingdoms would be a costly one, no matter who won."

"Smile, my love. You accomplished a great thing; you brought about an end to the heinous Temple of Styphon. A nest of vipers who have been leaching and living off the bounty of the Great Kingdoms for centuries."

Kalvan sighed. "It's been a long war, and part of me has a hard time believing it's finally over!"

"Well, thanks to your good work in Hos-Ktemnos and our alliance with Great King Phidestros, the Six Kingdoms are finally at peace."

"To peace," Kalvan toasted, everyone raising their cups, goblets and tankards.

"TO PEACE! TO PEACE!" some fifty voices called out.

"TO GREAT KING KALVAN!" another group shouted.

Kalvan sighed. "To the future," he said more to himself than anyone listening.

"Yes," Rylla seconded. "To our future!"

Kalvan took her in his arms and gave her a kiss that took her breath away.

"Is there a place around here where we can find some privacy?" he asked.

"Follow me, Your Majesty," she said with a little curtsy as she led him to their bedchamber.

The End